Available in June 2008
from Mills & Boon®
Special Edition

Undercover Nanny

WENDY WARREN

MILLS & BOON

Pure reading pleasure

First published in Great Britain 2008
by Harlequin Mills & Boon Limited,
Eton House, 18-24 Paradise Road, Richmond, Surrey TW9 1SR

ISBN: 978 0 263 86054 2

23-0608

Harlequin Mills & Boon policy is to use papers that are
natural, renewable and recyclable products and made from
wood grown in sustainable forests. The logging and
manufacturing processes conform to the legal environmental
regulations of the country of origin.

Printed and bound in Spain
by Litografía Rosés S.A., Barcelona

WENDY WARREN

lives with her husband, Tim, a dog, a cat and their recent – and most exciting! – addition, baby daughter Elisabeth, near the Pacific Northwest's beautiful Willamette River. Their house was previously owned by a woman named Cinderella, who bequeathed them a gardenful of flowers they try desperately (and occasionally successfully) not to kill, and a pink General Electric oven, circa 1958, that makes the kitchen look like an *I Love Lucy* re-run.

A two-time recipient of the Romance Writers of America's RITA® Award for Best Traditional Romance, Wendy loves to read and write the kind of books that remind her of the old movies she grew up watching with her mum – stories about decent people looking for the love that can make an ordinary life heroic. When not writing, she likes to take long walks with her dog, settle in for cosy chats with good friends and sneak tofu into her husband's dinner. She always enjoys hearing from readers, and may be reached at PO Box 1208, Ashland, OR 97520, USA.

This one is for the Ladies of Love –
Ginger Kentzell, Darla Lukenbaugh and Susan
Lute – fellow writers, sisters, soul mates. How
did we get so lucky? I love you, Ladies!

Chapter One

*W*ham!

Daisy June Holden slammed her fist into a stomach so dense it nearly broke her knuckles. Her victim jerked, but that was all. D.J. danced back, whirled and shot a roundhouse kick to his head.

Take that.

He never flinched.

Feet shuffling expertly, she ducked out of the way of a retaliatory punch and narrowed angry eyes at her assailant. *You're goin' down.*

His smirk pissed the hell out of her. She dove at him, throwing two unforgiving shots to his rib cage, an uppercut to the jaw and the final blow—a cruel, cruel strike to his groin.

Panting from exertion, D.J. hopped back, assessed her opponent's condition and allowed herself a brief victorious smile. *You lose, pal. Crime never pays.*

Wiping the sweat from her brow with a bare forearm, she used her teeth to tug the boxing glove off her right hand and flexed her fingers.

"Sheesh, D.J., have a heart, would ya?" Angelo Fantozzi,

owner-manager of Angelo's Gym Downtown, looked mournfully at the man-shaped punching bag he provided for his clients. Helping D.J. off with her remaining glove, he tucked them both under his arm and massaged her sore fingers. "You keep whaling like that on my equipment, I'm going to have to get all new stock. What's the matter? You get up on the wrong side of the bed or something?"

Immediately, D.J.'s stomach began to churn. Angelo was the best, a king-size teddy bear, but she had never discussed her problems with him. She'd come to the gym this morning so she could work out some of the tension that was turning her into an antacid junkie. When it came to conversation, however, she disliked turning herself inside out so other people could see her troubles.

No…that wasn't true. She didn't "dislike" it; she *hated* it. Chronicling her woes out loud made her feel weak, tragic.

Fixing her problems—that's what D.J. liked.

She glanced back at Angelo. He was waiting for a response, and he didn't look like he was going to take "No problem" for an answer, so she shrugged. "PMS."

Immediately the giant man turned beet red. "Oh, yeah, okay, well, whatever." He patted the air with a beefy hand and walked away.

D.J. smiled. Pity that her troubles couldn't be averted as easily as Angie.

Taking a deep breath, she blew it out slowly then rolled her shoulders. Angelo's punching bag wasn't the only thing going down. Thompson Investigations, the detective agency D.J. worked for—had worked for in one capacity or another since she was sixteen years old—was about to sink faster than stones in a river…unless D.J. found a way to keep it afloat.

Her stomach gurgled unpleasantly, making her regret the Danish she'd eaten before her workout. Wiping her face with the thin towel she'd slung around her neck, D.J. had made it halfway to the women's showers when the pager at her hip buzzed. Looking down, she read the numbers on the digital display, and her heart started pumping as if she'd begun her workout all over again. This was the call she'd been hoping for.

Rushing to her locker, she fumbled with the combination, dragged out her duffel bag and rummaged through its jumbled contents. Seizing her cell phone, she checked the pager again then punched in Loretta Mallory's home phone number—the private line.

D.J. had met with the elderly woman yesterday to discuss Loretta's needs, private-investigatorwise. The case she had in mind was a bit more involved than the missing persons or cheating spouse cases D.J. usually handled, but that was good; the fee would be greater than usual, too. Unfortunately for D.J.'s burgeoning ulcer, Loretta was also careful and conservative and had opted to sleep on her decision to use D.J.'s services.

A sudden case of cottonmouth made D.J. realize how worried she'd been that Mrs. Mallory wouldn't call, even to say she'd hired somebody else. Loretta Mallory was a wealthy woman, who could afford to pay top dollar, and D.J....

"I am a professional who can deliver the goods," she said under her breath, hoping the mantra would buck up her resolve in the event her prospective client required more convincing. Thompson Investigations needed this job like a calf needed milk.

The phone rang twice before a cultured but obviously elderly voice stated, "Loretta Mallory."

D.J. took a calming breath. Confidence begat power, and power was far more persuasive than desperation. Remembering that, she spoke as smoothly and evenly as any person with an urgent need could expect of herself. "Mrs. Mallory, this is Private Investigator Holden. I just received your page."

Bette Davis put it best: "What a dump."

D.J. stood just inside the door of Tavern on the Tracks, waiting for her eyes to adjust to the dim bar lighting. When they did, she almost choked.

The large square room was decorated in sixties-style restaurant chic—burgundy leather, tufted chairs that had been patched a few times too many, round wooden tables, threadbare navy-blue carpeting and red flocked wallpaper that looked as if it was molting.

At 4:00 p.m. only a few customers perched on the tall stools tucked up against a bar that ran almost the full length of the far wall. It looked like "happy hour" could use a Prozac here at the tavern. Fortunately that suited D.J. just fine this evening. She was looking for someone, and when she found him, she wanted his full attention.

In a ridiculously tiny but fashionably correct purse, she'd tucked a snapshot of the man she'd come to see—Loretta Mallory's grandson.

Maxwell Lotorto was the heir to the Mallory supermarket dynasty—Loretta's daughter's only child. Loretta had not seen her wayward grandson since he was a teenager, but she had a photo that was taken at his high school graduation—fifteen years ago. With no idea how to find Maxwell, Loretta had started interviewing P.I.s.

Standing straight and tall, D.J. squared her broad shoulders in a red dress that fit like a layer of glue. Fixing her gaze on the bar, she ignored the row of male backs on the customer side in favor of the man tending to drinks. Her brown eyes narrowed. Her heart rate accelerated. It always did when she was this close to victory.

The photo in her purse showed a young man with black hair. Dressed in a cap and gown for his high school graduation, he was tall with strong shoulders, but at seventeen he still had the lean, gangly look of a teenager.

The person behind the bar was all grown-up. And undeniably, heart-thumpingly masculine.

Maxwell Lotorto's looks were a striking combination of light and dark—dark hair, light skin, light eyes. He was a tall drink of water, too. Even at five foot seven and in three-inch heels, D.J. didn't come close to his height. For a moment she wondered if she had the right Max Lotorto. Then he looked up.

The dim room disappeared. Eyes the color of an overcast sky zeroed in on her like radar, and pure male heat radiated from their depths. He neither smiled nor acknowledged her in any other way, but the steadiness of his gaze made several of the other men at the bar turn to see what he was looking at.

D.J. struggled to maintain her concentration. She was here to do a job. *Finding* Max Lotorto was merely the beginning. Loretta Mallory would not pay a small fortune for a mere missing-persons gig; what she truly wanted was to have her grandson investigated. Evaluated. She wanted details, as many as she could get so she could decide whether to herd her AWOL lamb back to the fold. D.J. had opinions—mostly negative—about ordering an investigation before deciding whether to hook up with your own flesh and blood. But then again she didn't have millions to protect, and

Loretta was looking for an heir, not only someone with whom to share Thanksgivings.

More importantly, Loretta paid top dollar for services rendered, so D.J. intended to keep her opinions to herself and give the woman everything she asked for. Thompson Investigations had two weeks to cough up five months of back rent or they'd be doing business from the pay phone at Hot Dog Hut. If this job was successful, on the other hand, they'd be debt free—and then some—for awhile.

To investigate Maxwell to Ms. Mallory's satisfaction, D.J. knew she had to be very creative. Loretta wanted info that only a person close to her grandson could possibly know. Before she'd even gotten in her car to drive down here, D.J. had decided that by the end of the evening Mr. Lotorto was going to do one of two things: hire her to work for him or ask her out on a date.

Lifting her chin, she met his gaze squarely as she slipped onto a barstool. Then she breathed in deeply. Let the games begin….

Max watched the cat-eyed brunette seat herself at his bar with the same effortless grace she'd demonstrated on her walk across the room. Four of his five customers had turned to gawk at her the moment she'd strolled in. She hadn't noticed. All her attention had been on him. Flattering.

Glancing away from her wasn't easy, but he made himself do it. When their eyes had met and held, he'd felt a surge of pure male want, the kind that could make a man's desire circumvent his sanity.

Max decided to let the beauty wait a bit, checking first on his other customers, making sure they were all topped up. Harvey Newhouse looked at him like he was crazy. Raising his right hand to hide the gesture he made with his left, Harv pointed to the newcomer as if he thought Max might have missed her in the early-evening "rush."

"You want another beer, Harv?" Max wiped the bar in front of the older man. Scowling, Harv jerked his head to the right, another subtle cue.

Max ignored the directive, turning instead to Steve Shaynor, owner of the local feed and tackle. "How about you, Steve? You ready for another Dewar's?"

Steve scowled at the younger man. "You got a customer," he growled, and then, in a stage whisper the back row of an amphitheater could have heard, he hissed for extra clarification, "The girl."

"I believe they mean me."

She had the voice of a torch singer, and Max felt it wrap around him like a coil heater. He turned to her, resigned to the inevitable the instant he saw the humor in her up-tilted eyes and the wide unabashed smile. No question about it. He wanted what he saw.

Picking up a cocktail napkin, Max reached across the bar to set it in front of her. Her gaze fell to his forearm, bared by rolled-up shirtsleeves, and lingered there. He barely resisted a Cro-Magnon urge to flex his muscles.

Holding her gaze, he asked, "What can I get you?"

"Seagram's. On the rocks. With a twist."

She named a call whiskey. Expensive. Smooth. Strong. Definitely not for the faint-hearted.

Look all you want, Max, old buddy, but don't touch. Remember you've sworn off.

Deftly pouring her drink, he set it in front of her. "Enjoy."

"Thank you." She raised the glass before he could turn away. "Here's to good luck. May she continue to smile."

"Continue?" Picking up a clean bar towel, Max wiped out a shot glass—proper bartender behavior—but his eyes never left hers. "Have you been having a run of good luck lately?"

"Obviously." She tilted her head. The curtain of straight hair fell like a dark-chocolate waterfall, and her comment emerged half flirtatious, half factual. "I'm here, aren't I?"

Max laughed outright. She was something.

He leaned forward, folded his arms on the bar and said, "That may be luck…or just bad taste in drinking establishments." He'd lowered his voice so the regulars—who were all ears at the moment—wouldn't hear. Smiling into the amused brown eyes, he added, "If you need anything else, just whistle." Briefly his gaze dropped to her scarlet lips.

Taking his bar towel and his shot glass, Max turned away from temptation. *Smart move,* he congratulated himself, expelling the breath he hadn't realized he was holding.

So long, gorgeous, he thought, not without regret, certain his evening bartender, Dave, would arrive before she was ready for her second drink.

Damn.

D.J. realized she was staring after Maxwell and mentally shook herself. Raising the drink he'd set in front of her, she was shocked to see that her hand actually trembled.

Well, for Pete's sake! she thought disgustedly.

The man had thrown her totally off course. And she never lost focus when she was on a job. Never, *never!*

Taking a sip of the drink she had ordered simply to fit in, D.J. grimaced and tried not to cough. She wanted Maxwell's attention again, but not because she was gagging at his bar.

Setting the drink aside, she looked up to watch Max confer with another man who'd entered the area behind the bar. Facing her direction, the second man was in the process of tying an apron around his waist when he saw D.J. His eyes glinted with clear, uncomplicated interest, and he hitched his chin toward her. Max glanced back.

D.J. caught her breath. *If you need anything else, just whistle.*

Her lips slipped into pucker mode, but Max turned away again before she could generate any sound.

After another few words with the bartender, who had obviously come to take his place, he called goodbye to the regular customers and left.

D.J. stared after him in dismay. He was leaving? At…she checked her watch…barely four-thirty? That was not the plan.

So much for a knock-'em-dead dress and killer shoes whose only victims at the moment were her poor, pinched toes.

Sticking her thumbnail between her teeth, she started chewing. *Dang,* she hated failure, even little failures. Granted, she could spend the evening pumping the guys at the bar for information, but that would be admitting that Max Lotorto had gotten the best of her on the very first day.

She took her thumb out of her mouth as the new bartender

headed her way, an inviting smile on his classic hottie face. D.J. smiled only vaguely in return. Grabbing her purse, she took out several dollars, tossed them on the bar next to her barely touched drink and stood.

You snooze, you lose, Daisy June.

It was a plain fact that no one got anywhere by mulling her options over and over. Sometimes you had to act first, mull second.

If you need anything else, just whistle....

As she sauntered from the bar, D.J. puckered up and blew.

Max walked the seven blocks from his work to his home with a sense of purpose, thinking only about the night ahead. As much as he could, he kept his mind on images that were safe, like the inch-thick Black Angus sirloin and the ice-cold Olympia beer— still the best beer—that figured heavily in his evening's plans. And a muscle-relaxing soak in a tub that would, he decided, be as steaming hot as the brewski was cold.

And a cigar. Yeah.

A smile curved his lips. One of the mellow Cuban beauties he'd ordered off the Internet for his birthday.

If his plans seemed more suited to a phlegmatic retiree than a thirty-two-year-old virile male who could just as easily have been planning a night of outrageous sex, well, so be it. The one thing Max did *not* want to think about tonight—not even for a little while—was the lady in red. Too tempting. Too complicated. Strictly off-limits.

For the past several months women had ranked low on Max's list of priorities. Not that he would lack for female company if he wanted it. On the contrary, he knew that women were never very far away.

What he'd lacked in his life up to now was purpose. He'd made money; he'd traveled the world. He'd played hard with few regrets when the mood struck. But he had never felt a driving reason to get up every morning, to be responsible all day, to live for something larger than his own interests.

He had a reason now. He had four.

Unconsciously Max increased his pace, anxious to end the day and begin the evening.

Turning up the cracked cement path leading to his front door, he felt his shoulders begin to relax for the first time all week. To say the past three months had been chaotic was an understatement. Every day he'd felt like he was juggling balls that refused to stay in the air. As of yesterday, though, thanks to a goddess named Ella Carmichael, Max had finally been able to restore order to his home life. Tomorrow he would begin in earnest the extensive remodel he planned on the restaurant and bar he had recently purchased, but tonight…

Max grinned. Ah, tonight his biggest dilemma would be deciding whether to eat first or take his bath. Fitting his key in the front lock, he turned the knob and opened the door to his sanctuary.

"Give me back my wizard wand or I'll zap you with my laser stick!"

The shrill demand rent the air, slapping Max in the face like a stun gun.

"No! It's *mine.* You stole it from me, you poo-poo doo-doo brain!"

"You're not allowed to call me that! You're a poo-poo doo-doo brain, you poo-poo doo-doo brain *fart*head."

The arguing mounted rapidly in both urgency and volume. Max raised his hands as two small but surprisingly strong bodies hurled themselves at his legs with enough forward momentum to shatter his kneecaps. His breath hissed between gritted teeth as he held back the curse that wanted desperately to explode free. Small hands flailed about his legs. Max tried to grab at least one of them.

"Whoa!" he commanded when he trusted himself to speak without swearing. "Knock it off!" His demand went unheeded. Taking full advantage of his baritone, he hollered over the din. *"What is going on?"*

A pair of deceptively angelic faces surrounded by ruffles of blond curls looked up at him, for this one moment, silent. Then Sean's hand shot out, pointing at his twin brother, James. "He did it!"

And the quarrel raged again.

Max clamped a hand over the mouth of each twin. "Where's Mrs. Carmichael?" He'd hired the stalwart nanny three days ago because she had assured him that no domestic challenge was too daunting. She would easily—but with great love, of course—put order to the chaos that had become his life. Today was her first day, and upon waking this morning, Max had felt a degree of gratitude he'd never quite experienced before.

Slowly, with trepidation, he let go of James's mouth first. James was generally the more amenable twin, but you couldn't be too sure. Max looked at him with what he hoped was warning in his eye. *Don't mess with me, kid. Just give it to me straight.*

"She's in the kitchen, cleaning up the dinner."

Cleaning up the dinner. Max's brows swooped together. So, that's what he smelled. "Did it burn?"

James shrugged.

"Where are your sisters?" Before the boy could answer, the steel-haired dynamo who'd promised him a miracle marched out of the kitchen.

"Good, you're home." Built like a small tank in orthopedic shoes, Mrs. Carmichael nodded once, sharply. Her hands went to the apron tie at her back. Pulling the garment over her head, she shoved it at Max's chest on her way to the door. "Good luck."

"What?" Caught off guard, Max stared at the wadded-up apron.

"The girls are trouble, but those two—" she stabbed a quivering finger at James and Sean "—will be the death of you." Her hand grasped the doorknob.

Max felt the boys' shoulders tense at the housekeeper's harsh words, but he couldn't afford to stop and soothe them. Peeling the twins off his legs for now with the order to "Stay put," he followed the woman out the door, catching up with her on the front lawn. "Wait, wait!" When he touched her elbow, she whirled and glared at him. Promptly he let go.

"Dinner is burned," she said. "Somebody turned off my timer. And I hope you don't need clean shirts tomorrow, because the laundry never got done." She raised her chin, daring Max to complain. He didn't intend to.

"Obviously, this wasn't the greatest day…for any of us." From what remained of his humor, he summoned a smile. "I wouldn't want to repeat it myself. I tell you, dealing with contractors is a lot like dealing with kids. Everything happens on their time frame, they get to pout, and you're the one who has to pay for it all."

Mrs. Carmichael crossed surprisingly muscular arms over her

grandmotherly bosom. The curl of her lips said it all: tell me something I *will* care about.

Adrenaline pumped into Max's system. He rubbed his hands together, warming up for the old college try. "All right. First of all, do not worry about the dinner. We'll order pizza for the kids, and you and I can sit down and—"

"Dinner is the least of your concerns, Mr. Lotorto. Those two hooligans have been acting like wild animals all day." She pointed behind him to the two boys who had obviously not stayed put. "First they dug a hole in the garden—"

"No, it's a time capsule," James asserted, evidently certain this tidbit of information would cancel any wrongdoing. "We're puttin' Sean's dead lizard in it."

Max lowered his brow. "Shh."

"Then they put shaving cream on the windows—"

"Uh-uh, it was cleaning stuff. We were helpin' *clean* them," Sean whined in protest.

Max raised a finger to his lips. He could not afford to lose the only help he had. Returning his attention to Mrs. Carmichael, he tried to commiserate. Having lived with the twins for several months, it wasn't hard. "I can see how irritating that must have—" he began.

"And then they tried to set fire to the house."

"Fire?" Max knew these kids. They were boisterous, a bit too creative in their play, but ultimately they were good kids trying to find their way through circumstances that would have been difficult for anyone. They weren't delinquents. They had never deliberately hurt anyone or anything. "If they were playing with matches, I'll deal with them." He turned briefly to shoot both boys a warning glare. "I will definitely deal with them. But I think we ought to be careful about suggesting they *intended* to burn down the house—"

"They made a fire in the middle of their bedroom."

James ran forward, accompanied by his brother, and tried to speak again. Max pressed a hand over each boy's mouth. All he made out was a muffled "…campout…"

His head began to throb, right between the eyes. There had to be a way to deal with this firmly but calmly, rationally. "Here's what I suggest. I think we should all go back in the house, and—"

"They used a box of your cigars for kindling."

"—talk about—" He halted. "Cigars? Imported cigars? With a little hut…and a palm tree on the box?"

Mrs. Carmichael shrugged eloquently. "How should I know?" She shook her head. "No more box."

The throb expanded to the top of Max's head. He wanted badly to yell, but how could he? He was failing these kids.

The thought made him furious and frustrated, but not at them. They were innocent victims, loved by a mother who, unfortunately, had never been able to give them stability. So many times they'd been unceremoniously dumped in Max's life—a few days here, a couple of days there. But this time, they were here for good, and though they had known Max and loved him all of their lives, they probably sensed by now that the emperor had no clothes: Max knew how to be fun for a weekend, but he didn't know jack about being a parent.

No way could he do this alone.

His mind raced as he groped for a way to plug the hole in this sinking ship. Before he could make another gambit, however, the woman he'd hoped would be his salvation put her hands on her hips and said, "You won't like to hear it, people never do, but what those boys need is a good horsewhipping. I'd have done it, too, but they locked themselves in the bathroom."

Against his legs, Max felt the boys stiffen. Anger pumped more adrenaline into his veins. With her elbows sticking out and her slivered eyes spitting threats, Carmichael, the self-avowed *über*nanny, looked startlingly like Miss Gulch in *The Wizard of Oz* just before she took Toto away from Dorothy.

"Mrs. Carmichael," he warned in a low, cautionary voice, "try to remember what I told you."

She nodded. "Exactly. Bad blood breeds bad blood, and from what you said about their mother, those two are likely to be in prison before they're ten."

"Mrs. Carmichael—"

"You'll be doing yourself a favor if you let Social Services handle them."

Sean squeezed tightly against Max's knee. Max felt his anger reach frightening proportions.

Tightly controlling himself, he leaned down and murmured to James. "What did you call your brother?" James whispered in reply, eliciting a nod before Max straightened. "Mrs. Carmichael," he said, "you are a poo-poo doo-doo brain."

The woman's mouth opened and closed like a baby bird trying to feed.

"And just so that you and I completely understand each other, do not ever mention Social Services in connection with *my* children again, not even if you're standing on the other side of town in a soundproof booth."

"I quit!" the woman snapped, face growing redder with each second.

Maxwell smiled grimly. "Just when I thought we were getting along."

Mrs. Carmichael's nostrils flared, but she spun without another word and stalked to the maroon Buick she'd parked at the curb.

Max didn't wait to watch her get in. He turned the boys around, nudging them toward the house. On the porch, ten-year-old Anabel stood somberly with her arm around Livie, their baby sister. Garbed as usual in her thrift-store fairy princess costume, she had what appeared to be either makeup or strawberry jam all over her face. Her huge, worried eyes swallowed her face.

Max ground his teeth. Terrific. So much for setting a good example. They'd heard everything.

Tossing his ex-nanny's apron onto the sofa, Max clapped his hands with forced joviality. "So, who's starving? I'll order pizza."

Anabel was the only one who spoke. "We had pizza last night."

Fatigue pulled Max's body like gravity. Very little frightened him in life. He hardly ever panicked, and he hardly ever prayed. Hard work, truth, loyalty—those were the values he believed in. They ought to be enough to bring a man through most difficulties. Now he stood in his living room, with four pairs of worried eyes watching him, and directed this message heavenward: SEND HELP.

Chapter Two

Daisy June Ryder liked fashion. Before the business had started gasping for breath, and she'd opted to pay the past month's utility bills plus as much of the back rent as she could—which wasn't much, really—from her personal checking account, clothes and shoes had been her number-one material indulgence.

So when she dressed for success as a prospective baby-sitter, D.J. put on her favorite sixty-five-dollar Melrose Avenue jeans, an Anna Sui top that she'd bought at a second-time-around chic boutique and her Nine West boots.

With a name like Daisy June, a girl was practically forced to develop a sense of style.

Besides, D.J. was nervous, and clothes, she had long since discovered, could act the part of old friends. People might come and go, but her pink suede slides would follow her anywhere.

Yesterday evening she'd sat in a parked car down the block from Maxwell Lotorto's house and watched him engage in a confrontation with a stout gray-haired woman. Hunched low in the front seat of her Mustang, she'd watched four young children follow Max and the woman out of the house. With her window rolled down, D.J.

caught enough of the conversation to glean that the children belonged to Max, that the irate woman was either a housekeeper or nanny, and that she was quitting or being fired. Maybe both.

D.J. had never believed in angels or anything like that, but if she did, she'd swear one had been guiding her footsteps last night. She'd been in just the right place at just the right time to gather a solid foundation of information.

Standing in front of Tavern on the Tracks for the second time in fewer than twenty-four hours, D.J. attempted to quell that slightly sickening butterflies-in-the-belly feeling by calling it excitement. She'd spent years making her living by locating missing persons, some of whom had taken exception to being found. She had not yet, however, changed her identity or masqueraded as someone else to get the job done.

Today would be her first day "undercover." Today D. J. Holden, P.I., kick boxer extraordinaire—if she did say so herself—and undoubtedly the only woman in her yoga-for-relaxation class licensed to carry a concealed weapon, was going to be Daisy June Holden, career babysitter.

Without doubt, she was better suited to investigative work than to child care. She'd done a good portion of her own growing up as the only kid in the home of two much older adults, but she'd adored Bill and Eileen Thompson. She'd followed Bill around like a pup on a leash, absorbing knowledge about his private investigation business like soil absorbs rain—naturally, effortlessly.

She expected to expend a lot more effort learning to corral a bunch of rugrats.

Late-morning sunshine warmed the pavement of the small northern California town of Gold Hill, making D.J. squint. She left her sunglasses on top of her head, nonetheless, wanting to appear casual, eminently approachable when she walked into the restaurant that adjoined the bar. Tavern on the Tracks was comprised of two adjacent storefronts, each with its own entrance. On the right was the bar. On the left was a space that appeared to be undergoing renovations. A sign on the latter space said that an Italian restaurant would be opening soon. Yesterday D.J. had been to the bar; today she decided to investigate the restaurant.

Licking her lips, she walked across the threshold.

It was dark in the as-yet-unlit restaurant. She looked around, making out only shadow. It was *way* dark.

Standing still while her eyes adjusted to the dimness, D.J. let her ears do her investigating for her. Not only was it dark, there was a vaguely smoky, musty smell in the room that made her think of Mickey Spillane novels.

Until she heard giggles. Giggles and whispering that sounded distinctly juvenile.

As her eyes adjusted from outdoors to indoors, D.J. carefully approached one of the leather booths.

On the floor beneath the table, two squirmy, chortling boys huddled together like puppies.

She crouched down for a better look. "Hello."

When they saw her, the bolder of the boys put his finger to his mouth and hissed, "Shhhhh. You'll alert enemy forces."

"Sorry," she whispered back. "Why are you hiding?"

The other boy started to answer, but the first child clamped a hand over his mouth. "We can't talk to you until we know whose side you're on."

"Oh." She nodded. "I'm on your side."

"You gotta get under here then."

D.J. viewed the cramped space and gave a mental shrug. *If you can't beat 'em…*

She grunted as she crawled in beside her new comrades. With her five-foot, seven-inch frame hunched beneath the table, she felt like an arthritic turtle and knew she wouldn't be able to hold out long. "What's the location of the enemy forces?"

"They're over there." The curly headed self-appointed spokesperson of the duo pointed in the direction of the neighboring bar. "Eatin' stuff."

"Eatin' stuff." D.J. nodded. "Why aren't you two over there eatin' stuff?"

"Eatin' on a mission is sissy."

"But I'm hungry," his partner piped up.

D.J. looked at the other boy, physically a near carbon copy of his compatriot. Obviously brothers, they looked little like Max, which meant, she assumed, that they favored their mother.

Yesterday's discovery of the children and the apparently defecting caregiver had not told her everything she needed to know, but it had given her a place to start. Max Lotorto needed child care. His wife must have passed on or moved on, because he clearly had responsibility for these kids. Assuming the woman was alive, what had made her leave gorgeous Max and their four kids? Was she still in the picture at all? D.J. had no outstanding maternal instincts, but voluntarily leaving one's children did not sit well with her.

If the children's mother was alive, perhaps Max had some fatal flaw that had made the marriage untenable. That was the kind of information Loretta wanted, the kind of information D.J. had come to the restaurant to get.

The boys began nudging each other and whispering. "What are your names?" she asked them.

The gigglier, hungrier one started to answer, but his brother gave him an elbow shot to the ribs. "We're not supposed to tell," he said over his brother's cry of "Ow!"

"That's when we're outside," the other boy said, elbowing back.

A skirmish—one that would surely put D.J. at risk from a flailing appendage—seemed about to ensue, until a very deep, very authoritative masculine voice called out, "Sean! James! Where are you?"

"Shhhh," the boys hissed to each other. In a loud whisper the more dominant child commanded, "Change locations, change locations!" Both boys scrambled on their hands and knees to a new hiding place, presumably the next table over.

D.J. tried to scooch out, using her elbows and knees, but getting out from under the table wasn't nearly as easy as climbing beneath it in the first place, and a pair of work-boot-shod feet entered her line of vision before she had time to straighten.

A hand appeared before her face, palm up. She took it.

Work roughened but warm and large, Maxwell Lotorto's big mitt made hers feel small and feminine—quite a shock given that in elementary school the other girls had voted her "biggest girl's hand in fifth grade."

As her eyes adjusted to the light, she noted the surprise—then suspicion—in his gaze. He definitely recognized her from yesterday.

Letting go of her hand, Max watched her steadily, no doubt

awaiting an explanation, and D.J. would have loved to provide one, but her mouth was so dry she had to lick her lips again, and in truth she hadn't thought of an explanation for something like this.

Finally he spoke for her. "So why, he wonders, has the lady come back to hide under his table?"

"Good question." She had to smile, nodding her appreciation. "I'd start there. But I wasn't hiding, actually. I was becoming acquainted with two very personable young men. Yours, I assume?"

More giggling from the next table over. Hands moving to his hips, Max glanced the boys' way. "Get out here, you two. It's time for lunch."

The twin brothers scampered out to stand side by side before Max. "Go next door. Frankie made tuna."

"Yuck! Free Willy sandwiches." Once again Sean was not shy about his position.

Max shook his head. "Don't start. Free Willy was a whale."

James's eyes grew wide. "I'm not eatin' whale!"

While Max's body vibrated with the effort to maintain his patience, D.J.'s shook with the attempt to suppress laughter. The poor guy looked exhausted, which, for D.J.'s purposes wasn't such a bad thing.

Issuing his next directive as a not-to-be-flouted command, Max said, "Tuna is not a whale. It comes out of a can. Frank went to the trouble of making you lunch, so don't insult him. And FYI, I don't advise climbing under tables if you want to meet girls." His gaze returned to D.J. "They hardly ever hang out there."

James giggled. "She's not a girl."

While Max returned his attention to the boy, D.J. shivered for a reason most unprofessional. The man had eyes like a winter ocean: stormy and moody, beckoning with mystery and secret. His expression today was far less open than it had been yesterday, but when he held her gaze it seemed he was daring her to look away. As an investigator, D.J. felt enjoyably challenged. As a woman, she felt…ensnared.

That wasn't good.

"Lunch," Max told the boys again in a flat tone that brooked no refusal. "Ice cream later if you finish *everything*."

The boys looked at each other with huge, eager eyes. They raced off, leaving D.J. alone in the vacant restaurant with Max.

Her subject had dressed casually in worn jeans, a red cotton shirt with the tail out and his boots. He was in the mood for work, not play, a fact his next words confirmed.

"It's a busy day around here. What can I do for you?"

There's the door, what's your hurry, eh? Determined not to take offense, D.J. reminded herself she was also here for work.

Years of faking confidence until she'd actually acquired some made her back straight and her shoulders square. She smiled. "You can let me make your life simpler."

He reared back ever so slightly, but that hint of surprise told D.J. she'd just taken the upper hand.

"How," Max said, "do you propose to do that?"

"By working for you." D.J. tossed her head, flicking her dark hair behind her. "You probably don't remember me," she demurred, realizing full well that he did. "I stopped by your bar last night. I see you're opening a restaurant and you're going to need a staff. I've been involved in the restaurant business for years." D.J. looked him straight in the eye and refrained from adding, *but only if you consider how often I eat in them.* "I can do whatever. Wait tables, be a hostess." She glanced around. "Hammer a few nails." She didn't mention the children yet, or his need for child care. All in good time.

Max eyed her up and down, his scrutiny so blatant she didn't know whether to pose or cross her arms over her chest.

"You're not from around here."

"I was passing through town yesterday evening," she told him, using the simple story she'd concocted to explain her appearance in a small-town bar, dressed to the hilt, and her subsequent desire to look for work here. "I was on my way home from a friend's wedding. It was quite a bash. Naturally, I don't dress like that for job interviews."

"Where's home and where was the party?"

"Ashland." D.J. named a city south of Gold Hill. "That's where the wedding was. And I'm from Portland."

"Portland. Aren't there any waitress jobs in Portland?"

"Sure." Taking a deep breath, she put a sad little wriggle into the exhale. "But so are my fiancé and his new girlfriend."

As a little girl, D.J. had heard a story about an angel who wrote down everything a person said or did, recording the entries in a big book for God to read when He was deciding who got into Heaven and who didn't. There was a page for good acts and one for sins. If the angel existed and was listening to half of what she'd said so far today, she was in deep doo-doo.

The frown marring Max's handsome brow dropped lower. His lips pursed as he digested the information she was feeding him. She didn't want him to work at it too long.

"I really want to relocate to someplace peaceful, and I'm going to need a job right away. If you already have a full staff, maybe you know of another restaurant job in the area? I don't mind the dirty work. Even dishwashing is fine." She curled her polished fingers into her palm, hoping he had a nice big dishwasher in his kitchen. "Oh, and by the way," she said as if the thought had just occurred to her, "I baby-sit, too. I mean, if you and your wife or someone you know ever needs anyone."

Smooth, Daisy. Oh, smooth. Make him think it's not all about him. "I know this is a small town, and there may not be much work, so I'm willing to be flexible. And cheap for the first month trial period." *And if that don't grab you, Mr. Lotorto, I can't imagine what will.*

Maxwell's brow arched perceptibly with each fib she told. He was definitely mulling it over. "How flexible are you willing to be?"

Daisy shrugged. "Make me an offer."

Max wanted to bite the hook; she could tell. "How do you feel about full-time work with kids?" he asked.

She plastered an enthusiastic smile over her natural trepidation. "I love kids. Your boys are great."

"How do you feel about them 24/7?"

"So, just to get this straight. You want a babysitter? Someone to watch your children while you're working?" So far this was playing out the way she'd intended it to. D.J.'s maternal instincts were nil, but hanging out at the restaurant or at Max's home, watching the kids would give her a chance to observe Max up close and personal, and a few hours of playing cops and robbers under the tables wouldn't kill her.

Max frowned over her question. "No." He gave a quick, sharp shake of his head. "I don't want a babysitter. I need a nanny."

Good Lord. A nanny? Nannies were responsible for discipline. Nannies were responsible for feeding. Nannies…

Lived in.

"I could be a nanny," D.J. blurted before she let herself think twice. The investigator in her could no more turn down the opportunity to spend legitimate time in Maxwell Lotorto's home than her inner clothes hog would say no to free Jimmy Choo shoes.

"Do you have experience with kids?" Max's narrowed eyes suggested he might already be reconsidering his hasty overture.

"Do I have experience!" D.J. decided to lay it on thick. "I have thirteen brothers and sisters."

Max's astonishment was gratifying. "Thirteen?"

Give or take. A baker's dozen was probably a conservative estimate of the boys and girls with whom she'd spent her early, early years. The fact was they were all foster siblings, some of whom D.J. had known a month on the outside, and she hadn't seen any of them since she was twelve. She had never actually taken care of children, but growing up around them had to count for something.

Max ran a hand over his ink-dark hair and shook his head. "And I thought four was a handful."

"Are you on your own with your children?"

"Yeah. Our housekeeper…retired recently."

"Oh." Retired, huh? If that scene on his front lawn had been a "retirement," she'd machine wash all her hand-knit sweaters on Hot.

"Yeah. She was a great gal. The kids loved her. They're very loving kids."

"I'm sure they are." Poor Max. His page in the recording angel's book wasn't going to look any better than hers. "That must have been very hard, losing someone you all counted on."

"It hasn't been easy. I'm working a lot, trying to get this restaurant opened. School doesn't start for another few weeks, and I don't want to put the kids in day care." He was starting to appear endearingly less cocky, more earnest. "We've had some upheavals here lately. I'd like to give the kids continuity."

Which meant they hadn't had any for a while. D.J. filed the information away for Loretta. She'd have to probe later and get further details.

For some reason, a fresh pang of guilt squeezed her chest. She reminded herself that this was a job. A good one.

"Do you have references?" he asked.

"For waitressing, not for babysitting," D.J. said.

She'd already phoned Angelo at the gym and her neighbor Mrs. Pirello to tell them she might need a cover for a job she was working. They both owed her a few dozen favors and had family in the restaurant business. Devoted *NYPD Blue* fans, they had agreed immediately to help out.

"For waitressing I can get you a résumé. I don't have anything on me, though." Going whole hog, she grimaced, cheesily snapping her fingers. "Darn. Too bad I didn't think to slip a résumé into my suitcase. I packed quite a few clothes, because I decided to vacation in the Rogue Valley for a week before the wedding. I could have started right away."

He was still wavering, changing his mind about hiring someone with no experience. Never mind that the thought of caring for four kids could send her running for antacids; the fact that Max had second thoughts about hiring her made D.J. want to fight for the job.

C'mon, Maxie, give it up, she thought. Heck, if Loretta liked what D.J. had to report, Maxwell Lotorto and his kiddos would be richer than Oprah very shortly. Loretta wanted an heir, but she wanted one capable of running the family business. If Max proved to be responsible and genuine, with a head for business on his broad shoulders, then he would assume his rightful place in the family biz. He'd be able to hire a veritable Mary Poppins to be his nanny. A team of Mary Poppinses. D.J. figured Max might take exception to her subterfuge at first, but in the end he'd thank her. Who wouldn't?

With the goal of entering the Lotorto home uppermost in her mind, Daisy had to thank her lucky stars for what happened next.

A tiny girl not much higher than Max's knee, ran in from the lounge. The area all around her lips was stained red from something she'd eaten. Since she'd come from the bar, D.J. guessed she'd been filling up on maraschino cherries. There were tears in her eyes as she clung to Max's leg, and her bright red lips quivered.

"Sean says I ate Free Willy! I don't want to eat a whale!"

The tiny person let loose a torrent of sobs worthy of a Broadway star. Her hollering apparently drew the three other children. Even before Max could admonish the boys for goading their sister, they began to heatedly defend themselves while the elder girl patted the little one—maybe a bit too hard—on the back. As the little one cried, spurts of tears arced from her eyes as if they were tiny fountains. Then she leaned forward and barfed on Max's shoes.

Max looked down then up, locking gazes with D.J. "Get your suitcase and meet me back here at three. You're hired."

"And this is the master bedroom," Maxwell said, concluding an abbreviated tour of the rustic, ranch-style house set on two un-landscaped acres along Sardine Creek Road in Gold Hill, Oregon. "I haven't had time to move all my things out yet, but make yourself at home."

He'd rushed D.J. through the kitchen, living and dining areas and hadn't shown her the kids' rooms yet at all. For good reason, too, D.J. guessed. The house looked like a family of monkeys inhabited it. Obviously, Max had made a quick trip home earlier in the day to arrange the endless stacks of papers, books and games into some approximation of order; but riotous piles of loose things, and garbage pails overflowing with paper cups, cereal boxes and who knew what else, wouldn't win the Good Housekeeping seal of approval. The brief—very brief—glimpse he'd allowed her of the kitchen had almost made her call Loretta to quit.

Turning to Max, she plastered a game smile over her misgivings. She was no coward. If she had to, she could suck it up and restore order to this pigsty. "Thanks. I'm sorry to be kicking you out of your room."

Behind the fatigue, a flash of wry humor lit his light eyes. "I'd sleep in the backyard on a bed of nails if it'd help get this household on track."

"When did it go off track?" D.J. punctuated her question by swinging her suitcase onto the well-made bed. Clearly Max had taken more trouble with this room than with the others. If there'd been any reminders of the children's mother—photos, clothing— it was all gone now.

D.J. knew her curiosity was a tad more than professional. Aside from being big and strong and darkly gorgeous, Max appeared to have boundless patience with his kids. He really enjoyed them, which made D.J. endlessly curious about the woman whose absence was forcing him to secure child care. Where was she? Was she coming back?

Unfortunately, D.J. sensed already that Max was not a spill-his-guts-on-the-first-date kind of guy, so she would keep everything casual for the next day or so. It wasn't going to be easy. Protective of her own information, D.J. nonetheless had a natural curiosity about other people—how they'd been raised, what their families were like, how they lived. In high school she'd frequently been in trouble for talking too much, and in one of her first jobs, as a cashier, she'd almost been canned for interrogating her customers. She'd developed more subtlety since then.

To convey a relaxed attitude, she unsnapped her suitcase, intending to unpack while she spoke. "So are you completely on your own with the kids?"

"Yeah." Max had hesitated a second before he answered.

Taking a chance, she pressed just a bit. "Has it been that way for long?"

Max hovered near the door. He spotted some loose change lying on the dresser, scooped it up and put it in his pocket. D.J. sensed he was stalling. "It's a long story. I'll fill you in later. Right now I've got to get back to the tavern. My lead bartender fell off a damn roof and broke his ankle this morning, so I've got the night shift until he can work or I can find someone to cover."

"You're leaving?" The rush of pure fear that shot through her veins amazed D.J. Not being able to question Max further didn't bother her nearly as much as the thought of being left alone with the kids so soon. "Uh, I'd hoped you could stick around, acquaint me with the routine."

"You've probably gathered by now that there isn't one." He smiled, and for a moment the one-sided quirk of his lips completely distracted her. "Besides, with your background, you'll be able to teach me a thing or two. Thirteen brothers and sisters." Max whistled softly. "I was an only child, so to me four kids is the equivalent of a preschool. I was able to get hold of your former employers, by the way. They gave you glowing recommendations. Said you're a crackerjack waitress. Very organized and good with people. I'd say those are excellent qualities to apply to child care."

D.J. smiled a little weakly. "I'd say so."

Max leaned a shoulder onto the door frame. "Don't worry about anything. The kids seemed to like you."

Au contraire. The kids had stared at her with big eyes and distinct doubt when he'd introduced her as their nanny. She couldn't show fear, trembling and trepidation, though. Not after the song and dance she'd given him.

"Okay. Yeah, we'll have a great time. Hope your bartender's better soon."

Still seated on Max's bed a full ten minutes after he'd left the house, D.J. clasped her hands on her knees, back rigid as a steel girder. She felt as though she was waiting outside the principal's office. She couldn't seem to get the information from her head to her gut that from here on in *she* was the principal.

Max had started a video for the kids, who were still in the living room and still quiet, but she knew she had to get out there soon. For one thing, she'd conned him into believing her housekeeping skills were on a par with her child care abilities. Which they were.

Unfortunately.

Slapping her knees, D.J. stood and shook the nerves from her body. Time to sally forth and set a few precedents for running this house; she couldn't spend all her time corralling children. Matter of fact, she'd have to come up with a few clean-up projects to keep the kids busy so she could focus on Max when he was home.

Cracking her neck and rolling her shoulders to loosen up, D.J. commanded her feet to move toward the door. She'd work in a quiet yoga session later, but now it was time to get out there.

Wishing she'd thought to buy a couple of toys, utterly willing to resort to bribery right off the bat, she walked sprightly down the hall, clapping her hands as she neared the living room. "Okay, kiddos, ready to have some fun? I… Ah!" The sight that greeted D.J. stopped her dead in her tracks and elicited a swear word before she could censor herself.

Four children and one can of whipped topping had wreaked havoc on the already disrupted living room. Ribbons and clouds of the stuff covered the coffee table, sofa, windowsills. "What are you doing?" Heaven help her, but she swore again.

One of the twins responded. "You said a baddie."

Yes, she had. And now she was speechless.

"She sa-id—" The other curly headed brother began a singsong recounting of her indiscretion, using the word several times in succession.

"James, stop that," D.J. ordered.

"I'm Sean! And you sa-id—"

The youngest child, Livie, sat on the sofa with a huge teddy bear at her feet, clumsily ladling ice cream out of a half-gallon container. Both the bear and the child, D.J. noticed, had ice cream mustaches. "She said a baddie, she said a baddie…" Livie chanted, kicking her feet.

"All right, everybody *stop saying that*." All she needed was for Max to come home the first day to find that his kids had increased their vocabulary by one colorful curse.

Anabel, the older girl, sat in a chair, her eyes glued to the TV. One of the twins, the one who wasn't Sean, started squirting the table again.

"Hey!" D.J. sprang into action, hopping over assorted toys to grab the offending item from James's hand. "What is this?" She turned the plastic container over in her hands. "Squeezable mayonnaise?"

"We ranned out of whip cream."

"All right, give me anything edible." They stared at her dumbly. "Fork over the food!" She held out her hands and motioned to the little dears. "All of it. Right now." Collecting the can of whipped cream from Sean and the ice cream from Livie, whose lower lip started to quiver sadly, D.J. said, "There will be no more gourmet art as long as I'm here. Food belongs in bellies, not on tables or any other furniture. Is that understood?"

She received no response, other than big-eyed stares from the three younger children. Anabel continued to watch the TV. "Excuse me," D.J. said, stepping into her line of vision. "You seem somewhat normal. May I ask what you were doing while your brothers and sisters were destroying the living room?"

Brown eyes, large and beautiful behind a pair of silver-rimmed glasses, and dramatically more solemn than the dancing blue eyes of the other children, gazed at D.J. "I was waiting for you to come out of the bedroom."

Right. Anabel: one. D.J.: zero. "Well, I'm out now, so here's what we're going to do. We're going to clean up this living room. Then—"

"I'm hungry," James said.

Sean echoed immediately, "Me, too. I'm *starving.*"

Livie said plaintively, "Is it time for dinner *yet?*"

D.J. stared. Were they joking? You could start a burger franchise with what they'd spread on the coffee table. "Didn't you eat anything while you were doing that?" She pointed to what looked like a model of Mt. Everest.

Sean shook his head. "That was for Livie's bear. It's his birthday."

The little girl nodded hard. "He wanted to play ice cream parlor."

With a heavy sigh and a shake of her exotically dark head, Anabel slid off her chair to approach D.J. "I'll take these things to the kitchen," she said, removing the ice cream and other weapons of living room destruction from D.J.'s arms. "You'd better get the kids something to eat before they have a major meltdown."

The girl trooped off to the kitchen, and D.J. felt a ridiculous urge to call out, "Don't leave me!" despite the fact that Anabel, too, was only a child. But at least she seemed to know what she was doing. Taking a deep breath, D.J. said, "All right. We'll clean up here, and then we'll eat some dinner. Okay?"

Ending with a question was her first mistake. Sean leaped up. "Jamie's *starving,*" he informed in a sudden show of brotherly support.

"So's Livie." Jamie jumped up, too.

Swinging her legs, Livie picked up her previous chant. "You said a baddie…you said a baddie…."

D.J. wanted Max to come back. Right now. In the restaurant he had juggled all four kids, kept his sense of humor and managed to appear relatively sane. Of course, he'd had practice at this. He'd given her his cell phone number; she could call him for a little five-minute-advice session. She could imagine him responding in that half-wry, half-soothing tone he had and felt better already.

Unfortunately, she could also imagine him wondering what kind of wimp he had hired, and that did not sit well at all.

Whipped cream and mayonnaise slipped in glops from the table to the carpet. Livie's bear dripped ice cream onto the sofa.

The boys joined their sister's chant.

And D.J. realized she wasn't nearly as tough as she'd thought.

Chapter Three

Sunshine spilled across the green hills like drizzles of honey, sweetening the earth, kissing the children's skin as they romped and laughed in the afternoon rays. Daisy grinned at the children's antics.

"Anabel! Sean, James, Livie!" she called, waving them over. "Time for your music lesson."

Picking up her guitar, she lowered herself gracefully to the warm grass. Immediately the children scampered over. They looked so darling in the outfits she'd made for them. And you could hardly tell that the jumpers used to be a set of curtains hanging in her bedroom.

Positioning her fingers behind the frets, Daisy strummed a few chords from the children's favorite song. "You know this one, so I'll begin and then you join in. James, remember the line is *'jam and bread'* not *'yam and bread.'*" James flushed, but giggled along with the others. "All right, here we go."

Strumming the intro and nodding in time to the music, Daisy lifted her voice. "'Doh, a deer, a female deer…'"

Sitting upright on the couch, D.J. heard herself gasp as she came fully awake. Dazed, she looked around. The living room lights were still on, and the TV screen glowed with the image of Maria and Captain Von Trapp joining their family onstage for a patriotic rendition of *"Edelweiss."* Swinging her feet to the floor, D.J. calmed her labored breath.

Oh, dear God.

She'd popped *The Sound of Music* into the VCR after the kids had lost the bedtime battle, and the living and dining rooms had been restored—through a heroic effort of her own blood, sweat and tears—partially to order. Recalling that the lead character in *The Sound of Music* was a nanny, she'd hoped to pick up a few pointers. Her night had been torture.

After the kids started screaming for food, D.J. had discovered that there wasn't any. A few slices of bread, two eggs, a mostly empty box of corn flakes and a jar of peanut butter was all she'd had to work with. Her cooking skills were more practical than creative, so a trip to the market had been unavoidable.

And that was when the real trouble began. D.J. never again wanted to visit a market with anyone under six foot two. Never. Making the dinner, however, had made the nightmare of shopping seem like a stroll down a country lane.

No two kids had wanted the same thing. Their choices had ranged from chicken nuggets to French toast to corn dogs and tater tots. Anabel had thought they should have a roast, mashed potatoes and two vegetables because then all the food groups would be represented. D.J. had settled the dilemma by buying hot dogs with buns, frozen tater tots, chicken strips from the hot deli and a bag of carrots and celery sticks as a nod to the food pyramid.

It should have been easy. But the water for the hot dogs had boiled over, the tater tots had turned into tater rocks in the microwave, and Livie had pronounced the coating on the chicken strips "yucky," upon which she'd proceeded to peel off the crumbs, dropping them onto the already abused carpet. D.J. didn't even want to think about the damage four children and a bottle of squeezable ketchup had done.

Checking her watch, she gasped.

Midnight. For pity's sake! She'd spent her whole evening cleaning to establish her fake identity as a twenty-first-century Mary Poppins. Then she'd snoozed when she should have snooped.

Pushing herself off the couch, she turned off the TV and went to check on the kids. Relieved to see that they were still sleeping soundly, she decided to search the hall closets first, hoping to find photos, files, anything that might interest Loretta and tell her something about her grandson's potential as heir apparent and future CEO of the Mallory Superstores dynasty. The chaos D.J. had witnessed so far in his home life wasn't a plus, but she'd bet the mere fact he had children would tickle Loretta's fancy.

D.J. tried to picture the surprise and the smiles when Loretta realized she was a great-granny four times over and Max realized he'd never have to worry about finances again.

Opening the closet door, she scanned piles of hastily folded linens and towels, but nothing of real interest. She was stretching to peek at the top shelf when she heard the click of the front door.

Given the late hour, she shouldn't have been surprised by Max's arrival, but the sense that she was doing something wrong made her heart skip. When the living room door creaked, she reacted automatically. Shutting the closet door as quietly as she could, she ran on tiptoe to her bedroom. Standing in the dark with her ear to the closed door, she listened to the approach of Max's footsteps and waited for her runaway pulse to calm down. The closer the footsteps, the more nervous she became.

Uncertainty washed through her. Uncertainty and doubt and a sudden desire to run. She couldn't recall the last time she'd felt this nervous.

Bill Thompson, owner and founder of Thompson Investigations—and the man whose future she was currently trying to save—would read her the riot act if he knew she was "undercover." He'd always insisted on taking straightforward missing-persons cases, tracking down deadbeat dads or surveying cheating spouses. He'd taught D.J. it was possible to make a good living and do a good service at the same time without endangering oneself or others. D.J. used to tease him that he liked surveillance because it enabled him to make a living drinking coffee and eating his wife's homemade doughnuts while he sat in his car.

Now she wished she'd at least talked to him about this case before she'd taken it. But lately Bill seemed so distracted.

Bill and his wife, Eileen, had been her foster parents for eleven years—until she'd turned eighteen—and they'd been the only consistent family she had ever known. Nearly a year ago now, Eileen had lost her battle with cancer, and since then Bill spent most of his time traipsing off to visit distant relatives he'd never before mentioned and taking leisurely side trips to tiny towns with even tinier tourist attractions. He hadn't once mentioned their precarious financial situation to D.J. or that the rent was in arrears.

The somewhat scary, somewhat exhilarating truth was that she was on her own this time, and though D.J. trusted herself, she did wonder whether she'd seen a few too many *Charlie's Angels* reruns, because there had to be, oh, a zillion better ways to get the information Loretta wanted and to collect the big bucks than to move into her grandson's home under false pretenses. If the money wasn't so important right now, she might truly turn back. Maybe she'd slip Loretta's phone number to Max and tell him, "Listen, you look like you could use a nice inheritance. Go call your granny. I won't mention the TV dinner I found under the couch."

Another surge of anxiety pumped through her. The fact was she *did* need this money: she wanted Bill's business to be there, alive and kicking, so that things could go back to normal when he felt more like himself again.

So much had changed since Eileen died, but grief didn't last forever. Some day Bill would be ready to work again, and D.J.'s life would settle back into the routine she had come to know and trust. Working alongside Bill had grounded her, given her a focus and purpose that replaced the loneliness she had once believed might be her constant companion.

No, D.J. wasn't going to turn back from this job. It didn't matter whether Max was a decent guy or Attila the Hun; Loretta was going to get the most honest and detailed report as D.J. could give her.

Slowly, quietly, she turned the knob and opened the door…just a hair…to peek out.

Max had passed her bedroom to enter the boys' room. D.J. could neither see nor hear anything until he reemerged a minute later to check on the girls. Either Anabel or Livie must have stirred, because D.J. heard the soft sounds of an adult murmuring a child back to sleep. She closed her door as gently as she could, remaining very still, trying not even to breathe audibly.

Once more, Max passed her door without stopping. The hall

closet opened and closed, then footsteps faded away. D.J. waited a moment or two. When she was absolutely certain Max had vacated the hallway, she dimmed her light all the way, opened the bedroom door and slipped out as silently as she could. Positioning herself so that she had a clear view of the living room without making her own presence known, she watched Max toss a thin blanket onto the sofa. Before he sat, he studied the room, noting the books that were now *on* the shelves. With something akin to awe, he ran a hand over the newly cleared coffee table.

You should have seen it when it was an ice cream sundae. D.J. smiled, surprisingly touched when she saw him shake his head and smile at the order she'd restored. The room was by no means perfect; domestic details were not her forte. But the improvement was obvious and clearly a godsend to the overworked dad.

And Max did look exhausted as he reached into his pocket to extract keys, a wallet and some spare change. The coins and keys he set on the coffee table. The wallet he opened before setting it, too, on the table.

Resting his elbows on his knees, he linked his fingers behind his neck as if it ached and stared at the open billfold.

He's looking at a photo, D.J. concluded, certain she was correct when his features tightened and the muscles along his jaw tensed. She was on the verge of stepping forward—she wanted to see that picture!—when he sighed heavily and started to speak.

"I don't know how to do this, Terry. I swear, I have no idea how to do this alone." He rubbed his eyes. D.J. strained to hear the next whispered words. "The kids need you. I need you. Wherever you are, babe, you've gotta help us make this work." He ran his hands through his hair, mussing the black waves. Then he leaned back with his arms behind his head. As he closed his eyes, D.J. thought she heard him swear.

She stood motionless several more seconds.

Terry.

Babe.

Moving into Max's home had inspired a wealth of new questions, but so far no hard answers. If Terry was Max's wife, the children's mother, why weren't there *any* pictures of her in the house?

Moving as carefully as she could, D.J. crept back to her room, shut the door and sat on the bed in the dark. Her foot nudged the purse she'd dropped on the floor. Fishing blindly through the bag, she found a stick of gum, unwrapped it and popped it into her mouth.

The kids need you....

It was too soon to draw conclusions, and any decent P.I. knew that assumptions weren't worth the effort it took to come up with them, but D.J. would have bet her last stick of Juicy Fruit that Terry was the children's mother, that she had died and that her passing had been recent.

I need you...

Since she was on a roll, D.J. made another conclusion: Max still loved Terry. Very much.

Bringing her thumb to her mouth, D.J. gnawed on a cuticle, the very habit she'd tried to replace with chewing gum and frequent manicures.

Terry must have been beautiful. The children certainly were, and Max—

Biting her thumb so hard it hurt, D.J. scowled and whipped her hand down to her lap.

Gritting her teeth, she shook the pain from her thumb. Something about the way Max looked at the photo in his wallet had distracted her. She needed to concentrate on the relationship between him and Loretta.

Clearly, being the sole provider for four children was taxing Max to the limit. So, why hadn't he contacted his grandmother for help? He had to know that his mother's family made Donald Trump look like a slacker. Even if he'd never known Loretta up close and personal, surely no one would fault him for approaching her now.

According to Loretta, she and her daughter—Maxwell's mother—had been estranged for years before the younger woman's death fifteen years prior. Loretta had offered no explanation for the estrangement and had made it clear to D.J. that the topic was not open for query.

Loretta had not seen her grandson since he was a restless, and according to Loretta, hot-tempered teenager. She wasn't even aware that she was a great-grandmother. D.J. didn't have all the details about Max that Loretta had requested, but so far he appeared to be a man that would make a granny proud. Gut instinct told D.J. that Max was a good person.

She, on the other hand, was in his house, lying with every breath she took.

Undressing in the dark, conscious that her muscles were already protesting all the bending and stretching she'd done during her cleaning spree, D.J. hoped her conscience would bother her less in the morning.

Setting her internal alarm for 7:00 a.m., she lay on her back and stared into the darkness, waiting for sleep to overtake her. She had plenty to think about while she drifted off, but one image in particular kept coming back: Max on the couch, staring at the photo in his wallet and looking very much as though he was determined not to cry.

Rolling onto her side, D.J. scrunched the pillow till it suited her and closed her eyes. Her last thought before she fell asleep was that she doubted there was a man alive who had ever looked at her picture like that.

"Hey. What do you think you're doing?" Max's whisper held more than a hint of censure.

"We're watching," Sean whispered back. "She kinda spits when she sleeps."

"Come out of there. Right now!"

D.J. frowned, blinked and woozily lifted her head. The voices she heard were evidently not part of a dream. By the time her eyes focused, she saw the backs of three little people as they marched out the door, having been duly chastised by the frowning countenance of Maxwell Lotorto. He reached for the knob, but looked up to catch her watching him. A cautious smile replaced the scowl.

"Hey, you're awake."

Gingerly, D.J. sat up, pulling the sheet with her. Sneaking a glance at the digital clock on the nightstand, she almost groaned. So much for her internal alarm, previously as trustworthy as Big Ben. It was eight-thirty already.

"I hope the kids didn't bug you."

D.J. ran a hand through her hair. "No." She tried to smile, but it wasn't easy. Not only was she, the nanny, the last person up this morning, but also beneath the sheet, D.J. wore only a T-shirt and panties—no bra, no pajama bottoms. Granted, she was covered by a bedspread and a sheet hiked up to her chin, but she felt more self-conscious than she had the first time she'd stayed at a man's apartment overnight. "Sorry I stayed in bed so long. I'm usually up way before now."

He waved her guilt away. "You had a tough first night. At least that's what Anabel tells me."

The kid with her finger on the pulse of the food pyramid had ratted her out? "It wasn't bad." D.J. protested mildly, but if he already knew about James's collision with a spaghetti sauce display at the market, or about the scorched hot dogs she'd tried to convince the children were "cook-out style," she figured her goose was cooked.

"My brothers and sisters are all adults now. I'm a little out of practice with kids."

Max accepted that easily. "Tell me about it. I think I'm still there myself." Awkwardly D.J. laughed with him. "The teenage years." He shook his head, looking, D.J. thought, a bit green around the gills. "Can't say I'm looking forward to those. Especially with the girls."

D.J. arched a brow. "Why 'especially with the girls'?"

"Isn't it obvious?" He waved a hand in her direction. "Teenage girls want to talk about bras and boys. What do I know about that?" Taking a moment, he amended, "Actually, I know *a lot* about bras and boys, but nothing I want to tell Anabel or Liv."

Max looked so adorably cocky and disgruntled and paternal, D.J. wanted to laugh...until the talk of bras made her remember she wasn't wearing one under her thin muscle shirt. She tugged the sheet closer.

"Well, I think I'll get up now." She waited for Max to leave, but he seemed preoccupied, as if he hadn't really heard her, and he definitely wasn't leaving. D.J. tried again, prompting gently, "I need to get up, and I'm...not really dressed for company."

That got his attention. His gaze traveled down the sheet and bedspread as if it just occurred to him she might not be wearing jeans under there.

He turned red—actually grew red—beneath his collar. "Right. I've already got the kids' breakfast on the table, so take your time. When you're ready, we can have coffee. And a talk."

Smiling agreeably until he left the room, D.J. stayed in bed a couple of minutes after he closed the door. Criminy! She'd overslept, so Max had been forced to fix the children's breakfast, and still he wanted to have "a talk," surely about her staying on as a nanny. Either the man had an appreciation of equality that would make working women everywhere lust after him…or he was truly, truly desperate. Maybe both.

Her stomach growled loudly as she grabbed her clothes and headed for the shower. Maybe he'd take pity and feed her, too.

Heading toward the dining room, where the kids were squabbling over whose chocolate chip pancakes had the most chips, Max took a minute to draw a deep breath and clear his head.

She's the nanny, he reminded himself, striving to keep his eye on the big picture. Daisy Holden, as she'd introduced herself yesterday, would be a great fling, no doubt about it. And, frankly, he could use a good fling. With all the responsibility he'd assumed over the past four months, Max figured he *deserved* a fling. He'd earned a night—what the heck, maybe two—of carefree laughter and lust.

Not with Daisy Holden, though.

Long Thoroughbred legs and wide, sexy smile aside, Daisy Holden was going to make an even better nanny than she would a fling. And Max needed a nanny more than he wanted a lover. He needed someone with staying power in order to impress the social worker who'd been scrutinizing his home, his life, his bank account and just about everything else for the past month. A social worker from the Department of Human Services held his family in the palm of her hand. If he failed to impress her with his ability to create a stable home, he could lose the kids.

Briefly, Max closed his eyes, amazed by how quickly that thought could flood his body with fear. He wasn't perfect. God knew his parenting skills could use a shot in the arm. He lost his temper too often with the twins. He was a total pushover with Liv. He sometimes forgot that Anabel wasn't as grown-up as she liked to pretend and failed to anticipate her needs.

But he'd loved them all from the day they were born. The five of them made a pretty motley crew, but they needed each other. And they were fresh out of other family. If the state decided that

Max was not able to care for the kids on his own, the only alternative would be foster care.

When he pictured Livie being taken away—when he thought of any of the kids being separated from each other or from him— Max felt an overwhelming need to shove his fist through the wall.

Daisy Holden didn't know it yet, but she was their last hope. Two days ago they'd been falling apart faster than a house of cards. Last night he'd come home to a stocked refrigerator and a house that looked more like a home than it had in months. Nanny Holden might not be professionally trained, but she had experience; if he could keep her around, the threat hanging over them might very well be solved.

Pushing away from the wall, Max pressed on toward the dining room. He had a goal and he had a plan. The goal: to secure a commitment from Daisy Holden. Max wanted her signature on a year-long contract.

The plan: send the kids outside so he could have a little time and a little privacy to woo the nanny into staying.

Chapter Four

Ohmigod, the man can make pancakes. If he'd thrown a few sausages on the plate, D.J. would have followed him anywhere. Drawing her fork lazily through the remaining puddle of maple syrup on her plate, she watched his bottom while he cleaned the skillet.

Focus, Daisy, focus! she commanded herself. Ogling her employer's tush when she was supposed to be watching his children was not the rip-roaring start she'd intended today. Gamely, she reached for sticky plates.

"I'll take these," she said to the children.

One plate clattered to the table when Sean practically screamed, "I'm not finished yet!"

D.J. jumped back, surprised by his vehemence. Not finished? All he'd done was draw squiggles in the syrup for the past ten minutes. She wasn't sure how to respond. The only irascible children she'd ever spent time with were herself and a couple of foster siblings who made the cousin in *Harry Potter* look like Beaver Cleaver.

Fortunately, Max intervened. One good glare from over his shoulder was enough to make Sean lower his chin to his chest.

"Apologize to Daisy for using that tone. We don't scream at each other in this house. At least not much," he added, winking at Daisy.

While Sean apologized, D.J. nodded and faked a brief coughing fit into her napkin to hide the blush creeping up her neck. Yes, she actually felt her face heating from the single wink Max tossed her. It was upsetting. She wasn't a virgin, for heaven's sake, and she wasn't here to date him. But there was something disturbingly intimate about sitting at his breakfast table.

She'd never lived with a man or come close to marriage. She'd never dated anyone with kids. As a child, she'd bounced from one home to the next and had occasionally woken up wondering if she was having Raisin Bran with the Meltons that day or eggs and toast with the Donleavys. It wasn't until she'd moved in with the Thompsons that there was any continuity in her life. They had become her eighth and final set of foster parents.

Perhaps because she'd moved so much in her life, sharing a table with a family had always seemed like an intimate experience to D.J., one that subtly highlighted who truly belonged and who was just visiting.

"Bring me your plates," Max instructed the kids. "Then I want you to put all the toys that are in the backyard onto the patio so I can water the lawn." A few grumbles greeted his request. He silenced them with a raised hand. "Toys on the patio," he repeated. "Or no bike ride, no picnic, no swimming pool and no Game Boy. Now move it. Move it!"

D.J. felt a surge of foreboding—and quite possibly the pancakes—rise to her throat. Bike ride, picnic and swimming pool? She might know squat about the care and feeding of children, but sheer gut instinct told her those activities required supervision. More than that, they required an ability to corral children while performing physical feats. How was she going to do all those things *and* search the house for information on Max? Besides…

She couldn't swim.

While the children scrambled off their chairs with their breakfast plates and then hustled out the kitchen door, D.J. wondered how she was going to investigate Max when he decided to fire her.

Setting the plates to soak in the sink, he grabbed a towel and turned toward her. "I figured getting rid of the munchkins for a while would give us a chance to talk." He nodded toward her dish. "How was breakfast?"

"Terrific." She hopped up, plate in hand. "You're a good cook."

Taking the plate from her, he slipped it into the sink. "I like cooking for someone with a good appetite," he told her, his cloud-colored eyes and bourbon voice turning the comment into a skin-shivering compliment. "The kids play with more food than they eat." A lopsided grin tugged his lips. "Although you look a little kidlike yourself right now." Wiping his hand on a dish towel, he pointed to the corner of her mouth. "You've got a little chocolate there."

"I do?" Embarrassed, D.J. automatically sent her tongue in search of the smudge.

Max watched her efforts, but shook his head. "You're missing it. Here." Leaning in, he licked his own thumb then touched it to the corner of her mouth and rubbed. It was exactly what he might have done for one of the kids. And it was nothing like what he might have done for one of the kids. Tingles zigged down D.J.'s spine then zagged back up again. "Got it," he said, examining the spot that was now transferred to his thumb. "Hmm. Chocolate *and* maple syrup." He put the tip of his thumb in his mouth and sucked it clean. "Not bad."

Ohmigod.

The kitchen door banged open, nearly making D.J. jump in the air. Sean…or James…barreled in. "We found a snake!" He raced to a cupboard. "I need a jar."

Max caught the boy before he could begin his jar search. The elder Lotorto shifted gears a lot more easily than D.J. could. She was still vacillating between hyperventilation and not inhaling at all. "I don't think so, partner. No more pets. Besides, you're supposed to be cleaning up." Over the boy's fervent protests, Max guided him to the door.

"But he'll be gone if we don't get him now. James is holdin' him."

"Tell James to put the snake down, so he can pick up some toys."

"Awww, Uncle Max…"

"Sean, if I have to come out there—"

Uncle Max?

Max shoved Sean out the door, walked to the refrigerator and swigged orange juice from the carton as if it were a shot of something far more soothing. Midswig, he caught himself and swore. "Sorry." Setting the juice on the counter, he got a glass. "I lived alone so long, I've still got a lot of bad habits."

Uncle Max? *Uncle?* "You're not married?" D.J. blurted, realizing immediately she was going to have to work on subtlety. "I mean, I thought…I assumed you were married to the children's mother. That you were their father."

Max drank half a glass of juice then set it aside and frowned. "Their mother was my cousin." He smiled. "You thought I was their father? That makes sense. I suppose I was so relieved to hire you, the little facts slipped my mind."

"*Little* facts? Mr. Lotorto, that is not a little fact." Questions raced through D.J.'s brain faster than she could sort them.

Laughing, Max reached for her elbow. "Mr. Lotorto? You can't be *that* angry about an oversight." Holding her arm, he guided her calmly toward the living room. "Come on, let's sit down while we have the chance. Not even 9:00 a.m., and I'm beat already." His smile was tired as he pointed her toward the sofa and settled himself on a large chenille-covered easy chair. "Embarking on fatherhood and a new business at the same time isn't exactly what I'd planned."

"Why didn't you tell me you weren't the children's father?"

Facing her, he wiped the smile from his face and said, "I just didn't think about it. Honest. Does it make that big a difference?"

D.J. thought a moment and decided that yes, it made a very big difference, though she'd have a hard time articulating why. She knew that decent men, good men, accepted the responsibility of single parenthood. But how did one characterize a man willing to take in four kids he hadn't even fathered? Also, D.J. had expected Loretta to be mighty pleased at the news she had grandchildren. Now D.J. would have to find out whether Loretta was related to the kids at all.

"Actually, I'm not their uncle," Max said, rubbing the back of his neck. "Terry was my cousin. Let's see, that would make me…"

"A saint." D.J. gaped at the man before her. Good Lord, not only hadn't he fathered the children, he wasn't even their immediate family. Nor was he being paid. The foster families who'd taken her in had been compensated fairly well by the state.

"I'm their second cousin," Max corrected, quickly disabusing her of the saint notion. "Believe, me, Daisy, I have never been in line for canonization. I'm just a guy muddling through."

Exactly what she'd expect a saint to say. So Terry, the woman whose picture he'd looked at with such tenderness, had been his cousin. "Why?" she asked bluntly. "Why are you raising your cousin's children?" A thought occurred to her. "Is this a temporary setup?"

"No, it's not temporary." Max looked angry, even offended. "The kids are going to stay with me. Right here. I don't consider family a temporary arrangement."

Sorry. His tone might have cowed someone else into abandoning her questions. But if anything, D.J. was more curious than before. What made a single man willing to turn his life upside down?

"Where is your cousin?"

Max's jaw tensed. A distant, unhappy expression entered his eyes. "She passed away."

So this really was permanent. "Look, Max, I'm not implying you can't handle this, but aren't there other people who could help out? Other relatives?"

Max's expression turned more intense than she'd yet seen it. "I didn't mean to snap at you before, but you're not the first person to ask whether this is temporary. Or to suggest that it should be." He leaned forward. "The kids and I are on our own, Daisy. Except for you."

Nerves and a growing sense of foreboding made D.J.'s deliberate laugh a little too loud. "That's not saying much, Max. I'm a...a waitress."

"How dedicated are you to waitressing?"

"How dedicated?"

"Do you see yourself waiting tables a year from now?"

She hadn't seen herself waiting tables for five minutes. Not until the idea of going undercover had entered her mind. "I suppose I don't really have a career plan," she fibbed, since she couldn't tell him that in five years she planned to own one of the most successful P.I. firms in Portland, Oregon.

"Stay with us, then."

The pancakes D.J. had eaten seemed to fall to her feet. She didn't know how to respond, so Max filled in the silence.

"Let's sign a year contract—you, me and the kids. We'll jump into this thing together. We need you, Daisy."

Holy cow. *Holy cow.* He wasn't kidding. She'd expected him to ask her to stay a couple of weeks—three on the outside—while he looked for a professional child care provider. "But…I'm not a nanny," she stumbled.

"You're great. The kids like you. I like you. Last night I came home to a clean house and kids who were fed and in bed at a reasonable hour. It finally looked like someone knew what they were doing around here."

Visions of burnt hot dogs and fried chicken coating ground into the carpet came swiftly to mind. "But I'm not a *real* nanny."

Max shrugged. "If you want to get technical, I'm not a real daddy. Love and instinct cover a lot of mistakes." Max relaxed forward, elbows on his knees. "I like having you here, Daisy. You fit us."

As a professional, D.J. tried to ignore the highly unprofessional fingers of pleasure that skittered up her spine. She fit?

"The fact is I can't take care of these kids and run a business by myself. I need you, Daisy Holden, and now that I've found you, I don't intend to let you go." A smile, wry, attractive, almost infectious, spread across Max's face. "We haven't discussed hours or days off yet, but I'll give you a tip—you can pretty much write your own ticket. Anabel and the boys will be in school next month. I take Mondays off, and Livie can come to work with me one or two other days during the week."

"But I'm not a—"

"Also, I'll double what you could have made waiting tables at the tavern."

D.J. breathed in and out slowly. She couldn't very well tell him that the money didn't matter, not after the song and dance she'd given him about needing a job. What could she say? *"Thanks, but your grandmother has offered a lot more money for investigating you than you could afford to pay me for being a nanny."* D.J. shook her head imperceptibly. This is what happened when you lied: you had to think of more and more lies to cover the first one.

"Thank you for your faith in me, Max," she began hesitantly.

Max winced. "I hear a 'but' coming. Tell you what—don't say

it. Don't decide yet. I think fate brought you to me, Daisy June," Max smiled, but he didn't look as if he was kidding at all. "You showed up exactly when I needed you, even though you're not from around here. That's not the kind of divine gift I want to ignore."

D.J. was sure she'd stopped breathing—which, looking on the bright side, would effectively eliminate her ability to respond. Oh, what a tangled web we weave…

The slider to the backyard opened and closed. Small feet pattered across the linoleum floor and into the living area. Arms down by her sides, Livie ran with a bobbing motion that made her pigtails bounce. Pigtails that big, strong, masculine Max must have put in her hair. A fresh wash of tears streaked the four-year-old's face. Only when she reached Max did her arms rise in the child's universal language. *Lift me.*

Max rose and, with one fluid sweep, had Livie in his arms before he'd even asked what was wrong. When her tears turned to hiccuping sobs, he cupped the back of her head and pressed her close. The gesture was so protective, it almost made Daisy believe that nothing bad could ever happen to this child.

"What's the matter, baby?" Max murmured as she calmed a bit.

"I got bi-bi-bit!" Livie cradled her own tiny hand.

Shifting his hold on her slightly, Max examined the offended appendage. Clearly, he didn't see anything. "What bit you?"

She hiccupped several more times then managed to choke out, "A ladybug."

"Sweetheart, ladybugs don't bite."

"Y-yes, they d-d-do!"

As carefully as if it were spun from glass, Max lifted Livie's hand and healed it with a kiss. "That must have hurt really badly," he told her, looking into blue eyes that held his. "You're very brave."

The twins invaded the room next at their usual boy pace. Anabel followed more sedately.

The chattering about snakes, about who picked up more toys, about where in the yard they would bury a dead gopher if they found one, began immediately. Over the growing cacophony, Max's gaze met Daisy's. "Guess we better get this show on the road." He seemed resigned, a little frustrated, and maybe a tiny bit wary now as he looked at her. "I think I caught you off guard. I didn't even ask you if *you* like *us*. Let's shelve the conversation for now and pick it up again later."

He herded the kids to their rooms to get their swimsuits, while she followed ponderously, biting her tongue so she wouldn't admit out loud that yes, darn it, she liked them a lot.

Daisy poked her head outside the women's room at Wal-Mart and looked around. Ascertaining that the coast was clear, she emerged from the restroom, leaned against the wall near the door and unzipped her fanny pack. She had two phone calls to make; this was the first chance she'd had all day.

Max had stayed home from work, but instead of giving her the day off to make her decision, he expected her to accompany them all on an "adventure day."

Apparently, he'd promised the kids a day of fun, which, to accommodate their juvenile tastes, meant the aforementioned bike ride, a picnic and the activity they were currently pursuing—shopping for a bathing suit so Daisy, too, could partake of the community swimming pool.

Oh, joy.

Max had asked her to take the day to decide whether she'd stay or go. There was no decision to make. She wasn't a nanny. She wasn't even a waitress. She was a private investigator, and she was starting to dislike this job.

Max needed to look for real child care; he didn't need to be lulled into a false sense of security, thinking D.J. might actually accept the job permanently. On the other hand, if she told him she wasn't staying, he might find someone else and fire her before she'd collected all the information Loretta wanted.

Pulling her cell phone out of her fanny pack, D.J. dialed Loretta's number then checked her watch—2:00 p.m. They'd already gone on their bike ride and picnic. Max had bought them all sandwiches at a market deli, where the lady behind the counter clearly knew him and his charges and was blatantly curious about D.J. Max was saved an introduction when Sean or James—D.J. was still having trouble deciding who was who—informed everyone within earshot at the small, locally owned market that "This girl's our new nanny. She's prob'ly better than the old ones. We dunno yet."

During the picnic, which took place in a park next to a fire station, Max spread out a blanket while D.J. awkwardly handed out sandwiches. Awkwardly, because it failed to occur to her that the sandwiches needed to be unwrapped for Livie and the boys. Or that stupid, idiotic juice cartons spewed like damned geysers if you didn't hold them properly when you stuck the little straw in.

The boys had guffawed, Anabel had sighed in her too-grown-up way, which was going to doom her to perennial geekdom in junior high if she wasn't careful, and Liv had looked as if she was going to cry when she realized most of her juice was watering the park lawn.

Well, pardon me. I drink out of cups! Daisy had wanted to shout, but Max had come to her rescue by claiming it happened to him all the time, too. Then he shared his lemonade with Liv, whispering in the girl's ear that he would never, ever share his drink with anyone but his best girl.

D.J. pressed Loretta's number into her cell phone. She was ready to give Loretta the information she currently had, and as far as D.J. was concerned that ought to be enough. Loretta had wanted to know her grandson's personal habits, whether he was in a relationship and, if so, what kind of woman he was with—someone who might go after his money should their relationship falter, or a woman who was financially independent? She wanted to know if Max had a good work history. She'd asked D.J. to secure his TRW report and, if possible, copies of his tax returns for the past five years. None of those requests was out of the ordinary, but now D.J. realized that all Loretta would glean from that kind of information was a pile of facts.

Loretta needed to watch her grandson express amazement over the boys' discovery of a cricket and to observe his interest as Anabel painstakingly explained the difference between dry ice and the kind they had in the picnic hamper. She needed to be present when Max made Liv feel like the most important little girl in the world. Then Mrs. Mallory would know what D.J. had already discovered: Max was wonderful.

D.J. didn't want to be in his house under false pretenses anymore. She didn't want to lie to him eight sentences out of ten—even if it was for a pretty good cause. Max had integrity. D.J. had only known him two days, yet she admired him already. For the first time, she felt embarrassed to be investigating someone. She longed to talk the situation over with Bill, but he'd been away on another of his excursions when she'd left Portland. She didn't know where he was exactly. So D.J. lectured herself: *Max's opinion of you is irrelevant. This is a job; it's not personal.*

Punching the send button, she waited for the phone to ring.

Shifting to stand by the drinking fountain at Wal-Mart as three women and their children pressed past her on their way to the ladies' room, D.J. willed Loretta to pick up.

On the fourth ring, the housekeeper answered. When D.J. asked for Loretta, she was told that Mrs. Mallory was "out of town for the next two weeks."

"What? I wasn't told she was going out of town," D.J. protested. "Where can she be reached?"

"She can't, miss," the housekeeper answered shortly. "Mrs. Mallory left strict instructions that she is on vacation and does not wish to be disturbed."

D.J. scowled into the phone. "Excuse me? She and I are working together. She can't be out of touch that long."

The housekeeper insisted that Mrs. Mallory could do what she liked, whereupon D.J. copped an attitude at least as snooty as the housekeeper's and said, "Tell Mrs. Mallory that if she wants information about her grandson, she needs to get in touch with D.J. Holden ASAP." Then she left her cell phone number and rang off, feeling exasperated with Loretta and with herself. She should have asked Loretta many more questions the first time they met. How had she become estranged from her daughter, for instance, and why hadn't she tried to get in touch with Max before now?

It occurred to D.J. that at this point she knew more about Max than she did about her real employer.

Checking her watch, she saw that she'd been away from Maxwell and the crew for fifteen minutes. Hoping she could safely borrow five minutes more, she dialed Bill's cell phone. He had no idea what she was up to.

His phone rang three times before voice mail picked up. "Hi. You've reached Bill. I'm gone fishing. It'd be a crime against nature to leave my cell phone on when I'm exploring God's country, but you can leave a message. If the fish aren't biting, I'll call you back." *Beep.*

What? Now *he* wasn't answering his phone? "Bill, it's Daisy." She hurried to speak after the tone, using her given name because neither Bill nor Eileen had liked it when she called herself D.J. "Why didn't you tell me you were going fishing? You don't even like fish!" Taking a breath, she tried not to sound as frantic as she felt. It simply wasn't like Bill to disconnect completely. "Listen, where are you exactly? Call me on my cell, okay, as soon as you get this. I'm in southern Oregon, by the way. I took a job down here. It's a good one. I'll be home soon." She paused, wondering what else she should tell him: *I'm trying to save our business?* She didn't want to sound nagging or judgmental or paranoid, but she wished he'd acknowledge the financial trouble they were in. "Okay. Well. Call me."

Snapping her phone shut, D.J. slumped against the wall. Bill had always been such a rock. Now he wasn't even trying to save the agency he'd spent thirty-some years building, and she couldn't predict his actions at all.

Bill simply hadn't recovered from the loss of Eileen; that had to be the problem, and it was up to D.J. to help. Like her, he had no one else. Bucking up her resolve, she knew she wouldn't let Bill or the business down.

"Hey, there you are." Max rounded the corner with one twin hanging on his leg, another hanging upside down in his arms. Anabel and Liv brought up the rear. "The boys need to use the john. Will you watch the girls?" Anabel's wary expression said she wasn't at all certain D.J. was up to this task.

"I got a bathing suit," Livie announced gaily. "It's brand-new, and it gots *beautiful* flowers. I'll show you."

D.J. smiled. It was nearly impossible to hang on to tension when the winsome four-year-old blinked those blue eyes up at her. She wondered if Terry had been a devoted mother. The kids' basic happy natures and Max's love for his late cousin suggested that she'd done a good job with the kids.

"Did you get a bathing suit, too, Anabel?" D.J. asked the pre-teen, hoping to receive at least a brief answering smile.

The girl pushed her glasses up the bridge of her nose. "I don't need one. Uncle Max has a lot of extra mouths to feed now, and my bathing suit still fits."

Geez, Louise. D.J. glanced at Max, who rolled his eyes.

"You're very thoughtful, Anabel," D.J. commended. *And way more grown-up than you should be.* Anabel too easily assumed a parental role, which made D.J. wonder if she should amend her estimation of Terry. D.J. had been like that, too, as a kid. She'd figured out early on that she'd have to rely on herself. Did Anabel feel the same? D.J. made a mental note to get more concrete information about Max's cousin as soon as she could.

Max interrupted her thoughts. "Now that Livie's got a new swimsuit, when we come out, we can get one for you."

It took D.J. a moment to realize he was addressing her and not Anabel. "Oh, you know, about that—"

James squealed as Max dipped him toward the ground. This time D.J. was sure it was James. She'd realized she could distinguish between the twins if she remembered that James's hair was curlier.

Max swung the little boy like a pendulum, making him chortle. D.J. grinned. For a flash, she wondered what might have happened if she and Max had really truly met in a bar, no hidden agenda involved, with her in a red dress and him seeing her from twenty feet away and sending her a drink. On the house.

"So, you'll watch the girls while the fellas and I are taking care of business?"

D.J. nodded. "Sure. I'll be here."

Max gave her a lingering look that sent about a thousand butterflies swirling through her stomach. "I'm counting on it."

Chapter Five

"I don't have money for a swimsuit." *And if I did, it would be a tankini from Land's End, not the kind of one-piece people buy when they actually intend to swim.*

Daisy, the nanny, stood with her arms crossed, red Dansko sandal tapping the smooth floor. Three feet away, Max held up two hangers with the kind of solid, utilitarian swimsuits worn by Olympic athletes and members of the Polar Bear Club. *Yech!*

"I don't really need a suit, anyway," D.J. pointed out. "You're going to be at the pool. I can sit on the sidelines in case one of the kids decides not to swim. We could…color."

Max frowned heavily. "All the kids will swim. They love it. Livie's going to start lessons at the Y. You may be at the pool a lot."

He let the comment hang in the air. *You may be at the pool a lot*…as if she'd already agreed to his year contract. D.J. glanced at Anabel and Livie, trying to hide in a rack of clothing. The boys were a few feet away, scooting matchbox cars across the floor. All were within earshot, so she decided not to say anything now, but tonight she was definitely going to have to disabuse him of the idea that she was a permanent hire.

"I'm sure the pool has a lifeguard, right? And the kids can wear those floaty devices. So I'm good with shorts. I brought shorts."

"Daisy, if it's about money, I'll pay for the swimsuit," Max told her. "Think of it as an employer-supplied uniform. Look, as far as I know there's no lifeguard at the pool we're going to today," he told her when she looked as if she was going to protest again. "I'd feel better if I knew you were there."

Daisy cringed. She had to divulge her secret now: the only emergencies she felt capable of handling around a pool were re-filling a margarita pitcher and applying sunscreen.

"I can't swim," she said, her voice low, the words deliberately mumbled.

Max craned his head toward her. "Say again."

D.J. made a face. He'd heard just fine; the disbelief in his expression told her so. Raising her chin, she announced more clearly, "I cannot swim."

The entire Wal-Mart got quiet. That's how it seemed to D.J., anyway.

She was ashamed about very little in her life, but somehow her inability to execute a decent freestyle, or even to dogpaddle, felt embarrassing down to her core. The whole world knew how to swim. Every parent taught his kid how to float in a pool or at least sent the poor shlub for swim lessons. In her case, neither event had happened. Her birth family had spent too much time fighting or drying out in detox centers to recall they even *had* a kid. And her early foster families had neither the time or patience to show her how to swim when they had more pressing concerns, like teaching her not to mouth off at the slightest provocation or steal from her foster siblings. By the time she'd moved in with the Thompsons she'd been twelve and adept at avoiding issues that bothered her.

"I'm just not crazy about water," she told Max, willing him to drop the subject.

He didn't. "Are you *afraid* of the water?"

"No, I'm not 'afraid.'" For some reason she hated that word. "I don't like to get wet."

Slowly, he lowered the swimsuits he'd been holding for her approval.

D.J. felt a prickly heat fill her face. She just wanted to get out of here. Was that too much to ask for? "It's not a priority. I live in the Pacific Northwest. I don't need to swim."

"What do you do when you go to the coast?"

D.J. shrugged. She'd been working since high school. She'd only been to the coast a couple of times.

"What if you go sailing or take a cruise?" Max persisted. "You ought to be able to tread water, at least."

"Why? Because I'm going to fall in? How many people really do that? I don't think that's an issue."

Crossing his arms, Max wagged his head, a papa lion setting the standard for his pride. "Knowing how to swim is a safety pre-caution, if nothing else. You may want to go river rafting or kay-aking some day. You have to know how to handle yourself."

"If I have that much time off and that much money, I'll go to Nordstrom, thanks. I handle myself great there."

Max shot a quick look at the kids to make sure they were still close and still occupied. Then he focused again on Daisy. He felt his own stubbornness rise to meet hers. He got a kick out of this enig-matic woman. Her odd mix of toughness and vulnerability captured him. One minute she was all confidence and wry independence. You could see it by the way she swaggered in her jeans, the way she'd put her hands on her hips and cocked a brow in warning at the boys when they'd teased Anabel about having to wear glasses.

On the other hand, Daisy could seem utterly out of her element and uncertain. Max wanted to know what made her tick. He wanted to know what kind of woman dressed in designer jeans, a red tank top and a dozen skinny bracelets to go on a family bike ride, but seemed utterly absorbed in the activity and unaware of the looks every boy, man and old fart sent her as she pedaled past.

If he had hired her for the restaurant, they'd probably have a full house every night.

The fact that he'd seen other men ogle her was probably what had led him to pick out two of the more modest bathing suits on the rack. The long-legged beauty before him had never swum in the ocean, Max realized. She'd never been skinny-dipping. Right or wrong—and, okay, it was definitely wrong—he wanted to be the first one to introduce her to those pleasures.

The hours he'd spent with Daisy Holden had all of Max's senses stirred and shaken.

Returning the blue suit to the rack, he grimaced. It shouldn't even occur to him to touch the nanny; he sure as hell hadn't thought about touching Mrs. Carmichael.

Nothing regarding this situation with Daisy was normal. He wanted her signature on a year contract—though he'd settle for six months—because he knew the kids needed some continuity. So did he. Also, he needed to show the social worker that he had child care lined up, that the kids' welfare was his top priority and that everything was finally under control. That part made sense. But if he thought about it a little, how persuasive would Daisy be?

Max tried to picture Nadelle Arnold, the social worker with a bite like a Doberman pinscher, warming up to Daisy, and he couldn't do it. Nadelle was conservative and sharp as nails. From the get-go, Max had felt that the woman was looking for reasons to discredit him as a guardian. God knew he'd given her plenty of ammo. He had no experience taking care of kids 24/7; the house had been in chaos every time she'd arrived. Plus, he had thrown away a decent accounting job for a lifelong dream of opening a restaurant. Now he'd hired a nanny who was young, beautiful and had no formal nanny experience. Maybe he needed to have his head examined.

Daisy was still staring at him mutinously, arms wrapped so tightly around her waist she was probably cutting off her air supply.

"This one's red," he said, waggling the remaining suit. "You like red." He gave a nod to the top that showed off her curves. She'd been wearing red the first time he saw her, too. "Pick a suit. I'll teach you to swim." Before she refused—and she was going to, he could tell—Max sighed. "Fear of water could be a problem when you're taking care of four kids who love to swim, Daisy. We're an outdoorsy family."

"I said I wasn't afraid."

"Fear of drowning then."

"I'm not afraid of drowning! I just never…I haven't had…" He looked at her doubtfully, conveying his certitude that she was scared but didn't want to show it. The tactic worked. "Oh, fine, I'll try on a bathing suit!" She grabbed the red number out of his hand and quickly chose two other suits from the nearest rack. "I'll be back," she said, the implied instruction clear. *You stay here.* There would be no swimsuit modeling.

Attitude colored her every step away from him. She was peeved. Watching her stomp away, Max grinned. He had no idea if he'd saved himself and his family by hiring Daisy, or if he was setting up his own slow torture.

D.J. stood under the shower in Max's master bathroom. The tears that flowed down her face mingled with the streams of water from the showerhead. She cried silently so no one would possibly hear her, but she felt like six kinds of a fool, nonetheless.

D.J. remembered exactly the last time she cried, it happened that infrequently. And usually for a very good reason. When Eileen died—that was the last time. This time she didn't have a reason at all. Well…

Max had taught her to dog paddle. That was her reason.

Scrubbing her hair more vigorously than necessary, D.J. tried to put aside the image of his smiling at her fumbling attempts to swim without snorting a schnozful of chlorine. He'd smiled *patiently,* full of encouragement…the way he'd smiled at James when the less athletic twin had tried to dive like his brother, and the way he'd smiled at Liv in her water wings. The amazing thing was that D.J. hadn't felt diminished by his consideration; she'd felt nurtured. Held. Even when his hands hadn't been touching her. And when they had…

Lordy, Lordy. What was wrong with her?

Putting her palms on the slick, tiled wall in front of her, D.J. braced her quivering body. She was strong. She was independent. For years and years she'd viewed herself that way and believed her survival depended on her strength. She didn't know the shaky, glob of Jell-O feeling inside her, and she didn't want to know it. Max Lotorto was merely a man. This excess of emotion was absurd. She must be PMS-ing.

Turning off the water, D.J. wrapped a towel around her body and stepped from the shower. Max had said he wanted to talk to her after the kids were fed. Most likely he was going to press his point about a contract. Naturally she would not agree, but she wanted to be able to think clearly, unemotionally when they spoke, so that she could impress upon him the need to search for a real nanny. Immediately.

After today D.J. knew it was time to leave. With luck, Loretta would be satisfied with the information D.J. currently had and would offer appropriate compensation. Maybe the money wouldn't be as good as what they'd originally agreed on, but once D.J. was safely back in Seattle, she could get a second job to pay off the bills that were in arrears. It would all work out.

That was her chant as she dressed in a denim skirt and short-sleeved blouse. *It will all work out for everyone…It will all work out for everyone….*

She was about to leave the bedroom when her cell phone rang. Running to retrieve the phone from her purse, D.J. frowned at the name showing on her caller ID: the Oasis. What was that? The phone number had an unfamiliar area code.

She pressed the talk button. "D. J. Holden."

"Ms. Holden? This is Loretta Mallory."

Relief and adrenaline surged concurrently as D.J. hurried to close the bedroom door. She could hear the children playing in their rooms and had earlier left Max in the kitchen, working on the Italian meal he'd promised them. She assumed he was still there. "Loretta," she breathed as the door clicked. "Boy, am I glad to hear from you! Gotta tell you, I was a little worried when I spoke to your housekeeper. She wouldn't tell me a thing."

"Janelle is well-trained to protect my privacy." Loretta spoke with a lock-jawed stinginess that made nearly every sentence she uttered sound like it required exhausting effort. D.J. had thought she was used to the affectation, but this evening the older woman sounded more stiff-lipped than usual.

"I respect your privacy," D.J. assured her politely, "but when I'm working on a case, I like to keep in touch with my clients. Even if they're on vacation." When Loretta chose not to respond, D.J. asked, "How long will you be gone?" She lowered her voice. "I have some information—quite a bit, actually—about your grandson. I think you'll be very pleased. I'd like to give you the information in person."

"Impossible. Tell me what you've got."

"We can't meet in person?"

"No, Ms. Holden. I'm recuperating. I had minor surgery."

Recuperating. Loretta was recuperating? Then why all the secrecy regarding her location? If there was one thing that bugged the stuffing out of D.J., it was finding out that clients were lying or hiding important details. Quickly she put together the facts: ill matriarch is looking for estranged heir; ergo, matriarch could be *very* ill and trying to hide it.

D.J. didn't have the patience right now to muck around. "Loretta, are you ill?" she asked baldly, unmindful of her client's penchant for privacy. If D.J. was about to reunite Max with a dying grandma, she wanted to know it. She didn't want to spring it on him.

"No, I am not *ill,*" the woman snapped as if the very word was offensive. "I am the picture of health, Ms. Holden. What information do you have for me?"

Hardball, eh? For dramatic effect, D.J. allowed a sizable pause. "Where are you, Loretta?"

D.J. knew she was pushing her luck. She still wanted the money from this gig, but now she wanted to protect Max, too. The more information she had about Loretta, the more information she could give Max when the time came. Now that she knew him, she didn't want him to walk into a situation completely blind.

It took Loretta several long moments to decide how to answer. "Kindly remember that I am paying you, young woman," she snapped imperiously, but just as D.J. thought she might have to back down, Loretta sighed noisily, indicating she was about to speak again. "I am the CEO of a company founded by my husband. I worked as hard as anyone to make the business a success. I sacrificed. Yet after my husband died, I had to fight for the right to remain part of a company that would not have existed without me. In some ways, it is still a man's world…D.J." This time she emphasized the unisex initials. "Working in the industry you do, I expect you to know that. What you have probably yet to realize, however, is that power in business also belongs to the young. I am seventy-one years old. To protect my position on the board, I should not appear older than fifty-five. I had liposuction."

D.J. was momentarily stunned into silence. The way the conversation had been heading, she'd expected Loretta to say she'd had a facelift. But, "Liposuction?"

"Correct. I expect your discretion."

Realizing she had pressured Mrs. Mallory into a disclosure that was, after all, none of her business, D.J. agreed swiftly. "You'll have it."

Without further ado, Loretta said, "And now I believe you have some information for me."

"Yes." Unconsciously glancing toward the closed door, D.J. said, "I'm working for your grandson. I've had a lot of opportunity to observe him over the past few days."

"You're working for him?" Loretta sounded surprised and impressed. "How did this come about?"

"Max owns a bar in Gold Hill, Oregon. I applied for a job—"

"My grandson owns a bar?" Loretta may have tried to keep her tone neutral, but was unsuccessful at masking her disappointment.

"He's remodeling half of it into an Italian restaurant."

Loretta asked several questions about the restaurant, its location and D.J.'s initial impression of Max's work ethic, to which D.J. responded positively.

"And his personal life?" Loretta intoned. "What do you make of that?"

This was the only point at which D.J. seriously hesitated. Because the children were Max's cousins, she knew there was a fifty-fifty chance that they were Loretta's great-grandchildren as well. Naturally this information belonged in her report. Some instinct, however, instructed D.J. to withhold certain facts until she understood the situation better.

"Your grandson appears to be…responsible in all areas of his life," D.J. said carefully. "He's never been married, but he's definitely family oriented. In fact, there's a cousin—Terry—to whom he seems to feel a great deal of loyalty. I'm wondering if Terry might be related to you. Do you have other children besides Max's mother?"

D.J. waited with bated breath for the answer, but Loretta, too, seemed uncertain just how much information she cared to share with D.J.

"I have a son," she said at last, her voice low and halting. "He is not an especially happy topic."

Loretta moved the phone away from her mouth to cough. She spoke to someone in the room with her, asking for more ice in her water, and D.J. was afraid she'd ring off or at the very least try to steer their conversation back toward Max. When Loretta returned to the phone, however, her voice was stronger, and she picked up the topic of her son without further prompting.

"Jeffrey was a wonderful child. Bright. Creative. He looked very much like my father. Unfortunately Jeffrey became caught in the juvenile rebelliousness of the nineteen sixties. His father and I had started our business by then, and I regret to say we were caught off guard by Jeffrey's choices. Eventually he took up with a girl who called herself Echo and rarely bathed. They did have a child together, out of wedlock. His father and I tried to get Jeffrey to come home at that point. We offered him a job, but Echo, whose real name, I believe, was Lucille, refused to join what she called the 'slaving masses.' The last we heard she had moved to Europe to work as an artist's model. I've no idea what happened to her or the child."

"So you don't know whether Terry was that child?"

"I do not. Although in my opinion 'Terry' is far too prosaic a name for Echo to have chosen it. Do you have some concrete reason to believe that Terry may be my granddaughter?"

Though Loretta seemed to make a practice of sounding jaded, she couldn't mask the hopefulness that colored her voice. For the first time since meeting the woman, DJ was moved.

"Nothing solid," D.J. said honestly, tucking away the information that Loretta apparently was interested in as many new family members as she could rustle up. "So, as far as you know, Jeffrey didn't stay in touch with Echo or his daughter after they moved?"

This time Loretta's hesitation was more prolonged and more profound. "My son began a love affair with drugs that precluded any affection he had for a woman. Or for anyone else. His father and I barely heard from him in over a decade. He had no desire to be in touch, and most of the time we didn't know where he was. I have no idea why I'm telling you this." Once again, Loretta's voice became more faint. "My children have given me a good deal of pain," she said. "I'm sure I paid them back in kind. If this woman—Terry—is my granddaughter, I would like to know."

"Do you know where your son resides now?"

"Yes. He lives in Mexico, where as I understand it, he spends most of his time painting. He has no desire to come home or to work for Mallory's."

"And has no knowledge of his daughter?"

"He's never mentioned her."

"Would you be willing to have me contact Jeffrey?"

"Yes, if you're able to. He frequently chooses not to maintain phone service. Now I'd like to know more about my grandson."

D.J. filled Loretta in on general details about Max's appearance and personality and the fact that he owned his own home. She also told Loretta that Max was previously an accountant, which pleased his grandmother enormously.

"Why would he leave that to purchase a bar? If you haven't done so already, find out whether he's leasing or owns the building. If he owns it, find out what kind of mortgage he has. Look into the mortgage on his home, as well, and check into whether his car is paid off. Does he have any significant credit card debt?"

D.J. hesitated. She hadn't dug into any of that yet, and now she didn't want to. Her guess was that, with four mouths to feed, Max might show significant debt.

"Your grandson is a terrific person. That's really what you want to know, isn't it?"

"If all I were doing was inviting him for Christmas dinner, your informed opinion of his character might suffice," she said, confirming D.J.'s earlier estimation of the situation. "Fortunately for my grandson, I intend to make him a very wealthy and powerful entrepreneur. *If* he proves equal to the task. I am responsible for thousands of employees in two states, Ms. Holden. I simply cannot think only of Maxwell or only of my desire for family. And, yes, I do desire family." There was a brief but telling pause. "I desire it very much. However, I've not had the greatest luck in that area, and I've no wish to be devastated again."

"I understand." D.J. truly did understand all about family and disappointment, and her empathy for Loretta's point of view rose a notch. But to dig into Max's finances, now that she'd made him trust her…oh, brother…like his *friend*… It felt wrong.

"I'm not asking you to prove he's Donald Trump," Loretta assured, sounding, for once, wry rather than imperious. "I simply require a modicum of evidence that his decisions are sound and reasonably conservative. It is my fondest wish to see my grandson in a career that I can attest will never fail to fascinate him…or to reward him financially. He and any future offspring will be, in the common vernacular, set for life. That is, if he has offspring. Is there a woman he's particularly interested in?"

"Not that I know of."

"Thirty-two, and there's no woman. Most members of our family partner, for better or worse, while still quite young. Have you any reason to believe my grandson is gay?"

D.J. choked. "No," she squeaked when she caught her breath. "I have no reason to believe that."

A knock sounded on the bedroom door, making D.J. jump.

"Daisy?" Max's deep voice reached through the door as if he were standing in the room. "If you're ready, I need you to hold down the fort while I make a quick run to the market."

"Uh…yeah. Okay!" she called.

"Is that him?" Loretta sounded breathless.

"Yes," D.J. whispered into the phone, surprised by Loretta's anticipation. "Listen, I've got to go. I'll call you back. Are you going to be at this number for a while?"

"Daisy? Did you say something else?" Max was still outside her door.

"Are you calling me from his restaurant?" Loretta asked before D.J. could respond to Max. In a voice that was almost girlish, she added, "I'll admit to you, I decided to have my surgery now partly in anticipation of meeting my grandson."

"Really?" The surprising confession was rather sweet, but D.J. had no time for confessions at the moment. To Max she called, "I'm just…getting dressed. I'll be out in a second!"

When Max had walked down the hall, she hissed to Loretta. "I've got to go. I'll phone you tomorrow or the next day at the latest."

Loretta agreed, and D.J. ditched her phone, then exited the room to help Max "hold down the fort." She had a sneaking suspicion, however, that her fort was in a lot more trouble than his.

By the time Max returned from the market, D.J. and the children were happily engaged in a kick-boxing lesson on the front lawn. It seemed to be as good a way as any to help the twins re-

lease some of their mind-boggling energy, and it encouraged all
four children to listen to and follow instructions.

D.J. took extra time with Anabel, who, as bright as she was,
could barely remember left from right when she had to coordinate
arm and leg movements. Refusing to allow the ten-year-old to run
away when she became embarrassed, D.J. continued to work with
her until Anabel's pride supplanted her frustration.

All the kids, however, wanted to abandon the lesson the moment
Max slammed the door on his minivan. D.J. made her junior war-
riors stand in formation until she released them from their practice.
The power play kicked her up a notch as an authority figure. Besides, it was fun to watch them wiggle as they fought the urge to bolt.

The moment she let them move, they ran headlong for Max,
who had been watching them—and her—with a huge grin on his
handsome face.

"Uncle Max! We learned how to 'fend us against 'tacks!" Livie
practically burst with excitement.

"Yeah, I saw as I was driving up." Max had no problem trans-
lating the little girl's abbreviations into something that made sense.
Juggling his grocery bags, he managed to tweak Liv's nose.

The boys demanded his attention next, showing off the muscles they were sure they had built. Max exhibited suitable admi-
ration then winked at Anabel. "You were looking good over there,
Bel. You may have found your sport."

Anabel delivered the first full-fledged smile D.J. had seen from
her. It disappeared, however, when the twins nudged each other
and taunted, "Anabel wants to be on the dance squad." They fell
into each other's shoulders, giggling as Anabel's cheeks went
nearly the color of Max's burgundy van.

"I do not!" she denied heatedly. "You're two grades behind me.
You don't know anything about it!"

By this time, D.J. had come closer. "Is the dance squad something they do at your school?" she asked. Anabel merely shrugged,
glaring the twins into silence.

D.J. made her first eye contact with Max. Regarding the dance
squad, he added his shrug to Anabel's. Then his smile broadened
again, and this time it was just for her. "You've got some pretty
fancy moves, Daisy June. Are you as dangerous as you look?"

D.J. felt herself blush. To counter her self-consciousness, she said, "You have no idea."

Max gave her a long slow nod of such appreciation, D.J. actually felt goose bumps race along her arms and legs.

Oblivious to the undercurrents between their guardian and their nanny, Sean and James began clamoring to know what was in the grocery bags.

"I told you I was going to bring a surprise, didn't I?" Max asked. The children nodded eagerly. "Have I ever lied to you?" A chorus of "No" sang in the air. "All right, then."

Setting the grocery bags on the ground, he made a big production of reaching into the larger of the two bags and withdrawing a bunch of green leaves with long stems and presenting it as if it were a brand-new play station.

"That's what you brought us?" Sean's wrinkled nose indicated blatant dissatisfaction. "What is it?"

Max blinked as though disbelieving his ears. "This is a fresh herb. What are the two most important herbs in Italian cooking?"

"I dunno," Sean answered, eliciting a look of such pain from Max that everyone, D.J. included, began to giggle.

Max's lower lip quivered, and he looked like he was surely going to cry. "Have I taught you nothing?" he complained. "Anabel, make me proud, baby." He waggled the bag of greens.

"Basil and oregano are the two most important herbs in Italian cooking." She pointed. "That's basil."

"Yes!" He punched the air.

"It's not our surprise, though," Anabel announced with great certainty.

Max looked at the herbs, then back at the children. "Oh." Returning the herbs to the bag, he made still another production out of rummaging for a package shaped like a very small toothpaste box, which he held up for their examination.

"What's that?" Livie asked, wrinkling her nose exactly like Sean.

"This, my children...owners of my heart...angels in the flesh... is anchovy paste." He extracted a small tube from the box. "*This* is your surprise."

There was confused silence all around, except for D.J., who erupted in laughter.

Cocking a brow, Max stood, holding up his delicacy. "You think this is funny?"

"What's an-chovy?" James grimaced as he tried to pronounce the word.

"Anchovies," D.J. answered for Max, "are small salted fish, and they're nasty. Only someone with a criminal mind would squish them up and stick them in a little tube. And only an uncle with a warped sense of humor would tell you *that's* your surprise."

Shaking his head as if he were trying to get water out of his ear, Max said, "Excuse me? *Warped sense of humor?*" He tapped his chest. "I'm a riot. So take that back or I'm going to make you eat anchovy paste until you say you like it."

The kids didn't understand exactly what was transpiring between their nanny and their uncle, but their glances bounced between the two adults with much interest and intermittent giggles.

D.J. noted the mischief and challenge in Max's eyes; she noted the spark of pleasure and told herself that her natural spunk was what made her rise to his challenge. "I will never eat anchovy paste. I will never, *ever* say I like it, and I will not take back what I said about your sense of humor. Basil and anchovy paste are only gifts if you're Luciano Pavarotti and it's dinnertime in Tuscany."

"Yeah!" Sean was delighted to agree with his nanny.

"What?" Max looked at the traitor with genuine surprise. "You don't even know what she said!"

"But he knows I'd never make him eat fish paste."

Max turned to D.J. with narrowed eyes. "You're diverting my children's loyalty." He advanced several soft, measured steps. "Take it all back."

D.J.'s hands settled confidently on her hips. She raised her chin. "Uh-uh."

Like gun fighters squaring off, they sized each other up. Max nodded slowly. "You know anything about wrestling?" he asked.

D.J. shook her head. "Nope. But I know about kickboxing. And it's only fair to warn you—I'm a fighting machine."

The setting sun glinted off Max's smile. "Thanks for the warning." Without wasting another moment—or warning *her*—he broke into a sprint, heading right toward her.

D.J. turned and ran. The children ran with her, laughing and squealing. "Run!" "Don't let him get you!" And from Livie, "You can't make her eat yucky stuff!"

"Traitors, every one," Max growled. "I'm going to make you *all* eat it!" He chased the lot of them in zigzags across the yard, pretending to get more and more frustrated when he couldn't catch anyone. Finally he saw D.J. more or less open and beelined toward her. In a classic wrestling move, he had her pinned to the lawn in no time flat.

"In wrestling," he informed her, his breath coming in warm puffs as he lay half on top of her, "we call what just happened a takedown. What do you call it in kickboxing?"

"I've never done it before," D.J. panted, the lawn warm on her back, Max's eyes gorgeously gray-blue above her. "I kickbox rubber dummies."

"Rubber dummies." He used one hand to brace himself above her, his arm grazing her ear. His other arm wrapped around her waist. A slow smile crinkled his eyes. "Where's the fun in that?"

It felt to D.J. that they stayed in that position a long, long time. At one point she could have sworn his face was moving closer, but then four more pairs of arms and four more sets of legs appeared to come out of nowhere, tangling with theirs. Hoots and shrieks of laughter enveloped them as the children fell on Max. Quickly he propped himself on his hands, push-up style to avoid crushing D.J.

"Time out, time out!" he hollered, but within seconds he and D.J. were laughing as hard as the kids.

D.J. hadn't discovered anything Loretta wanted her to, but she'd found out something about herself: she was enjoying being part of a family much, much more than she'd ever thought she could.

Chapter Six

A thorough investigation of the grocery bags revealed that the "surprise" Max promised the children was actually a whole chocolate cake with fudge frosting and chocolate kisses pressed onto the tops of each of ten rosettes. To earn the treat, they had to take turns sweeping the back patio, which they'd quickly turned into a highly unproductive game. Max didn't seem to mind. His true motivation had been to keep the kids occupied while he put the finishing touches on dinner. He'd asked D.J. to hang around and help him.

D.J. knew what she had to do as far as her P.I. job was concerned: find out whether the children and Loretta were related through Terry. If she decided to fulfill Loretta's request by ferreting into Max's personal finances, she could do it on her own, once she left his home and his employ. That led to the next item on tonight's agenda: make Max understand that he had to begin searching for new child care. Immediately.

She'd never taken a psychology class, and self-help books made her gag, but D.J. was clued in enough to realize that her aversion to marriage and family was a direct result of her past. Not that she thought Max had marriage on his mind. God knew he had enough to think about without adding romantic entanglement, particularly with a woman who had child-care skills only slightly better than the average turtle.

But *she* was attracted to *him;* there was no denying it. And the feeling, untimely and senseless as it was, seemed to be growing.

At the age of twenty-six, nearly twenty-seven years old, she'd had only a couple of longer relationships, one that had ended when her boyfriend moved home to Ohio, and one she'd enjoyed very much until she discovered that her police officer boyfriend tended to confuse the words "separated" and "divorced." When he'd referred to his "ex-wife," he'd really meant "the woman I might divorce someday if we get around to it, but then again maybe not."

Looking back, D.J. blamed herself and an uncharacteristically romantic imagination for her failure to see the situation clearly. A lady P.I. and a rugged male cop had seemed like a match made in pulp fiction heaven: they were two individualists who would share a second-floor apartment, keep their own voice mail and send out for pad thai. A couple living independent lives.

A little too independent.

For the first time, she'd let her guard down and started thinking about life in the long term. Big mistake. The evening she attended a holiday party thrown by one of Brian's friends had opened her eyes.

She'd spent two hours dolling up, because she had wanted to make a good impression on his friends. Left in the kitchen to help the hostess place crudités around a bowl of artichoke dip, D.J. learned quickly that Brian's "ex" had attended the precinct Christmas party with him the night before. Paring knife in hand, the lady of the house had regarded D.J. with a mix of pity and disdain that had made her feel as welcome as ants in the babas au rhum.

D.J. had ended her relationship with Brian the next day, but she'd felt stupid and small, and she hadn't dated in the two years since. If she ever dated again, she'd promised herself, she'd do such a thorough search on the guy, she'd know what he'd eaten for breakfast the morning of their first date.

Honest to God, she didn't want a whirlwind, sense-robbing romance. But something funny…something disturbing…happened to her when Max drew her into his circle with the children: she

got a pain deep in the center of her chest, a physical pain that felt
scary and ominous and…

Sweet.

She couldn't explain the warring thoughts that eddied in her
mind, and wished she were the type of person who confided her
most confusing feelings to others, but that had never been her
way. She believed no one would understand, anyway, unless they,
too, had packed their bags a dozen times during childhood and
moved from foster home to foster home. Twice D.J. had been told
a couple wanted to become her "forever family" only to have the
placements interrupted when the prospective parents changed
their minds.

D.J. knew she hadn't been the easiest kid, but that hadn't
blunted the feeling of rejection, nor the deep fear that she might
be somehow incapable of fitting into a family. With the second
halted adoption, she had stayed up all night, staring blindly at the
dark ceiling, terrified by the thought that when people got to know
her—really know her—they either saw or sensed something that
warned them away. Something she wasn't aware of and so might
never be able to fix.

After her tussle on the lawn with Max and the kids, she'd
needed time to collect herself. She'd felt dizzy, and not just because she'd had the wind knocked out of her. The stronger her feelings, the more vulnerable and exposed she felt, and she couldn't
accept that. She *chose* not to accept that. With apologies to Dr. Phil,
she wasn't willing to let go the hidden insecurities of a lifetime.
Insecurities bred defenses, and D.J. liked her defenses.

So while the kids were outside pretending to sweep and Max
was working magic with anchovy paste in the kitchen, D.J. had
excused herself briefly to tidy up.

Trading her grass-stained white jeans for a rather conservative
denim skirt and an eyelet top, she studied herself in the mirror and
decided the effect was right: very innocent. Wetting her mussed
hair, she combed it quickly into a sleek chignon.

Now, entering the kitchen to help Max with dinner, she knew
she needed to be more impartial, to keep the atmosphere as im-
personal as possible.

The first thing D.J. noticed in the kitchen was the remarkable aroma. Next her senses were assaulted by Max in a dark-green apron with Hug the Chef splashed across it in bold yellow. He'd crisscrossed the apron's skinny ties around his flat belly and lean hips, managing to make even an apron look sexy.

Ignore it.

"Wow, something smells good," D.J. said brightly. And impersonally.

Standing at the stove, Max turned. His gaze swept over her, and she was forced, yet again, to ignore the physical reaction she had—correction, that her *body* had—to his attention.

"So, what can I do to help?" she asked.

Setting a wooden spoon on a small dish atop the stove, he shifted to lean a hip against the counter, casually crossing his arms and legs. "Do you know your way around a kitchen?"

"I know where the stove and refrigerator are."

"Good enough." He beckoned her over. "You can stir the marinara while I make salad dressing."

"You make your own dressing?"

"Just like Paul Newman," he quipped, untying his apron as she approached the stove. "Turn around," he said.

"What will you wear?" she protested as he pulled the green neck loop over his head.

"I'll be fine. Your outfit is prettier than mine." He winked at her. "Turn."

Accepting that it was futile to argue with Max when he'd decided something, D.J. turned, reaching for the waist ties, but Max beat her to it. Reaching beneath her arms, he belted the apron around her once…twice…three times, bending close to her each time.

"All set." He stepped back.

When D.J. turned, she expected to see that smoldering look in his eyes, but he was holding up the wooden spoon and smiling as if he had nothing more than dinner on his mind.

She, on the other hand, could feel herself reddening. To cover the moment, D.J. took the spoon and glanced into the pot on the stove. "So, what is this? Canned sauce?" She knew the answer, of course, but felt most comfortable with Max when they were trading quips. It helped keep a certain…distance.

He responded to her question as if it had caused physical pain.

"Daisy. When you are in my kitchen, kindly remember you are talking to the only son of an Italian father and that my Italian grandmother lived with the family."

"And that means…?"

"That means Chef Boyardee was considered heresy in my family."

"Oh. Too bad. I like SpaghettiOs with the little cut-up franks."

Max winced. "I'm going to forget you said that. This sauce is made from fresh tomatoes. It simmers for hours. Sometimes overnight. There are wines that don't have the bouquet of this sauce."

"Not given to exaggeration, are you? How did you make it so fast if it has to cook that long?"

"I make it in large batches at the restaurant and bring it home."

"I thought you had a chef at the restaurant."

"I do, but I make my own marinara. And lasagna. When we officially reopen I'm going to introduce this town to a Bolognese that will make them weep."

"A bowl o' what?"

Max pressed the heels of both hands against his eyelids. "To think I almost hired you as a waitress. Where have you worked?"

"In a…Thai restaurant mostly," she improvised. "I like Asian food." That seemed safe; she'd ordered enough Thai takeout to have some idea of what she was talking about. "So what is it— Bolognese?" She pronounced the word correctly this time. "Sounds like a dance."

Max raised a brow. "Very good. That's truer than you realize. All sauces are a dance. A relationship of flavors." Pulling a tablespoon from the drawer, he dipped it into the pot and blew gently on the hot marinara. "Like in a marriage."

"Marriage? You think marriage is a dance?"

"Absolutely."

"Meaning what? One person leads and the other follows?"

"No." He pulled a face. "Meaning that the parts complement each other and the whole. They blend. They mingle. Like in a sauce, no one ingredient overpowers the other, but over time the individual seasonings are better together than they could ever be apart."

D.J.'s mouth went dry. "That sounds like a lot to live up to."

Max shrugged. "The good stuff in life always takes work,

right? And time." He held the spoon of sauce to her lips and ordered, "Taste."

D.J. didn't want to taste; her belly rumbled with a butterfly sensation. She talked to overcome the nerves. "You really get into cooking analogies, don't you?"

"Ah, Daisy, girl, cooking—and eating—are about much more than food." He inched the spoon closer, urging her. She leaned forward self-consciously, his gaze following her. The moment the sauce hit her taste buds, her eyes widened. "Well?" he prompted.

"It's good." In truth, though, it was better than merely "good." Angelo at the gym, who ate Italian food every day of his life, would have palpitations over Max's sauce. D.J. took another taste and thought she could eat it every day of the week, too. The most disturbing thought flashed though her mind: she was beginning to think she could do most things with Max every day of the week. "It's very, very good," she said, trying to contain herself. "Your granny taught you how to make this, huh?"

Max grimaced. "Don't say 'granny.' Call her Nonna. Makes me sound more macho. And, yeah, she did."

"Nonna does not make you sound more macho. Sorry to break that to you."

Grinning, Max tapped D.J. on the nose with the spoon handle then deposited it in the sink. He moved away from the stove to collect the ingredients for his dressing.

Taking advantage of the increased space between them, D.J. tried to relax while Max smashed a piece of garlic with the flat of a knife. She watched curiously as he rubbed the clove around the inside of a big wooden bowl. Now that he'd brought up the topic of family, she couldn't ignore the opportunity to fish for the information she needed. She was still here on Loretta's dime, and Lord knew she could use a distraction from his absurdly sensual a-sauce-is-like-a-dance-is-like-a-marriage theory.

"So Max," she began with what she hoped sounded like casual interest, ignoring his question in lieu of her own, "Did you come from one of those huge Italian families, like the kind you see in the movies?"

"You mean like in *The Godfather*?" He smiled at her.

D.J. laughed. "Sorry. Is the image of a big Italian family a cultural stereotype? I was thinking of *Moonstruck,* actually," she admitted. "Cher had all those aunts and uncles."

"My father was an only child."

"Really." D.J. was sure her heart missed several beats. If his father was an only child, then… "Terry was your cousin on your mother's side?"

"Right. Use that wooden spoon to give the marinara a stir every now and then, okay?"

She did so absently, her mind rapidly sketching the Mallory-Lotorto family tree. Loretta's son, Jeffrey, had a daughter; now D.J. was certain that child was Terry. Loretta claimed that Jeffrey had never had contact with his daughter, but then she'd been pretty out of touch with Jeffrey herself.

"Were you close to Terry's parents?"

Max was bent over the counter, mincing fresh herbs as he spoke. "Barely knew them. My uncle Jeffrey, Terry's father, never married her mother. He didn't have much to do with Terry for the first few years of her life. Then Lucille—that was Terry's mom—met someone she fell hard for. He was wealthy and liked to travel in style, and he wasn't keen on taking a three-year-old with them. So Lucille pretty much dropped Terry on Jeffrey's doorstep and said, 'Your turn.'"

Apparently Lucille…Echo…had made the transition from hippie to yuppie after splitting with Terry's dad.

Max paused to eyeball measure olive oil and balsamic vinegar. "Jeffrey called my mom and asked if we'd take Terry. He hadn't lasted a day with her. He couldn't handle kids. According to my parents, Jeffrey couldn't handle much of anything back then."

"Did Terry stay with you?"

"For six months that time. Up till then my mother had been afraid she'd never meet her only niece. At first she was thrilled. She asked her brother to stay, too, but he declined. Then Lucille's relationship fizzled. That started a pattern. She would come to collect Terry and settle down—I use the term loosely—in some new town. As soon as Lucille found a new man, Terry would be back with us."

"Let me guess," D.J. said, seriously disliking the picture Max painted. "Terry would just start feeling secure again when her mom would show up boyfriendless and depressed and wanting her daughter."

Max looked over. "You got it."

"How many times did that happen over the years?"

"Too many to count."

"Your parents were okay with this?"

"Hell, no." Max finished the dressing by whisking sugar and mustard into the oil, vinegar and herb mixture. His expression turned as sour as the balsamic vinegar, and he tapped the whisk much harder than necessary on the side of the bowl. "My parents were furious that Terry was shuffled around like a piece of luggage. They begged Lucille to let Terry live with us full-time."

"Did she?"

"I think she considered it for a while, but then she married again, got pregnant and came to get Terry. The whole family moved to Europe. I didn't see Terry again until she was seventeen."

"What was she like then?"

"Independent. Funny. Jaded. Way more cynical than she should have been." Max wiped his hands on a dark-green dish towel. His gaze seemed faraway. "She'd gotten into drugs by then. She struggled with them on and off until the day she died."

D.J.'s stomach dropped sickeningly. "How *did* Terry die?"

Max turned to her, looking more tired and bleak than she'd ever seen him. "From a drug overdose. Five days out of rehab."

"Were the kids—"

"They were with me. Terry was at a friend's house."

Silence fell on the kitchen for several long moments. The only sound came from the sauce bubbling gently on the stove and the muted voices of Terry's children in the backyard.

D.J. struggled—hard—with a surge of anger that threatened to obliterate the compassion she had previously been feeling for Max's troubled cousin. "So you picked up where your parents left off."

"What do you mean?"

"Taking care of children for someone who had no business having kids in the first place."

D.J.'s unequivocal condemnation obviously surprised Max. She knew she should tread more softly—she was here to gather information, not pass judgments—but Terry's drug abuse hit too close to home for her to be objective.

"Terry wanted nothing more than to be a good mother." Reproach, albeit calm, colored Max's voice. "She *was* a good mother when she was clean."

"How often was she clean? Was she on drugs when she was pregnant?" Loretta would want this information.

Turning toward D.J. fully, Max narrowed his eyes. "None of the kids was born addicted if that's what you're implying."

D.J. crossed her arms, stubbing the toe of her shoe into the linoleum. "I'm not implying anything. It just seems you want to whitewash your cousin's behavior." Oh, well. So much for not passing judgment.

"Wrong." Max issued a quick, irritated denial, then paused. He was clearly frustrated and he was angry, but not necessarily with her. Passing a hand over his face, he calmed himself, then met D.J.'s gaze as if he wanted to imprint his next words on her brain. "I realize it's hard to feel compassion for addicts when they've got kids and they relapse, but I don't have that luxury. I need to understand why someone who wanted nothing more than family panicked every time she got close. I've got to feel compassion for her because someday I'm going to have to explain her behavior to four kids."

The children's innocent faces came to mind, leaving D.J. with an uncomfortable sense of shame for her fierce judgments. At their ages, she, too, had wanted to believe the best of her mother. She'd seen Joan only a handful of times after entering foster care yet she had clung tenaciously to the faith that one day her mother would come for her. While other kids rode bikes or played with dolls, D.J. had spent hours alone, constructing scenarios in which her mother appeared at the foster home, prepared to steal D.J. away if necessary, like Sally Field in *Not Without My Daughter*.

Joan never had shown up, however. The few times the social worker had taken D.J. to see her mother, D.J. had recognized the smell of alcohol and the disconnected, drugged-out look in her mother's eyes.

If D.J. judged Terry's relapse, she had good reason: she understood firsthand the scars a mother's absence left. Especially a mother who was an addict. "What did you tell the kids when she died?"

Max plowed a hand through his hair. "She'd been in rehab a few times. They were so little. We always told them she was sick and needed to be where the doctors could see her every day. Anabel asks the most questions, of course. I planned to postpone telling her the truth until she was twelve or thirteen, but I doubt she'll wait that long." His stormy eyes showed how little he looked forward to that moment.

Compassion did flood D.J. then, but the feeling was all for Anabel and Max. How well she remembered being ten, the age Anabel was now. That was the year she'd been legally relinquished for adoption, the year she'd finally understood her mother wasn't coming back, ever.

Anabel was much better behaved and so much smarter than D.J. had been. At ten D.J. had been a loose cannon, firing at everyone within range. The only thing to worry about with poised, self-contained Anabel was that she might hold her emotions and her questions inside.

After what seemed like minutes, during which Max and D.J. were each lost in their own thoughts, the buzzer on the oven sounded, startling them both. At the same time, they realized the sauce had started to boil. Max bounded forward to reach for the knob on the stove while D.J. plunged the wooden spoon into the marinara to keep it from scorching. They bumped each other, Max's arm grazing D.J.'s breast and stomach. D.J. jumped back, bringing the spoon with her and splashing spaghetti sauce over the white stove.

D.J. yelped, and Max took the spoon, tossing it onto the spoon rest so he could examine her arm. "Did you burn yourself?"

"No. I just got sauce everywhere."

Max shook his head in relief. "You scared me."

"Sorry. I got really startled."

He smiled. "Me, too. It was probably what we were talking about. Our nerves were already on edge."

D.J. nodded. Her nerves were still on edge, and the fact that he continued to hold her arm didn't help any.

Max seemed to notice he was holding her about the same time D.J. did. He looked at her, his eyes still troubled, and she felt a guilty ache in the pit of her stomach, knowing he must think she was a world-class witch for criticizing his cousin.

"Well. My arm's okay," she said, gently pulling free from his grasp.

He released her, but didn't move away. "Daisy, you're not the only one with strong opinions about the way the kids were raised. I've got a social worker breathing down my neck. I get the feeling she thinks I may be only slightly better a parent than Al Bundy." Briefly he told her about Nadelle Jacobs.

"You're not the children's legal guardian?"

"Terry brought it up before her last stay in rehab. I didn't want to hear her talking 'negatively,' so I told her I'd always be here for her and the kids, and we left it at that." He shook his head. "I was an ass. It would have been a lot harder for Nadelle if I had something on paper."

"You said there were no relatives to help you, but is someone challenging your custody?"

"Just the state." His gray eyes turned stormy. "You saw what it was like when you first got here. Nadelle has seen us when it was even more chaotic. The kids grieved hard for the first month, and things were pretty out of control. I had just bought the restaurant and was having trouble—plumbing and electrical and permits." He made a dismissive gesture with his hand. "It's all par for the course, but I was needed in two places, and I wasn't here as much as I should have been. The kids kept acting up, I had trouble hanging on to a nanny, and the last time I saw Nadelle Jacobs, she asked me to consider the benefits of a two-parent family for the kids."

"She wants you to relinquish them for adoption?" D.J. could feel her blood pumping in response to this new information. "Hardly any families adopt four kids at once, Max, especially older kids. It could take years unless she splits them up. Splitting siblings happens more than you think. And where are they going to live in the meantime? Foster care, right? I bet she wants to put them in foster care." Where they would quite likely also be separated. D.J. felt her energy turn almost hyper.

Max eyed D.J. askance. "You know a bit about the system."

"Well…I've met a few foster kids." She'd told a number of untruths to cover her bases since she'd met Max, but that, at least, was honest. "I know foster care is necessary in certain cases, but it isn't perfect. Some kids have brothers or sisters they see way less often than their school friends."

"Yeah, well I'd go to prison for disposing of Nadelle Jacobs before I'd let anybody separate these kids." Max's grim humor nonetheless underscored the steadfastness of his commitment.

Immediately D.J. thought of Loretta…and the security implied by all that money. Resources like Loretta's would surely impress a social worker. "Max, aren't there *any* other relatives who could help you?" she prodded, fishing to see what he knew.

In the hesitation before he answered, Max realized the oven was still on. With a curse D.J. suspected had nothing to do with the food, he twisted the temperature knob, grabbed a padded mitt and opened the door, forcing her to back out of the way so he could remove a slightly burned pan of lasagna.

Max set the pan atop the stove and tossed the mitt aside. He poked at the burned section of cheese with a fork and muttered, "Anabel won't eat anything burned. She says it causes 'carbon poisoning.'"

D.J. watched him work. He might want her to believe the pause in the conversation was due to a burning dinner, but she realized in those few moments that he absolutely was hiding something. She waited until he had excised the offending piece of cheese, then said, "So, no relatives? Terry's mother or father?"

Max backed away from the oven, his jaw clenched, black hair mussed from raking his fingers through it. When he spoke, he stared at the lasagna, not D.J. "Terry's mother is dead. Her father lives in Mexico somewhere and doesn't want to be bothered. He's never seen his grandchildren, never sent a birthday card. It about killed Terry every time she called to tell him he was a grandfather, and the best response he could give was 'Okay.'"

"That's awful."

"Yeah. Unfortunately she married men who weren't much different from her father."

"Do the children have different fathers?"

"Anabel's father lives in Ireland. I think he's been married twice since Terry. She always had trouble getting him to stay in touch. As for the twins and Livie, I don't know where their father is. He left Terry to become a performance artist. He said the pressure of kids stifled his creativity."

Terry's experience left D.J. with a sour feeling in her stomach and anger at the men the young woman had chosen so unwisely. "Well, what about…other grandparents?" she ventured. "Or, I don't know, even great-grandparents?"

"Fresh out. There's no one." Max's response was swift, decisive, and untrue. The enmity behind the denial was unmistakable. "I told you once before, Daisy, I'm it. And you're the only help I've got."

He stepped toward her, his hands on his hips, eyes stern and demanding. "It's time to finish that conversation we started this morning. Nadelle is coming next week for another 'home visit.' She has to see that I've got this situation under control. Do I? Are you staying? Because I don't think I can make it any plainer than I already have—I need you." He took one more step in her direction. D.J. watched the rise and fall of his chest. "Six months," he bargained, his eyes softening now, but watching her no less closely. "Give me six months. Once you have, I bet you won't want to leave. You're going to love us."

A smile tugged stubbornly at D.J.'s lips. One minute Max was hard and forbidding; the next, charming. Both facets, she knew, were genuine. He could play like a kid and show affection with the ease of someone who trusted in the world. But in a fight for someone or something he loved, she had no doubt Max would be severe, even ruthless if need be. Loretta would probably like that.

Before she could report again to Loretta, however, D.J. had to deal with the matter at hand. She didn't want to see the children separated any more than he did. She didn't want them to leave the only father figure they'd ever known or the place they called home, whether it was chaotic or not. A social worker might have a degree, she might understand the mechanics of early childhood development, but D.J. had personal experience. She knew that Anabel and Livie and the dynamic duo belonged with Max. She knew they needed consistency. She knew they, above anyone, needed the answer she was about to give.

"I can see you want the best for Anabel and Livie and the boys. I see that every moment you're with them. And, let's face it, you're desperate, but I'm still flattered that you think 'the best' could be me." He wanted to speak, but D.J. wouldn't let him. "My answer is no, Max. It has to be, and there's nothing you can say to change my mind. I'm not a nanny. I never said I was. As a…waitress…you know, you have the freedom to move around, and…and…"

D.J. realized she was twining her fingers, and halted the nervous action immediately. She had nothing to be guilty about. In this moment, at least, she knew she was doing the right thing.

With more confidence, she completed the sentence she'd started. "I like my freedom. I've always been that way. I'm not a nester. I'm not that type of person. Not like you." She smiled into a handsome face that watched her with burgeoning disappointment and no small amount of frustration. "You and the kids, you need someone who'll stick. You can't count on me for that. I will stay through next week, though, if you still want me to. I'll be here when the social worker comes, and we don't have to tell her I'm not staying forever, you know? If she requests another visit after next week, I think you should play hardball. Tell her you're hiring a lawyer. Tell her someone from the media contacted you and wants to do a story about harassment of single-father households." *And by then if all goes according to my plan, you'll have Loretta and a whole lot of power on your side.* "I know you have the restaurant to open, but I bet we can find you a real nanny by the end of next week." By the end of next week, he'd be Loretta's acknowledged heir if D.J. had anything to say about it. He could hire a dozen nannies.

A brief, benign smile curved Max's lips but barely made it to his eyes. "You've given me a lot to think about," he said, then winked and pointed at her. "I'm going to take you up on your offer to stay another week. Thank you. I think we'll handle Nadelle by taking this a day at a time for now." He twisted his wrist and checked his watch. "Better get some food into these kids so she can't add malnutrition to her list of grievances." He offered another smile that merely skimmed the surface. "You mind calling them in while I toss the salad?"

"No." D.J. shoved down the discomfort she felt as she turned toward the kitchen door. She refused to regret doing what was right. Right for them, right for her.

When she stepped onto the patio, the first thing she saw was Livie trying to wield a broom three times her height. An uncommon rush of tenderness flooded the corners of her heart not filled with guilt. It would be better if Max pulled away. She'd said good-bye too many times in her life to get sentimental about it, but D.J. sensed that saying goodbye to this family would be hard, much harder than it ought to be.

Chapter Seven

A warm oven and the August night made Max's living room unreasonably hot, at least as far as Max was concerned.

He shifted uncomfortably on the sofa, once again his bed for the evening. Reaching behind him, he walloped his pillow three times then folded his arms behind his head, leaned back and sighed heavily. If he slept five minutes tonight, he'd be a grateful man.

He had controlled himself admirably, he thought, when Daisy declined his job offer. He'd remained jovial in front of the children, asked polite questions about Daisy's favorite foods, her hometown and her taste in music. He'd even made chocolate chip cookies with the kids after dinner. His intention there had been to send Daisy into the other room to watch TV so he could gain a little distance from her, but she'd remained in the kitchen to help. She'd gotten flour on her face and had snitched raw cookie dough with James even though Max had warned them all about salmonella. At one point he'd turned around from putting cookies in the oven to find James and Daisy with cookie dough stuffed in their cheeks like wads of tobacco. They'd looked at him with wide, innocent eyes, lips shut tight, and when he asked whether they were eating dough *again,* they'd wagged their heads in an identical, exaggeratedly innocent fashion.

The memory sent a fresh wave of desire and frustration crashing through Max's body. He wanted Daisy here.

He wanted Daisy everywhere.

Everything he'd told her was true: she fit them. But how could he expect her to feel the same? She was right. He'd roped her into this gig because he'd been desperate and she'd been available, but she wasn't really a nanny and had never claimed to be. She'd been honest; he couldn't fault her there. Her lack of guile was one of her most appealing qualities.

Max stared at the darkened ceiling of his living room. Somewhere in the vicinity of where he was lying, there was a water spot that indicated a roof leak he'd have to find the time, money and energy to repair before the rainy season began. At the moment, the lingering aromas of chocolate, butter and vanilla made the place seem homey, but in stark daylight nothing would distract from walls that needed paint, carpets to be replaced, shingles to repair and grounds he intended to landscape if he ever found the time to begin. What did he have to offer a woman at this point in his life?

Whoa. Involuntarily Max's body jerked. He meant, what did he have to offer a *nanny?*

Max ground his teeth. Ah, he was a damned liar; he didn't mean that. When Daisy made it clear she wasn't staying on to take care of the kids and that there would be no changing her mind, Max's defenses dropped and he began once more to feel the desire she ignited in him. He was viewing his house, his life, the kids, everything now through the eyes of a man who wanted a woman.

Max bought this place a year and a half ago when he left Silicon Valley to begin a new life away from traffic and noise and the constant striving for more, bigger, better. He'd become a successful corporate accountant after college, but managing other people's finances had become as soul fulfilling as counting backward from ten, over and over and over. He'd taken a week's vacation to go rafting along the Rogue River with a buddy and had felt the first real happiness he'd experienced in a long, long time. Max had been in a relationship at the time with another accountant in his firm.

When he arrived home, full of enthusiasm for southern Oregon and a life outside the city, his girlfriend had seemed more stunned than anything else. But when he shared his dream of opening a family-style restaurant in a town she'd never even heard of, she'd let Max know loudly and clearly that she didn't appreciate the "phase" he was going through and suggested counseling for his "mood swings."

One month later Max returned to Oregon alone to buy this small farm with its heirloom apple trees and cedars, its broken-down chicken coop and a herd of cows lowing in the pasture next door. Owls hooted at night, and the mostly flat acres behind the modest structure he called home bore more than one calling card from the neighborhood deer. The first time Max put his hundred-dollar loafers down on deer poop, he remembered his girlfriend's advice about finding a good therapist and wondered if she'd been on the right track.

But the truth was he loved it here. He believed his parents would have loved it here. By the time he'd moved in, Terry had been doing well after her fourth stay in a drug and alcohol treatment facility. She'd sworn she was ready for a new life, and Max had offered her the use of his home, thinking that a small southern Oregon farm would be a great alternative to city living for her and the kids. Back then he hadn't even been thinking about starting a family of his own. Now he had one, but without the woman. Sometimes he felt as if he'd been thrown into the ocean without a life preserver when all he'd wanted was a slow cruise down a lazy river. He hadn't even had a date in the past year and a half.

He hadn't had sex.

Couldn't say he hadn't thought about it, of course, but at first he'd been too busy to think about dating, which required more effort than he felt like giving it, and then with the kids…

Max sat up, peeling off his T-shirt and tossing it over the back of the couch. It was too damn hot in here.

Ever since Daisy had walked into the bar, sex had been on his mind again. Now that he knew she wasn't going to be his permanent nanny, his defense against his own interest was crumbling. He'd planned to hire only locals to work in his restaurant; now he was thinking he ought to make an exception in Daisy's case. Having an affair with one's restaurant employee wasn't as bad as having an affair with a nanny, was it?

"Get a grip, man." Sitting up, Max buried his head in his hands. Daisy had as good as admitted she didn't have staying power. She wasn't a nester. Any man with four kids and half a brain would look for a mother type the next time he got involved with someone.

Then again…

People changed. He had. A year ago, he'd cared first and foremost about his own comfort. He'd moved because it had suited *him*. When his girlfriend balked, the relationship ended. Buying this property, he hadn't given a rat's hind end about school systems or libraries or the proximity of playgrounds. He'd eaten what he wanted, when he wanted, yet now—

Ah, all right, so his and the kids' diets were still crap, but at least now he complained about it.

Heck, he watched Daisy—all the damn time when she wasn't looking. He noticed things. Her eyes sparkled, and her luscious mouth curved softly every time she looked at Liv. She grinned when the twins were hunting trouble. Sometimes she aided and abetted. And she was concerned that Anabel had responded only minimally to her overtures.

Max sat up straight. Despite what Daisy June Holden told him about herself, her actions suggested that she was mommy material, or his Italian nonna couldn't boil water.

Feeling triumphant because his thoughts had taken him exactly where he wanted to go, Max rose from the sofa and headed toward the kitchen for a glass of milk and a few of the cookies they'd made earlier. What he needed to do was take the pressure off Daisy. She saw herself as a waitress, not a nanny. All right. He'd work on finding a new nanny, even if he had to import one from England. He'd give Daisy the restaurant job she'd been after in the first place, and he'd begin exploring a relationship between them. He didn't want to be cocky, but he really didn't think she'd take that much persuading. The temperature rose several degrees when they were together.

Picking his way toward the kitchen in the dark, Max brought his foot down on a plastic toy with sharp edges on top and, apparently, wheels on the bottom. He had just enough time to holler

"Ouch!" when his foot slid out from under him. He flailed his arms, looking for balance, but lost the struggle and fell flat on his butt.

Afraid he might have awakened the household, Max stifled the curses rising inside him and remained still, listening for the sound of someone—Daisy, perhaps—rushing to his rescue from the hallway. When no one came, his mood skittered quickly from pissed off to self-pitying to philosophical. The Universe had spoken: maintain your focus, watch your step. Better yet, don't walk around in the dark.

Max arose, moving much more thoughtfully through the rest of the room. He was going to get through this next week with Daisy, let her help him get Nadelle and the Department of Human Services off his back. He'd start looking for a new nanny, and then—and only then—would he entertain thoughts of, well, entertaining Daisy.

That seemed like a very wise plan…until anticipation began to skyrocket inside him, he tripped on another toy and figured the universe wasn't quite through with him yet.

Stretching in bed after a good night's sleep, D.J. moaned and congratulated herself on clearing her conscience the night before. She may not have told Max the *whole* truth, but at least she'd taken herself out of the Daisy-for-permanent-nanny campaign.

Flopping onto her back, she reached her arms over her head and tried to gauge the time by the cool light filtering through the window shade. It had to be early. Last night the digital clock radio had been moved from the nightstand to the living room because Max had to be up extra early to meet with the plumber and contractor and to accept delivery of equipment for the kitchen at his restaurant. He'd said he'd be gone before D.J. and the kids got up this morning, so she and the kidlets were going to be on their own. All day. Fortunately she had a plan.

With the social worker making a home visit next week, D.J. decided that she and the children would spend the day making this place shipshape. Granted it would take more than a weekend warrior to turn this pumpkin into a golden carriage. For today, she'd settle for polishing the edges off the Green Acres look. Number one on the agenda: do something about the thoroughly disgusting chicken coop the rug rats had shown her yesterday. She might be a city girl with little fondness for any fowl that wasn't fried, but she'd bet her last pair of 501 jeans that any enclosure filled with hay and chicken droppings would be a red flag to a social worker who cared about germs and environmental hygiene.

Before they could get started on work, though, D.J. had to get up and make a good breakfast to fuel her little workers' tummies until snack time. Fortunately, she had a plan for that, too. Though she was no better a cook today than she'd been yesterday, she'd fallen asleep last night mentally reviewing her own favored breakfasts and coming up with ways to make them kid friendly.

Sitting up, she threw off her light covers, rather looking forward to the challenge of the day. While the kids were working outside, she planned to sneak back into the house to look once again for evidence of Max's financial status or anything she could find that might satisfy Loretta.

D.J. was about to slip out of bed when the sound of the TV alerted her that once again the children had arisen before she. Drat. Her nose told her that someone had already started breakfast. Or, rather, had burned it. The aroma of scorched something filled the house.

Springing out of bed, she pulled on her jeans and a T-shirt and hurried barefoot into the living room. "'Morning." The curly heads of the twins turned sleepily in her direction. The boys were watching cartoons, but Liv and Anabel were missing. Afraid the scorched smell might be one of their experiments—as per their inquiry last night: "What happens if you set fire to Jell-O?"—D.J. tentatively asked, "What's going on?" and was relieved to no end when the dangerous duo informed her that Anabel was in the kitchen, making breakfast. Livie was still in bed.

Entering the kitchen, D.J. was surprised to find the meticulous Anabel surrounded by food in various stages of preparation. Eggshells filled the sink, while a large glass bowl and whisk dripped yellow beaten eggs onto the laminate countertop. Slices of bread—some burned, some as yet untoasted—sat on plates, and a stack of paper towels drained what must have at some point been bacon. Now it would have hard to positively ID the twisty, charred strips.

Anabel stood at the electric stove, trying to make…an omelet?

"Anabel," D.J. ventured, "how are you doin' in here?"

"Fine." Her voice was thin and strained, and she did not turn around, preferring to concentrate on adding shredded cheese to the almost-dry skillet in which her omelet was scorching. At least she was carrying through on a theme.

"Wow, you're certainly busy this morning." Wading in amongst the food, D.J. approached the jeans-and-T-shirt-clad girl until the omelet was in full view. Ugh. She'd added chopped tomato with the watery seeds floating among the egg and hunks of raw carrot and celery. She'd used so many eggs that they appeared to be glued to the bottom of the pan, though they were still raw on top. "Veggie omelet, huh?" D.J. asked brightly.

"Someone has to make sure these kids eat their vegetables." Anabel grunted as she struggled with the cheese grater.

"Yeah. Well, that ought to do it. Listen, I'm not the greatest cook, but would you like me to lend a hand?"

Bacon grease had splattered Anabel's glasses. "No, thank you."

Blunt as ever. Setting aside for the moment her absolute unwillingness to eat the mess in that pan, D.J. tried to put herself in Anabel's shoes. Not eleven years old, the girl obviously viewed herself as the "mommy" of the family and probably had done so for some time, even before Terry passed away. Anabel yielded control of most situations to Max, but she wasn't about to trust a stranger. D.J. wished she had been able to make the requested pot roast instead of chicken nuggets and burned hot dogs for the first meal she'd shared with the family. That alone might have brought Anabel around a bit.

Perhaps she could redeem herself this morning by saving breakfast.

"I think I'll make more bacon," D.J. announced heartily, rubbing her hands together. "I'm really starved this morning. We can have BLTs with our omelets. How does that sound? That would sneak in a couple extra servings of veggies for the little kids, you know?" She lowered her voice for this last part, trying to turn Anabel into a comrade.

Rubbing cheese off the grater, Anabel answered, "I was going to make whole wheat toast."

"Okay. I'll use whole wheat bread for the BLTs. And we'll toast it. Gotta have toasted bread at breakfast."

"There's no more bacon."

"Really?" She'd used a pound of bacon? They had just bought it. "Hmm. Well." Determinedly cheerful, D.J. checked the fridge. "We've got ham. HLT's? Ham-lettuce-and-tomato. Get it? That'll give us a little variety. Like a breakfast buffet. Have you ever been to a breakfast buffet, Anabel?"

"The ham is for our lunches."

So much for small talk. "We can get more ham."

Anabel rolled her eyes. "I guess. If you don't mind wasting all of Uncle Max's money."

Livie's appearance saved D.J. from a smart-mouthed retort that would prove conclusively who the adult was around here—not she. Liv trudged sleepily into the kitchen in her footed pajamas, a Pooh Bear blankie trailing dismally behind her.

"I'm hungry. It doesn't smell good in here."

D.J. might have laughed, but she saw Anabel's lips thin into a tight, angry line. Walking over and bending toward the sleepy little blonde, D.J. insisted, "Anabel's gone to a lot of trouble to make omelets, and I'm going to make HLTs. Know what they are?" Silky ringlets bounced as Livie shook her head. "Fried ham, lettuce and tomato sandwiches, like a BLT, only—" She broke off as Anabel tossed a kitchen utensil into the sink with more force than necessary.

Turning away from the stove, the older girl announced, "It's done. I'm not hungry anymore. This was too much work!" She ran out the kitchen door and down the rickety porch steps to the backyard, ignoring D.J.'s call to wait.

D.J. was certain she should follow, but first she had to save the frying pan and quite possibly the kitchen from going up in flames. Smoke rose from the skillet and electric burner where stray bits of cheese had landed during Anabel's furious grating.

Muttering a curse she wouldn't have used in front of Livie had she had a little time to think about it, D.J. raced to the stove and grabbed the pan—barehanded, yet another thing she wouldn't have done had she taken time to consider. Yelping, she let the pan clatter to the stove, turned the knob beneath the burner and hunted for a towel or potholder, anything with which to remove the increasingly smoky frying pan.

Livie stood with huge eyes right where D.J. had left her, which was a good thing, because at least she was out of the line of fire, but then the boys raced in from the living room to holler that their show was over, and they were *starving to death*.

"Pee-euwww! Something stinks!" James broadcast as if no one else had noticed, and then Sean looked toward the stove and said, "Cool! Lookit all the smoke!"

Daisy found the drawer with the potholders and muttered a quick, "Thank you," about two seconds before the smoke alarm began to buzz. Livie started to cry, and the boys covered their ears with their hands, grinning at each other as they wailed in a pitch remarkably like the smoke alarm's.

Oh, yeah, she'd have the family under control and the social worker eating out of the palm of her hand in no time.

"That's really good, James. I'm sure we'll—achew!—have this henhouse looking like the Marriott Hotel in no…no…no—achew!—no time." D.J. watched the seven-year-old gather stray chicken feathers, putting them all into a big paper bag. Until today she'd had no idea she was allergic to chicken feathers. Now all she'd had to do was step inside the dark and cramped chicken coop to realize she had an aversion to nearly everything about it.

"You're not supposed to clean hen droppings. I *told* you," Anabel informed her caregiver for the second time that afternoon. It so happened D.J. was doing just that, and after a day filled with similar unpleasant and laborious tasks, Anabel's prissy superiority was enough to make D.J. want to scream.

The preteen had acted either sullen or downright disapproving of D.J. since breakfast. D.J. was tired of it. What kind of idiot did Anabel think she was, anyway? *"You're not supposed to clean hen droppings."* Right. Like the chickens would care. If the social worker saw this mess of a coop, she'd whip the kids away from Maxwell and send them to a nice foster mom in the city so fast it would make his head spin. D.J. had been surprised to discover that the chickens were on Max's property to begin with. She'd thought the rooster calls she heard each morning were coming from the neighbors' property. It was only today while exploring the pasture behind the house that she realized the chickens lived here. She questioned the children and discovered that Anabel arose early each morning to collect eggs. How was the social worker going to react when she found out that Max made Anabel walk into a dirty old chicken coop and touch eggs that had chicken poo on them? *And* you'd think Anabel would like doing her chores in a nice neat henhouse for a change.

"We're cleaning this place up, and I don't want to hear another word about it," D.J. said through gritted teeth as she tried not to sneeze again.

She glanced at James, who was staring intently at a chicken feather while running one finger up and down the silky plume. Sean had decided to play "Harry Potter" while cleaning the coop and was waving a feather, muttering things like "Disappearo!" to make the droppings vanish magically. Livie, garbed in her princess costume, played alone outside the small outbuilding.

"You kids keep picking up the stray feathers." D.J. hadn't allowed them to touch the germ-ridden doo. Darned maternal, if you asked her. Wiping her brow with the back of a gloved hand, she said, "I'm going to take this bag of trash to the garbage."

Stepping out into the daylight, D.J. squinted as she waded through about a dozen displaced chickens on her way toward the house, which was a short uphill hike from the hen yard. She hadn't even had a chance today to slip back into the house and hunt for evidence of Max's financial position. She may as well have hired on as a nanny or a farmhand because that seemed to be the only way she'd been earning her wages of late. And Max was paying her fairly well. This morning he'd given her a check, which she planned to repay with the money she received from Loretta.

"I must have been out of my mind when I let him talk me into staying," she muttered, nudging a stubborn hen with the toe of her MUDD boot. A rickety fence and gate separated the area where the chickens lived from the rest of the property. The hen was sitting right in front of it. "Shoo! Shoo!"

The hen squawked and ran away. D.J. enjoyed the minor victory until she felt something slam her in the back. "Ow! What—"

Furious squawking ensued. Instinctively, D.J. dropped her

trash bag and turned to face her attacker, but this wasn't the kind of opponent on whom kickboxing would be effective. A giant rust-colored chicken flew at her again, hitting her feet first and trying to peck her anyplace it could.

"Ow! Get away…you…crazy…ouch! Dang it!"

The kids ran out of the coop, hollering. "What's going on?"

"Stand back!" D.J. ordered, her arms crossed in front of her to fend off the flapping wings and sharp pecks that kept coming. "This chicken's gone crazy!"

"That's Frankie!" Sean's voice broke through the squawking.

"He's not a chicken. He's a rooster." Anabel sounded absolutely disgusted. "Stop it, you're going to hurt him!" she cried when D.J. tried to kick the mad bird away between flying attacks.

D.J. was no coward; she'd been telling herself that most of her life. But she wasn't a dummy, either, and she knew when to retreat. Turning, she unlatched the gate and took off.

That's how Max saw her when he came home: running toward the house, with an insane rooster chasing after her and four children running and shouting behind the rooster. The hens were scattering, too.

The expression on Max's face as he rounded the corner of the house to investigate the noise would have been comical had D.J. possessed even a shred of her usual humor. Unfortunately, she was fresh out, so when Max shouted, "What's going on? Why are those chickens out of their yard?" D.J. merely hollered back, "I quit!" as she raced past him without breaking stride.

"Just a couple more. You're being very good," Max murmured as he gently dabbed D.J.'s scratches with antiseptic, then placed Disney character bandages over the worst scrapes.

D.J. felt humiliated. Bad enough to be attacked by an overgrown chicken; now Max was trying to tend the wounds she'd received from the rooster's pecks and her own misguided attempt to give the bird the slip by running behind a hedge, which had turned out to be part rosebush and part thorny blackberry bramble. She had looked like an absolute doof in front of the kids and Max. She had the impression the chickens didn't think much of her, either.

Now Max was speaking to her very…slowly…and…very…patiently. That was the most humiliating thing of all. "Will you please," she requested through gritted teeth as he used Donald Duck to patch a particularly mean scratch on her ankle, "remember that you're speaking to another adult and not to Livie?" She sounded rather mean-spirited, she knew, under the circumstances, but she hated feeling out of control, and this day had been one long lesson in total surrender.

Sitting on his haunches on the hard linoleum of his kitchen floor, Max watched Daisy try not to cry. He believed he understood the tender-tough woman enough now to know she was not crying over the cuts stinging her arms and legs.

Max had experienced a pretty miserable day at work, encountering all sorts of problems with city permits and building codes and mistakes that threatened costly delays to his restaurant's grand opening. He'd come home for a few hours of peace on his farm before he returned to work and had been envisioning a long walk around the property, or a nap if he could squeeze one in. Instead, he'd arrived home to absolute chaos, with his nanny at the center of it.

He recalled the sight of her in her designer jeans and one of the brightly colored tank tops she favored—and looked damn good in, her long, long legs pumping and gorgeous arms flailing as she tore across his yard like the hounds of hell were pursuing her. Within a minute of viewing the situation, Max had had the startling revelation that he was right where he wanted to be. Right where he was supposed to be.

His life was a series of surprises, punctuated by childish laughter, shrieks, snotty noses and wet, sloppy kisses. Plus bursts of love and protectiveness so fierce he hardly recognized them as coming from his own heart. For months he'd been trying to make everything run smoothly. Obviously that was where he'd gone wrong. Smooth was no longer an option.

Joy was. He felt joy when he surrendered to fatherhood.

He felt joy when he surrendered to his growing feelings for Daisy Holden.

Watching her run from the cranky old rooster he'd inherited with the house made Max plunge deeper into lust and affection. He liked watching her; he liked listening to her. He plain liked being near her. Of course, she'd been screaming, "I quit," as she ran from Frankie, but Max didn't intend to take her seriously.

"I think most of your cuts are from the blackberry brambles," he said, somehow managing to maintain a straight face while Daisy's gorgeous cheeks turned red and her brow puckered in irritation. He guessed she was recalling her own unwitting dive into the bushes and perhaps also the fact that the rooster had been too smart to follow.

"Those blackberries are a hazard," she insisted, adorably grouchy. "And the other bushes camouflage them. It's very unsafe for children."

Max nodded. Wisely, he chose not to mention that the kids knew not to get near the brambles without gloves, or the fact that they'd all had a great time picking berries that summer. "Do you think you have any cuts under there?" He pointed at her shirt. Was it horrible of him to hope she had maybe one teensy scratch under the fuchsia tee?

Innocently D.J. stretched the collar of the top away from her skin and peered down. Max had to fight not to join the inspection. "I think it's okay," she murmured, "but that rooster is nuts." Letting go of the shirt, she glared at Max. "Criminally insane! Why do you keep an attacking chicken?"

"Frankie is a little territorial, but I've never seen him attack before. He seems to get along fine if he's not antagonized—"

"I did not antagonize that bird!" D.J. insisted. "I told you before, I was cleaning the coop, trying to tidy up around here, *trying to help,* and all of a sudden Freddie—"

"Frankie."

She waved her hand. "The monster bird comes out of nowhere and goes nuts on me."

I can hardly blame him, Max thought, although when he had the opportunity to go nuts on Daisy Holden he planned to do so in a more mutually enjoyable fashion.

"That useless piece of poultry is off his rocker! I swear, he thinks he's in an Alfred Hitchcock movie." D.J. spoke dramatically, using her hands in a way that reminded Max of his Italian nonna when she was reading the riot act to his grandfather. "Not to mention that big fat fowl is an ingrate. I cleaned his coop from top to bottom. You could eat off the straw."

Max coughed, trying to hide a smile, but Daisy caught him. "What? Why are you laughing? Max," she warned, when he declined to speak.

"Okay, Daisy June," he drawled, wondering who had chosen a country name for a girl who was all city, "it's like this—chickens don't like perfectly clean coops. It's not even good to have a *perfectly* clean coop. The, eh, poop…acts like an antibacterial agent on the eggs."

There was a long pause. An adorable wrinkle appeared between D.J.'s brows. "Poop does."

"That's right."

"You're telling me," she said slowly, "that I spent all day picking doo off of straw for nothing?"

"Not for nothing. I appreciate the intention, even if Frankie won't."

"That's it!" She flung her arms in the air. "I don't know what I'm doing here. What was I thinking? Coffee tables turned into ice cream sundaes—"

"I beg your pardon?"

"Detonating smoke alarms—"

Max frowned. "Is there something you haven't told me?"

"—and I can't cook."

"I can."

"I do not belong here. Not for any reason—"

In one swift move, Max reached for the arms of her chair and yanked her closer, his arms and body trapping her. Their eyes met and held in the half-second hesitation before Max gave her the longest, hungriest, most thorough kiss he'd given anyone in years.

Chapter Eight

Desire made D.J.'s chest fill with heat and her arms and legs feel weak. This was not normal physical desire; this was a kind of yearning that unsettled and prodded her.

For the first time in her life D.J. understood the phrase "fireworks went off," in relation to a kiss.

Max's mouth slanted over hers. His lips were warm and seeking, his touch commanding as he cupped the back of her head, slipping strong fingers through the hair at her nape. He didn't merely kiss; he tasted and tested, telling D.J. without words what, actually, she'd already suspected—as lovers, they would be dynamite.

When he was through, he sat back on his heels. His hand lingered along her jawline, then dropped. Max's lips remained parted and relaxed, his gaze smoky blue gray and steady. All in all, he appeared confident, calm. No regrets at all.

D.J., on the other hand, felt her blood boiling in her veins. The energy contained in her lithe body threatened to catapult her from the chair. Now she recognized the unsettled feeling that lived behind all yearning—the threat of loss.

"What are we doing here, Max?" she whispered shakily. She

inched away from him. "Was that something casual? Because our lives are in very different places, you know, and—"

"Shh." He frowned. "Or I'll have to kiss you again." A slow, gorgeous curl shaped his mouth. "At the moment, our lives are en-twined." He crooked a brow, indicating the very modest space between them. "And I'd say we're both in the right place at the right time. I like having you here." He sounded gruff, as if he thought that ought to be reason enough for her to stay.

"It was wrong for me to agree to this. I'm not supposed to be here…" She heard the words coming out of her mouth and realized almost belatedly that she was about to tell him the truth about why she was here. *Why?* another voice inside her head shouted. *You've been lying to him. He's not going to like that.*

He will when he finds out that his grandmother wants to make him an heir.

The simple fact was D.J. *had* to tell him the truth; she couldn't breathe with him so close to her, looking at her…the *way* he was looking at her.

"I want you to stay, Daisy." Max interrupted her thoughts with a voice that barely rose above a whisper yet managed to reverberate through her body. He moved forward until their breaths mingled. His gaze touched her mouth for a moment, then his eyes bore straight into hers. "I know you didn't come to town intending to be a nanny. Quit that if you want. But don't quit me, not yet. Because we're just beginning to get to know each other, and I think that's something you *will* like."

Brow pursed in worry, D.J. tried to speak, to tell him that she wouldn't stay, that he shouldn't expect that from her. But Max, probably aware he wasn't about to get the answer he wanted, shook his head and reached for her before she could get the words out. Pulling her forward on the chair, he rose to meet her. "Warned you," he growled, proving conclusively that the magic of their first kiss was no accident.

"All right, you've got to stop doing that," D.J. gasped, barely able to breathe when Max stopped kissing her this time.

Max shook his head slowly. His hands slipped to her shoulders, where he trailed his fingers up and down her bare arms. "Nah." He grinned. "I like it. So do you. Admit it."

Goose bumps shivered along D.J.'s flesh as if the temperature was twenty degrees. She didn't even feel the scratches anymore. "L-liking it is not the p-p-point. I mean it, Max, cut it out! This is no way to prepare for a—*yipe!*—home study." His thumb had brushed the side of her breast—so briefly it *could* have been an accident.

"What's a home study?" he murmured, clearly focusing more on her lips than on the words emerging from them.

"It's the social worker's visit. You do remember that you have a social worker showing up in less than a week, don't you, and that's why I'm here?"

"Can't remember a thing right now. How come you can?"

It wasn't easy. D.J. actually grew dizzy as Max leaned into her so his lips could follow the same path as his fingers. He nibbled the curve of her neck. Her voice trembled. "M-Max, you need to s-s-stop. Really… Okay, now you're tickling my neck, and I…I've never liked that." She felt like melting butter as waves of thrilling sensation made her weak. In another second she would be incapable of thought. The knuckles of his left hand brushed slowly down her right arm while his lips moved to her left shoulder. "Maxwell! You're forcing me into some highly—" she gasped "—unprofessional…" gasp "…nanny…" gasp "…behavior." As he attempted to give her a hickey, she couldn't help but giggle. "I m-m-mean it! M-M-M-Max! *Mr. Lotorto!*"

That got his attention. He let her go, the disgust on his handsome face almost comical. "Mr. Lotorto?" Rising to stand in front of her, he shook his head. "I suppose you're right. We haven't even been on a date, and here I am, practically mauling you."

Primly D.J. smoothed her hair behind her ears. "That's right," she agreed in a small voice, willing her goose bumps to recede.

"So what are you doing tonight?"

D.J.'s gaze jerked up. "Wha—"

"Yeah. We'll get a sitter, go into Ashland and get a bite to eat. There's a great place called Lela's. Tokie, a friend of mine, works there."

"Tokie?"

"You'll like her. I'll give her a call, see if she can get us in."

Her? D.J.'s brow puckered with a whoosh of jealousy she was helpless to prevent.

Max noticed and smiled. A little smugly, she thought. "Tokie's just a friend."

Good. "I don't— That's hardly— I don't care what she is. To you. That's not my business." D.J. compressed her lips and raised her chin. She sounded like a constipated nun, but she couldn't help it. It was either that or agree so fast to his plans for the evening it would make his head spin. She needed time, definitely needed time to compose herself, reclaim her own thoughts and evaluate her goal and purpose for being here. At the moment everything was too damn fuzzy, even her heartbeat.

Max walked across the kitchen, opened the fridge to pour a glass of lemonade and offered a drink to D.J., who declined, fearing she might dribble down her shirt. She watched the muscles in his throat move as he swallowed. He was behaving completely casually now, as if seducing nannies was a regular occurrence in his life. The thought irked her.

"I realize you haven't asked for my advice. But I would say that kissing people in your employ is not what should be on your mind right now." D.J. knew she sounded more stilted than concerned. "How many people in your employ *have* you kissed, anyway?"

Setting the lemonade on the counter, Max looked at her without speaking for a long moment. Then he crossed to her, staring unflinchingly, with nothing to hide. "I've lived in Oregon a year and a half. Haven't had a girlfriend since I left California. Haven't wanted one. Definitely haven't considered dating any of our previous nannies, although Mrs. Carmichael did make a very fine tuna casserole…she crumbled potato chips over the top." He leaned down, a hand on either arm of D.J.'s chair, his nose only a couple of inches from hers. His voice was low, silky and deep. For her ears only. "I'm well aware of what *should* be on my mind right now. That's not a problem. Getting you out of my mind has been the problem. I've decided not to fight it. So listen closely—I don't care whether you're the nanny, a Radio City Rockette or the school superintendent. I want to get to know you better. *Much* better. Will you join me at Lela's, Daisy June Holden?"

D.J. swallowed hard enough to hear the noise she made. "Okay."

* * *

"Your friend Tokie is very nice," D.J. said, aware that she felt somewhat begrudging about the admission, because Tokie was also beautiful and utterly charming. "Is she dating anyone?"

"Nope." Max took her arm as they strolled down A Street after dinner.

"Oh." D.J. felt the thud of disappointment. She told herself not to be stupid, but in fact she would have enjoyed hearing that Tokie was "off the market."

The food at Lela's had been delicious, but D.J. had found it impossible to take more than a few bites of each course. Her stomach had done flip-flops through the whole meal.

All afternoon and all through dinner, she hadn't stopped thinking about Max's lips and his hands—and what it would be like to be held by him and to wake up laughing next to him and to touch, long and soulfully, into the night.

"So what qualities do you look for in a man, Daisy June?"

The question, rife with implications, set her heart on a hard, fast thump. D.J. could feel the tension in Max's arm as he waited for her answer, and the further proof of his interest made her spirits skyrocket.

"I like 'em tall," she said, slanting an assessing glance at him. "Because I'm tall, and I like to wear heels."

"I've noticed. Height is an important consideration in choosing a mate. What else?"

D.J. realized he wasn't going to let her off the hook easily. And suddenly she wanted to tell him more and hear what he had to say. The problem was she didn't know what she looked for in a "mate," and she realized with a clarity that had escaped her up to now that she'd never dated anyone thinking he might become a lifetime partner. She never read bridal magazines. She scoffed at reality TV shows that purported to find someone a husband or wife in six weeks. Really, how could anyone decide whether to get married after a handful of dates? People could lie. They could pretend to be someone they weren't. Or people could be utterly genuine and still not reveal their every lump and bump and fatal flaw in six piddly weeks.

Watching a very popular reality dating show while eating an

oyster po'boy one evening, D.J. had found herself talking back to the TV with her mouth full. "Oh, fuh Goth's sake, don't get engathed!" she'd tried to yell at the screen as one young woman swore to the host that she was ready to marry her bachelor, a man she hadn't even dated exclusively yet. Shaking her head while the girl pledged her fidelity to a stranger, D.J. had sat back on her sofa and considered starting a Web site offering her investigative services to anyone who planned to appear on a dating show. She could have a tagline like, Don't Just Date Him, Investigate Him.

Thinking it over, D.J. respected Loretta's caution. Anyone could seem warm and fuzzy or upright and responsible *temporarily*.

"I don't believe in forever," she blurted aloud to Max, surprising herself because she hadn't *planned* to say that.

They had just reached his car. He stopped, turning to her on the sidewalk. "So you don't believe in marriage?"

D.J. picked her way carefully across her words. "I don't think people should assume they'll be together forever. It's not realistic. A lot of women think they're in love with a man simply because they've made love or they assume that strong feelings in the moment mean they should start ordering their bridesmaids' dresses. But feelings change. People meet new people or they just want to move on, and you can't spend your whole life being resentful because of it." She shrugged, the very soul of philosophy. Then she folded her arms and hugged her chilly self, though the late-summer evening was still warm.

Max stood by the car, staring at her, a bemused furrow between his brows. "Every guy's dream date," he muttered. Resting a hand on the hood, he leaned against the car while he assessed D.J.'s point of view. "All right, let me get this straight. You think it's unrealistic for two people to promise each other a future together. Or to hope that they'll be able to keep that promise all their lives."

"Exactly. 'Hope.' You see? You said it yourself." D.J. seized on his last word. "A person might have a hope, but that shouldn't be confused with a guarantee or, for that matter, even a likelihood. In fact, the very word *hope* suggests something uncertain. Because if it were certain, you wouldn't 'hope,' you would 'know.'" She began to warm to her argument. "Sometimes you think a situation is permanent and then you find out that people have limitations. They get stressed or angry, or they move away, or whatever. Your so-called permanent situation is over, and maybe you would have been better off not obsessing about forever in the first place."

Max's eyes had narrowed a bit more with every word she spoke. Then his brow cleared with the suddenness of a Seattle rainstorm, and he actually smiled. "Okay, we agree. You're one weird chick, but we agree." He grabbed her arm again. "C'mon."

Disappointment coursed through D.J. She had expected him to argue—a little, anyway. If he agreed with her already, then what had all that "Daisy, I want you to stay," been about? She started to feel angry. "Where are we going?"

"Somewhere we can't talk." He pulled her along A Street to Pioneer, where they merged with a maze of tourists visiting the Oregon Shakespeare Festival. The only thing he said as he hustled her along was, "You must be the only girl in fifty-two states who never thinks about forever."

D.J. glanced up at him, but the crowd was noisy and Max's expression bland. She couldn't tell whether he intended this last comment positively or not, and she was left with a prodding discomfort as they walked uphill to the Festival's theaters. At the brick courtyard in front of the box office, Max led her through a crush of people to find a small patch of grass. She eyeballed the space.

"There's only room for one," she protested, frowning. "Why do you want to sit here?"

Max pointed to a raised stage fifty feet away. "There's going to be a music and dance concert in a few minutes." He dropped to the grass with his long legs outstretched. D.J. saw pure mischief in his eyes as he looked up and patted his lap. "Have a seat, Daisy June."

Funny, he hadn't intimidated her at all before they'd kissed. Now she felt a maddening blush creep up her face. To cover the embarrassment, she raised her chin haughtily. "I'm not going to sit on your lap in front of all these people. Do I look like I'm five?"

Ever so slowly his gaze traveled her length before returning to her face. "Not hardly." He spread his legs, making space for her, and though his expression had turned utterly benign, D.J. thought she'd never seen anything sexier. She'd have bet her last pair of Skechers that he knew exactly what he was doing, too.

She itched to upset his equilibrium as much as he was upsetting hers. If she demurred again, he'd know he was affecting her more than she apparently affected him.

Determined to behave as casually as Max, D.J. sat in the vee of his legs, facing forward toward the stage with her back to him. She feigned blithe unawareness that they were touching in intimate places, even though her intimate places responded loudly and clearly to the feel of Max snuggled around her. Instead of attempting conversation, D.J. busied herself by arranging her skirt over her outstretched legs. Relief mingled with disappointment when she felt Max lean back, leaving her free to sit up without his hands anywhere on her person.

The lawn in front of the stage, indeed the entire area, was packed with people, some of whom were eating boxed dinners or licking ice cream cones as they watched musicians take their positions at the far end of the outdoor stage. Truly, D.J. was almost as close to total strangers as she was to Max. No one looking at them would know their physical proximity was sending heat waves through her body. With an effort, she tried to focus on something else.

Children. There were children everywhere and so many babies crawling about it was hard to tell who belonged to whom. She thought about Anabel and Livie and the boys and felt a pang of guilt that they'd had to stay at two different neighbors' homes—the boys in one location, the girls in another—while she and Max enjoyed an evening out. Liv would probably love to watch dancers; she wore her fairy princess tutu every chance she got.

On the verge of breaking her silence to ask whether Max had ever brought the children here, D.J. had to hold her question for later as the woodwinds heralded the start of the show.

The dancers, six in all, had just taken the stage when Max sat up, and D.J. felt his arms wind around her, pulling her against his chest.

What a sneak! His hold was relaxed and comfortable, not sexual, and there was not a thing for her to protest, except the fact that she couldn't concentrate for the first fifteen minutes of the show. Once she became used to his touch again and realized his hands were going to stay put rather than shift around, she began to watch the music and dance concert the festival sponsored as a prelude to its outdoor show. According to the green fliers the costumed ushers passed out, tonight's concert complemented its current production of *Much Ado About Nothing*. The dances were vibrant and funny and sexy and finally very, very passionate. Dressed in colorful unitards and broad belts from which long, filmy strips of fabric hung, the performers' lithe bodies arched and twined around each other. They moved fully and freely, committing their bodies and hearts to each step and to each other. D.J. didn't dare glance back at Max.

By the time the concert was over, she was enraptured and profoundly moved by the statement she believed the music and dances made—that love was funny and quirky and wild and untamable. Several times she'd felt the urge to get up and join the dance, and she wondered if others experienced the same reaction.

As the people around them rose for an evening of theater or window-shopping, D.J. stayed put, following Max's lead. When the lawn had cleared considerably, she felt his lips brush her ear. "Have you ever seen a production of Shakespeare?"

D.J. shook her head.

"Some people," Max said, still in that low, ear-tingling hush, "think Shakespeare wrote the sexiest romances in history."

Even in the mellow light of evening, it must have been eighty degrees out, but D.J. felt a flesh-tingling shiver race across her skin.

Max said nothing else, merely released her and rose, moving in front of her and extending a hand to help her rise, also.

"Where are we going now?" she asked as he walked her away from the theaters and into Lithia Park.

"I could use a little exercise after dinner and sitting for forty-five minutes. Couldn't you?"

Yes, she could, but his continued mellowness was driving her crazy! Had he not felt what she had sitting on the lawn, wrapped around her? Had he done this so many times before that he wasn't affected the way she was? Was she just another body?

D.J. walked by Max's side, beginning to feel unreasonably moody. Despite his whispered comment about sexy old Shakespeare, she had, apparently, won her argument about the ephemeral nature of love. Her stance hadn't bothered Max for long; he was, even now, whistling one of the tunes they'd heard during the show.

Feeling rather stoic, she walked by his side, telling herself nothing had changed. She hadn't believed in permanence before she'd kissed Max, and she didn't believe in it now. He couldn't convince her otherwise. The fact that she wanted him to at least *try,* well, that was just one of the foibles of human nature.

"Have you been to Lithia Park?" he asked, leading the way down a flight of cement steps and past a lovely picnic area.

"No," D.J. mumbled, gazing too long at a couple lying on the grass, smiling into each other's faces.

"There were torrential rains here in 1997. Lithia Creek overflowed, and a good part of the park was destroyed. The stores on the plaza were flooded, as well."

"That's terrible," she mumbled dutifully. The man and woman on the lawn threaded their fingers together, then looked at their linked digits as if they'd invented hand holding. And Max was discussing natural disasters.

They walked down a trail and into the park. "There's a duck pond a little to the north of here and another, larger pond up the hill to the south. The park plays host to a number of mallards and wood ducks. Last summer I spotted a blue heron sunning himself with the turtles at the upper pond."

D.J. nodded. *Blah, blah, blah, blah, blah.* She may as well have been home, watching an episode of Animal Planet.

She listened with half an ear to his running commentary on Lithia Park: "Originally intended to be a mineral-springs resort… monkey puzzle tree by the tennis courts…Japanese garden up ahead on the right…." All the while she grew—unfairly, to be sure—more and more perturbed. When they reached a grove of maples and Max led her between two trees to show her how to identify a maple by examining the pods, she blew her stack.

"Thanks for all this *fascinating* information—really, I mean it, but to tell you the truth, Max, I— *Mmm-nn-mmph-hmphnnnnn… Mmmmmm."*

Max had one hand on the small of her back and one hand on the back of her head as he kissed her. He smelled clean and woodsy like the monkey puzzle tree. Standing together like twined branches, the broad-fingered maple leaves ruffling above them, D.J. felt perfect. Perfect.

"Not too interested in ducks, are you?" Max murmured when they broke free.

"About as much as chickens." Whereas a moment ago D.J. had felt as if she'd swallowed a lead balloon, now she felt buoyant and exhilarated.

"Trees, either," Max murmured, his lips still grazing hers.

"Some." D.J. breathed the response. All the reasons for not doing exactly what she was doing seemed hard to grasp at the moment.

"Thank you for joining me tonight." Max's hands slipped to the small of her back. He held her in a loose but sexy embrace, a smile playing about his mouth as he gazed at her.

"You're welcome," D.J. said. "I had a really good—wait a minute!" Reaching for his hands, she pulled them from around her back. "Damn, I lost focus again. We're not supposed to do that."

"What? Kiss?" Max pursed his lips. "You're wrong. You're not allowed to ride bikes, camp out or walk a dog through this park, but kissing's okay."

D.J. looked him square in the eye. She was no tease. "I'm not going to have an affair with you," she said firmly.

Max took the information in stride. Gazing thoughtfully into the distance, he reached up to rub his chin. "Puts me in a kind of awkward position then, because I definitely intend to make love to you."

There went her pulse again. She affected a frown and pointed a finger in the vicinity of his chin. "That's exactly the kind of thing that's going to get you into trouble, Max."

"Reason, please?"

"You're supposed to be preparing for a home study. That means you have to be serious. You have to present an environment suitable for child rearing." Folding her arms, she lowered her voice. "Jumping the nanny does not create a suitable environment."

Max smirked. "Well put." His eyes narrowed. "Refresh my memory. How is it you know so much about social workers?"

"I… Well, it's…obvious, isn't it?" she hedged, still reluctant to talk about her past. "Social workers like married couples," she said as if it were the most obvious thing in the world, "not single men who are carrying on with their nannies."

The corner of Max's mouth quirked. His nod was exaggerated. "I see. Okay." His tone and outstretched arms suggested total surrender. "I'll marry you."

"What?"

"Listen, if it's the only way to get you in the sack, I don't mind."

"I…beg…your…pardon?"

"It's no problem. I'm an excellent cook, so you won't have to worry about that. You're good with the kids—I have no complaints. I would like to be there, though, next time you read John Grisham to them at bedtime. I like Grisham."

D.J. fought a rising tide of conflicting emotions. Despite everything she'd said or thought about marriage, including her belief that "forever" was a fairy tale, she didn't want Max to joke about marrying her.

"Not funny?" Max said, reaching over to rub a thumb over her frown. "Okay, kiss me. If you do, I promise to behave."

"I already kissed you," D.J. muttered.

"No. *I* kissed *you.*"

She crossed her arms. She wanted to be angry, to believe he was an inveterate flirt and nothing more, but sustaining a soothing disdain was impossible with Max's eyes sparkling at her and his sexy mouth quirking just enough to make him look wonderfully wicked. "How long are you capable of behaving, Max? An hour? You're starting to remind me of the boys."

"I don't know whether to be flattered or insulted."

"I'll make a deal with you," she said, an idea beginning to form. "You behave yourself for—" she squinted, assessing him "—forty-five minutes, and I will kiss you when the time is up."

Max's eyes widened. "Interesting. What do I have to do to prove I'm behaving myself? List your criteria."

"It's not tough. I'll ask you a few questions and you answer them. *All* of them. No double entendres, no evasions, no touching for the full forty-five minutes."

"Answer some questions?"

"Answer them honestly and completely. And no touching."

"And then we kiss."

"*A* kiss. One."

He smiled. Dangerously. "On the mouth."

D.J. pretended to consider this condition a real burden and seriously hoped no one ever heard about her investigative tactics on this case. "Fine."

Max extended his hand. "Deal." As D.J. moved to accept the handshake, he whipped his arm back then wagged a finger at her the way she'd wagged hers at him. "Ah-ah-ah. No touching, Daisy June." Shaking his head sternly, he clucked in disapproval. "Got to watch you like a hawk."

Chapter Nine

Lithia Creek flowed steadily over smooth rocks and a mossy bank. The constant, pleasing sound defined the area as much as the lush, generously treed landscape. D.J. sat on a wooden bench, watching Max try to skip stones down a particularly calm segment of creek. "The forty-five minutes doesn't begin until you sit down," she reminded him. She would have been content to sit here and simply watch him, but the sky was beginning to show signs of twilight. And she had business to conduct.

Brushing his hands against each other, he wandered back to the bench and sat. "What's on your mind, Daisy Sunshine?"

Tilting her head, D.J. regarded him silently. "On her mind" was settling the situation between him and his grandmother. Tonight. Department of Human Services would not remove children from an affluent home in which there were two loving adult family members and a veritable cornucopia of housekeepers to provide backup child care.

D.J.'s work would be done here when Max and his grandmother reconciled. Then she could leave.

Or she could pursue a relationship with him—without an obstacle course of lies between them.

For one thing, she was not "Daisy Sunshine" or even Daisy June; she was D. J. Holden, a woman who lived alone in a Portland apartment that contained a single bed, a thrift-store futon and a battered coffee table left by the previous tenant. She cared more about fashion than decor because clothes were portable, and her nesting instinct was nonexistent.

Maybe she was playing with fire, but it wasn't enough that Max wanted "Daisy." *If* D.J. decided to make love with Max, she needed to know for sure that he wanted her as she really was—a little cynical and a little too unsentimental, lacking a past that might have provided a reason to believe in fairy tales.

She wasn't sure why the candor was important; it wouldn't change the quality of their lovemaking, which she expected to be pretty dang good. It just was important, that's all.

"I want to know more about you." D.J. plunged into the conversation she hoped would provide the final information Loretta needed to accept her grandson. She intended, too, to prepare Max to meet his grandmother, so it wouldn't come as a total shock. "You told me about Terry, but what about other family, Max? Are you all alone in the world except for the kids?"

"You realize you just made me sound like Little Orphan Annie?"

"Oh." Chagrined, she felt herself color. "Sorry, I—"

"It's all right, I'm teasing." He smiled at her, raking long fingers through the dark hair that was already mussed by the Ashland breeze. "I do come from a small family, but maybe that was one reason we were so close. We lived with my father's parents in a house my mom and dad eventually purchased from them. I don't recall it ever being a problem—living with multiple generations. Did you grow up near your grandparents?"

Repressively, D.J. wagged her head. "This is about *you*. We have an agreement."

Physical awareness flared in Max's eyes. "You drive a hard bargain, Ms. Holden. Then again, so do I. You'd better be ready to uphold your end of the deal." He lowered his voice. "And remember, one kiss can last a very…very…long time."

Dangerous desire flooded D.J.'s every cell. She coughed a bit to steady the beat of her heart. "So. Your father's parents lived with you?"

Enjoying the fact that he had unsettled her, Max continued. "Until they passed away. After that it was just my parents and me. So, in a way, you're right—when my parents died, I think I did feel a little like an orphan."

D.J. told herself to ignore the tingle of kinship that tried to wriggle through her. Feeling "a little like an orphan" did not make them soul mates. "How did your parents die, Max? They must have been young."

"They were." The rush of the creek seemed to grow louder as Max paused. "My father had a problem with his heart valve that required surgery. He could have gone in, had the procedure right away, but he had a new employer. He didn't want to take off work until he had sick time accrued." Love, more than judgment, colored his words. "My father was a blue-collar guy. He was a butcher, like his dad. Taking care of his family was the guiding principle of his life."

The news that Loretta's daughter had married a butcher surprised D.J. "Your father postponed surgery so he could work more, and that's why he died?" Why hadn't Max's mother approached Mrs. Mallory for help with their financial situation until her husband was well again? Independence was one thing, but risking everything you loved because you were too proud to ask for help—

"I think every decision my father made was intended to benefit my mother and me. He was a good man who acted with integrity." Max interrupted her thoughts in a tone that was almost forbidding. Belatedly she realized her question had come across like a judgment.

D.J. frowned. "I'm not saying your father lacked integrity," she said carefully, "but do you agree with his decision? I mean, what good is it to sacrifice yourself and then lose everything you wanted to protect?" That was as close as she dared come to saying, *If money can save your life, and you have a wealthy relative, pick up the phone.*

"Look, Daisy, the fact is in most of this world people think of themselves first. My father put principles above his own interests. He erred in judgment, but that's all."

"Yes, but he died. That's not what you or your mother wanted. Maybe absolute integrity can't be the basis of every decision."

"Or maybe it should be."

They were leaning toward each other on the bench now, both frowning. D.J. thought Max sounded like Tom Cruise in *A Few Good Men*. "That's fine in theory, but in practice don't you have to allow a little flexibility in your philosophy for human failings? Who can live up to a perfect standard?"

"I'm not talking about perfection. I simply believe that if integrity were a guidepost for more people, my father may not have made the decision he did. He was trying to compensate for the pain his in-laws caused years before."

"What do you mean?"

"My parents came from different social circles. In other words, my mother's parents had one and my father's didn't. My grandfather worked for my mother's parents. That's how my mom and dad met. My mom was seventeen, just graduating high school, an English-Irish-American rose who fell hard for the son of an Italian butcher. My grandfather moved from Italy as a kid and never had more than an eighth-grade education, but he had a dignity the Mallorys could never understand. My dad had more education, but he was as simple as his father, in the best sense. I think that's what drew my mother to him. She said she'd had a knot in her chest all her life, and it untied the moment she met my dad."

D.J. listened avidly, trying to plug this information into the bigger puzzle. Loretta had obviously left out a few important pieces. "Did your maternal grandparents…the Mallorys…did they try to stop the relationship?"

Max's lips twisted into a cynical smirk she had not yet seen on his face. "Yeah, just a few times. They took my mother to Europe for a mandatory vacation, then they refused to pay her college tuition unless she went somewhere out of state. When she got a job and registered at a junior college so she wouldn't need their money, they went ballistic and threatened to fire my grandfather unless he persuaded his son to break off the relationship."

"But your grandfather refused?"

"He told the Mallorys the choice to have a relationship or not would ultimately belong to their children. Then he convinced my dad that getting between a girl and her parents was wrong. My father tried to break it off, and my mother tried to stay away, too, because she did love her parents. The breakup didn't last long, though."

Loretta, Loretta, D.J. thought, *you sure created a lot of drama.* "What happened?"

Max took time to watch a family stroll past, eating caramel apples. "We should get one of those."

"We're not hungry." D.J. knocked on the back of the bench to command his attention. "Continue the story."

Crossing his arms and ankles, Max leaned back against the bench. "If you're going to deny me a caramel apple, you'd better be prepared to deliver one sweet kiss."

"Just finish the story."

Complying, Max said, "My mother tried to distract herself by working and taking a large course load in college. She still refused to let her parents pay her tuition, so she attended the community college to study psychology."

"And she and your dad stayed away from each other."

"For as long as they could stand it. Mom had juvenile diabetes, and she became lax about taking care of herself when she was under stress or working too hard. A few months into her first year of school, she got pretty sick. My grandfather heard about it at work and told my dad. He rushed to my mother, and the experience cemented what they already felt about each other. They were together from then on."

"And your grandparents? How did they handle it?"

"They handled it great. My grandfather quit the Mallorys before they could fire him."

"Mmm…actually, I was referring to your maternal grandparents."

D.J. couldn't miss the way Max's whole body tightened. "Then you should have specified 'the Mallorys.' They never deserved the title of 'grandparents.'"

Uh-oh. "Did you see them much when you were growing up?"

"My mother took me over a couple of times. Once we were turned away at the door. By the housekeeper." He glared at his watch. "How long have we been here? Gotta be close to forty-five minutes by now."

D.J. checked her own watch. "Twenty minutes." She could see Max preparing to seduce her out of the final twenty-five minutes. "Are your…the Mallorys…still alive, Max?"

"He died. The old woman is still around. If you're not going to kiss me for another half hour, I'm going to walk down to Rocky Mountain Fudge and get one of those caramel apples. I'm getting hungry."

"You couldn't be. That dinner was huge."

"Yeah, and I ate half of yours, too, so you've got to be ready for an apple." He started to rise.

"Max!" With both hands, she grabbed his arm and tugged him back to the bench. "You have the attention span of one of the twins. I haven't asked *that* many questions yet."

"You sure as hell have." His eyes narrowed. "And after we kiss, you're going to tell me why." He slipped his arm from her grip and grabbed her hand. "Come on, let's get high on sugar."

"No." D.J. tugged him down again, ignoring the roll of his eyes. "It'll be too distracting, and you can't talk with your mouth full of caramel."

"Sure I can. My mouth is really talented." He waggled his brows like Groucho Marx.

"Obviously, you forgot what I said about no distractions. Our deal was only good if you stayed on track, so—"

"So the last time I saw the Mallorys, I was fourteen and they were 105. At least, that's how it seemed to me," Max continued as if he'd never been off topic. "My mother took me over for a little Christmas cheer. I suppose she thought they might have mellowed over the previous decade."

"Had they?" D.J. almost dreaded the answer.

"Toward me," Max said, surprising her. "Granny Mallory thought it would be peachy to have me to Christmas dinner."

Relief coursed through D.J. "Well, that's great. People do change—"

"Yeah. In this case from bad to worse. She invited me to dinner and invited my mother to leave. Thought it might be too 'upsetting' to the old man to open old wounds around the holidays."

Loretta, you weenie. "Some women are afraid to confront the men in their lives," she attempted to assuage his resentment. "Especially women of that generation."

"Loretta Mallory could scare a pit bull into giving up its teeth. I may have been young, but I could read her insincerity without any trouble. She was all about power. My mother could come back into the family *if* she was willing to play by Loretta's rules this time and if she was willing to eat crow."

D.J. felt heartburn building inside her, and it wasn't from the house-cured lox at Lela's. Could the woman Max described be the same woman D.J. had met and on whose behalf she was now working? Or had the impressions of a fourteen-year-old been skewed in support of his parents? She hoped for the latter, for all their sakes. "How was Christmas?"

Max pulled a face that mirrored his words. "You think I stayed? I couldn't get out of there fast enough. My mother never forced the issue after that, and I never heard a bad word from her lips about her parents. But I don't think anything short of Loretta apologizing to my mother on bent knees could have induced me to visit again."

D.J. thought for a moment. If Max hadn't stayed for Christmas, there was no way to know definitively whether Loretta had had good intentions or ill that year. Even if he wasn't entirely off base in his estimation of his grandmother's meanness, he hadn't seen her for…sheesh, eighteen years. Perhaps now she wanted to make amends—not only to Max but also to her daughter and son-in-law through Max. Perhaps that's why she had contacted D.J.

"You said your father might not have worked so hard if things had been different between your mom and her parents."

"My mom was a good woman. Good soul. She didn't want anyone to hurt because of her choices, so as much as she loved Dad, she always felt terrible about the split between her and her parents. My father saw the pain she went through, and he worked extra hard to be worthy of her, I think, and worthy of her sacrifice, because her lifestyle changed appreciably when she left her parents. It was even a joke between them—that she'd married on the wrong side of the tracks—but there was too much truth in it to be funny when Dad postponed his surgery." Shifting on the bench, Max leaned down, picked up a broad maple leaf and twirled it slowly between his fingers. Evening light made the late-summer leaf appear velvety soft. "My mother was lost when he died. They were each other's best friends. I was in college. I wanted to take some time off after the funeral, hang around, make sure she was okay, but she refused to let me stay home." A reflective smile touched his lips. "She said if I missed one day of school because of her, she'd use my father's favorite meat cleaver to chop my entire CD collection."

"You're lucky to have grown up around that much love."

"Yep." His gaze slanted toward her. "Go on." When D.J. looked at him quizzically, he said, "You've asked me everything else, don't stop now."

"New deal," D.J. offered because she felt guilty and because she had indeed been about to ask the difficult question Max anticipated. "Just ten more minutes of questions. That's a good ten minutes less than our original bargain."

Arching a brow, Max looked at his watch and very deliberately set its timer for ten minutes. "Shoot."

Softly, D.J. obliged. "How did your mother die?"

"Her diabetes got out of control. I wasn't there, so I'll never know exactly what happened, but I do know she increased her hours at work and volunteered more to take her mind off things. I suspect she wasn't taking care of herself or checking her blood sugar like she should have. Dad used to remind her constantly. Her kidneys had already been compromised from a rough patch she'd had in her twenties. By the time I graduated from college, neither of her kidneys was doing her much good. When she finally told me she needed a transplant, I got tested, but I wasn't a match. She didn't get a donor in time."

Max did not take his gaze off the leaf, nor did he stop twirling it. D.J. had yet to think of him as a lonely person, but in this moment he exuded a quiet grief that made him seem isolated, even in a park filled with people. From deep inside her came a longing to tell him she understood what it was like to feel alone in a world full of families. The urge unsettled her, and she was almost thankful when a new thought intruded, though this one sent a chill through the very heart of her.

"Her mother…Mrs. Mallory…was she tested?"

Along Max's well-sculpted jaw, a muscle tensed before he

spoke. "It was the one time I was willing to contact her. My mother didn't even know. The old man had died by then, but…" Max didn't know quite what to call his grandmother. "*She* was traveling in Europe. I chased her by phone through five countries. By the time she got the message we'd already had the funeral. I don't know what she would have done if I'd gotten hold of her in time."

D.J. stared at the ground, her heart pounding. *Thank God.* Thank God Max didn't have that grudge to hold. And Loretta, she wondered, how had a mother felt to discover she might have been able to save her estranged daughter but had never been given the chance? It began to make more and more sense that Loretta was trying to make up for past mistakes and long-held regrets now, in the waning years of her life.

"So you haven't seen Mrs. Mallory since you were a boy, but you know she's still alive?" D.J. felt a little guilty for asking questions to which she knew the answers, but it was time to make Max discuss Loretta as she was today, not as he remembered her.

He gave the leaf a final twirl then stood. "Don't know." He walked to the edge of the creek and dropped the leaf, watching it waltz down the river with the water leading. Turning back toward D.J., he said with finality, "And I don't care."

"Max," D.J. admonished, "she's still your grandma. She's the children's great-grandmother."

"Grandma?" He gave a snort of laughter. "Not quite the image Loretta projected. Listen, the old broad made her bed years ago. It's got silk sheets. Mine has cookie crumbs and juice spills and usually a toy stuck between the pillows."

"But—"

"Hey, I never even got a birthday card from her, Daisy. Neither did Terry. You think I'm going to expose my kids to the crap she put her own children, not to mention grandchildren, through?"

"She may have changed—"

"I wouldn't go to Vegas on those odds." He shook his head. "Look, I think it's great that family loyalty means something to you. It does to me, too. Which is why I want nothing to do with Loretta Mallory. And now this discussion really is over."

"Max, she could help you."

"For God's sake!" he exploded.

"Stop swearing." Rising, D.J. squared off with him. "You know it's true. Oh, don't scowl. You have to think realistically. She's a wealthy woman…you said that yourself. No one will challenge the custody of a loving man with a very wealthy relative who's willing to help out."

"Who said she'd be willing to help out? I don't even know if she's alive. And," he added as D.J. opened her mouth again, "assuming she is too arrogant to have died, I don't want her anywhere near my kids until they're old enough to fend for themselves."

"Your kids aren't even teenagers. If Mrs. Mallory is alive now, she'll surely be gone by the time they're grown up."

"Tough break." He brushed past her, toward the walking path. "Let's get out of here."

"Max!"

"Daisy, what the hell is it to you?" Rounding on her, Max glared. "You're not staying. You've been looking for a way out since you got here."

"I never said I was a nanny! But I…I care about the kids."

The emotion left his face, if not his body. With visible effort, he schooled his features into a sober mask. "Well, that's real nice."

An insistent, metallic beep knifed into the tension between them. It took a while for them to realize the sound came from Max's watch. They both knew what that meant: he'd satisfied the conditions of their deal.

For a long while they were able to do little more than stare at each other. Then Max said quietly, "I think I'll take a rain check on that kiss."

D.J. was at the Rogue Valley Mall the next day, buying a new pair of shoes for each child while Max worked at the restaurant. He'd given her money this morning when, after a very silent breakfast, she'd suggested the boys' hard-used sneakers should be replaced before the start of school in September and before the social worker paid her visit. Somberly agreeing, Max gave her money for the girls, as well. That brief exchange provided the most conversation between them since their argument last night.

The evening before had proved unsettling on a few accounts.

First, D.J. could no longer convince herself that Max was going to feel joyous relief upon meeting his wealthy relative. Even as he carefully calculated the money needed for four pairs of budget shoes, she knew he'd rather cobble the footwear himself than work for Loretta. Second, if Max was uninterested in Loretta's money, he wasn't likely to overlook the fact that D.J. had lied to him. She'd lied a lot. Unless…

Unless she convinced Loretta to kiss some serious butt so her grandson would forgive her. That was D.J.'s new current plan: convince Loretta that Max was worth fighting for. Even temporarily groveling for. The way D.J. saw it, the older woman wanted an heir and she wanted a relationship with her great-grandchildren; that had to be worth eating a little crow.

Still, D.J. knew she had her work cut out for her. She was being paid for investigation, not mediation, and she wasn't entirely certain how she was going to approach her employer.

She figured she was entitled to the tension headache she sported as she herded the children out of the largest discount shoe store in the mall and toward the food court. Thankfully, even Anabel was excited about her purchase, and there was enough money left over for the snacks D.J. had promised if everyone was cooperative about sticking their little feet in the shoes.

Trying to decide between hot pretzels or ice cream, the kids trotted happily ahead of her, Anabel carrying her own bag and D.J. wrestling with the others when her cell phone buzzed against her hip. Transferring the bags to her left hand, she checked her caller I.D. and stopped dead. "Bill!"

Dropping the bags, she opened the phone and called to the children at the same time. "Wait up. I have to take a call." D.J. didn't miss the subtle roll of Anabel's eyes or the boys' eagerness to continue on toward the food court, but at least they all stayed put where she could see them.

"Bill," she barked into the phone, "where are you? What have you been doing? Why haven't you called me?"

His characteristic chuckle undercut her anxiety. "Good girl. *Where, what* and *why*. If you add a *how* question, I'm going to think I really did teach you a thing or two about investigating."

Under the circumstances—utilities barely paid; a job she was about to blow completely unless some miracle occurred; and emotions that made her feel as if she were walking a tightrope—D.J. found it hard to appreciate her former foster dad's cheerfulness. "Okay, *how* could you not give me a heads-up that you were taking off?"

"I left a message, Daisy Girl. It was on my machine."

"'Gone fishing'? What kind of message is that? You don't even like fish." She snapped her fingers and pointed, indicating to the boys that they needed to stay closer to Anabel.

Bill laughed again. "It's a metaphor. You know, 'gone fishing.' On holiday. Taking a long siesta. A person should take a vacation every now and then, don't you think? Good for the blood pressure."

A vacation? With the wolf, as it were, beating down the door of his business? Of course D.J. wanted Bill to enjoy himself, but the business he'd nurtured for thirty years was in peril, and he persisted in behaving as if everything were perfectly fine. That was more worrisome than whether he felt entertained.

"Bill," she said, picking up her parcels and resuming the walk to the food court, as the children had begun to drift in that direction, "you do realize that we're a little…behind in our accounts at the office?"

"Haven't looked at the books lately, honey. Say, where are you? It's noisy."

"I'm at a mall. I—"

"Good for you! I was just thinking we haven't seen any new shoes around here for a while."

"I can't afford new shoes at the moment. Bill, we—"

"What did you get, then? Come over to the house tonight. I'll make the pork chops you like, and you can show me what you bought."

Like when Eileen was alive. "I can't, Bill," D.J. said, kindly but loudly enough to be heard above the noise in the mall. "I'm not in Portland. I took a job in Gold Hill. Remember? I left that on your machine."

"You did?" He sounded positively upbeat. "Well, good, good. What kind of job? I always thought you'd be great in sales."

"Sales?" Oh, no. He was really, really out of it. "No, not sales. It's a P.I. job, Bill."

"Oh." D.J. couldn't miss the disappointment in his voice. "Same old, same old," he muttered.

"What?" With the food court in sight, the children headed immediately for the ice cream kiosk. D.J. followed. "Hang on," she said into the phone. Digging into her jeans pocket, she handed Anabel the remainder of the money Max had allotted for their excursion. "You can order a single scoop each."

"With toppings?" Anabel asked.

D.J. looked at the prices and tried to remember what she had in her wallet. She thought she was going to be on the phone a while longer, so she said, "Two toppings each," in the hope that would keep everyone happy until she and Bill were squared away.

"Hey, are you working for an ice cream parlor?" Again hopefulness filled Bill's voice.

"No!" With all the kids happily pressed against the glass that divided them from the ice cream, D.J. stepped back a bit so she wouldn't be overheard. "I'm working for Loretta Mallory. You know who I mean? The owner of Mallory Superstores." She waited for a response, but he said nothing. "Can you believe it? Mallory Superstores! This job could pay out really well, Bill, and we need the money. You must have forgotten to cut checks for the past few months. Were you aware of that?"

"Maybe," he muttered. "What are you doing for the Mallory woman?"

"I'm working undercover."

"Undercover?" She paused and this time Bill didn't disappoint her. She could hear the frown in his voice. He'd always said undercover work was too dangerous and should be left to the "professionals."

"Undercover as what?" he demanded. "What's this woman got you doing? You should have checked with me."

D.J. didn't point out that he had made that virtually impossible. She had always been ultraindependent, anyway, but now she realized how much she'd missed hearing the protectiveness in Bill's voice. For the first time in days she felt as if some things, at least, were back to normal.

"It's nothing dangerous," she said, not adding that though the work wasn't physically dangerous, there were other hazards. Emotional hazards. She watched Livie's eyes light up as Anabel handed her a cup of pink ice cream covered in multicolored sprinkles and jellybeans. Liv's greedy grin could make D.J.'s heart melt faster than a Popsicle in the sun.

"Well, what are you doing?" Bill asked impatiently.

Falling in love, D.J. thought before she could edit herself. James's mouth formed an awed *O* as the girl behind the counter ladled crushed Butterfingers extragenerously over a scoop of rocky road. Waiting his turn, Sean was so eager he practically vibrated.

"I'm a nanny," D.J. said.

For several moments only silence greeted her. Then, "Nanny," Bill said, as if he couldn't figure out how D.J. and that word could fit into the same sentence. "For kids?" His surprise was certainly justified. She'd never even babysat in high school. "Who are the parents?"

"Parent," she corrected. "Max Lotorto, Loretta Mallory's grandson."

"A man? A single man? You didn't move in, did you?"

As succinctly as she could, D.J. explained Loretta's original request and described Max's character and situation.

There was another lengthy pause as Bill mulled the information over. "Four kids," he murmured. D.J. began scoping out nearby tables as the children completed their orders and Anabel counted out the money. Bill's low chuckle stole her attention. "That must be keeping you busy. So, where are you? In case I need to reach you for anything."

"Gold Hill."

"Never heard of it."

"It's a little town in southern Oregon. Has a creek running through it. Listen, Bill, I'm going to try to get a little advance on my fee here. I'll send it to you."

"What for?"

"So you can pay the gas and electric at the office. They'll be due next week," she said clearly, as if she could imprint the instructions on his mind, like a to-do list. Maybe Bill truly was going slightly senile. A frisson of fear went through her. He sounded like his old self one minute, then seemed disconnected the next. "How is everything at the house, Bill? Are you...you know, paid up on everything there?" His personal finances had never been her business before, but it looked like someone might have to keep tabs on him from now on. He and Eileen had never had children, so that left D.J.

He answered heartily. "Fine, everything's fine. Went up near the Idaho panhandle and met a second—or maybe it was a third—cousin on my mother's side. Wish you'd come with me one of these times, Daisy girl. It's important to meet your relations."

D.J. refrained from pointing out that the distant relatives Bill had been popping in on were barely relations of his, much less hers. At any rate, she thought they ought to be focusing on business not road trips. "I've got too much to do to get away right now, Bill. Business has been down, don't you think?"

"There are always lulls. That's all the more reason to take off while you can. Are there any good lakes where you are?"

"I don't know, Bill, I haven't had time to go to lakes."

He made a tsking sound. "Too bad. Well, I'd better go, Daisy June. Chores pile up when you've been out of town. You take care of yourself, honey."

"Wait. I want to ask you—" The line went dead. Frustrated to the point of exasperation, D.J. considered calling him back. She wanted an answer about his home accounts. She would have liked a little advice about the tangle in which she currently found herself, too, but perhaps it was better not to worry Bill right now.

Slowly she closed her phone and joined the kids at the ice cream counter. Now that she'd spoken to Bill, she felt depressed—more concerned about him and, strangely, more alone than she had before he called. She also felt an uncomfortable queasiness in the pit of her stomach. At first she wasn't sure quite what the feeling was, but it grew quickly, and she identified it finally as fear. She told herself to shake it off, but the vague, distasteful sensation felt as if it had come home to roost.

"Everybody set?" she asked as Anabel paid for the treats. "What did you get?" D.J. asked her, thinking she, too, could use a little sugar.

"I got vanilla with fresh strawberries," Anabel said.

D.J. stared at her. There was such a thing as being too good. When the girl behind the counter asked D.J. what she wanted, she ordered a chocolate-peanut-butter cup with hot fudge and cookie crumbles. Grabbing as many napkins as she could hold, D.J. guided them all to a large table, where the children immediately dug into their treats. It took D.J. a little longer to put the first spoonful in her mouth. Her stomach was beginning to feel too unsettled. Probably an ulcer in the making.

In the past when she'd imagined doing undercover work, it had seemed exciting and creative, not…dishonest.

It's not personal. It's business. D.J. remembered that line from a movie. *It's not personal. It's business.* Unfortunately, she had crossed the line—she who rarely got personal about anything—and she was paying for it with the kind of heartburn an antacid would not cure. For the first time since she'd boldly knocked on the door of Bill's office and stayed, she wondered whether she was cut out for this kind of work.

Watching Anabel carefully scoop strawberries and small dabs of yogurt onto her spoon, keeping herself and the table around her wonderfully clean while the other kids managed to drip more than they ate, D.J. thought about the task that awaited her once they reached home.

Utterly by accident last night, she had come across a steel file box on the floor of the linen closet, under a hastily folded quilt. If the box yielded information about Max's financial profile, she would have hit pay dirt. D.J. hadn't had the time or privacy to look inside the box last night, and to tell the truth she'd felt relieved not to have to. After she'd gone to bed, though, she'd had a long, hard talk with herself.

Last night, she had turned Max off by pressuring him about Loretta. D.J. knew in her gut that he shouldn't hide from a heritage like his. But it also made her sick to think that he was angry with her, that in doing her job she had alienated him.

It's not personal. It's business. She had no reason and no right to feel bereft. Maybe her concern over Bill was making her soft.

There were only two outcomes to this situation as far as she could see: Max and Loretta reconciled and everyone was happy. Or, Max found out D.J. was working for Loretta and decided that D.J. was the liar of the century. Then Loretta decided D.J. was a failure at her job because instead of merely investigating, she'd stuck her big nose in, and D.J. and Bill's business went under and no one would talk to her ever again.

D.J.'s stomach did a somersault. No way could she eat. Glancing at Anabel, who was eating her vanilla with strawberry slices and hadn't dropped a bit, D.J. thought, *Maybe I'm wrong. Maybe you can't be too good.* Perhaps she should have been more like Anabel all her life. If she had, she might have thought twice about taking this job.

Pushing her ice cream to the center of the table, she said, "Who wants it?"

Chapter Ten

The kids were sugar-bouncing off the roof of the minivan before D.J. rolled into Gold Hill.

"I wanna show Uncle Max my new shoes!" James called from the rear seat.

"He's working," D.J. answered, not sure whether she did or did not want to see him, given the tension between them. Tension equaled stress, yet in a way this particular tension was rather…exhilarating, too. "You can show him when he comes home tonight."

"But I want to show him now," James persisted, "while they're new."

"They'll still be new tonight, Jamie."

Sean piped up. "What if our old sneakers fall apart and the house catches on fire and we all gotta get out, so me and James put on our new shoes and run outta the house, but then we fall in the mud and then when Uncle Max gets home he wants to see our new sneakers, but they don't look new anymore?"

D.J. looked in the rearview mirror. All the children except Anabel were awaiting a reasonable answer to what they obviously considered a reasonable question. Anabel merely rolled her eyes.

"You make an excellent point, Sean," D.J. said. "Unusual, but excellent. Tell you what, we'll check all the smoke alarms when we get home. Then you and James can play quietly in your room—maybe work on a puzzle or color—some activity that won't require you to wear your old shoes out of the house, so they won't fall apart before your uncle gets home, thereby relieving you of the necessity to put on your new shoes, which will keep them beautiful until he sees them."

"Does that mean no?" James asked in a genuinely puzzled tone. He looked so cute, D.J. wanted to jump into the back seat and hug him.

"I want the cherries from Uncle Max's bar," Livie said in a singsong voice while she stared dreamily out the van window.

"I want French fries!" Sean enthused.

"I want to see Uncle Max and tell him I missed him all day," Anabel said sadly.

Well, that did it. Instead of proceeding to Sardine Creek Road—and the silver box that awaited her examination—D.J. headed for Tavern on the Tracks.

"So this bison is staring at me as if she'd like to kick me clear into Wyoming, and I'm thinking, I'm going to kill the other vet if he ever decides to show up, but in the meantime I've got to decide whether I want to stick my hand into a pregnant bison that's breaching and really pissed!" Cleo Marks laughed as she ran a hand through the blond hair she'd cut into perky half-inch spikes.

She has a well-shaped head, Max found himself thinking inconsequentially as he sat across from Cleo in a booth in his still-unopened restaurant.

Max hadn't seen Cleo in over a month, but as much as he liked her—truly enjoyed her company—this afternoon he was having a hard time hanging on to the thread of the conversation. He'd felt down, frustrated and angry since his evening out with Daisy.

"So anyway, I decided, 'Clee, don't be crazy. Use a tranquilizer.'"

Max frowned. "Wouldn't a tranquilizer slow down the birth?"

Cleo cocked her head, her hazel eyes wide and guileless. "I wasn't going to use it on the bison, silly. I was going to take it myself." She waited for Max's reaction then tilted back in her chair and laughed with unabashed heartiness.

The frown that had marred Max's brow all day finally smoothed. Cleo had been his next-door neighbor since he'd moved to Gold Hill. She had degrees in both wildlife biology and veterinary medicine, and she was one of the most genuine, unaffected people Max had ever met.

"So what's coming up next for you?" he asked, knowing Cleo liked to travel for work. There was always a new adventure around the corner.

Cleo stretched her arms above her head, then rested them on the back of the booth. "I think I'm going to stay put for a while, actually. Dr. Frank asked me again to join his large-animal practice. He wants to retire next year, so I'm thinking about it."

"Really? I'd finally have a neighbor who actually lives in the house next door?" he quipped.

"Could be."

"Uncle Max! Uncle Max!" A veritable chorus accompanied the kids' stampede into the restaurant. As usual, Max felt his spirits rise at the sight of his family.

Daisy trailed behind.

"Munchkins!" Cleo was out of her seat, arms thrown wide as the children appeared beside the booth.

Four wide-eyed children came to a halt, went silent briefly as they recognized Cleo and then burst into chatter.

"Cleo!"

"Cleo's home!"

"I saw your horses in the pasture!"

"Biscuit came to the fence, and I fed him a carrot!"

"*I* gave him *two* carrots."

The children vied for the attention of the neighbor whose farm animals had kept them entertained and helped them heal when they first came to Gold Hill. Cleo had been Max's greatest help after Terry died, using her animals to reach the grieving siblings.

As usual, Cleo seemed able to focus on all the children at once, nodding and murmuring responses very seriously as the kids clustered around her. Max simply sat back and smiled. In under a minute, Cleo was seated again, with Anabel and the twins on either side of her, and Livie on her lap.

He smiled as Cleo entertained the kids with tales of her recent trip and pulled small, thoughtful gifts from the large tapestry bag she habitually carried. Max had asked her once what was in there, and she'd dumped it on the table where they were having coffee, displaying the usual purse items, plus a gallon-size plastic bag of cut apple, mini carrots, glucosamine sulfate for the horse who has everything, veterinary salve and bovine eye ointment. She was a unique girl, Cleo was.

Max seemed to be surrounded by unique girls.

Walking slowly to the table as if her eyes hadn't yet adjusted to the dim interior, Daisy approached the table with an expression as wary and hesitant as her pace. Max almost rose to turn on a few more lights but reconsidered. If Daisy was having trouble seeing them, well…he didn't mind the advantage. He could look at her all he wanted without being caught until her vision sharpened again.

Max was aware, however, that he was nursing a churlish annoyance where Daisy was concerned. While he'd been lusting after her the other night during dinner, she'd spent that evening bugging the hell out of him over a family issue that didn't even affect her. Or did it?

He'd convinced her to stay on by playing the custody issue card. Once that issue was squared away, she could leave without guilt, which, apparently, was her goal.

Because he knew that he was way more ticked than he ought to be under the circumstances, Max watched Daisy only until she made eye contact with him. Once she did, he gave her a curt nod, but looked away.

Yeah, real mature, but what the hell.

Cleo gave Sean a fat, unusual-looking pencil made from a Montana tree. "See this rough, bumpy side of it?" Cleo ran a finger along the barrel of the pencil. "This is the actual bark. This is almost exactly what you would see if you were standing right in front of the tree trunk."

"Wow." Sean's eyes grew round.

Max leaned forward, exhibiting considerably more interest in the souvenir than he actually felt. Daisy stood by the table for several seconds, saying nothing, until Cleo glanced up and said, "Hello." Cleo's tone remained as pleasant as always, but curiosity lit her eyes. She raised a brow at Max, expecting an introduction.

Daisy, obviously ticked that he hadn't offered one, stuck out her hand. "Daisy June. Nanny. And you are?"

Max looked up, surprised by her tone.

"Cleo Marks. I'm—"

"Our *very* good friend." Max interrupted smoothly, watching Daisy's gorgeous eyes spark with what looked a whole lot like resentment even as her lips curled up politely. "Cleo owns the property next door to us. You've probably seen her horses in the pasture." Max paused significantly. "We've missed her." His voice was silky smooth and deliberately misleading.

Cleo's brow, which had hitched when Daisy introduced herself, now spiked humorously. "You did? That's very nice."

Anabel squeezed Cleo's arm. "We always miss you, Cleo. When can you come over? I want to show you my model horse. It's supposed to be National Velvet. Uncle Max bought it for my birthday."

"I bet it's a beauty. Good gift, Uncle Max."

"Come see for yourself," Max invited, lounging casually on the other side of the booth. "As I recall you've got a birthday coming up in a couple of days. Have dinner with us tonight, and we'll celebrate. We're having your favorite," he tempted.

"Slippery shrimp and pot stickers?" Cleo said doubtfully. "Uh-uh. You're just saying that."

"Uh-uh," Max teased her. "I was planning to stop by General Yee's on the way home from work."

"Oh, boy! Can we have tomato noodles, too?" James bounced on his knees in the booth.

"And orange chicken," Sean added, trying to hold the pencil Cleo had given him between his upper lip and his nose.

Anabel and Livie added their requests. Max answered everyone affirmatively, but his attention never wavered from Daisy. Even when he wasn't looking directly at her, he could *feel* the tension emanating from her strong, curvaceous body.

Well, well, well.

Max had to school himself not to grin. Daisy June was jealous. Had to be. Of course, that notion didn't exactly mesh with his previous theory—that she couldn't wait to be free of the lot of them—but he was humble; he was willing to revise his first guess.

You are a puzzle, Daisy June. And I want to put the pieces together.

"What do you want, Daisy?" he asked smoothly, ostensibly referring to dinner.

She tossed her head, and her mink hair, pulled into a high ponytail, whipped sassily behind her. "Nothing for me, thanks. In fact, if it's all right with you, I have a few things I'd like to get done tonight. Since you're going to be home, I think I'll take a few hours to myself."

She wanted the night off? Max felt his frustration rise again. He couldn't have misread the classic signs of jealousy…could he? Was he that far gone?

"Go ahead," he mumbled. Fairly certain he looked as disgruntled as he felt, he rallied by throwing an unabashed wink at Cleo. "We'll hold down the fort."

"*Uh-uh*, you were *not* planning to have Chinese. You're just saying that!"

D.J. simpered as she stood before the mirror in Max's-slasher room and brushed her hair. Switching parts, she became Max, winking at the lovely Cleo. "Uh-uh. I planned to get take out Chinese all along. Isn't that a coincidence?" D.J. seductively narrowed her eyes at the mirror. "I *lo-o-ove* slippery, slimy… sick-o… shrimp!"

All right, so she was padding her part, but sheesh. Could the two of them have been any sappier?

So much for D.J.'s assumption that responsible, dedicated Maxwell had put his own life on hold for the sake of the children. So much for her belief that he'd been celibate while focusing on the care of four needful orphans who required his time and attention. Celibate—ha! Max was likely as celibate as a rabbit. He'd probably been having an affair with "Clee," über farm girl, since he'd moved to Gold Hill. Small-town women were notoriously racy.

"Cleo. What kind of a name is that, anyway?" D.J. groused, hearing strands of her hair snap beneath the punishing strokes of the brush. "*Cleee-o*," she trilled. "Clee-o-patra." Of course she knew she was regressing to the behavior of a six-year-old and that people named Daisy June shouldn't throw stones, but she was beyond maturity and reason at this point. She was…

Jealous.

Abruptly she lowered the brush and gave her image a hard stare. Good grief, that's what she was, all right—green-eyed, energy-robbing, head-achingly jealous.

And angry.

And resentful.

And hurt.

Max had almost had her convinced that she could become indispensable to the children and to him, but it wasn't true. She wasn't "special." If anything, she'd been a temporary fill-in while Cleo, the horse whisperer, was out of town.

Compressing her lips in a firm, tight line, D.J. shook her head. It shouldn't bother her. Nothing about this situation should tweak her emotionally at all. She was here to do a job, and let's face it: she'd do it a whole lot better without the distraction of a transient flirtation…or some misplaced feeling of guilt because she had started to like Max too much to investigate him.

"Well, boo-hoo-hoo. Time to wake up and smell the caffeine, D. J. Holden. When you leave here, you're not coming back. And you're not taking anything with you except a very healthy check from Max's granny. It doesn't matter whether Max loves Loretta, hates her or can't remember her name. That old broad is going to get all the information she wants, because *this is only a job. Max is a subject.*"

D.J. set her brush on the dresser and frowned at her reflection, horrified to see tears gathering in her eyes. Damn!

If it were only Max's reaction to Cleo that she had to contend with, D.J. could have told herself he was a testosterone-driven snake who'd flirted with the nanny because his regular squeeze had been out of town. She certainly couldn't feel too horrible over losing a guy like that. But, try as she might, she could not expunge the image of Sean and James and Anabel and Livie racing to Cleo with arms and hearts open wide, crawling all over the other woman in an effort to get closer. Or of Max smiling indulgently at them all. That's what really hurt—and she was so stupid for feeling this way. But what really, really hurt was that as soon as they'd spied Cleo, no one—not Max and not the children—had even remembered that she, D.J., was there.

Placing her hands over her face, D.J. shook her head. This was exactly the way she'd felt when the Lindstroms had said they were going to adopt her and then backed out because Mrs. Lindstrom found out she was pregnant. D.J. had trusted her heart to someone else, and the result had been disastrous.

Pressing her fingers hard against her eyelids, D.J. released her breath with a sound that fell somewhere between a sigh and a groan.

She shook her head again, harder this time, as if she were trying to get water out of her ear…which couldn't be so far from the truth, because she'd have to have fluid on the brain in order to sucker herself into a family fantasy again.

D.J. had been ten when the social worker on her case had popped in for a visit. Surprising D.J., she'd explained what adoption was, then asked D.J. how she would feel about the Lindstroms becoming her parents forever. The Lindstroms had sat there, too, in a pleasant kitchen that smelled perpetually of cinnamon, smiling at her with what appeared to be hope in their chinablue eyes. To this day, what D.J. remembered most was the smell of cinnamon, the color of the Lindstroms' eyes and the taste of her own fear, because she'd felt sick to her stomach suddenly, like she was going to vomit Trudy Lindstrom's snickerdoodle cookies all over the kitchen table.

She'd nodded in response to the social worker's question and everyone had seemed pleased. It was only later, alone in her bed, that she'd stared at the dark ceiling and realized that if the Lindstroms were going to adopt her that meant her own mother wasn't coming back for her. She'd started "acting out" the very next day. It couldn't have been a month later that the social worker had come for another visit, explaining that the Lindstroms were going to have a baby of their own and that "under the circumstances" they thought Daisy June might not like having another child in the house. She'd been placed with new foster parents the next week.

The Department of Human Services had stuck her in counseling shortly thereafter, which in retrospect was, of course, a good thing. At the time, though, nothing could have assuaged the feelings of loss and betrayal, grief and self-loathing D.J. had feared might kill her.

Thank God she was all grown-up now, with a decent understanding of what had transpired sixteen years ago and the awareness that she no longer had to live with those feelings. If she chose to avoid situations that called the feelings to mind again…that was her business.

Checking her watch, D.J. muttered firmly, "Enough of this. Let's get going."

Max had arrived home only a couple hours after D.J. returned with the kids. He'd decided to shower and change first then pick up the Chinese food and a birthday cake for Cleo. He'd asked the children if they wanted to drive into town to help him choose the cake, a few decorations and a gift. Naturally, they had been enthusiastic.

D.J. had retreated to her room while Max herded the kids into the van. She paid attention now to the sound of their chatter, silenced when the van door slid into place. She waited for Max to slip into the driver's seat, heard that door close, too, heard the motor start and the van tires crunch across the gravel and twiglined driveway. Then and only then did she leave her room.

Even though D.J. knew there was no one in the house, she glanced up and down the hall. Creeping carefully to the closet, she extracted the steel box and took it to her room. She set it on her bed and unlatched the top, feeling relief and anticipation and still a niggling discomfort as she viewed the contents. Files. The entire box was filled with files.

Carefully labeled, the manila folders contained warranty booklets, medical records for Max and the kids, paid utility and credit card bills, even Max's bank and loan statements, and the last two years' tax returns.

Bingo. Just the information Loretta wanted.

Digging into her duffel bag, D.J. pulled out her digital camera. She tried to remain businesslike and impartial as she laid various folders open on the bed, but she *had* to scan the contents so she knew which files to photograph, and her own interest was undeniably piqued. What information would she—and Loretta, of course—be able to draw by viewing these files?

D.J. began by photographing the most recent credit card bills.

Apparently, Max possessed only two pieces of plastic. From there, she moved on to loan and bank account info, then snapped the paid utility bills and, despite her sane voice, which said, "Knock it off," she carefully examined the cell phone charges to determine whether Max had made repeated calls to one number…Cleo's cell, for example.

But no, Max appeared to be the soul of moderation in all areas. Before she was done, D.J. had formed a solid opinion of Max's spending habits. What she discovered was that he'd made a generous living as an accountant and was irreproachably responsible where money was concerned. Nonetheless, his life had changed considerably over the past year, and his finances were obviously stretched to the limit due to the opening of the restaurant and the arrival of the kids.

Pretty much what she'd expected. His bank account had taken a hit during the last several months. His restaurant accounts were not included in this set of files, but D.J. guessed that the bar didn't do that well. In fact, if he'd taken responsibility for the children prior to buying the Tavern, D.J. would have said he hadn't shown the greatest judgment in leaving a well-paid accounting position for the personal dream of running a restaurant. His savings, though more than respectable for a single man, weren't going to stretch much farther with four growing bodies to feed and clothe. Or a nanny to pay.

Department of Human Services wouldn't have to hire an investigator to gain access to this information; all they'd have to do was ask.

As far as D.J. could see, there was no doubt about it Max needed what Loretta had to offer. D.J.'s only concern was whether Loretta would judge her grandson's CEO potential based on his decision to leave a secure accounting position in order to become a struggling entrepreneur.

Checking the camera to make sure she had all the photographs she needed, D.J. patted the files back into place, wiped the metal box and returned it to the closet. Then she went to her room, grabbed her camera, cell phone and purse and headed to her car.

Cleo gazed at shiny multicolored letters that spelled out Happy Birthday on the wall behind Max's chair. Crepe paper streamers and half a dozen balloons decorated the dining room, where the remains of a devil's food cake with white icing and teeth-jarringly sweet pink frosting flowers sat upon the table. The kids had given her a bottle of perfume that smelled like berries and a yellow candle that smelled like vanilla.

Stretching out along the sofa, her elbow digging into the cushion, Cleo propped her head on her hand to afford herself a clear view of Max. Seated on the chair kitty-corner to the couch, he had spent the past ten minutes since the kids went to bed alternately glancing at his watch or the clock on the mantel or peering out the living room window. His nanny, Daisy, had not joined them for dinner, and Cleo thought it was pretty clear that despite his desire to be a good host, Max had been distracted all evening by the other woman's absence.

She sighed. "Thanks for a great night, Max. Having a birthday party was a really thoughtful way to welcome me home."

Car headlights beaming up Sardine Creek Road caught Max's attention. He cracked his knuckles in frustration as the vehicle passed the house without slowing. Absently he nodded at Cleo. "Sure. Sure, Clee."

"Yep. I love birthday parties. Very cool." She gave him a big, glowing smile he barely noticed and added, "It might have been even cooler if it had actually been my birthday, but, oh, there I go splitting hairs."

Max nodded. Then he frowned. In the darkening room, illuminated only by the light spilling in from the dining room and several flickering candles, she saw Max finally register what she was telling him.

"Isn't your birthday in a couple of days?"

Blandly, Cleo shook her head. "A couple of days and three months. What's up with you, Lotorto?"

Max wiped a hand across his face. It wasn't Cleo's birthday. The information smacked him between the eyes, which was probably where he deserved to be smacked. Man, could he have been a bigger putz?

"Clee, I'm really sorry. Honestly, I thought—"

She waved the hand that was resting on the curve of her hip. "I don't expect you to remember my birthday. I've only known you a year and a half. Besides I had a good time. I just think you should tell me what the heck you're up to."

Max agreed. His behavior today warranted an explanation to the neighbor who had rapidly become his friend. The problem was…he didn't want to give her an explanation. It would make him look like a jackass.

A jackass with a crush on his nanny.

Max cracked his knuckles while he hesitated. Cleo winced. "Sorry. Bad habit." He looked at his hands. "Have I been—"

"All evening." She pushed herself to a sit. "Listen, Max, I told you when we met that I'm a really good judge of character. I knew right away you and I would be buds, but I gotta tell you, today felt a little weird. You know? Like at the restaurant. When you first asked if I wanted to come to dinner, I thought you had an ulterior motive."

Guilt swelled in Max's breast. She was right, and he chose not to insult her further with some lame excuse. Out of curiosity he asked, "Why did you say yes?"

"Because I wanted to find out exactly what your motive was." She smiled mischievously. "And I like slippery shrimp."

Max wagged his head. In the candlelight he studied Cleo's honest face and bright, curious eyes. It was 9:35 p.m. the last time he'd checked. Cleo had been here approximately three hours. She was pretty, fun and intelligent. She was straightforward and independent. Yet not once tonight had he felt anything stronger than friendship.

He'd barely been able to get his mind off Daisy all evening.

Rubbing his eyes, Max tried, rather unsuccessfully, not to wonder where Daisy was or whether he'd completely misread the jealousy he could have sworn he'd read in her expression this afternoon. He sighed and studied the far less complicated woman before him. "Cleo," he said, a flare of regret coloring his tone, "how is that you and I never…" Before the words were out, Max stumbled, aware suddenly that he could hurt Cleo unintentionally.

"How is it we never hooked up?" she finished for him, quite easily. A smile pushed dimples into the spot below her high cheeks. "You're not my type, Max."

That was blunt. Though the information didn't particularly take him aback, he was curious. "Who is your type?"

She answered without missing a beat. "Your nanny."

Forty minutes ago, after putting the kids to bed, Max had poured brandies for both him and Cleo. He hadn't touched his yet; now he reached for it and guzzled.

Setting his glass on the table, he let the surprise sink in. "Okay. I am not sure what to say."

Cleo looked at him levelly. "It's just information, Max. Is it going to get in the way of our friendship?"

"No." His reply was swift and sure. She was too good a neighbor, too good a friend to lose.

Cleo nodded. "Good." Reaching for her own brandy, she sat back, curling her legs beneath her. "Okay, your turn."

Max cocked a brow.

"I confessed," she said, swirling her drink. "Now it's your turn. Who are you attracted to? And you may as well admit that it's Daisy…that is her name, right? Because I saw the way you looked at her."

Max palmed his brow, squeezing his temples, where a massive headache was about to begin. "Obvious, huh?" Cleo shrugged, and he shook his head. "I can't be attracted to my nanny. That is not kosher."

"Why not? It worked for Jane Eyre and Mr. Rochester." Cleo leaned forward. "Know how I see it? Solid relationships don't come around that often—whatever your persuasion is. Real passion on every level—physical, emotional, intellectual—is pretty rare if you ask me." Cleo tilted her head. "Are you attracted to her on every level?"

Max thought about it. "I don't know her on every level. What I know I'm attracted to. And the rest…" He stood, shoving his fists into his pockets. Decisively he stated, "I want to find out about the rest. All of it." He paced the room. "I shouldn't even be thinking about a relationship right now. Especially not with her." His voice dropped to a growl. "She's not really a nanny, you know."

Cleo put a hand to her throat. "Gracious!"

Completing his first trip across the room, Max turned and began another leg. "Yeah. She applied for a job as a waitress…or a babysitter. I'm not quite sure." He thumbed his chest. "*I* asked her to be a nanny. And she only agreed to take the job temporarily. For all I know, *temporary* is a trend with her."

Another car cruised up Sardine Creek, and Max turned toward the window, hands on his hips as he watched it, too, pass the house. He cursed under his breath. "She's probably gone already. Hell, I bet she packed her bags and took off. I should have checked her room for a note." Stabbing a finger in Cleo's direction, he said, "She guaranteed me the next two weeks…I think she said two weeks." He scowled. "What time is it now? Almost ten—"

"It's 9:47."

"Right. And where is she? Who knows! Is that the kind of person I want to get involved with? Not that I'm looking for anything permanent." He held up a hand. "I'm not looking for anything permanent."

"Well, I'm glad you got that cleared up." Cleo slapped her knees and stood. "I'm gonna go." She rubbed her belly. "I'm full and sleepy." Gathering the gifts the children gave her, she walked over to Max and gave him a peck on the cheek. "G'night."

He walked Cleo to the door. "I'd have to be crazy to turn something simple into a giant headache."

"That's why God made people who make Tylenol."

Despite her protest, Max accompanied his neighbor to the car he always insisted she drive if it was going to be dark when she headed home. Houses were separated by some acreage and no sidewalks on Sardine Creek.

Max leaned into the car window. "Ring once when you get home, so I know you're safe."

"I live next door, Max."

"Yeah, and you never lock the door. Ring once." He tapped the window frame and straightened. "Thanks for listening, Clee." Looking gruff in the moonlight, Max issued a brusque nod. "I'm a lot clearer now."

"Really?" She started the car. Just before pulling away, she leaned her head out the window. "Oh, listen, for what it's worth I think you're full of it, and when Daisy comes back tonight, you'd be an ever bigger ass *not* to go for it. 'Night."

* * *

D.J. returned to the house shortly after 10:00 p.m.

What a night! She'd phoned Loretta with her information, and the woman had practically machine-gunned questions into the phone. D.J. had felt as if she was being interrogated by the FBI. Most of the questions had been about the children—their hobbies, habits and attachment to Max. Loretta had been ravenous for details and had driven the conversation. Being a control-loving pain in the rear came naturally to the elderly woman because she'd had to take care of herself and her company for a long time now, but her genuine excitement was palpable.

Still, D.J. felt uncomfortable.

She'd tried to hint that Max held a few resentments about his mother's background and that Loretta might have to tread carefully. The news did not go over well. Loretta had turned irritable and even more commanding. D.J. had backed off, reminding herself that her job had been to provide information and information alone; what Loretta did with the information and what Max did about Loretta was not her business or her responsibility.

It's not personal….

This afternoon had taught her an excellent lesson in never ever, ever—did she mention "never"?—mixing business with pleasure. Period, end of story, no exceptions to that rule.

Trudging up to the house, she noted that all the lights were out and felt relief over not having to make polite small talk with Cleo. She refused to speculate on what the evening had been like and instead wondered if there was any food left.

After making contact with Loretta, D.J. had decided to kill time by going to the movies. She'd bought a hot dog, soda and box of Milk Duds, but she'd made the fatal error of buying a ticket to a romance, which had somehow given her a stomachache even worse than the one she'd had this afternoon. The dog and popcorn wound up in the trash, the Milk Duds in her purse. The couple in the movie had made love about a dozen times…maybe that was a *slight* exaggeration, but by the time the show ended, D.J. felt as if she needed a long, hard kickboxing session and an ice-cold shower. She'd driven around, listening to hard rock on her car radio and singing at the top of her lungs just to distract herself. Now she was starving.

And very, very glad Max had, apparently, gone to bed. He'd been bunking in with the boys instead of crashing on the sofa the last few nights, so she planned, after letting herself into the house, to ferret through the kitchen for anything but leftover slippery shrimp, take two Tylenol and crawl into bed. She only hoped her mind would quiet enough to let her get some sleep.

Unsure of how long ago Max had retired, and aiming to get her food and sneak to her room without being seen or heard, D.J. chose not to turn on the living room lights. Instead she walked softly across the carpet and into the kitchen. The light from the open refrigerator illuminated boxes of leftover Chinese food as well as meat loaf from the night before and the usual staples, but also a half-eaten cake on the kitchen counter. Dark chocolate crumbs mingled with soft white icing.

Decision made. D.J. needed a disgusting splurge to quell the continued misgivings that filled her with anxiety. By the time she left the kitchen, she had a soup bowl filled with cake, a big slab of mint-chocolate-chip ice cream and a drizzle of chocolate syrup on top. If that didn't take care of the itchy feelings that made her want to scratch all over, nothing would. The drapes to the living room window were open, so she decided to flop on the couch and gaze at the stars as she took the first sloppy bite.

When the lights went on in the room, her heart bounced; when a deep, wry voice sounded practically in her ear, she nearly rocketed off the couch.

"Welcome home," Max said from a chair tucked into the corner of the room between the reading lamp and the bookshelves. "You're fired."

Chapter Eleven

Chased by surprise, the cake went down the wrong way. D.J. choked and coughed, trying to catch her breath.

She cast a perturbed glance at Max, noticing that he didn't exhibit much remorse for startling her half out of her wits. He did, however, move to sit beside her on the sofa, taking the bowl from her hands and thumping her on the back for good measure.

"Relax," he advised.

"Relax?" she gasped when she finally could. "Do you always sit in the dark, waiting for unsuspecting guests to enter your home?"

"You're not my guest," he reminded her with challenging matter-of-factness. "You're my employee."

"Not anymore. You just fired me. And might I add, *you big fat ingrate!*"

Max was seated close enough on the couch to smell the mint ice cream on D.J.'s breath. "I fired you because you've been MIA for—" he checked his watch "—four hours."

"I was not missing. I told you I had things to do."

Narrowing his eyes, Max growled, "What 'things'? The stores around here close at six."

Slapping a hand over her mouth, D.J. gasped, "Oh, I'm sorry, I didn't realize I had a curfew! If I'd known I could have told you to…*stick it in your ear.*"

"Nice talk. They teach you that in nanny school?"

"I didn't go to nanny school. I'm—"

"I know, I know…you're not a nanny! How about Courtesy 101—you ever take that course? Because there they teach you to *phone if you're going to be gone for four hours!*"

"I figured you had better things to do than watch the clock!" They were both leaning forward now and both so angry they could have blown steam from their ears, though they modulated their voices to a loud hiss to avoid waking the children.

"What are you so upset about?" D.J. demanded to know. She assessed Max with a suspicious glare. "Did your girlfriend leave early?"

"No, she did not. As a matter of fact, Clee just left. She said to tell you hi." He jerked his head toward the bowl he'd set on the coffee table. "You're eating her birthday cake."

Daisy flicked a glance at her abandoned dessert. "No-o-o," she droned, "I was choking on her birthday cake."

An expression of such clear disdain crossed Daisy's face that Max's attitude took a sudden swing…for the better. In fact, he had to force back a rather smug smile.

Hell, he loved it when she did that—tossed her head like a sassy colt and gave him her best "I couldn't care less" look. Because that's when he knew she did care. He was learning to read her.

Daisy had stayed away tonight until she was sure Cleo had gone.

A swell of masculine satisfaction made his chest feel heavy, in a good way. A very good way.

Max had spent the past twenty minutes since Cleo had left asking himself, *Why Daisy Holden?* If he wanted a relationship, why not find someone simpler, less elusive, more open?

Because.

The answer was sitting right in front of him, with blazing eyes, a temper that could flash like wildfire, smiles that enticed like sugar. The woman was a pain in the keister precisely because she was too maddeningly contradictory to ignore. She possessed a tough independence that reminded Max of the type of woman who generally kicked everyone else's butt on the Survivor reality show. But then, usually unexpectedly, she exhibited a gentleness that stole his breath and put a hunger in his belly.

Max felt he already knew a fair amount about her; now he wanted to know *why* she felt uncomfortable openly showing her vulnerability…*why* she didn't want to stay when he could see that the kids touched her heart…*why* she didn't want to start a relationship with him when he knew damned well that he ignited her passion.

What he wanted most of all right now, though, was simply Daisy. Naked.

Abruptly changing the tactics he'd used thus far tonight, Max settled into the sofa, his arms spread along the back. "Did you have dinner?"

Daisy's brows swooped down. "You want to talk about food?"

"I just realized how unfair it is of me to sit here, very comfortable, very full, arguing with someone who, for all I know, is half-starving. What's the story?" He lowered his voice…just enough. "Are you hungry, Daisy?"

D.J. wasn't born yesterday. She'd seen that look in a man's eyes before—the slit-lidded, partially smiling suggestiveness that told her to read between the lines. What was up with Max that he could argue and appear genuinely angry one minute and quite obviously hot for her the next?

What was up with her that she felt exactly the same way?

Daisy looked at the arms Max stretched across the sofa and at his hands. Strength—it was there in the carved biceps revealed by his short-sleeved polo shirt, down to the granite-sleek forearms and the hands that looked so secure and comfortable when they were carrying the kids, but so very tempting and dangerous now when she imagined them exploring her body.

Max picked up the bowl on the coffee table. With clear intent, he scooped up a bite of cake and ice cream and aimed it slowly, tantalizingly for D.J.'s mouth. It wasn't even the cake that appealed anymore, hungry as D.J. was. The light in Maxwell's eyes, the ready-to-spring coil of energy that lay beneath the facade of laziness in his posture, the sheer blatant *wanting*—that's what poured gasoline on D.J.'s fire.

She licked her lips because suddenly they were too dry for her to speak. "Max. Put the spoon down."

He shook his head, barely enough for her to see the movement. "Uh-uh."

Damn. She wanted him, wanted to feel his body wrapped all the way around hers. She wanted to feel his weight and experience his power, and ordinarily she never wanted to yield her power to anyone else's. Never. With Max she thought she might be willing to lose control. Or unable not to.

The cake and ice cream inched closer. D.J. watched Max's face. Max was watching the spoon. A second before it would have met her lips, a thick sticky drop of chocolate syrup blopped onto her bare chest above the scoop neckline of her T-shirt. D.J. felt the cool chocolate sauce and then, immediately following, a drop of cold, cold ice cream. A moment later, while she was looking down at the chocolate sliding toward her bra, she heard Max's voice— as mischievously hot as the ice cream was cold.

"Oops."

The rat; he'd tilted the spoon!

"I assume you have a reason for doing that?" D.J. kept her own voice silky. The best way to prepare oneself to yield all power, she decided, was to wield a little of her own first. Unexpectedly, the thought—both thoughts, actually, the wielding and the yielding— excited her.

She put her hand around Max's and guided the spoon all the way to her mouth. Slowly…very, very slowly and, if she did say so herself, sensuously, she ate the ice cream and cake off the spoon, keeping her eyes on Max the whole time. She watched his eyes narrow, his breath quicken and his nostrils flare before she released his hand and looked at the rivulets of chocolate running down her chest.

"Can't reach?" he asked huskily, the wry question laced with the strain of keeping his lust in check.

D.J. treated him to an equally wry glance that smoldered. "My tongue is fairly talented, Maxwell," she all but purred, "but no, I can't reach it."

"That does it." He tossed the spoon onto the coffee table, where it was still clattering as he reached for her.

D.J. didn't protest a bit; she merely clung to Max while he yanked her close enough for them to feel the heat coming off each other's skin. He stared at her…maybe an instant, maybe an hour… until her fingers dug into his arm and her lips parted with an urgent need to kiss him. But Max had other ideas.

Before he kissed her on the lips, he had business to conduct with her chest. Couldn't leave it all sticky and chocolaty.

Holding her shoulders, Max bent Daisy back until she half reclined against the cushions. With one hand firmly on the middle of her back and one caressing her stomach, Max kissed chocolate syrup and ice cream off the milky skin that had been driving him crazy since that first night in his bar. She was warmer than the dessert, but just as soft, just as sweet…and far more addictive. He felt Daisy's fingers tighten on his arms as his tongue flicked over her skin. When he reached the neckline of her shirt, he lifted her slightly and used one hand to tug the hem of her tee from the waistband of her shorts. Vaguely he thought they should turn off the light, but selfishly he wanted to see her.

She sat up, offering help rather than protest as together they peeled her shirt over her head. Max wasn't entirely surprised to see an ivory lace bra that looked as if it had been traced onto her breasts. The blush of her nipples was easily visible yet tantalizingly protected. The sight was so damned beautiful Max almost hated to alter it by removing her bra. Almost.

The trail of chocolate he'd eliminated above the neckline of her shirt picked up again to run between her breasts. Max made quick work of it, then unhooked her bra and gave himself a gift that made it feel like Christmas, his birthday and the Fourth of July all rolled into one. He was a kid again, a tremulous, freaking teenager as Daisy's bra fell away and her firm, perfect breasts were freed. Max reminded himself to breathe, had to clench his teeth to keep from swearing at himself. It hadn't been *that* long since he'd seen a breast. It had been eons, though, since he'd wanted to touch a naked body so badly. *This* naked body. Only this naked body.

Holding himself in check as much as he could, he avoided her breasts for the moment to concentrate on the trail of chocolate dripping between them. Once more moving with as much leisure as he could muster, Max lowered his head to Daisy's gorgeous bosom and, beginning at the bottom of the chocolate trail, licked his way up. He touched her skin lightly, teasing her, stopping once to draw a lazy circle with his tongue. Once or twice his hands tightened on her as his body ached to surge ahead, but he exercised sterling control. He was going to take this slow. Slow and easy. He expected her to call a halt to the proceedings before they went too far, which meant he'd spend the night under a cold shower, but he intended to make every moment before then worth it.

At the very first touch of Max's tongue, D.J. felt a hot chill zoom through her body, as if she'd been pierced with flame and ice. She longed to arch and writhe, but controlled herself until her shirt came off, then lay back with gritted teeth and a firm commitment to remain calm and enjoy a taste—just a taste—of Maxwell Holden.

D.J. closed her eyes so she couldn't see the hunger on Max's face. The hunger could undo her completely; the heat in his gaze made her feel more wanted than she'd ever felt in her life. And that was dangerous. Misleading.

The moment her breasts were exposed to the air, the big, broad hand that supported her back seemed to burn into her flesh.

Don't look at him...don't look... D.J. commanded herself, keeping her eyes tightly shut. *You could be anyone...he isn't particular...you could be...*

She gasped. Couldn't help it. When his tongue touched her utterly bare torso, and his free hand clamped over her hip, she felt possessed—by him, by lust, by a power greater than anything she'd ever known.

It isn't that big a deal...it isn't...it isn't...it—

"Oh!" His mouth had claimed her breast entirely. She arched, and Max shifted his hand from her hip to her stomach, fingers dipping underneath the waistband of her shorts. It was a tight fit. Feelings began to course through D.J. like the blood in her veins. She reached down, unbuttoned the shorts, and Max didn't waste a moment unzipping them. His touch became bold. D.J. moaned. The feelings assailing her seemed to belong and not belong at the same time. She felt united with Max in play she wanted to continue, but even as the intimacy of his mouth and hands relentlessly increased, she began to feel, almost intolerably, more and more alone. One of Max's knees slipped between hers, and she followed his unspoken instruction, parting her legs, feeling her body gladly open to welcome his fingers even as her heart tried and tried to block him out.

But Max couldn't feel what her heart was doing. He responded to the signals the rest of her body sent out, and they told him to keep going.

D.J. felt the tension in her nerves and muscles mount, building rapidly to the exploding point. Max moved up her body to kiss her full on the lips, which was too much and not enough at the same time. If the emotional paradoxes of sex with Max didn't kill her, the effort to control herself surely would. So she stopped trying.

With his mouth on hers and his hand working magic, D.J. yanked Max's shirt from his waistband, letting her fingers explore his sleek torso and deciding somewhere in the part of her that was still thinking, *Nothing will ever, ever, ever feel this solid or strong or perfect again.*

She felt his back, his rib cage, the muscles of his stomach as he held himself above her, and his chest…his marvelously sculpted, hair-dusted chest… When she touched the hard, masculine nipples and felt him contract, her own desire pulsed afresh.

At the very moment she decided to drive him wild, too, and began to fumble for his belt buckle, Max touched a spot that started to send her over the edge, loosening her control over the scream she'd been trying to contain. He pressed hard against her—hand, body, mouth—absorbing her noise and movement, frustrating her and driving her further into passionate madness.

It took several moments for D.J. to regain her senses, and even then she felt as if she'd only regained half of them; the rest still belonged to Max. He was poised above her, watching her, his hands still on her, though he'd finally lifted his head so they could both breathe again.

"I have never wanted a woman like I want you right now." Max's voice was roughened by the sex he hadn't yet had. "You are beautiful."

It was a strange moment to have a personal revelation, but in truth D.J. realized for the first time that she had never completely believed the good things people said about her. But Max could have had anything he wanted a moment before; he could have pressed his advantage then. He could press it now, too, she supposed, but somehow she didn't think Max had ever resorted to trading flattery for sex.

Her heart skipped. "You're beautiful, too."

He settled her against the sofa, slipped his hand from beneath her back and smoothed her brow. "And yet," he said in a rich, low hum, "the lady is frowning. What's wrong? And I should tell you that I am not man enough to hear you say, 'Your technique.'"

That brought a smile to her face, as he'd intended. She seriously doubted that his ego could bruise so easily, in this arena at any rate. Still, she said, "I think you know your technique is, to put it mildly, not a problem."

He allowed himself the smallest smirk before pressing, "So what is? Because I see the wheels turning, Daisy, and while there's a time for analysis and contemplation, this isn't it."

True enough. He was still waiting his turn. Pretty patiently, too. D.J. hesitated. Maybe she should bury her misgivings, seize the moment. After all, in for a penny, in for a—

"You're doing it again." He leaned over her. "Speak. The first thing on your mind. Say it." He growled good-naturedly when she hesitated, "Right now!"

"Cleo!"

Max reared back, enough to give her some breathing room. "Damn." He sat up all the way, plowed fingers through his hair, shook his head…and began to chuckle. "Damn."

D.J. sat up, too. She looked around for her shirt and her bra. Passing on the bra, which she was suddenly too angry to fumble with, she jammed the top over her head.

When she had trouble finding the armholes, Max tugged the T-shirt into place. "I can't believe I'm helping you get dressed," he muttered, wry humor lacing his tone.

D.J.'s head emerged from the neck hole; the shirt settled where it belonged. "I can't believe you're laughing at my answer," she said, glaring at the man who persisted in jerking her feelings all over the board.

Max was getting to know that glare well, so he sighed, accepting the need for a little explanation. "Cleo is a neighbor and friend.

Period." Okay, so that was a very little explanation, but he didn't want to tell all of Cleo's business. The important thing for Daisy to know was that he had misled her. Deliberately.

He reached for her hand, felt her stiffen and decided immediately, *No way, baby. We're not going back to that again.* His tightened his grip, refused to let her erect her wall. "I wanted to get closer, and you were pulling back. It seemed easy for you to talk about leaving, and…" He shook his head. "I didn't like that. I owe you and Cleo an apology. I used my friendship with her to make you jealous. At least, I tried to."

It was as if gray clouds parted to reveal a sky that was bluer than it had been. D.J. realized quickly that she didn't feel suspicious of answer at all—only awed and guiltily delighted. She tried to frown. "You certainly do owe Cleo an apology, you…you… cad."

Max's lips twitched, but he managed to maintain a more or less sober countenance. "You're right," he nodded, "I am a cad. I'll apologize properly to Cleo tomorrow. For now…" He raised her hand. Touching her knuckles to his lips, he looked up at her from beneath lashes a man had no right to possess. "Forgive me?"

He pressed a soft kiss to the back of her hand. Then another kiss. And another…traveling up her arm. When he reached the middle of her forearm, D.J. said breathlessly, "You're not going to apologize to Cleo this way, I hope?"

"I was thinking more along the lines of a free dinner for two when the restaurant opens."

"For two?"

"Guest of her choice. I can guarantee she won't choose me."

Max danced his fingers lightly along the inside of D.J.'s arm. She was sure he noticed the goose bumps his touch left in its wake. "You never dated Cleo, right?"

"Daisy June," he grinned, "you're jealous."

"Not even," she said, knowing she was lying. Knowing that he knew. She stuck her nose in the air. "I'm only thinking of Cleo."

"That's a beautiful thing. You can phone her tomorrow, make sure I apologized to her prettily enough. Right now, though, I'd rather have you think of something else."

As he was already exploring her taut stomach—beneath the

T-shirt—her question was pointless, but she asked for the hell of it. "Like what, for example?"

"Mmm, like this, for example." He lowered his head, and she sucked in her stomach, glad finally for all the crunches she'd performed; his tongue circled her belly button while his thumbs rhythmically massaged her muscles.

As fingers of heat shot through her body once more, she manacled his wrist in a grip that seemed to surprise him. "I don't think so," she growled.

Max raised his head, brow arched, to gaze up the length of her body. "'Scuse me?"

Using the strength she'd gained in four years of regular gym attendance, D.J. pulled him up so she could talk to him eye-to-eye. "I don't want to do this, Max." She spoke in a voice that was caramel smooth. All womanly silk and matter-of-fact. The flicker of frustration and—yes, she saw it—flash of anger in his eyes did not bother her.

"We've already been down this path once tonight. Once is enough. For me, anyway." D.J. kept her face a blank canvas. She was moving into rough waters, and she didn't mind a bit. The little thrill of danger that skittered along her nerves excited her.

Still holding his wrist, she sat up. Her free hand patted her shirt primly into place. "You understand, don't you, Max? I simply don't like to repeat myself."

"What the hell—"

"You, on the other hand," she continued as if he had not spoken, "currently run no risk of repeating yourself. Because you haven't experienced anything."

His eyes narrowed.

D.J. reached down and gave the zipper on her shorts a neat one-handed tug up. "See, I just don't think you know me well enough yet. I may appear to live spontaneously, but at heart I like order. In certain instances you might say I'm almost compulsive about it. Like when it comes to taking turns." She reached for his belt buckle. Pulled the tail free of its loop. "It drives me *crazy* when someone takes cuts. The rules for that are very clear. After one person has taken her turn, it's time for the next guy in line to step to the plate. Am I making myself understood?"

Max glanced from the wicked solemnity in her cat-tilted eyes to the hand that was, even as he watched, loosening his belt and heading for the button on his jeans. Yeah, she was good. Popped that one open in a single move. Her clever, graceful fingers were on his zipper when he grabbed her so that they were holding each other's wrists, each restraining the other.

"I would love to." His voice was rough with desire and discipline. "Believe me, you have no idea how much," he added to remove the furrow of self-doubt that arose between her pretty brows. Daisy June Holden could morph from vixen to kitten in a second, and Max wanted to why. He wanted to know everything about her. Briefly, he thought about making love to Daisy until she was too mindless to hold on to her secrets, but he'd stopped her for a reason, and the reason was a good one.

The kids were asleep in the house. And, yes, they'd been there while he'd pleasured Daisy, but he'd been in control—or pretty much so—the entire time.

If Daisy made love to him right now, there would be no holding back. He didn't think he had that kind of fortitude.

"What's the matter?" Her voice had lost too much of its confident caress.

Max kissed the worried furrow. "Nothing is the matter. Not with you. The kids have only been in bed about an hour."

"Max, the kids sleep like logs. They never even get up to pee."

"True, but—"

"You were willing to risk it a few minutes ago."

He didn't want to explain about being the one in control. "I think we've pressed our luck all we should tonight." He raised the hand that was being held by hers, turned it until he was able to kiss her knuckles.

Daisy's furrow melted. Her brows and her lips curved. Her eyes began to sparkle again, and she nodded with deep satisfaction. "You're scared."

"What?"

"Yeah, you are. Chick-en. You know that if I make love to you, you'll lose it. You'll moan—" with her thumb, she began to stroke the wrist she still held "—groan…probably holler." Her voice was infused with teasing. And truth. "You're afraid you'll wake the whole house, because big, strong Maxwell will be under my command."

Max's jaw was clenched tighter than the skin on a drum. She had no idea how greatly her words resembled foreplay…or maybe she did. Her eyes glinted with irresistible mischief, and her lips curved knowingly.

There wasn't much Max could have said in that moment to convince her she was wrong.

Because she wasn't wrong. Desire that was almost impossible to control surged inside him already.

Call it male pride, but he refused to admit he'd lose control if she took the reins in their lovemaking. He bent his mouth into a deliberate smile. "Sweetheart, if we continue what we started, you'll raise the roof before I will." He leaned forward. "Guaranteed."

D.J. couldn't believe the excitement that flooded her from a few well-chosen words and a look that could ignite water. She volleyed right back to him. "Remember what I said about taking turns—the next party is mine. And I promise to help you reshingle after *you* shout the roof right off the house." Lord, she was asking for trouble. Never in her life had she promised someone sexual fulfillment! She was enjoying herself immensely, though, and something told her that she could keep her word. Or die happy trying.

She and Max stared at each other, still in physical gridlock with their hands around each other's wrists, and all of a sudden D.J. had the wackiest idea.

"Let's arm wrestle."

Max cocked his head, sure he hadn't heard correctly. "What?"

"Yeah. We'll arm wrestle. If you win, I'll accept that we're calling it a night because of the kids, and I won't call you a chicken again. If I win, you let me do whatever I want to you…but you can't make any noise. Which shouldn't be a problem since according to you, you're so self-composed you'll be quiet as a mouse."

"I didn't say I—"

"Oh, come on now, partner. Don't waffle." D.J. ignored the jangle of nerves that tried to warn her. If Max took her up on her dare and she actually managed to win, she would have to make good on her promise to make him holler. How the heck was she going to pull that off? Good thing she was having too much fun goading him to back out now. She felt possessed by some new, outrageous D.J. she hadn't met before, and she decided to get as much mileage out of it as she could. "Haven't you ever arm wrestled a girl before?"

"I can't say that I have," Max murmured smoothly. "You have great arms, but you're not going to win this, you know."

She shrugged. Max released his hold on her wrist, and she followed suit.

He nodded. "Coffee table? We can sit on the floor."

"Fine." Smiling, and without taking their eyes off each other, they slipped to the floor. "Marquis of Queensbury rules?" D.J. asked.

"That's for boxing."

"I was just trying to be polite."

Max grinned. "Let's sweeten the pot, shall we?"

"Spell it out."

"If you win, you have your way with me—"

"And you don't make a peep."

"And I don't make a peep. If *I* win, we have a conversation right here on the couch. My turn to ask you anything I want to…while my hands are exploring your body."

D.J. hesitated. He could ask *anything?* She mulled it over briefly, then shrugged. Theoretically he already could ask anything he wanted; whether she answered fully was another matter. "Okay. I'm going to win, anyway."

Max shook his head.

They clasped hands, elbows on the coffee table. Beneath the arc of their arms, they curled their fingers into each other.

"Who's going to say go?" Max asked.

"Let's see…I am—go!" D.J. threw her weight onto their arms. Max was definitely taken by surprise and gave a few inches before he recovered.

Digging his elbow firmly onto the table, Max looked at Daisy in amazement. Her head was bent, her teeth gritted. She was serious about winning, and she was strong. He was impressed. In fact, his muscles were working hard just to hold his ground.

"You do this often?" he asked through a clenched jaw.

"No." Beads of moisture appeared on her upper lip.

"Where'd you get your muscles?"

"Workouts."

"What kind?"

"Be quiet!"

Max grinned. Perspiration was dampening his skin now, too. He routinely hefted fifty-pound boxes at the restaurant; nonetheless he had to work to prevent Daisy from gaining too much ground.

Muscles bunched, jaws clenched, breath grew labored. The sight and sound of their working bodies was darned erotic, at least as far as Max was concerned. And then, abruptly, sanity hit him upside the head: *Why* was he trying to keep Daisy from winning? What kind of idiot turned down a night of lovemaking with the woman who fascinated and beguiled and made his heart flex like it was showing off?

He looked at Daisy, noted the way her eyes focused unwaveringly at a point on the table, the curl of her lips as she unconsciously bared her white teeth. Even her high ponytail quivered as she maintained a steady effort to keep her hand erect. Max saw the tension in her graceful neck and the surprising curve of her biceps, and he decided that he liked the way her fingertips dug into the back of his hand. If she put half that energy into making love—

"Aw, darn it!" he exclaimed as his elbow slid out from under him. Daisy took the opportunity to slam his hand onto the wood.

"Woo-hoo!" She thrust triumphant arms into the air.

"No fair," Max complained mildly. "I slipped."

Daisy pointed both index fingers at him from above her head. "You slipped," she sang out, then hitched both thumbs back at herself. "I won. I'm the best!" She punched the air. "Who's the best? I'm the best. Who's the best?" She cupped a hand around her ear. "That would be me!"

"You're going to wake the kids," he admonished, then nodded broadly. "You are the best all right. And now that you've won fair and square…what are you going to do with me?"

Daisy stopped smiling.

Chapter Twelve

D.J.'s arms fell to her sides. Her smile dropped, too. For a while there, she'd forgotten why she was arm wrestling.

The steamy, speculative gaze Max trained on her made her belly rumble with the kind of hunger a slab of chocolate cake would not satisfy.

"What's the matter? You look nervous." A lazy smile framed Max's mouth.

"Nervous?" About to deny it, she lowered her eyes demurely and smiled. "Well, maybe a little."

She sat up on her knees. Max Lotorto was sexier than any man she had known. When he was tender, she melted; when he flirted, she became light-headed. She loved his voice and his manners and his honesty and his humor.

But she'd fibbed about being nervous. She wanted to touch Max, to make him crazy, more than she'd wanted anything in a long, long time.

In a calculated move, she placed a hand lightly on the front of his shirt...toyed with one of the buttons as if she wasn't quite conscious of what she was doing.

She'd won the bet: he had to remain perfectly silent while she did…whatever she wanted. She coaxed her lips into a coy smile. She was going to make Max Lotorto holler.

"Can you blame me for being nervous?" she asked, idly slipping his shirt button from its hole. "You were very…*very* good at what you did. You seemed to know exactly what I liked." Her fingers wandered into the patch of chest hair she was itching to tangle with. Releasing another of his shirt buttons so her other hand could join the play, she glanced up. "I'm not sure I can match your…expertise."

Max's breath came in stronger puffs, especially when she came into contact with his left nipple. "You're doing okay so far," he rasped.

"I am?" She grinned, pushing him back until he lay on the floor. "Oh, good."

D.J. knew she would return to Portland when this job was done. That was a given, but she tried not to let that knowledge ruin the moment. She wasn't a three-bedroom, two-bath, kitchen-with-a-center-island kind of girl. Even though she cared for the kids—more and more all the time—she wasn't a minivan mom, and that's what they deserved. She *needed* space to be alone with her thoughts and her restlessness when she felt the need to be.

Still, she wanted this time with Max, told herself she deserved this kind of passion at least once in her lifetime. She'd been honest with him…. He knew what to expect from her…and what not to….

Max's muscles tightened with D.J.'s hands on his flat belly. The response, immediate and involuntary, made her shake the thoughts away. Leaning forward, she placed tiny nibbling kisses over Max's tummy, needing the sensuality of touch more than she'd ever needed it in her life. The tip of her tongue flicked out with every kiss, and then, when she was sure he could barely tolerate the effort to remain still, she unbuckled, unbuttoned and unzipped his pants, splaying open the denim to her liking.

Then D. J. Holden gave Max Lotorto a hickey. Where he'd never had a hickey before.

He managed to control himself almost until the action was complete. But a moment before D.J. was absolutely certain she'd branded his low, low, low belly with a purple mark that announced, *D.J. was here,* she felt big, firm Max hands on her shoulders. He drew her up with a mutter that sounded half like the groan she was after and half like a curse.

"That does it." Shifting his body for leverage, he reached one arm under her, sweeping her into a cradle hold. "That really does it." He planted a smacking kiss on her lips and carried her through the living and dining rooms, a look of grim determination visible in the shadows of the dimly lit house.

They were at the door to the garage before she had time to contemplate his intent. With his arms full of her, he instructed, "Open the door."

D.J. might have asked why before complying—she wasn't in the mood for a drive, after all—but she was in the midst of a passion haze that made her will unusually pliable.

Moonlight slanted through two windows to reveal a surprisingly tidy and clean garage with a car she hadn't seen before, and never would have guessed belonged to Maxwell Lotorto, family man: A 1960 Bentley with a fabulous iridescent slate-gray paint job.

"Gorgeous," D.J. breathed. Moonlight glinted off the classic auto, making the dark paint resemble the black sands of Hawaii. "I want it."

"I thought you'd like it," Max murmured close to her ear.

"Love it."

"I've been wanting to show you."

"If I'd known, I'd have asked to see it."

"I bought it years ago." His voice remained low and husky. "Refinished it myself. It's the one piece of my old life I couldn't part with."

D.J. looked up at Max. Pride and sentiment. She liked that in a man. "Bet you didn't bring me here just to show off your wheels, though, did you?" She smiled.

He smiled in return and shook his head. "Have you ever been in a Bentley?"

"No."

"This isn't what I intended for our first—"

"Quiet. I hear the leather is really soft."

"Very. Especially in the backseat."

"Set me down, Max. I want to see the Bentley."

Smoothly Max lowered her feet to the ground. D.J. made a big show of opening the front door and peering inside the car. She ran her fingertips lightly over the broad steering wheel and the real wood dashboard, but she didn't slide into the driver's seat, as she would have under normal circumstances. Instead, she opened the rear passenger door, inspected the beautiful workmanship there, too—the door handles, the wood panels, the plush carpet.

"What kind of condition was she in when you bought her?"

"Poor. Which was one reason I could afford it. And, actually, the car isn't a *her*. Saunders is all gentleman."

D.J. raised a brow. "Like his owner?"

"I'm not feeling very gentlemanly right now."

Didn't look very gentlemanly, either, she thought. His shirt was unbuttoned, pants unzipped, and his eyes smoldered. No, Max Lotorto looked very, very much like a man who was trying not to rip her clothes off and have her on the floor of his garage.

"Pardon me, Saunders," she said, raspy and breathless as she climbed into the back of the cavernous Bentley. Smoothing a hand across the seat, she nodded. "Yeah, nice leather. Real soft." Scooting, she relaxed against the far door to face Max. "Big back seat."

She held out her hand.

A warm glow from the interior car light joined hands with the moon to illuminate Daisy's face and body as she beckoned to him. Max joined her without words. Their kiss was long and deep, stoking their physical hunger. For two people who had been hovering on the edge of wanting since the moment they'd met, the tumble over the precipice was rapid and breath stealing.

Clothes were fumbled with. Arms and legs tangled. D.J. giggled when Max's shirt got stuck on his wristwatch. Then she began in earnest an assault to make him get noisy. Really noisy.

Taking advantage of her on-the-bottom position, he maintained control by moving out of her reach so he could remove her pants before she could attempt to discard his.

Try as Daisy might to be the lover in charge, she couldn't hold her ground when every move he made had her body quivering like a bow. By the time Max had her completely naked, she'd still managed only to get him down to his jeans, yet already she was writhing beneath him.

D.J. bucked under Max's touch, believing that unless he was

inside her soon, she'd feel an emptiness in her body that would never go away.

Born of instinct or experience, he evidently knew not to wait. As he began to answer her body's hunger, D.J. felt a loss of control so complete, so pervasive that it frightened her. She actually felt herself pushing him away.

Max tensed. His harsh breathing grew even more ragged. "What is it? Am I hurting you?"

Yes. But not physically. D.J. hurt in a way she couldn't explain.

Looking up at him, at the handsome, concerned, passion-filled face so close above hers, she shook her head. "Don't stop."

Once more Max moved against her, and D.J. grasped at him almost convulsively—shoulders, hips, all the strong flexing muscles she could find as she urged him more deeply inside. Some confused, frustrating part of her wanted the physical pleasure to go on and on, while she wished for the emotional ache to end.

They matched each other move for move, galloping relentlessly toward a climax D.J. believed she needed to keep from going insane until abruptly, deliberately, Max stopped moving. When D.J. arched beneath him, he held her hips. Refusing to allow the last moment to be the mindless release she obviously wanted, Max reached down to hook her knees, raising her legs and continuing with wicked, excruciating slowness. "Feel me," he murmured.

D.J. felt. She felt as if she was dying and coming alive and falling apart all at the same time. She sincerely thought the sensation might kill her if it went on for much longer, but Max would not rush.

Finally she lost it—lost control, lost reason, lost a sense of where she stopped and Max began. She felt as though she was giving up everything that held her together and kept her sane as her body exploded in a shower of blinding lights. In the midst of her surrender, Max sacrificed control, too. Gone were the slow and measured movements. Yielding to his own body's need, Max thrust until he reached the release that had him hollering as she'd promised he would.

D.J. felt no sense of triumph, however, because she was hollering, too, until Max leaned over her and covered her mouth, smothering both their cries.

* * *

"You shouted, 'No.'"

"What?" D.J.'s hoarse voice crackled. She barely had the energy to respond. She wanted to lie silently a moment while she gathered the scattered pieces of herself together. She wanted to regroup so she could be glib, sophisticated, casual about this encounter before she made a graceful exit.

She'd just had the most powerful sexual experience of her life, and she felt awkward as hell.

Max had carefully disengaged from her body before he spoke, but now he leaned above her, thigh pressed against hers, knee wedged deliberately, D.J. thought, between her legs. He left her little option but to lie there a while longer, and D.J. had the distinct impression that Max's position was due as much to a desire to make sure she didn't try to beat a hasty escape as it was to the limited opportunity for side-by-side reclining in the Bentley's otherwise spacious backseat.

"So what did it mean?" he asked, voice deep and private.

At first D.J. thought Max wanted an emotional definition to pin on their act. Then she realized he was referring again to her vocalization.

She really, really wanted to get dressed. Pushing a hank of hair behind her ear, she demurred, "I didn't say, 'No.'"

Max's fingers followed hers, tucking more loose hair behind her ears. His touch was gentler. "Yes, you did. You shouted it."

Lordy, Lordy, she really wanted to get dressed and get out of the car. Maybe even get out of the house for a while. She needed air. She needed to think.

Affecting the most casual, no-big-deal sigh she could manage, she said, "I have no idea what I said—"

"Shouted."

"Well, whatever. If I said—"

"Shouted."

"Fine! If I shouted, 'No,' it was just typical…sexual contrariness."

In darkness she felt Max's displeasure. "Typical sexual contrariness. What is that, Daisy? Enlighten me."

"Do you mind if I enlighten you fully clothed? Your garage is drafty."

She read a number of emotions in Max's answering scowl—guilt for making her lie in a drafty area, reluctance to let her go, frustration over her evasiveness.

Reluctantly he let her up, helped her locate her clothing, and exited the vehicle to give her privacy and to put on his own pants while she dressed in the backseat. When she was finished, she slid to the door.

Max offered a hand to help her out, but she pretended not to see it, preferring to get to her feet on her own. She needed to come back to herself and knew she couldn't do it if Max touched her. Anywhere. For any reason.

She avoided looking at his face, but could feel his tension. He knew her action had been deliberate. She didn't have to see him clearly or hear his voice to know he was angry and hurt.

D.J. felt bad, but she had no idea what to say. The need to put distance between herself and Max burned inside her now almost as strongly as the need to make love had burned moments before. She didn't understand it herself, and she definitely didn't want to talk about it.

Max shook his head. "This is the first time I've felt like apologizing after making love."

Guilt rose in a nauseating wave. "Don't be silly."

His hands shot out so quickly in the dark that she wasn't able to avoid his grasp as he took her arms and turned her fully toward him. Ordinarily that kind of action would have elicited from her one of the self-defense moves she'd learned over the years. Remorse alone kept her docile as he growled.

"Don't do that, Daisy. Don't brush me off like I can't tell how sorry you are about what just happened." In the shadows she saw him jerk his head toward the car. "Whatever is eating you now, what happened in there was mutual."

"I didn't say it wasn't."

For a long moment there was silence except for the sound of their breathing.

Max knew he was manhandling Daisy, but he was so peeved, he didn't give a rip. What the hell was with her? They'd just had the greatest sex of their lives, and now, two seconds later, she was pulling away.

As usual.

Getting close and pulling away seemed to be a pattern with Daisy Holden. Or maybe the problem was *he* kept getting close while Daisy was just having a good time.

Quickly Max tried to replay those first seconds after making love. He'd wanted to talk, wanted to know what was going on inside her head. *Cosmopolitan* magazine would make him man of the year for that kind of attitude. Daisy acted like he'd asked to read her diary.

He studied her through the shadows, hoping for solid eye contact and possibly a smile to indicate the wall she was erecting had a chink or two that might give him a toehold.

She stared at his chin. No chinks, just wall.

Fine.

He let her go. A little surprised by the sudden release, Daisy took a wobbly step back, and Max forced himself not to reach for her.

"I'm sorry for everything that happened tonight." His voice was tight, flat.

Daisy brushed a hand over her forehead. "Max, I told you, that's...silly. I don't want an apology—"

"You're not getting one. I'm not apologizing to you. I'm saying I'm sorry it happened. And it won't happen again."

When D.J. rolled her shopping cart out of the local Gold Hill grocery store, she felt tired to the bone. As it was only 11:00 a.m., it was utterly unlike her to feel ready to crawl into bed again, but last night's emotional scene, the subsequent lack of sleep and the miserable morning she'd had so far made her want to bury her head under a pile of pillows.

The fact that she wanted to hide pissed her off. She wasn't the type of person who hid.

"How come your doughnut's got pudding in it and mine doesn't?" Sean, walking alongside the cart with James, eyed his brother's treat as James squeezed the pastry to make the custard squish out. "That's not fair! I want a pudding doughnut, too." He looked back at D.J.

She'd bribed the children—shamelessly—when they'd entered the store: "Cooperate *quietly* with the morning's shopping, and everyone gets to pick out a doughnut. One episode of misbehavior—from anyone—and the deal is off."

The kids had kept each other in check while she'd shopped for snacks to serve during the home study visit this evening.

"You wanted chocolate, and that's what you got, kiddo. Enjoy it." D.J. muttered her response. She simply didn't have the energy to argue. She and Max had traded no more than a dozen words this morning, and those were all in regard to Nadelle's visit.

It had been Max's idea to have dessert, though D.J. would have thought of that on her own. She remembered a few of her foster families putting on a show for the social workers who had come for their periodic check-ins. D.J. had almost said as much, just to make civil conversation, or, actually, to get him to make eye contact for more than a second and a half, but she wasn't going to sell herself out just to get her one-time lover to talk to her. Nadelle's visit had her antsy, and it would have been nice to share some of the jitters with Max, but there'd been a layer of ice beneath the unimpeachable politeness to which he'd treated her this morning.

Sean stopped dead in the parking lot, stamping his boy-size tennis shoe. "I don't like chocolate!" He glared at his brother. "Uncle Max says you have to share."

Sitting in the front of the cart with her own sprinkle-covered doughnut clutched protectively against her chest, Livie's eyes were wide. Anabel was busy wiping powdered sugar off her nose and glasses and seemed content to mind her own business this time around.

D.J. felt an unreasonable surge of irritation toward Max. He wasn't even here, yet his rules of conduct suffused their day. He was so upright, so Dudley Do-Right, that unlike a *normal* man, he couldn't allow her the space to pull back a little, to regroup and reevaluate their relationship. For a moment there in the car—and she nearly blushed to think about *that* in the light of day—she could have sworn he was going to murmur something unrealistically emotional. Like *I love you.*

He'd looked at her and made her feel almost ashamed because she couldn't, wouldn't claim a bunch of feelings simply to justify the fact that they'd gotten…carried away.

That's the conclusion she'd come to this morning, at any rate, while he moved stiffly and politely around the kitchen before he left for work, making the kids French toast and asking how they'd slept and what they planned to do today.

That weird, pins-and-needles desire to run toward and away from him at the same time had assailed her strongly once again.

"James, you *gotta* share, or I'm tellin'!"

With big blue eyes trained on his brother, James stuck his tongue as far into the center of his cream-filled doughnut as he humanly could.

Furious, Sean started to lunge over the shopping cart. D.J. grabbed him by the collar of his shirt. "Hey! We are not fighting in a parking lot, especially not over one less ounce of sugar than you would normally eat." Sean whined and squirmed. *"Hey, listen up!"* What D.J.'s parenting skills lacked in finesse, they made up for in volume. "I told you each to choose a doughnut for yourselves, and you did. One each. If you don't like the one you chose—and you *do* like chocolate, Sean, don't pull that malarkey with me—tough. In life sometimes you have to live with your choices, even if you regret them." She swiveled to catch James with a cream-smeared grin on his gamin face. "And you—" she pointed at him "—do not have to rub it in. I want everybody to be quiet and eat their doughnuts or I'm throwing them all in the trash." That got Livie's and Anabel's attention, too, and the girls immediately started to protest. D.J. cut it short. "I don't want to hear anything but chewing until I get these groceries loaded into the car."

Miraculously her orders were followed, which gave her time to recognize their boomerang effect: she could be talking to herself about Max. For the fact was, she'd decided years ago that her relationships with men, with anyone, would be played out on her terms, according to her comfort level, and if that meant risking anger from someone who wanted more from her, well then, so be it. Now she had to live with the consequences of that choice.

"I'm not wrong," she muttered, opening the rear of the Max's van and plunking grocery bags into the back. Some people willingly signed up for chaos and roller-coaster emotions and the continuous stomachache that went with it all. She wasn't one of those people.

Sean had chosen chocolate, and he was stuck yearning for Bavarian cream now that he'd seen it.

D.J. had chosen balance and emotional predictability. Now she was stuck yearning for another taste of Max.

A yearning she would probably have to learn to live with.

Slamming the rear door, D.J. made sure the munchkins were all settled in their seats, then slid the side door closed and jogged the shopping cart to the return strip. She was halfway back to the minivan when she saw something that made her halt in her tracks and whip her sunglasses to the top of her head.

A limousine in Gold Hill. A limousine whose passenger was handing money to a short, steel-haired woman and issuing instructions as the latter stood by the open rear window.

D.J. watched the uniformed lady march off to the pharmacy located next to the market. Then she watched the handsome, elderly, blond woman lean back against the seat. The smoky rear window rolled up.

Loretta.

D.J. raced to the minivan and darted to the driver's side before glancing back. The limo carried Oregon plates, not personalized. Evidently, Loretta had come down from Portland after D.J.'s last phone call.

With her pulse pounding, D.J. got in the minivan and started her up. She didn't pull out, though.

The kids were chattering more or less happily among themselves. Sean was trying to convince the others that UFOs were real and that he was going to photograph one as soon as Uncle Max bought him a camera. D.J., who had replaced her sunglasses, stared intently in the rearview mirror.

"Aren't we going to go?" Anabel asked. She'd eaten half her doughnut and fastidiously wrapped the rest in a paper napkin. "It'll be time for lunch soon. I want a Cobb salad."

D.J. spared the ten-year-old a brief glance. "We'll go in a minute. I need to…put on some lip gloss." She dug one-handed into her purse, and without taking her eyes off the rearview mirror, slicked clear gloss over her lips—a few times. Then she took out mascara, raised her sunglasses and applied that. Any excuse to keep an eye on the limo.

Finally, as the children were becoming restless, Loretta's house-keeper returned with a small package from the pharmacy. She got into the front seat next to the driver, and the limo pulled slowly out of the lot.

"Okay, let's go!" D.J. backed out of her space, then threw the minivan into Drive and followed the long, black vehicle, determined not to let it or Loretta out of her sight until she found out exactly what Loretta was up to. *Drat the woman!* Had D.J. said, *"Gee, why don't you come to Gold Hill unannounced"?* Had she suggested that Loretta pop in to see how things were going?

No and *no.* Good Lord, Max would freak out if he found out about Loretta without D.J. preparing him first.

D.J.'s heart pounded harder as she cruised slowly a couple of car lengths behind the limousine, waiting to see which way it would turn as it exited the lot—toward Max's home, toward the restaurant or away? D.J. itched to call Loretta on her cell phone and scream, "What the blasted hell do you think you're doing, lady?"

And that's when D.J. realized that her chief fear at the moment was how Max might react when he realized she'd been working for Loretta—and lying to him—all along.

She wanted to be the one to tell him. Actually, her hidden agenda the past couple of hours had been to avoid having to tell him at all. She'd been fantasizing about keeping her true role in this drama a secret.

Her stomach roiled, and she wished she had the time to return to the market for an antacid. She couldn't remember ever having so many stomach problems. If this was what loving Max was going to do to her, then—

She slammed on the brakes, causing a noisy protest from her passengers, especially Anabel, who mentioned something about whiplash, despite the fact that they'd been traveling less than five miles per hour. "Sorry," D.J. muttered, forcing herself to take a slow, deep breath to counteract the dizziness that assailed her.

Dear God…love? That wasn't possible. She abhorred the free and easy use of that word.

Caring for Max. That's what she'd started to do; she'd started to care for him, because…he was a good man. And he was sexy.

And he made great love. And she was in a vulnerable position, because she was out of her usual element.

The driver of a green truck that looked old enough to be a set piece from *Petticoat Junction* honked behind her. D.J. forced her attention back to driving and to Loretta.

The black limo turned right. D.J. followed at a reasonable distance.

"Uncle Max's house is the other way," Anabel piped up from the second row of seats.

"I know that," D.J. said, gritting her teeth as her already-tweaked nerves took another hit. The kid could sound just like the school librarian D.J. remembered from third grade—prim, instructional…

Uncle Max's house.

Not "our house," D.J. realized, but "Uncle Max's house." She glanced in the rearview mirror. Anabel sat with her hands clutching the rolled-down top of a white paper bag containing the remainder of her doughnut. She'd been the only one to request a bag. She resembled, D.J. thought, an old woman on a bus, gripping her purse. Protective, watchful. Alone.

Abruptly D.J. understood why Anabel could irritate her so easily: Anabel was D.J. at the same age, telling the world how to behave, because she didn't trust it to behave properly on its own. And for good reason. In Anabel's relatively brief life, the world had not behaved as it should. It had left her, at far too tender an age, parentless and scrambling to figure out how to protect herself and her siblings. It had burdened her with cares no child should have to face and with insecurities no child could possibly know how to assuage.

A rush of compassion filled D.J. for Anabel and then, unexpectedly, for the younger self she'd never completely accepted. Surprised, almost embarrassed by the sudden revelation, D.J. had to blink back tears behind her sunglasses.

"Where are we going?" Anabel asked, and for the first time in a long, long time D.J. recalled her own juvenile need to know where she was going and with whom at all times.

"I want to pick up a couple of other things," D.J. prevaricated, unsure of how far she would have to follow Loretta.

"For the lady coming tonight?" James asked.

Flicking a glance in the rearview mirror, D.J. nodded. "Right."

She knew the children had met Nadelle before and that Max had explained that the woman wanted to make sure he was giving them a good home.

"She's a social worker," Anabel said, a definite edge of childish distaste souring her tone. "I know what that is."

"What is it?" D.J. asked softly.

"Someone who makes decisions about where kids should live. If they don't like the people you live with now, they can take you away and put you in foster care. A girl in my grade is in foster care."

"What's that?" James asked.

"Someone's gonna take us away from Uncle Max?" Sean's question and his understanding were sharper than James's.

Livie started to whimper.

Crud.

"No one wants to take you away from your Uncle Max." D.J. spoke quickly and authoritatively. "Social workers do look out for the welfare of children, but they only remove you from your home if they think you aren't being well taken care of." *Jeez, that sounded sterile.*

"Uncle Max takes care of us!" Sean said with his characteristic tough-guy, ready-to-rumble stubbornness.

"Yes, he does," D.J. agreed. "He takes care of you all very, very well. Which is why the social worker's visit is only a formality." They didn't understand that. D.J. tried to lighten things up. "It's part of her job, that's all. She's paid to visit families. She just wants to say hi, and then she'll fill out a report saying you're all very happy and stuffed full of good food. And, Livie, you can show her your princess costume and your favorite books. It'll be fun." Like going to the dentist, D.J. thought, giving them all a big smile in the rearview mirror.

Sean and James looked substantially relieved, and Livie's whimpering turned into periodic sniffs, between which she nibbled the sprinkles off her doughnut. Anabel turned her head to gaze out the window, a troubled frown tugging her brows behind her glasses.

Between the limo ahead of her and the children behind, D.J. felt like a rubber band ready to snap. She'd have to give Max a heads-up about what just transpired, so he could reassure the kids again. It wouldn't look good for them to be rude or even overly quiet when Nadelle showed up.

Her stomach churned afresh at the thought of talking to Max again. She was definitely going to stop for an antacid…right after she found out where Loretta was headed.

Chapter Thirteen

"You delivered the wrong bread, Dave. I ordered ciabatta, not sourdough." D.J. saw that Max held a cell phone in one hand and a large oblong loaf of crusty bread in the other. He looked harried and irritable, and was bobbing the loaf as if he wanted to toss it like a football. "No. No. We *used* to serve sourdough. I'm opening an Italian restaurant now. I want the ciabatta and your rosemary-olive loaf…. No, *no* sourdough…."

Watching from the door of the newly renamed Nonna's Cucina, D.J. noted the exhaustion on Maxwell's face and felt the now-familiar guilt fill her chest. She was about to give him four more things to worry about.

"Yeah, bring the first order today," he said into the phone. "I want to get my regulars used to the changes before the official opening…. Either I'll be here or have your driver check in with Laurence in the kitchen…. All right. Thanks." He flipped the cell phone shut, chucked the bread onto a table and sighed.

The restaurant was scheduled to open in five days, a couple of weeks later than Max had originally planned, and his schedule was as full as it needed to get. As his nanny, D.J. ought to be keeping the kids out of his hair, not standing with them inside the glass-doored entrance to Nonna's. Rather than lightening his load, she was about to give him another burden. It couldn't be helped, though. It really couldn't.

D.J. had followed Loretta's limo to Gold Hill's only hotel, where it had parked to emit Dame Mallory, her housekeeper, the driver and more luggage than the hotel had likely seen since it opened in 1949.

What the devil was the woman up to?

Thankfully, the children had been occupied with their own conversations and with what remained of their doughnuts, so D.J. had been spared a plethora of questions. They hadn't even commented on the limousine.

After confirming in her own mind that Loretta was, in fact, staying at the hotel, D.J. had driven another block to a take-out chicken place, where she'd bought enough broasted chicken, plus all the fixings, to feed Max and the children for a week.

Now she was standing in his restaurant with four lunch-ready kids, a huge bag of chicken and biscuits that gave off a heavenly aroma, and the hope that she could pull off one more lie so she could hustle back to the hotel to confront Loretta.

The very sight of Max, in casual, low-slung jeans and shirt-sleeves rolled to expose his muscular, smooth-haired forearms, made her wish nothing had gone wrong last night. She wished she had every right in the world to approach him now with a kiss to erase the lines on his brow and a whisper to promise a little tension-relieving play later on tonight.

The moment he was off the phone, the kids raced to him. He showed a moment's surprise, chased swiftly by frustration, which he masked nicely. Unfortunately, it only took his looking up and seeing D.J. standing a few feet away to increase the tension on his face. Even his broad shoulders stiffened visibly.

D.J. took a breath. "Hi," she greeted softly, wishing she could wind back the clock, wishing he still looked at her with warmth and pleasure creating sparks deep in his eyes.

Awkwardly she cleared her throat. "The kids really wanted to see you. They were hoping to have lunch with you." After she'd planted the idea in their heads. "I brought the food." She lifted the still-warm bags. The promise of broasted chicken and all the fix-ings did not erase the irritation that settled around his mouth.

"Daisy, I'm a little busy here."

"I know." She stepped toward him. "Hey, rug rats, why don't you take these bags to a booth? Anabel, there are napkins and plastic utensils inside, if you'd like to set the table. I'll be over in a minute."

"Daisy—"

"I know this is bad timing." Quietly she circumvented his pro-test while Anabel led her brothers and sister to a booth. "I did the dumbest thing. I bought a bag of corn nuts—you know, those re-ally hard fried corn kernel things?—and I bit down and out came a filling and I think part of my tooth, too. It really aches." If God was keeping track of her fibs, she was in so much trouble. "I found a dentist who can see me today—right now—so I thought if I brought lunch, you know, my treat… Maybe you could use a little break?"

The frown over Max's brow deepened.

"I'd put it off, but when the extra-strength aspirin didn't work—"

"I don't want you to put it off." He sounded disgusted that she would assume so. "Do you need a ride? How much pain are you in?"

He was going to kill her with decency. Guilt skyrocketed again. "I'll be fine once I get this handled," she said assuredly. He certainly couldn't go with her to see Loretta. "I can drive myself. I'd rather. That way the kids don't have to go. I'll come right back after—"

He waved away the offer. "Wait and see how you feel."

They stared at each other silently. Max looked as if he wanted to say something more, something about last night perhaps? D.J. found that she wanted him to talk, to break the ice that secrecy and evasion had packed around their relationship. Inside her, there were words that itched to rush out. She wanted to apologize for pulling away and for misleading him; she wanted to erase the dis-trust and consternation she put on his face last night.

Mostly she wished desperately that she and Max had met some other way, because right now there were so many lies between them, she didn't know how she'd ever explain them all away.

The truth about what she was doing here: That was the one thing she could give.

Which was why she needed to get to Loretta ASAP and find out what the woman's intentions were. Even if she had to return the retainer Loretta had given her, even if she didn't make a dime off this job, D.J. couldn't let Loretta contact Max before she herself had told him the truth.

"I…I'm sure I'll feel better when I get back," she said. "I bought a lot of snacks for tonight, so…that's covered, anyway."

He nodded. "No corn nuts, I hope."

"No." Weakly, D.J. smiled. His straight-faced humor made her ache. "No corn nuts." *Max…Max…* She wanted to tell him she would be with him tonight one hundred percent, making certain the social worker knew what a great permanent guardian—no, *father*—he would make. Making certain Nadelle Jacobs knew how hard he worked to hold the family together. She wanted to promise him nothing would come between him and his children and to tell him she would be at his side tonight come hell or high water.

She wanted to tell him she was on his side, period.

Maybe she would have found the words. Even with all the awkwardness between them, maybe she would have found the words to tell him how much she cared if the door hadn't opened just then. And if Max's gaze hadn't lifted. And if she hadn't turned to see a luscious blonde standing just inside the door, smiling like a Crest commercial.

If sheer jealousy hadn't sliced quick and hot as a lightning bolt through D.J.'s gut, maybe she would have found the words and the courage to tell Max how much he and the kids meant to her.

When the gorgeous blonde smiled, the hair on D.J.'s arms hurt.

"Hi, I'm Kirsten. Are you Max?" Dimples dented Kirsten's cheeks as she looked past D.J.

"That's me. Glad you could make it, Kirsten. Make yourself comfortable in one of the booths. I'll be with you in a minute. And thanks for being prompt. I appreciate it."

Who, D.J. thought without a shred of softer feelings, *is the cheerleader? My replacement?* She watched with mounting discontent as the miniskirted Britney clone took herself to a booth.

"Don't worry about coming back here after your appointment. Just go back to the house."

D.J. turned. Max's expression was shuttered and neutral. *Tell me she's interviewing as a waitress and not your new nanny*. Since D.J. had no idea how to ask that question, she offered instead, "You know, I could stay a little longer…to watch the kids…if you need me to. I'll call the dentist—"

"Not necessary. They're here now, and it looks like lunch was a good idea." He nodded toward the booth where the kids were already devouring chicken and biscuits with honey. Max was going to have such a mess.

"Maybe I should—" D.J. began, but Max put a hand lightly, platonically on her back.

"If we're not at the house when you get there, give me a ring on my cell phone. And here." At the door he reached into his pocket, then dangled keys in front of her. "Take my truck and leave the minivan."

Feeling absurdly domestic and just as absurdly hoping that Kirsten had heard their little exchange, D.J. dug in her purse and handed Max the van keys. D.J. couldn't help but wonder if he'd have kissed her now had last night ended differently.

She hesitated at the door long enough to feel truly awkward. Because he, of course, made no move toward her at all, and she, by lingering, hinted that she wanted him to.

"Gotta get going," she mumbled, shoving out the door. "This tooth is a major headache."

Only a few minutes later, D.J. stood before Loretta's door at the Gold Hill Hotel. The manager had properly insisted on phoning the room, so Loretta knew she was there. It took two knocks for Loretta's housekeeper to answer.

Gray-haired and uniformed, the woman was as dignified as ever. "Good afternoon. Mrs. Mallory is having tea on the patio."

Leading D.J. through the room and outside again, the decorous housekeeper settled D.J. with a cup of tea from a service they must have brought with them. The cookies, however, D.J. recognized from the local market.

"Have a cookie, Ms. Holden," Loretta said by way of greeting, "and then you can update me on the case."

"I'll pass on the snack, Mrs. Mallory, but I'd sure like you to tell me what you're doing here."

Displeasure pursed Loretta's lips, forming a ring of lines that negated the effect of those pricey Botox injections. She seemed as willing as D.J. to forgo the niceties. "*I* hired *you*. Let's keep that in mind, Ms. Holden, shall we?" With forced calm, Loretta sipped her tea.

"As I understand it, you hired me to give you information about your grandson so that you could decide whether to bring him into the family business." With a deep breath and a quick prayer, D.J. tried again to steer the conversation. "I assume your being here means you've made that decision?"

Loretta set her teacup delicately on the saucer and the saucer smoothly on the table. Not a hair of her exquisitely dyed and coiffed head was out of place. She gazed levelly at D.J., hazel eyes faded but sharp. For a moment D.J. thought the woman was going to kick her out in the most polite manner. Instead, to D.J.'s relief, she was coldly honest.

"We're both intelligent women, Ms. Holden, so we won't dither. The job for which you were hired required a less…personal approach than you have given it."

D.J. felt her ears turn red. Loretta couldn't know about last night. "If you're referring to the fact that I took the nanny job—"

Halting D.J.'s momentum, Loretta raised a thin but foreboding hand. "We won't argue. You've given me some information about the existence of my great-grandchildren, for which I am grateful and for which you will be paid today. I emphasize the words *some information*. If you think I'm unaware that you withheld knowledge the last two times we spoke, then you underestimate me. People in my employ do the job for which they were hired, Ms. Holden. They do not alter their job description as they see fit."

D.J. felt her chest constrict. There was something ominous about this conversation, more ominous than simply the fact that Loretta had guessed D.J. was holding back. "I told you what—"

"What you thought I needed to know. Do not insult me by claiming you told me everything. I want *specific* details about my grandson's finances, past and present. I want details about his choices. I want as much information about my great-grandchildren and their status as possible."

"Their status—"

Loretta gestured to her housekeeper, who turned to remove

something from a drawer. "I've already seen the…shack…my grandson calls home. On a road called Sardine Creek." She wrinkled her thin nose. "More disturbing, he left an apparently excellent position as a corporate accountant to run a *bar.*"

"He's opening a restaurant. Next week, in fact."

"Yes. An *Italian* restaurant in a tiny town whose claim to fame appears to be that one of its main streets is named after a canned fish. My grandson's decisions lack distinction. I assume the decision to serve pasta in a run-down bar is an homage to his paternal grandparents." Loretta's attempt at an indulgent shrug lacked conviction.

"Every decision Max makes is thoughtful and well planned."

Loretta's smile turned knowing. "Spoken like a woman, Ms. Holden, rather than an investigator. I hired you to gather information, not interpret it."

Since Loretta didn't want to "dither"—and since D.J. loathed, absolutely loathed being backed into a corner—her private investigator uttered a very unladylike word when she could have said, simply, baloney. "You wanted interpretation. You weren't content with facts. You wanted to know what Max was like. You wanted to know what kind of worker he would be and what kind of family member and what kind of father and whether he'd reject you if you approached him with the idea of joining your company. I don't know what all this ice-matron crap is about right now. If you think he's such a loser, what are you doing here?"

The housekeeper had approached with a large flat checkbook, the kind that let you know someone wrote a lot of checks. She handed her employer a heavy gold-plated pen. Loretta accepted the writing implement, but kept her shrewd gaze on D.J. Fire glinted in her eyes, but she was far *less* furious than D.J. had given her reason to be. "There is always hope, Ms. Holden, isn't there? Despite my dislike of my grandson's choices, I am prepared to accept them, but I am concerned with the attitude that fuels them. He appears to have developed a disdain for the finer things in life. Things to which my great-grandchildren are perfectly entitled. I expect Maxwell to make his decisions based on sound reasoning rather than the emotion *du jour.*"

D.J. shook her head. "If you're implying Max is flighty, you couldn't be more off base. The man is a rock." She leaned forward, speaking with conviction. "He's assumed sole responsibility for four kids who aren't even his immediate relatives. I mean, they're what? Second cousins? I'm never sure how you figure that out, but whatever their blood tie is or isn't, Max is like a father to them. He *is* a father to them. Plus he's opening a restaurant, a very good restaurant—"

Loretta smiled thinly. "A spaghetti house."

"Fine Italian dining in a family atmosphere! Have you ever tried his marinara?" She slapped a hand on the table. "No! It's awesome." D.J. was flat-out ticked by the woman's attitude. "What's with you, anyway? You hire me because you want an heir, then you come here yourself. Yet now you act like you couldn't care less whether Max follows you to Portland or not."

Loretta was silent for a time. "I care. Regarding the question of nature versus nurture, Ms. Holden, which do you think is a more powerful influence?"

Momentarily D.J. was taken aback. Not because she hadn't considered the issue—how could she avoid it, given her background?—but because she hadn't anticipated discussing it today or with Loretta.

"I think we each make our own decisions about who we're going to be."

"That's too easy an answer," Loretta snapped.

D.J. shrugged. "Easy or not, that's the answer I've got. What's yours?"

Loretta's eyes narrowed. For her own reasons she decided to answer, rather than push D.J. further. "Biological predisposition and environmental factors will have their way with us, whether we emulate our upbringings or rebel against them. I grew up poor and uneducated, Ms. Holden. I was determined not to stay that way. In my case, rebellion against my environment and my heritage were a boon. My own children rebelled to their detriment."

D.J. might have argued that last point, but she was caught off guard by Loretta's personal revelation.

With a flourish, the woman signed the check she'd made out. "How did you rebel, Ms. Holden? How has your background affected your choices? What made you decide to…march to your

own drummer, as it were? Because you certainly seem to have es-
chewed fidelity to authority."

The "authority" being Loretta, of course. D.J. bristled. There
was something calculating, something almost condescending
about the way Loretta angled her gaze at D.J., as if she knew much
more than she was saying. Resentment and something more—an
incipient sense of panic—tingled in D.J.'s veins.

"Have you hired another investigator, Loretta?" It was a hunch,
one which Loretta's unshrinking gaze confirmed.

"I have."

D.J.'s blood ran cold; her imagination ran wild. Had the investigator discovered and reported the full extent of her relationship
with Max? Was that even possible without a telephoto lens? Or
X-ray vision? And what of her own background and her history
as a perennial foster child? Had Loretta dug into D.J.'s past? The
possibility stirred a host of unquiet emotions, not the least of
which was an embarrassment that made D.J. want to cringe. "Has
your new investigator been spying on me?" The question escaped
through clenched teeth.

Loretta winced, but it was a mock expression. "Spying. Really,
Ms. Holden, I'm amazed that someone with your professionalism
would use such a word. When you refused to be forthcoming with
the information *I was paying you to gather,* I hired another investigator, yes. But not to investigate you. You are none of my business." Her eyes narrowed shrewdly. "Unless, of course, you
develop a relationship with my grandson that affects his decision-
making process."

Loretta was waiting for something, most likely confirmation
that D.J. was personally involved with Max.

Keep waiting, D.J. thought, staring the woman levelly in the eye
and remaining mum. The only reason she didn't give the old broad
a taste of her temper was that Loretta was right: D.J.'s professionalism on this job sucked. Still, everything could turn out fine if Loretta would act like a grandmother instead of a CEO.

Unconsciously, D.J. chewed the inside of her lip. She should
have listened better or dug deeper when Max told her there was
no love lost between him and his grandmother. Perhaps she'd
given too much weight to the blood tie. The fact that Max had a

biological relative who wanted him had driven D.J. to assume the reunion would be worthy of an *Oprah* segment. She'd made, however, a critical mistake by assuming that Max's estrangement from his grandmother was solely an extension of the estrangement between Loretta and her daughter. That didn't jibe with the reasonable and compassionate person she knew Max to be. He was loyal and stubborn, yes, but she saw him as someone who would rather mend a fence than perpetuate a feud. Obviously, he'd encountered Loretta's coldness and decided to avoid frostbite.

"Did you cut your daughter off when she didn't toe the line?" D.J. jumped way, way into the deep end, but she wanted to gain control of the conversation and didn't particularly mind if she had to infuriate Loretta into dropping her guard.

And the elderly woman was infuriated. The skin around her tightened lips turned white. "Is that what my grandson told you?"

"He didn't have to tell me anything. You told me you made decisions you regretted. Now you want your family back." She was putting words in the proud woman's mouth, but she had to find out what, exactly, Loretta wanted—merely an heir apparent or a grandson? "I think you have a really good chance at recreating the family you lost. But not if you talk to them the way you just talked to me."

For good or bad, her words had an effect. Something sparked in Loretta's eyes when D.J. told her she had a chance with Max. Of course, that emotion—hope or sentiment or whatever it was—yielded to sheer irritation when D.J. called her on her attitude. "Max isn't someone you'll be able to push or belittle into toeing the line. He's a really good man with a lot of self-esteem and as much confidence as you have. He's as independent and opinionated as you are, too. Not too hard to see you're related. He's got all your good attributes and a stubbornness that makes him persistent."

"A winning endorsement," the older woman said tightly. "But is he independent enough to turn his back on what I have to offer?"

He was. D.J. knew it. But… "He won't jeopardize the children. Keeping the kids together under one roof is his first priority. He'll do whatever it takes to maintain the family."

Loretta's ears practically perked. "My granddaughter's children. Is he lacking the funds to provide for them? Does Maxwell fear he may not be able to care for so many children?"

"No, not at all. And your great-grandchildren couldn't be in better hands. After love, food and shelter, kids don't need that much, anyway, do they? Max knows he can provide for their basic needs and then some. But the state is involved because Max was never named a legal guardian."

"The state. By that you mean…"

"DHS. Department of Human Services. What they see is a single guy juggling fatherhood and a new business, and Oregon is a conservative state. The DHS doesn't always make its decisions based on love or on what the child would like. They'll reshuffle a family like a deck of cards if they think they have a good reason. A child's future can be affected by a single social worker." D.J. knew her perspective was colored by her own experience, but so be it. She didn't trust this Nadelle person, not if the woman couldn't see that the children belonged with Max. If D.J. did nothing else here today, she wanted to win Loretta's help in securing Max's guardianship.

Once again she'd gotten the woman to think. The wheels in Loretta's head went round and round. Obviously her second investigator had not reported that Max was being visited by a social worker, but that didn't surprise D.J. Why would he have looked into that? Loretta's faded tongue darted out to lick her coral lips. "My great-grandchildren are the chief reason I came here, before I resumed contact with Maxwell. I wanted to see for myself how they've been cared for, who they are becoming." She looked more closely at D.J. "I can give them everything. It is my understanding that they currently run barefoot like farmers' children, that their play area is inhabited by chickens."

D.J. tamped down her own dislike of the nasty birds to give a more accurate portrayal. "The property Max bought came with a coop and some chickens, which he kept. The kids love it. They gather eggs and clean the coop and learn responsibility. As far as running around barefoot, I can vouch for the fact that they have shoes and wear them." For the first time today D.J. believed she might actually be making headway with the other woman. Loretta appeared to be more musing than judgmental. A kernel of hope popped open in D.J.'s chest. Perhaps she could salvage not only this situation but her own part in it, as well. Perhaps, when all was said and done, Max would understand why she had tricked him and would find it in his big heart to forgive her. Whether she could have a future with him was another story, but at least he would know she had done her best to preserve his family.

Leaning forward, D.J. spoke directly and earnestly to Loretta. "With your support, Max wouldn't have to worry about the social worker who's been breathing down his neck. A strong financial profile can go a long way toward balancing deficits, like the absence of a two-parent household. I think all it will take to get Nadelle off his back once and for all is the knowledge that you'll be involved in your great-grandchildren's lives. That you'll support Max's custody."

Slowly, contemplatively, Loretta nodded. "That was my thought, as well." She ripped the top check from the page in the book. D.J. expected her to hand it over and to say the interview was finished. Instead, Loretta ripped the check into many small pieces and commenced writing out a new one. She passed it across the table. D.J. took one look, and her jaw dropped.

Loretta merely arched a brow. "You've proven helpful, more helpful than I thought."

The amount on the check would more than pay the outstanding bills and overdue charges waiting at the office. In fact, it would provide a nice cushion until D.J. could get them another job, assuming Bill's lack of interest in working persisted.

The check was a good thing.

And yet it burned in D.J.'s hands.

It felt wrong to take it now, before she'd had a chance to talk to Max. Perhaps it was wrong to take it at all. Her head spun with the complexities of the web she'd woven. Work ethics demanded that she warn Loretta before she confessed that she'd been investigating Max. But what if Loretta balked at that? What if she wanted to approach Max first? As her paid employee, D.J. would have to acquiesce, wouldn't she?

With concern about Bill—and guilt that she was not protecting him or the business he'd invited her into—gnawing at her stomach, she handed the check back to Loretta. "I can't take this. Not…yet."

Loretta made no move to take the slip of paper.

"I've got to tell Max that I was sent to investigate him. I want to tell him that's why I became his nanny, and I want to do it before tonight."

D.J. expected anger or an outright order to do nothing of the sort, but Loretta maintained her cool. She sipped her tea, then broke off a small piece of cookie and nibbled. "Why," she asked when she had politely swallowed, "do you wish to do that, Ms. Holden? What's the rush?"

Realizing that she still held the check over the table and that Loretta was clearly making no move to take it back, D.J. lowered her hand to her lap. "Your grandson and I are not romantically involved." It was true…mostly. She'd be lucky if Max ever spoke to her again after tonight. "I made a tactical error when I took the position as his nanny. I've become emotionally invested. I'd like to tell him the truth before he finds out—"

"From me?"

"Well…"

"Why is it important that you tell him before tonight?"

"Max has a meeting with the social worker tonight. She's going to evaluate his home, determine whether he has adequate child care. Hiring me prevented him from hiring a real nanny, someone who would stick. I want to help him, and I think to do that he needs the whole truth. I think I owe it to him."

"And?" Shrewdly, Loretta read that D.J. was still holding back.

"I'd like to tell him about you. I'd like to pave the way, so to speak, by telling him you'll support his efforts to secure permanent custody of the kids."

A weighty silence ensued while Loretta delicately worked on her cookie. D.J. ground her teeth, endeavoring to remain silent while Loretta considered her answer.

"The truth should be told when it would be of the most benefit. There's really no need to be hasty. Or to antagonize Maxwell by making him feel everyone concerned has manipulated him. I think it would be particularly imprudent to incite him prior to this important meeting, don't you? Let's allow him to put his best foot forward and see what this social worker has to say."

There was a certain logic to Loretta's train of thought. But the logic was just convenient enough to make D.J. uncomfortable. If she followed the other woman's advice, she could stay mum until this evening was over. Guilt swelled as she told herself it might truly be in Max's best interests not to have to deal with lies and Loretta before his meeting with Nadelle.

She raised the check again, this time laying it on the table next to the shortbread cookies. "I can't take this. Not until I've spoken to Max about everything that's happened."

"Rubbish. Be a businesswoman, Ms. Holden. Practicality won't preclude your also confessing your part in this little drama to my grandson, if you feel you must. You did your work, however you feel about it at the moment. If my grandson is half the man I hope him to be, he will understand and applaud your efforts to reunite him and the children with their heritage." She raised one of her artfully penciled brows. "You don't believe you can erase your actions by refusing your fee, do you? Our lives are comprised by a series of choices. Owning them, as they say in the common vernacular, determines our character. Don't disappoint me, Ms. Holden. Honesty seems to be your trademark. Continue the trend."

She was good. D.J. nodded. "You're right, of course. All the way down the line." Gazing at the check, Daisy June Holden sighed. She'd never thought to see that many zeroes on one paycheck. Practicality had been carved into her by nature and by necessity. Before meeting Max, there hadn't been a romantic or sentimental bone in her entire body, and if she'd found one, she'd have considered it broken. Did she have a good reason, then, a logical reason given the circumstances, to change her tune now?

No. She really didn't.

"It would be almost hypocritical not to accept my fee," D.J. murmured, still eyeballing the seductive numbers on the check. She looked up again. "So I will. But *only* my fee, not several thousand dollars more than we agreed on in the beginning. And not until I've spoken to Max and returned the salary he paid me to be his nanny."

Laying the check between the plate of cookies and the sugar bowl, D.J. stood. "Thank you for seeing me, Mrs. Mallory. I'll be in touch tomorrow, if that's agreeable to you."

Loretta did not stand. She viewed her original private investigator with an admirable poker face. "I won't contact Maxwell myself until tomorrow. I'll expect your call and will have another check ready for you."

D.J. nodded. As if by mental telepathy, the housekeeper appeared to escort her to the door.

D.J. slipped her sunglasses on as she walked back to Max's truck. She'd done the right thing regarding the check and even had renewed hope that Maxwell's attempt to secure custody of the children would be aided by Loretta. But her stomach still churned, and it took the full length of the parking lot to realize why.

Loretta had decided to remain mum about her presence at least through tonight. She seemed to have a good reason—to avoid upsetting Max before this evening—and she'd made a decent case for D.J.'s doing the same.

The conflict in D.J.'s belly reflected the battle being waged in her mind: should she confess all to Max as soon as possible or excuse herself from the truth for one more night?

Turning the key in the ignition, she started the rough-running vehicle and eased out of the parking space, knowing in her gut that it was time for the truth and wishing she could tell it in a way that would make Max look at her the way he used to. She had a sick feeling, though, that the truth, no matter how it was couched, would drive the final, intractable wedge between her and Max.

·Most likely she'd be leaving Gold Hill soon, possibly as early as tomorrow. Depending on how she left things with him, she could be going home with the glittering hope of seeing Max and the children again sometime…even only as friends. Or D.J. could go home with a nice check from his grandmother and the memory, only, of feeling her heart open for a brief moment in time.

Chapter Fourteen

D.J. drove around, exploring the back roads from Gold Hill to Jacksonville and trying to kill enough time to make her trip to the dentist plausible.

Wheat-colored grass blew in the late-summer breeze on either side of the two-lane road. Leaves the shade of limes had turned, here and there, into the pale yellow that signaled an early fall, and large homes on even larger parcels of land invited the passersby to think of families with long pasts and long futures.

D.J. tried to enjoy the scenery, but mostly she rewound her meeting with Loretta and played it over again in her mind.

As it turned out, Mrs. Mallory was no Grandma Walton. The warmth the woman had exhibited today wouldn't heat a doghouse in June. Still, she'd softened as she'd done once before when D.J. spoke of her great-grandchildren, leaving D.J. with the hope that Loretta would, at least, come in handy if Max's custody was threatened. So, D.J. concluded, her employer's lack of maternal cuddliness did not fully account for the dull, flulike heaviness dragging on D.J.'s limbs.

Sighing, she fiddled with the radio in Max's truck. She'd spent

a lot of years learning to like herself, creating a strong and bal-
anced "D.J." out of a chronically frightened and pissed-off Daisy
June. Most of the time now, she walked through her days feeling
a power that pleased her. Today, though, nothing in her life seemed
right. She felt weirdly off-kilter, as if she was physically tilted. It
was strange, and she wanted the feeling to stop.

When she'd started this job, she'd figured Max would leap at
the chance to be an heir. She knew better now. His farm was run-
down, yes, but it was also home. Running a restaurant in a small
town was labor-intensive work with a potentially modest payoff,
but Max wasn't about the payoff. If he and Loretta couldn't connect on an emotional level, D.J. understood they wouldn't connect
at all. Making contact and discovering they disliked each other
could cause strife in both Max's and Loretta's lives. The fallout
would certainly affect the children.

The desire to control the outcome of this scenario felt like an
anchor around D.J.'s neck.

She cranked up the volume on a Martina McBride tune, letting the singer's strong belt act as a cathartic for her own churn-
ing feelings.

Lies and emotions, she thought, lies and emotions. The one got
you into trouble, the other troubled you. She shook her head, making a mental note to stop at the pharmacy for an antacid on her way
through Gold Hill. Her only consolation at this point was that it
would be a relief to tell Max the truth. At least then the awful tension would end. So would her contact with Max, but that had been
written on the cards right from the start. Tomorrow she could head
back to Portland, straighten out Bill's finances and dive back into
work; she'd take anything but an "undercover" job.

It was late afternoon when she pulled the truck onto the gravel
driveway of Max's Sardine Creek home. A roll of antacid tablets,
already opened, was tucked in her jeans pocket. She'd stopped by
the restaurant, intending to pick up the kids, but Max's bartender
informed her Max had already headed home. When she arrived at
the farm, she expected to find the kids playing outside and Max
indoors, working on his new menu or perhaps setting out the
snacks for Nadelle's visit. Instead, the scene out front added ad-
ditional weight to her already burdened spirits.

Max was in the front yard, carrying Sean and James like footballs as he jogged across the grass, approaching a defense line that included Anabel, Livie…and Cleo.

The woman's laughter rang like a deep bell. She looked great in jeans and a shirt half tucked in, half out of her beltline. Cleo held hands with the girls, forming a straight line that stumbled in an awkward horizontal pattern to keep Max away from the goal line, which was marked, D.J. assumed, by the rags they'd laid on the ground.

Livie was grinning so hard it looked as though it hurt. Even Anabel—chronically worried, too-serious Anabel—had a smile on her face. Her glasses were askew halfway down her nose. For the first time since D.J. arrived, Anabel looked as if she wasn't holding back. She looked like part of the family. Suddenly D.J. remembered that Anabel had a different father from Livie and the twins. In that moment she recognized the little girl's sense of isolation and the similarity of it to her own.

On leaden legs D.J. moved toward the front walk, toward the laughter and the fun.

Childish squeals filled the air; for a moment, they were the only sound in a perfect world as Max lowered his head and ran like a bull toward the giggling all-girl defense line, the twins bouncing joyfully under his arms.

Somehow the goal was scored, ending with three males and three females in a tangled heap on the grass. D.J.'s body remembered the first time she and Max and the kids had played like that, like a litter of puppies, and the longing that sliced through her left a physical pain. She considered slipping by them, into the house, while they were still engaged by the game, but Cleo saw her and waved.

"Hey, Daisy! Come help us. The women's team needs you!"

With the twins hanging off him and Livie hanging off the twins, Max sat up. His eyes met hers, and though they lacked the warmth of former days, they weren't completely cold. He said nothing, however, giving her only a short nod.

A big fist squeezed D.J.'s heart. In a flash she was eleven again, living with the Murphy family and feeling awful because they and their five children played charades every Saturday night while she sat on the sidelines pretending disinterest; she hadn't known how to play and hadn't wanted to admit it. She'd tried to tell herself she couldn't feel rejected if it was her choice not to join in, but even at eleven she'd sensed that wasn't the truth, not by a long shot. Now she was beginning to understand that rejection began with a sense of isolation that lived in a person's soul. Outside situations might pull the bandage off the wound, but they didn't cause it.

Yeesh, get over yourself, Dr. Laura. D.J. shook her head in disgust. No way was she going to start getting philosophical; that wasn't her. *Back to business, D. J. Holden. You have a job to finish and, by God, you're going to do it well.*

She raised her hand and touched her jaw, finishing the play she'd started. "Thanks, but I'm a little sore. I'm going to take an aspirin, then putter around the kitchen awhile." Lifting her hand again, this time in parting, she walked through the front door, pleased that the house she'd tidied earlier was still organized. She was determined to put together a tea to convince the toughest social worker that Max's kids were living like the children in *Mary Poppins.*

Memory united with purpose to kick adrenaline into D.J.'s system as she embarked on her mission to leave Max's life as neat as his house when she left here.

D.J. was dressing a dessert plate with alternating rings of chocolate and vanilla cookies, like she'd seen at Loretta's, when Max walked into the kitchen. Nerves rippled along her arms; she took a deep, calming breath.

Moving straight to the sink, he shoved a glass beneath the tap, filled then drained the tumbler in a few long swallows and finally turned toward D.J. "So, how did it go?"

D.J. kept her gaze on the box of sugar-dusted lemon cookies she was trying to open, but she'd already seen enough of Max to devour the details: wavy hair mussed handsomely…perspiration on his forehead…grass stains on the polo shirt that circled his strong forearms and tucked neatly into the waistband around his flat stomach. He was handsome enough to be a model, but his clear eyes bespoke an integrity that turned prettiness to substance, sheer good looks to depth and intensity.

"It went fine," D.J. said, cursing the cookie company for making boxes that trembling fingers couldn't open.

He nodded. "How's your tooth?"

"Better." She plucked ineffectively at the edge of the box and grew frustrated. "All—" she gritted her teeth "—better. What kind of glue did they use on this thing?"

"May I?" Max reached for the cookies, quickly lifting the flap. "Where do you want them?"

D.J. frowned. "I must have loosened it for you."

"Must have. Do you have another plate?"

She reached for a white plate with a blue floral pattern on the rim. "I thought I'd use this."

"My parents' wedding pattern," he said, a nostalgic smile curving his lips. "My mother loved those plates."

"Oh! I didn't realize they were so special. Is it all right to use them?"

"We used them all the time. And broke plenty of them through the years. My mother bought them one at a time at the local market. Twenty-five cents a plate with a ten-dollar purchase."

"Your mother paid twenty-five cents a plate for her wedding china?"

Max took the dish, shook out a good portion of the cookies and popped one in his mouth. "She celebrated over every dish she was able to add to her collection. She always said she loved these dishes more than if they'd been Lenox."

D.J. didn't take the information lightly. Max's mother had probably eaten her baby cereal out of a bone china bowl. Yet she gave up her lifestyle, apparently without regret. "Your mother really, really loved your father," D.J. murmured, more a compliment than a question.

"They were soul mates."

Soul mates. Max said it so matter-of-factly. If D.J. had said it, she'd have felt…like a dork. "Why do people use that phrase?" she asked, shaking her head. "'I've found my soul mate.' What does that mean?" As far as D.J. could tell, calling someone a "soul mate" was chiefly a way to deny the randomness of the universe.

Casually, a man used to working around food, Max arranged the cookies as he spoke. "I think people say it when they meet the person who makes them feel whole."

"Ohmigod." Unable to help herself, D.J. rolled her eyes. "That's a dangerous thing to say in the twenty-first century." Following his lead, she opened the cans of frozen lemonade and dumped them into a big plastic pitcher as she spoke. "Shouldn't a person feel whole all by himself? Or herself? Isn't that why there's a self-help section at Barnes & Noble?"

Max grunted with laughter. "No. That's what a lot of people have made a lot of money trying to sell us. But no, I don't think that's what we *should* feel."

D.J. was genuinely surprised. "You think people should be empty without someone else to complete them? That's not healthy."

"Did I say 'empty'?"

She waited, but he didn't elaborate. "Okay, what *are* you saying?"

Taking his time, Max palmed two of the remaining cookies in the box. He turned, leaned against the counter and ate half a cookie before responding. "I think people should be *almost* whole…with one small piece missing."

"Why?" D.J. shook her head. That seemed almost cruel. "Life is hard enough. Why should you have a missing piece?"

"So that you'll keep looking."

Again she waited. Again he was in no hurry to elaborate, just stood there and ate the other half of his cookie. Finally D.J. exhaled in frustration. "For?"

On the surface Max appeared very relaxed. His legs were crossed at the ankle as he leaned against the kitchen counter. He tilted his head as he regarded her. So casual. But thoughts she could not begin to read made his eyes appear dark and bottomless. When he answered, his voice was low, like a hum.

"For someone who can help you navigate a world that doesn't always make sense. For the one person who makes your body heat up and your spirit calm down." Stillness seemed to surround Max as he spoke; stillness filled the kitchen. "You sleep together at night, wake up beside each other in the morning and one day you know that's the only way you *can* live. After a while you realize you're not sure anymore whose heart you feel beating. You need each other and don't feel weak because of it. The need makes you stronger."

Max watched D.J. a long moment, his eyes still unfathomable, before he concluded, "That's a soul mate."

D.J.'s chest constricted. She felt hypnotized, foggy, drunk. Deep inside was an emotion that burned hot and acrid—anger? Frustration? She wasn't certain. All she knew for sure was that she couldn't breathe.

Did Max truly believe what he said? Did he expect life to give him that much? D.J. didn't; she'd never hoped for such a thing.

"That's a fantasy." Dismayed that she'd spoken her thought out loud and that her voice emerged as an angry, sandpapery scratch, she clamped her lips shut.

Expressions chased each other across Max's face; the one that settled and stuck was cynicism. A wry kind of cynicism— but certainly not about the picture he'd just painted; his cynicism was for D.J.

Tossing his remaining cookie back into the box, he dusted powdered sugar off his hands, closed the flap neatly and set his water glass in the sink.

"It *is* a fantasy." He surprised her by agreeing in an easy tone. When he turned her way, he had the kind of smile people wore when they were done with a conversation they didn't particularly like. "As fantastical as a trip to the moon."

He nodded toward the plates of cookies, strawberries and grapes she'd set out. "Thanks for doing that. I appreciate your help." Plucking at his shirt, he excused himself. "Nadelle will be here in an hour. I'm going to wash up, then get the kids cleaned." With a nod he headed toward the door then stopped and glanced back. "Oh, by the way, after Nadelle leaves we're going to head over to Cleo's for a cookout and to see her new horse, so don't worry about dinner."

He seemed utterly relaxed again, acting as if he had few cares. D.J. didn't even try to speak as Max exited the kitchen. *I didn't tell him about Loretta.* That was the first thought that made it through the numbed maze of her mind. *I didn't tell him about Loretta, and I didn't tell him about me. And it doesn't really matter.*

Loretta was right: after Nadelle's visit—that was soon enough to confess all. In the end, the timing wouldn't matter. D.J.'s relationship with Max would be over when she walked out his door. All she'd have left would be the memory of him and his kids.

Getting down to business, D.J. set out glasses, making sure not a single water spot was in sight. The kitchen counter got an extra scrub, and the coffee table in the living room was treated to an extra helping of lemon-scented Pledge before the kids were ushered carefully to the bathroom for their own polish. The cookie plates, covered in plastic wrap and strictly off-limits to little fingers, were set out.

When D.J. looked at the table, she saw her own past and every foster family who had ever prepped for a social worker visit. Always the objective had been to make the living room evoke coffee hour after Sunday church. That was pretty much how Max's living room looked now—tidy and benign and very, very friendly. D.J. decided she'd done a good job.

Before Max emerged with the children, she washed up and changed clothes, too. Removing from the closet an outfit she'd bought specifically for today, she slipped into clothes the likes of which she hadn't worn since her first year of junior high. At that time she'd been living with the Offenbachers, who were Pentecostal and made sure all D.J.'s skirts were exceptionally roomy and fell below the knee. D.J. had always felt like a refugee from the cast of *The Sound of Music* while she'd lived with the Offenbachers, and she felt a bit like Sister Maria right now.

Her pale-blue blouse and matching cotton skirt did little to enhance her dark looks. After bangle and earring removal and the addition of a simple, low-heeled pair of sandals, D.J. felt very much like Daisy June Holden again. It was a disturbing, but as far as she was concerned, necessary sacrifice to help Max convince Nadelle that he had trustworthy childcare.

When the doorbell rang, she raced into the living room, ignoring Max's disbelieving glance when he saw what she was wearing, to arrange the children attractively and stand at attention behind them. They must have looked like the family Von Trapp when Nadelle got her first glimpse of them.

The introductions were stiff and formal, despite Max's relative calmness. When he suggested they all take a seat in the living room, D.J. felt herself turn into a kind of home study coordinator, telling the children where to sit, pouring lemonade, preparing a small plate of treats for Nadelle instead of allowing her to choose her own cookies if she wanted them, and then gratuitously complimenting the woman on her outfit, which consisted, basically, of a sundress and wrinkled linen blazer.

Max looked at her as if she was off her rocker, and, indeed, she felt a bit wacky. Nadelle's presence, the very first sight of her clutching an ivory folder with the children's files and a yellow legal pad on which to scrawl her own notes, made D.J.'s insides quiver like jelly. A terrible metallic fear filled her mouth. While the others sat, she excused herself in a voice that was about an octave higher than usual.

"I forgot the Nutter Butters!" she exclaimed as an excuse to retreat temporarily to the kitchen. God help her, she sounded like Carol Brady on helium.

"I think we're fine," Max said. The table was bulging with treats already. Both Nadelle and Max were staring at her curiously, but D.J. insisted.

"I'll be right back."

Taking refuge temporarily in the kitchen was the only solution D.J. could think of to wait out the shakes that had claimed her body.

Clutching the kitchen counter, she lowered her head and took long, deep breaths. Before she had time, however, to evaluate her own breakdown, Max entered the kitchen.

"Are you all right?"

She straightened and turned, Carol Brady smile at the ready. "Fine! I'll just get the cookies, and—" She reached up to a cabinet.

Max grasped her arm. It was the first physical contact they'd had since their tryst in his Bentley. Unfortunately, its potential effect was lost on her. One look at his sober, concerned, annoyed expression made her feel almost paralyzed.

"Don't lie to me." Max cut to the bone in a low, uncompromising tone. "There's a lot I don't know about you. What I *do* know is that this Stepford Wife impersonation is a load of crap. Where is it coming from, Daisy? What's happening here?"

Mutely, she shook her head. She didn't know. "You should be in the living room," she said, her voice quavering with her nerves. "We don't have time—"

"Nadelle is speaking to the kids. She'd already warned me she'd want to talk to them alone. I suggested they tell her about

Cleo's horses while I went to the kitchen for a bowl of chips. So either she knows we're trying to butter her up or she thinks we're compulsive snackers."

Tears sprang to D.J.'s eyes. She felt herself losing control as her whole face started to crumple. As she covered her face with her hands, Max's arms enfolded her.

He asked for nothing as he held her, but she spoke anyway, her words wet and muffled. "I'm sorry. I'm ruining everything."

Once uttered, the apology seemed to break the dam around D.J.'s heart. Suddenly she understood some of what ailed her, and the reasons came in a wash of images and sensations from the past. *I'm ruining everything.*

That's how it seemed to her, how it had always seemed. All the moves, all the partings, beginning with her removal from her family of origin, had felt like her fault. How could she have believed anything else? In every school, every church, in every McDonald's she'd ever entered, there had been children whose families did not turn their backs. How could she help but believe there was something inherently wrong with her?

How could she have prevented the fear that had coursed through her body every time a social worker had arrived for a home study? Until Bill and Eileen took her in, D.J. had lived every day with the threat of rejection and yet another huge change hanging over her head.

The truth, she realized now, was that she had never stopped feeling that way. Even after Bill and Eileen had taken her in. Some feelings, apparently, never went away; they merely hid…until a new circumstance made the body, if not the mind, remember.

"Talk to me, Daisy," Max murmured to the top of her head while he stroked her back.

"You shouldn't be gone this long. Really, it's not good." She managed to choke out the warning against his shoulder.

Max held her upper arms, squeezed them gently. "Talk to me."

She let it out then, in a stumbling, apologetic confession—the fact that she had been a foster child. He accepted the revelation with unmasked surprise, listening closely as she insisted that she knew how tenuous a placement could be…that she was terrified Max and the kids could be parted.

Max let her speak without interrupting. When she ran out of steam he held her arms, looked directly into her eyes and reassured confidently, "No one is going to take these kids away. Or separate them. Nadelle won't recommend that. I was concerned when I first met you, yes, when I couldn't keep a nanny to save our lives. The house was a constant wreck; the kids kept getting into trouble. I was the skipper of a sinking ship, and there wasn't a first mate in sight."

With the thumb and then the knuckle of his forefinger, he wiped tears from her eyes, gently. So gently. "Look around you, Daisy. This house, the kids…me…we're doing great, and it's because of you."

"That's not—"

Max gave her a little shake when she immediately began to demur. "You were the answer I hadn't found before. You jumped in and shouldered the burden. You make us laugh, you cook—not well, but you do cook. You try harder than anyone I've ever known. I've watched you act out stories for an hour. I've seen you concentrate like a researcher on the verge of discovery when you're making pancakes."

Max smiled as he described D.J. as she was, truly, not the perfect nanny, but someone he had quickly come to trust with the people he loved the most. "When the arm on Livie's doll broke for the hundredth time, I could tell you were thinking what I was thinking—time to throw it out. But you took one look at Liv's face, and the next thing I knew, the doll was wearing a silk sling." He reached up to smooth D.J.'s hair, frowned and released her ponytail so that her hair cascaded freely.

D.J. reached back to stop him, but Max was adamant. "We'll get through this being exactly who we are. You don't have to pretend. I like Daisy June Holden the way she was the day I hired her."

Max teetered on the brink of closing the gap between them. He gazed at her with that half-candid, half-contemplative expression that made her ache to pull his head toward hers and kiss him until "strong and silent" turned into "mushy and groaning."

Max's words meant more to D.J. than she could possibly have told him. They'd have meant more still if he truly knew her. She longed to tell him about Bill and the struggles that they currently faced. She wanted to confess to Max that she feared she would not be able to save her foster father's business, and she wanted to confess that she feared for herself if she couldn't go to her job, the one constant in her life. She wanted to tell someone—Max—how frightened she was that she might be losing the closest thing to a father she had ever known.

She longed to say the things she'd never said to anybody, to confess her weaknesses and her concerns and to find out how that felt.

Max seemed to realize he was still playing with D.J.'s hair about the same time she realized she liked it.

"We'd better get back in there," he said, pulling back and nodding toward the living room. He put his hands more platonically on her shoulders and gave them an encouraging squeeze. "We'll all be fine. We'll have a little conversation and eat way too many cookies."

Releasing her, Max stepped back. He gave her a wink. "If you get nervous, I'll be there."

D.J. summoned a smile, because he deserved one. She had to dig down to her toes to find the strength to push her own emotions to the side so she could accompany him to the living room and act like a proper nanny. Max appeared certain that's all it would take to please Nadelle. What could she do but follow along? And hope.

Deep down, though, in her gut, she felt the stirrings of an intuition she'd never thought she possessed. Maybe it was simply her normal cynicism overwhelming positive thoughts, or all her turbulent emotions causing a meltdown, but somehow D.J. didn't think their time with Nadelle would be as simple as Max predicted.

Chapter Fifteen

As it turned out, the meeting with Nadelle was a breeze.

Tall and slim, Nadelle had pulled her graying brown hair into a simple long ponytail held with a turquoise clip. She wore an ankle-length, lackluster sundress and brown sandals. She appeared approachable, if businesslike, and she gave the children her full attention when they spoke.

Thankfully, the social worker managed to glean information about family dynamics and the children's life without conducting an inquisition. She took few notes and when she did, she was discreet, writing on the pad on her lap without breaking eye contact with the person to whom she was speaking.

D.J. was still uncomfortable. She couldn't shake the feeling of foreboding. She ate several cookies, one after the other, in the hope that her mouth would be too full to have to do much talking.

"And how long have you been a nanny, Ms. Holden?"

Hastily swallowing the jam-filled sugar cookie she'd stuffed in her mouth, D.J. glanced at Max to determine whether he had a preference as to how she answered. He was sharing grapes with

James, however, not looking her way, and she figured her options were limited, anyway: lie or don't lie.

Taking a sip of lemonade, she cleared her throat. "I've worked around children most of my life. This is my first nanny position."

Nadelle's pale eyebrows rose. She made a note on her legal pad. "How do you like it?"

"Love it," D.J. said enthusiastically. "The children are wonderful."

"So you plan on staying?"

The million-dollar question, right off the bat.

This time Max jumped right in. With a brief, reassuring smile in D.J.'s direction, he responded to Nadelle. "Daisy came to my restaurant looking for a job as a waitress. I pressed her into being a nanny. The kids happened to be in the restaurant that day, and I saw immediately how good she was with them. I'd already hired a couple of women who treated children like cattle you had to herd or they'd get lost or out of line. Daisy talked to the kids. She listened. She has tremendous compassion and she thinks creatively. I practically bulldozed her into being our nanny, at least until I could find someone like her if she decided not to stay."

Dizzying shivers trickled down her body. Did he truly believe she had those qualities?

There was little time to wonder. Nadelle had another question. "What do you think is the most important aspect of good parenting, Daisy?"

Almost immediately D.J.'s shivers converted to a prickly panic. Good parenting? How could she know? She'd never had—

You had Bill and Eileen. The answer came as if someone else had put it in her head. *You've watched Max.*

D.J. took a breath and responded honestly, remembering and appraising.

"C-commitment," she said, as nervous as if she'd been standing before an audience of one thousand. "I think, really, to be a good parent you have to be willing to turn your life upside down for the sake of the child. Your needs have to come after his when it's necessary." Her heart thumped as she spoke. "It seems to be necessary a lot." She bit the inside of her lip. "And…love…you have to love unconditionally, hang in there even when you think you'd rather not. I think…" She looked at Max, who watched her with a sober expression on his impossibly handsome face. "I think it takes someone incredibly unselfish to be a good parent. I think it takes someone strong."

Nadelle nodded, scratching notes. "If you could instill any virtue into the children in your care, Daisy, what would it be?"

D.J.'s gaze remained locked with Maxwell's. "Kindness. Integrity." *I'd want them to be just like Max.*

From that point on, the interview with Nadelle focused mostly on Max and the kids and could almost have been termed chitchat. D.J. remained silent, mostly, talking to the kids when they got a little loud and briefly responding to a question during a conversation about the *Harry Potter* books, one of which she'd read to Anabel and the boys.

The interview concluded with a tour of the chicken coop. D.J. stayed behind to clean up.

Carrying plates and glasses into the kitchen, she realized she was trembling. The meeting had gone well as far as she could tell, but she felt shaky, out of sorts, nonetheless. She thought about Bill and Eileen…about the way Max described her first meeting with the kids…about a life spent dreading change and then accepting it and finally embracing it.

Moving on was D.J.'s MO. She changed apartments more often than most women changed hairstyles…and that was without leaving Portland. Maybe change had become a habit.

And maybe it gave her a sense of control. These days it was always her choice to pick up and go.

In either case, no one really cared how itchy your feet were when you were on your own. She'd always considered her mobility to be a sign of independence and freedom. Now, for the first time, she had an image of herself dancing atop the surface of her life, never settling in, never relaxing.

Nadelle had left without requiring a clear answer regarding D.J.'s future plans. When Max had responded in D.J.'s stead, he'd avoided committing her one way or the other.

Mechanically, she put the remaining cookies in a jar shaped like Miss Piggy and set the used glasses in the dishwasher. Too many cookies and too much worry made her feel nauseous. When Max and the kids went to Cleo's tonight, she'd pack, load up her car and get to bed early. She'd tell Max the whole story first thing to-morrow morning, before the kids were up. After that, she'd head to town, tell Loretta that she'd spilled the beans and then point her car north, back to Portland. She'd be on the interstate before he could tell her to get out.

Plans. She had plans, and that was always good.

Deciding that by far the best thing she could do for herself would be to stop thinking, D.J. dove into housework with the verve of Heloise.

Max, the kids, and Nadelle had been gone long enough for her to completely clear the living room and to wonder why the chicken coop tour was taking so long, when the front door opened and closed.

He entered the kitchen as she started the dishwasher.

D.J. felt her pulse skitter when he leaned a hip against the sink and stared at her.

"Did Nadelle leave?" she asked to fill the empty space while Max merely stood there.

"Yeah."

"Are the kids outside?"

"I took them over to Cleo's."

"Oh! Well…" She turned from wiping the sink to look at him. "Why aren't you at Cleo's?"

Folding his arms, Max stared at her a long moment. "How come you never mentioned you were in the foster care system?"

D.J. snapped to attention, her back and shoulders stiff. "I didn't think it had to do with anything."

Rather than challenging her, Max asked, "What happened to your parents?"

His voice was gentle, his gaze nonjudgmental, but D.J. hated the question. She felt trapped by a past that branded her, made her feel inferior to anyone whose parents had chosen to stay with their children. In better moments, she simply felt different. This was not one of her better moments.

"They took a powder."

He tilted his head. "When?"

Grabbing the damp dish towel she'd tossed over the kitchen faucet, D.J. began wiping the sink a second time. The occupation was not as effective as kickboxing, but it would have to do. "What difference does it make?" she snapped repressively, then found herself grumbling, "My father took off, and my mother wasn't viewed as a 'fit' parent. She liked booze and marijuana. The DHS gave her a few chances to clean up and get me back, but she preferred scotch and soda—hold the soda. End of story."

Max mulled over the information. D.J. sensed immediately that he was thinking of his cousin and knew she was right when he began gently, "Sometimes people are incapable—"

"Look, my mother never went to rehab. I don't know about your cousin, I don't know what her story was—and probably you don't, either, when you get right down to it. But what I do know is that people make choices. My mother *made a choice*. She didn't want kids, so why bother to clean up her act?"

D.J. heard the bitterness in her voice and wished—she wished with all her might—that she could relay this information impartially. She wished she could sound wonderfully forgiving or even calmly neutral. In truth, she rarely thought anymore of the man and woman who, with an act that had probably been more careless than loving, created a child neither had wanted.

Standing before Max, however, before a man who had been loved and who knew how to love, she felt belligerent, defensive, confused. She wanted conflicting things: to appear dispassionate *and* to have someone, Max, ease the two-decade-old ache of being unwanted. And that was ridiculous…and self-indulgent… and more than a little pathetic. Old baggage was the kind of thing you either dropped all by yourself or lugged around uselessly forever.

Wagging her head, she forced a laugh. "Oh, boy, listen to me. I'm tired. Look, I don't really care about any of this stuff, anymore. I never even think about it; *that's* why I didn't mention it. It's just not pertinent."

Max's expression had barely changed while she'd stumbled around her words. When she finished, he moved forward, ignoring her compressed lips and frown, until there wasn't enough room to slip the dish towel between them.

His eyes were kind…and serious. "I'm sorry your parents were selfish. I'm sorry they didn't know how lucky they were when you were born."

Instantly D.J.'s eyes burned with tears. She swallowed hard to hold them back and started to speak, to change the subject before she made a complete fool of herself, but Max wasn't finished.

"I'm sorry," he said, raising his hand to her cheek, "that your family didn't get to know the woman you've become."

D.J. wasn't sure what cracked her composure more surely, Max's sincerity or the touch that sent waves of reaction crashing through her blood.

He looked as if he wanted to say more, but in lieu of words, raised his free hand to her other cheek and cupped her face, gazing at her.

Heat, a powerful heat that ached more than her past, made D.J. feel dizzy. When Max moved forward, she met him halfway.

Her arms slid like smoke up his back even as their lips touched. Whatever else Max may have said was lost in the blaze of mutual need that blocked out every concern save the need to get closer… to touch more fully…to feel more naked mentally, emotionally, physically.

They were alone. Warm, summer-evening light bathed the house and the moment in a time-suspended glow. Their desire was dangerous for its ability to make them forget.

Max forgot he was due at Cleo's.

D.J. forgot she was leaving tomorrow.

Neither remembered the anger or guilt or frustration that followed the last time they made love. All they knew, as they gave in to a need that was gloriously mutual, was that being together had the power to turn a life with missing pieces into one solid whole. At least for a while.

"Thanks for watching the kids, Cleo. We'll be over in a few minutes. Want me to bring anything?"

Propped on an elbow in the middle of Max's bed, D.J. watched him clamp a cordless phone between his shoulder and ear while he shook out a pair of stiff 501s. He sounded so absurdly nonchalant. He sounded so…*dressed*.

Ending the call and setting the phone aside, he found the underwear they'd somehow kicked halfway across the room. He stepped into the briefs and then the jeans, turning to D.J. while he buttoned the fly. "I can't believe these words are coming out of my mouth, but you'd better get dressed."

D.J. sat up, dragging the sheet with her. "I don't know how you can talk on the phone while you're naked."

"I can do a lot of things well when I'm naked."

Allowing herself a long moment to drink in the sight of his sculpted bronze chest, she nodded in agreement. "You're a pretty confident guy, aren't you?" she said in a challenge.

Max shrugged. "Gotta know what you do well." He moved toward the foot of the bed, staring down at her with a more sober expression. "I'm confident about some things. Not so confident about others."

"Like what, for instance?"

"Like you, for instance."

She knew what he meant, but answered as if he'd been referring to what had recently taken place in his bed. "If you're fishing for compliments, Mr. Lotorto, I'm happy to tell you that I agree with you. You do a lot of things well naked. *Very* well."

While he wasn't precisely displeased with her response, he'd clearly been referring to her reluctance to stay with him, to open up verbally and emotionally. D.J. willed him not to push her, not tonight when she wanted nothing more than to snuggle down into the bed, the memory of his tenderness and his passion still fresh in her mind and her body.

She was grateful when his expression cleared. He reached down, scooped something off the floor and dangled it from one finger...her bra. "Although I much prefer taking this off you, would you like me to help you put it on?" He waggled a brow.

D.J.'s smile covered a myriad of less happy feelings. Lord, she was going to miss him when she left here. And if he looked at her with distrust and outrage, as she knew he would after she admitted all the lies she'd told him, it was going to put a crack in her heart she figured she'd never completely patch.

She wouldn't dwell on any of that now; she wouldn't ruin the memories she was storing up to take with her.

"I've been putting my bra on all by myself since the days before I really needed one," she retorted cheekily. "I don't think your motives are pure, mister, so I'm going to decline. And you'd better get going or you're going to have to explain to Cleo why you're so late."

As if it were a slingshot, Max sailed the bra her way. It landed on the rumpled sheet. "You seem to think I'm going to Cleo's alone. You're coming, too."

Max's tone sounded fairly dictatorial, not something she was used to from him. "No," she said firmly. "Cleo invited you and the children."

"What are you talking about? Get dressed."

Snatching her bra and putting it on beneath the sheet, which elicited a roll of the eyes from Max, D.J. remained stubborn. "I'm going to get dressed, and then I'm going to go into town, rent a video and watch it in peace."

"Daisy—"

"No." D.J. searched the floor near the bed for the rest of her clothes, retrieving items one at a time and putting them on under the covers while she spoke. "I don't want to fight with you again, especially not now. Just go before anyone gets suspicious about your absence, and I'll see you…tomorrow morning. I'm going to turn in early."

"I thought you were going to watch a video."

"A short video, and then I'm going to turn in early!" she snapped, searching the floor beside the bed for the skirt she'd hastily discarded.

Max walked to the door, bent to pick up D.J.'s skirt and brought it to her. "Frankly, I think you should burn this damn thing," he said, fingering the washed-out blue cotton before handing it to her. He sat on the bed, staring long and hard until she met his gaze. "Look," he said, "I don't want to fight with you after sex, either, but it seems to be a pattern we're falling into. Maybe we ought to just get used to it." With the tip of a forefinger, he raised her chin. "You are coming to Cleo's, where we are going to have a great night…unless you can articulate in fifty words or less exactly why you don't want to be there."

"I'm still leaving."

Every muscle in Max's body appeared to contract at the same

time. "You really do need to work on the timing of your announcements."

"It's not an announcement. I already told you, so this is just a reminder." And though she longed *not* to have to say it, D.J. knew it was the one piece of truth she could offer tonight.

Unsure of what she expected exactly, D.J. was disconcerted by the keen stab of pain that hit her solar plexus when Max visibly relaxed and shrugged. "I've decided to live in the moment, anyway. Get dressed. We'll eat too much barbecue, look at a sweet mare and roll in the hay. Literally." With a quick wink he rose from the bed to retrieve his shoes. "I'm going to get a fresh shirt." He headed for the boys' room, where he'd stowed most of his things when D.J. moved in. "I'll meet you at the front door in ten."

Chapter Sixteen

It had become Max's habit over the past two months to stop by the bakery for a Bismark bar and a tall cup of strong black coffee that he could take with him to work. Somehow the sugary breakfast made the problems with contractors go down easier. The coffee kept him alert.

"Same as usual, Max?" Dorla Howard, a stout, graying, sixty-something, whose family had owned the bakery for forty years, greeted him from behind the tall glass counter. Dorla and her sisters, Fran and Esta, still made all the pastries themselves.

The sisters' melt-in-the-mouth doughnuts held little appeal this morning, but Max decided that the best way to deal with his turbulent feelings about his relationship with Daisy Holden was to go about his business as usual. At least until he could think of something better to do.

And he *was* thinking. The wheels of his mind were turning at high rpm's as he considered what to do about a woman whose secrets stood in the way of love.

"Yep, same as usual, Dorla. Thanks." Max stood patiently while

Dorla plucked a doughnut out of the case and turned to pour his coffee. Inside, he felt anything but patient.

He could love Daisy, love her for a really long time. Like, forever.

Discovering she'd been a foster kid filled in one piece of the puzzle: she was afraid to be part of a family. Afraid it wouldn't last. Yeah, it seemed like a pat answer, but it made sense. He refused to believe she didn't *want* to stay. He *couldn't* believe that, not the way she acted with the kids.

Not the way she *re*acted to him. There was no way she'd convince him with words alone that she was ready to end their relationship. It was too good, too damned good to walk away.

The buzz against his hip told him someone was trying to contact him on his cell phone.

He glanced at the caller ID. Nadelle.

Quickly he snatched the phone off his belt and flipped it open. Tucking it against his ear, he nodded at Dorla, mouthing, *Thank you,* as she snapped a plastic lid on his coffee and passed it across the counter. He handed her exact change as he answered the phone.

"Hello, Nadelle, glad you called." He'd thought about the social worker last night as he'd watched the kids play at Cleo's. His heart had caught several times when he realized he didn't know what the next step should be in his quest to secure permanent custody of the children. Pure love and family loyalty aside, his new awareness of how the foster system had affected Daisy made him more determined than ever not to let a single *T* go uncrossed as they closed this case once and for all.

Despite his greeting, Nadelle apologized for phoning so early.

"Hey, it's fine." Max brushed the apology away. "I'm already on my way to work. I was going to call you, anyway, when I got there."

"We have a problem, Max." Nadelle leaped in, but her customary brusqueness was buffered by her obvious reluctance to have the early-morning conversation. "There's an issue we need to talk about regarding your case. Do you have time?"

Max felt his heart thud uncomfortably. Leaving his breakfast where it was, he turned slightly from the counter, sidestepping the next person in line. "Go on."

As Max listened to the somber woman on the other end of the

line, anger ignited in his belly, kindling rapidly to a rage he hadn't known he possessed. At first he listened only, not trusting himself to speak. Then he lowered his head, made sure he was out of earshot from the bakery's other customers and said in a rough growl, "You're telling me that someone who hasn't seen the kids—ever— is challenging my custody? That's insane!"

Nadelle tried to calm Max down, but they both knew it was a lost cause. Max asked a few questions, to which Nadelle promised to find answers, and they agreed to speak again later in the day.

Snapping his cell phone shut, Max left his breakfast on the counter and exited the bakery in a red haze of fury. He wasn't sure where to go, what to do first…whom to kill…until he saw the limousine.

"Mr. Lotorto?"

The dignified male voice belonged to a uniformed man who regarded Max with trained neutrality from his position beside the long, black vehicle. Opening the rear door, the chauffeur gestured politely, indicating that Max should please get in the backseat.

It took Max maybe five seconds to realize whose car, whose servant and whose request this was.

"Bite me."

Max didn't move, though, while Loretta slid across the seat to the open door. When she poked her imperious head out of the car, he was surprised to see she hadn't changed much in a decade. Just showed what clean living and the best plastic surgeons could do for you, he supposed.

She looked as much like a queen as ever, but unlike the old days when, as a teenager forced to visit the grandmother he disliked, Max had tried his damnedest to irritate Loretta with "low" language, today she showed no irritation over his crudeness.

"Kindly do not abuse my staff" was her only rebuke. She watched him a long moment, no messy emotion marring her nipped-and-tucked regality.

She eyed him up and down. "You've filled out since I saw you last."

There was plenty Max wanted to say, but all of it was contentious, and he didn't want to give her any more ammo to take to her lawyer—the one she'd hired to steal the kids from him. With Herculean effort, he curbed his tongue and waited.

Loretta's smile was strained. "I can get out of the car, Maxwell, and we can have a discussion on the main street of this charming town. Our other options are for you to join me here or meet me at my motel. Either way, we have a great deal to discuss."

D.J. was a goner.

Standing on Max's weathered wooden porch, she sipped a cup of hot coffee and poked her bare foot idly against a spot of dry rot. The morning breeze carried the scent of jasmine and roses from a trellis against the side of the house. She wondered if Max had planted the flowers. He'd shared his plans to rebuild the porch and to landscape when time and money allowed, but standing here, leaning against an aged wooden post and watching the kids pluck the last of the summer blackberries, D.J. thought the farm was perfect just as it was.

Yes, she was a goner all right.

Last night, after experiencing her first cookout, she, Max and the children had returned home warm, relaxed and happily full-bellied. Together she and Max had settled the kids in their rooms for the night. A sleepy James had blinked up at her while she'd tucked the covers around his waist. "You're pretty," he'd murmured, then put his arms around her neck for a sweet, sweet kiss. He'd fallen asleep before his head touched the pillow again.

D.J. had swallowed a lump in her throat. Then as she and Max had walked from the boys' room to the one shared by the girls, Max had taken her hand. He hadn't said anything, simply took her hand as if tucking these kids in was something they'd done together for years.

Her body had tingled with pleasure at his touch even as her heart softened with a tenderness that was altogether new. Never had she experienced such pure and searing sweetness. She'd wondered if Max would come back to her room once they made sure everyone was comfortably in bed; the thought had brought with it an intoxicating rush of anticipation.

Alas, the twins had had other plans.

Sean had called out for water, and when Max and D.J. headed

back to the boys' room, they found James awake again, too. Max
had been sleeping in the twins' room for the past couple of weeks,
and once again they'd expected to share the top bunk "like in a tree
house" while Max slept on the bottom. They'd opposed vocifer-
ously when he announced he was going to sleep on the sofa.

Finally D.J. had unwittingly solved the dilemma by starting to
yawn. As happy as she was, she was still exhausted. Max sighed
and told the boys, "All right, I'll be back in two minutes. I know
when I'm licked." In the hall, he'd leaned close to D.J., adding for
her ears alone, "And though I'm not opposed to being licked, I
thought it might happen tonight in a different context."

That had definitely woken D.J. up again, but Max had put both
hands on her shoulders and pushed her gently toward her room.
At the door, his hands had slid leisurely to her waist. She'd turned
into his arms. Without a word uttered, their lips had met in a lingering good-night kiss.

Even now, the memory warmed D.J. far more than the morning sun. But that wasn't the only recollection currently tugging
on her heart.

This morning Liv had climbed into D.J.'s bed, claiming she
was "lonely." Max had already left for work, and D.J. sighed as
the little girl snuggled spoon fashion. They cuddled in utter con-
tentment for several long minutes, and then Livie asked if they
could have blackberry muffins for breakfast, "Like my other
mommy used to make."

Her other mommy.

The words that would have panicked D.J. a day earlier had, this
morning, turned her blood to honey. Her whole body had grown
warm and liquid and sweet.

She'd spent an hour on the Internet this morning searching for
muffin recipes.

Muffins, for crying out loud.

Generally by eight-thirty in the morning, she'd have had a good
workout by now, read the police blotters in several local papers and
picked up a breakfast burrito from her favorite deli.

But muffins? She'd never made one in her life. Never had any
desire to try.

Now she wanted to make blackberry muffins that were just like the ones Terry had made.

Now D.J. could spend half the morning with a cup of caffeine, watching four kids outfitted in a variety of oversize kitchen mitts, gardening gloves and snow mittens. While the others monkeyed around, Anabel diligently sought the last of the season's blackberries.

Someday, D.J. thought, *I'm going to make that girl giggle.* Someday she would tell Anabel about losing her own parents at a young age. She would explain that she, too, had developed a cool demeanor, had learned to keep herself distant from others and to pretend that while she liked people well enough, she didn't really *need* them.

Someday she would explain to Anabel how wrong she'd been.

Between last night and this morning, everything had changed. Everything.

D.J. still had to tell Max that his grandmother had hired her and that she'd never been a "real" nanny. She had to admit she'd been a fake from the start—except with regard to her feelings. Her time may have been bought by Loretta, but her feelings had been her own, and she'd given them to this family. The heart she'd protected for years was wide-open and throbbing now, and in her gut D.J. knew there was no turning back.

Not after last night.

Yes, she still needed to tell Max the truth, but now she couldn't imagine leaving here, making room for some other woman to help him paint the new porch…and cheer the boys' soccer games…and watch Anabel graduate as her class's valedictorian.

She wanted the right to worry out loud that considering how adorable Livie was, she would never make it to "sweet" sixteen without being kissed.

D.J. wanted to go to sleep beside Max every evening and to awaken smooshed against him each morning, crowded by a bed full of children who'd migrated during the night. She wanted to call Max in the daytime for no reason at all except that they both needed to touch home.

Home.

For so long she had been in limbo, wondering where she would move next.

This morning, for perhaps the first time in her life—certainly for the first time in her memory—she felt as if there was nowhere else she had to go. Despite all the sane and logical reasons for moving back to Portland and focusing again on her career, D.J. couldn't imagine ever being happy again if she was away from Max. Away from the family.

Away from her heart.

At the far end of the front yard, the boys were picking mostly dried berries now, calling them shrunken heads, then dropping them on the ground and stomping on them. Livie was squealing loudly, but without much conviction, and Anabel was ignoring her younger siblings entirely.

And D.J. stood stock-still beneath the porch, her heart pounding too hard because she knew she might be on the verge of experiencing that blessed completeness at last…not because of a place, not because of a career…but because of Max and four motherless kids.

Suddenly feeling almost buoyant, D.J. knew what she had to do. After telling Max the truth about her sudden appearance here, she would give him the *whole* truth—not only the part about how she'd lied, but also the part about how she was starting to love. Leaning against the porch post, for a moment D.J. relied on it to hold her up. It wasn't every day that a woman was willing to gamble that maybe, just maybe she had a future with five people who had been strangers only a short time ago.

Close to laughing from the sheer unlikeliness of it all, D.J. called in the crew.

She made them wash their hands at the garden hose, then gave them the choice of helping her in the kitchen or watching *Finding Nemo* until the muffins were done. The boys chose the movie, Livie said she wanted to help, and Anabel said nothing, clearly wavering.

As the other children stampeded into the house, D.J. pulled Anabel aside and effusively admired her bag of berries. "Wow. We wouldn't be able to make muffins at all without these. You did great."

Shy pleasure lit Anabel's face until she slipped her guard back into place. D.J. felt a momentary letdown, but recalled that she'd spent most of her own growing-up years feeling not only out of place but superfluous. Inspired suddenly, she took the bag of berries and weighed them in her hands. "I bet we could get…what? Five or six muffins out of these?"

"Five or six!" Anabel was incredulous. "I picked enough for a dozen muffins, at least!"

"Really?" D.J. frowned. "I'm not very good with measurements. To tell the truth, I've never made muffins before." She fingered the plastic bag, pondering. "Livie said your mother made blackberry muffins. Did you ever watch her?"

"Sure."

"Would you show me how to make them? I have a recipe we can refer to, but I'd much rather learn firsthand from someone with experience."

Anabel rolled her eyes. She took the bag of berries and sighed loudly, but a tiny smile tugged at her mouth as she entered the house. D.J. read the response as, *I guess I have to do everything around here.*

Following the girl, D.J. felt a burst of confidence and hope. She would win Anabel over…it might take a while, but she would do it. And if she could win Anabel over, then the future with Max, who wasn't nearly as tough a customer, looked pretty good, indeed.

"I want butter."

"I want jam!"

"Can I have both?" James squeezed in beside Livie and Sean at the kitchen table, inhaling the sweet, buttery aroma of piping-hot muffins.

The kitchen was a wreck; D.J. couldn't seem to get the hang of putting one ingredient away before pulling out another. The breakfast table, however, looked exactly the way a breakfast table should—laden with platters of eggs and fruit, glasses of milk and orange juice, and a basket of muffins. D.J. wanted to freeze the moment. She wanted to snap the picture so she'd remember it always.

She had created a family moment.

As they took their seats, D.J. passed the muffins and sneaked a glance at Anabel. The girl wriggled with uncontainable energy. When her siblings *Mmmmm'd* and smacked their lips over her creation, Anabel beamed. Then D.J. selected a muffin, took a bite and solemnly declared it, "The best muffin I've ever had in my life. My compliments and a round of applause to the baker."

Rising, she led the others in a standing ovation that puffed Anabel up like a bespectacled peacock. The girl's eyes crinkled behind her glasses, and she appeared, for the first time since D.J. had met her, truly happy.

D.J. felt her throat clog with emotion. She figured this ranked with one of the most fulfilling moments of her own life. Who'd have guessed? As they sat down and dug into the eggs, she found herself retelling the moment in her head, imagining Max's reaction and his pleasure when she told him she'd finally gotten through to Anabel.

Happily splitting and buttering a second muffin to share with Livie, D.J. tried to imagine, too, Max's reaction when she told him he didn't have to look for a new nanny…that she'd stand beside him hook, line and sinker until his custody of the kids was a done deal in the eyes of the Department of Human Services. And after that…

Well, after his custody was a done deal, D.J. figured she and Max could negotiate new terms regarding her stay on here…for as long as they both felt good about it. Something told her she'd feel good about staying here for a long, long, long, long time.

Handing Livie the halved muffin, D.J. sat back and watched the four-year-old press her tongue flat against the buttered surface. Sean poked his fingers into the top of his second muffin to pull out the berries. James and Anabel focused intently on their eggs.

Breakfast, she thought. Who knew it could be so fascinating?

When Max walked into his house shortly before ten in the morning, the first thing he noticed was the heavy, sweet aroma of something baked, followed by happy chatter and shrieks of childish laughter from the kitchen. He paused a moment inside the front door before heading toward the scent and the sound.

When he saw Loretta this morning, anger and shock had frozen his system. After all these years…

Seeing her hadn't packed the punch that speaking to her had, however.

His devoted grandmamma was threatening his custody of Terry's children—unless Max chose to move into Loretta's home with the kids *and* work for Mallory's Superstore chain. That was the deal. Anybody who knew Max, and knew him well, could tell her it was never going to happen. But the deal made perfect sense to Loretta, who was a controlling, narcissistic, interfering old—

Max shouldn't have been surprised that Loretta would stoop to threats and manipulation to get what she wanted—someone in the Mallory gene pool under her roof and working in her business. Her son and daughter had bailed on her; however, in her eyes, her grandson and great-grandchildren were still up for grabs.

She hadn't changed. Ownership, possession, was everything to the old woman. Not once had she asked what Max wanted out of life, what the kids were like or what they might need.

"Mallory's will stay in the family. It's the children's legacy. And yours, Maxwell, if you are smart enough to recognize that."

If he was "smart enough," huh? And if he wasn't smart enough to see things *her way,* she was going to help him by threatening his custody of Terry's kids. Thanks, Granny.

Steeling himself, Max walked toward the kitchen. His footsteps fell heavily; his lungs felt like steel, incapable of expanding enough to allow a full breath. He did not want to upset the kids and wished he could get over this next hurdle without involving them. But it was impossible. After this morning's meeting with Loretta, Max felt he had to act now or explode.

When he reached the kitchen entry, the sights, sounds and aromas of a big homemade breakfast were everywhere. Anabel and the twins were clearing the kitchen table and chattering with each other; at the sink, Livie stood on a step stool with her hands under the running faucet while Daisy helped her clean up, rubbing Liv's hands with soap and complaining happily that the little girl might have to learn to live with purple fingers.

The scene was so homey, so close to what he'd hoped to create for himself and the kids that Max felt his fury arise afresh, and he became afraid he might not be able to contain it. His dream of family and permanence had grown sharper and clearer over the past several weeks, but it had been burned to ash this morning. It would not rise again.

Because he was unable to stop himself, Max allowed his gaze to travel over his children's nanny and to note every detail. Dressed in a thin, sleeveless red turtleneck and blue jeans that ended just below her knees, she stood at the sink in bare feet. She wore an ankle bracelet, but her hair was scooped into a haphazard ponytail. She looked like a young mom, though the lithe grace of her long arms and legs made her seem more like a model-turned-young-mother.

Watching her stand in his kitchen as if she belonged there forever made Max's desire flare. And that infuriated him further. Everything he wanted was right here in his humble, rundown farmhouse—a good life, a worthwhile life that was within arm's reach, but out-of-bounds. Out-of-bounds for good.

"Uncle Max!" When she spotted him, Anabel rushed over, more bubbly than he'd seen her in months. "We made muffins," she told him, eyes sparkling behind her glasses. "With the blackberries from our hedge."

"I picked 'em!" Sean said, galloping over.

"Me, too!" Joining his brother, James grabbed Max's legs and hugged hard. Max felt a swift, fierce rush of love and protectiveness.

Liv turned around on the step stool, ready to barrel over to him, too, soapy hands and all, but Daisy stopped her. "I'm washing my hands," his tiniest cousin called out. "'Cause they look like blackberries!"

A lump filled Max's throat. Love and fear and bitterness turned his blood to an unhappy cocktail that felt more life robbing than life sustaining. Just the thought, the threat of losing these kids could bring him to his knees.

He shook his head; he needed to stay clear, focused. Anyone who threatened his family had to learn that when pushed hard enough, Max shoved back even harder. He detested threats.

He detested liars.

Like a homing pigeon, his gaze landed on a pair of cat-green eyes. Holding on to Liv, Daisy was flushed and smiling.

And as innocent as her phony name.

He didn't bother to smile back, but tried not to allow any less appealing expression cross his face, either. He wasn't about to start a scene until the kids were out of the house. He had no idea at this point what Daisy would say or do. He didn't know her at all.

Max's gut tightened. He thought of her body, of the times he'd held her, felt her quiver in his arms…and then he recalled that first night of lovemaking. Something had been wrong. She'd shown all the passion he'd hoped for from her, but she'd been holding back, too, trying to resist. It made him sick to his stomach to think that she'd given him her body to get…what? Information? To retain his trust?

How could he have been so damn wrong about someone? He felt a rush of self-loathing almost as strong as the fury he felt toward her…almost as strong, but not quite.

"Try one of our muffins," Anabel said, taking his arm and tugging him toward the table.

Max resisted the tug, but turned his full attention toward her, schooling himself to behave as he ordinarily would. The effort seemed monumental. "I can't right now, sweetheart, but I'll have one for lunch." He placed his hand on the top of her head, like a cap, letting it rest there. "Cleo is out front. She's waiting for you all. Why don't you take her a muffin?"

She nodded vigorously, beaming. "We made extra."

"Where are we going?" Anabel asked, puzzled.

"Over to her place. She's having a couple of goats delivered. She thought you might like to meet them, and she could use some help keeping the chickens out of the yard while the goats are being dropped off. You think you kids can help her?"

He didn't have to ask more than once. The lure of baby animals was too much to resist, even for the proud baker, who offered a token protest, saying she should probably stay to help Daisy clean up.

"You go," Daisy insisted before Max had a chance to respond. "You made most of the breakfast. I'll handle the cleanup."

Anabel flushed with pride at the comment. "If you're sure."

Max observed the exchange with a jaded eye. It seemed she and Daisy had come to a better understanding than they'd had only a day before. Even that made him angry.

Stay away from my kids, he wanted to growl, but couldn't. Not yet.

He had been impulsive from the moment he'd met Daisy June Holden, and it had cost him dearly. He would pay still more before it was over, but Daisy would pay, too. He'd make sure of it.

"Better hurry," he said to the children. "The goats will arrive in just a few minutes."

There was immediate action. The twins raced to the front door
and out into the yard, greeting Cleo, who had come to his rescue
this morning, no questions asked. Max had offered only the spar-
est details about his grandmother's reappearance in his life and
what that could mean to his custody hearing. Cleo had listened,
offered help in any way he needed and agreed immediately to
spend an hour or two distracting the kids this morning while he
dealt with his phony nanny.

Max watched D.J. help Anabel bag a couple of muffins for their
next-door neighbor. Cleo was due to leave town again on business
in a couple of days. Once more Max would be completely on his
own, attempting to take care of four kids and to open a restaurant.
It couldn't be helped. Eventually he'd find a babysitter, the older
kids would start school in the fall…life would settle into a predict-
able routine.

God willing.

When the door closed behind the children, he remained where
he was, several feet from Daisy…D.J. He said nothing, choosing
to see how she intended to handle the moment between them now
that Loretta was in town. Loretta claimed she hadn't told D.J. that
she planned to contact Max this morning, which meant that as far
as D.J. knew, her cover was still intact. So how, he wondered,
would she play the game today?

Standing on the other side of the table, a dishrag in hand, she
smiled, more tentatively than usual, he thought. "This is a surprise," she said. "What brings you home so early?"

He had to hand it to her: she appeared to be the picture of the
sweetly anticipating lover, showing equal parts pleasure and shy-
ness at seeing him unexpectedly.

"What brings me home?" he murmured. "Business. Strictly
business."

"Problems with the restaurant?"

He shrugged casually. "Nothing I can't handle." Taking a few
steps to lean against the counter that ringed the kitchen, he crossed
his arms. "Business problems really aren't that difficult to cor-

rect when you think about it. Even if they seem complicated at first."

A small frown pinched the delicately arched brows. "Really? Seems to me the opposite is true—if a business problem seems simple, look out, because it's bound to be complex."

"Then you're not thinking about it properly." Max forced himself to focus on her character—as it had so recently been revealed to him—and not the face that had fascinated and captivated him from the first. "In business, you keep a cool head," he said, aware that he was speaking to himself as well as to her. "You commit yourself to your best interests. Base your actions and decisions— all of them—on experience and reason, not emotion. No matter what, you keep emotional and physical drives out of your business dealings."

Using the dishrag to wipe her already dry hands—clearly a nervous gesture, Max thought—she laughed. "This is an awfully serious conversation for the morning."

He smiled. An unpleasant smile. He could feel it.

Uncrossing his arms, Max moved slowly toward the table, his gaze intent upon her. Her discomfort was palpable. Guilty conscience? If so, he wasn't impressed.

Reaching into his back pocket, he pulled out his wallet and began to extract bills. While he counted out money, he spoke. "A serious conversation," he agreed in a murmur. "But appropriate. We have outstanding business, you and I. I believe I owe my children's nanny some money."

"Money? You didn't come home for that, did you—to pay my wages?"

"You've earned them, haven't you? You've been working hard. Harder than I even realized. Staying here, working for me when you're not really a nanny, a point you made clear right from the start. I appreciate your honesty about that, by the way."

He was baiting her, enjoying it and in a vicious way, hoping she'd evade the truth so he could continue to build the list of grievances against her.

D.J. clutched the towel in her hands, giving her restless fingers something to grip while her mind raced at a tiring pace. Something was wrong, very wrong. Max was smiling, his shoulders were relaxed, but his casualness was a veneer and nothing more. Beneath the smile there was tension and—D.J.'s heart began to hammer—anger.

He knows.

Quickly she warned herself not to jump to conclusions. It would be foolish and dangerous to make assumptions based on appearances. No matter how many times she told herself she was prepared to give Max the truth, facing him while wanting him the way she did tended to blunt her courage. She didn't want to rush an explanation because she was afraid. If she could just find the right way to tell him, to make what she did sound…less bad than it was…

Loretta wouldn't have contacted him yet, D.J. comforted herself. *Not without telling me first. Not while I'm still in the house.*

Taking a steadying breath, she said carefully, "I know I've mentioned a few times that I'm not a nanny…and that I wouldn't stay. But…" She felt shaky and reminded herself not to palaver. Fear made her belly churn, but she was clear enough to realize that the fear came from the past, from her history. She could get past that now. She *could.* Max and the kids wanted her, as she'd never been wanted before.

"I didn't realize how much I'd enjoy taking care of children. These children." The edges of her smile wavered with anxiety and emotion. She pressed past both. "I didn't know how fulfilling it would be."

Max swore in his head and had to clench his teeth not to let the oath explode from his lips. He watched the uncertainty in Daisy's gaze, the tentativeness of her smile and knew now that baiting her had been a mistake. He couldn't take another lie, would never be able to tolerate another phony come-on. She had played him for a fool right from the start. He'd let circumstance and his own desire blind him.

"How much?" he demanded, the words growled hard and low.

"How much?" Wagging her head a little, obviously confused,

D.J. looked for a reference point. "How much? You mean, how much do I enjoy—"

Whipping several more bills from his wallet, Max slammed them onto the table. He was through with games. "How much will it take to get you out of our lives? For good."

Chapter Seventeen

D.J. Holden had faced some angry people in the past, but standing in front of Max and his rage was another story. It was entirely possible she was going to throw up before she managed an explanation.

"You spoke to Loretta," she said, not a great opening, but it cut to the chase and was all she could manage at the moment.

Max stood before the money he'd slapped onto the table, his expression rich with disdain. He said nothing, a silence that was both deliberate and challenging.

He wanted her out, out of his home and his life, out of the children's lives. Despite her pledge not to react as she might have in the past, D.J. felt herself grow numb in the face of his rejection. She recognized clearly the paralyzing coldness that crept into her when she was about to be cast off from a family and told herself that this was different, that she was not a child anymore. This was about choices she had made as an informed adult, choices that only she could explain.

"Loretta hired me to find you because she wanted an heir. She wanted you." D.J. began at the very beginning. "You're her grandson. I didn't know there was any enmity between you."

"The fact we'd been estranged for a decade didn't clue you in?"

"She said she wanted to make you CEO of a multimillion-dollar company, Max. I thought you'd be really…happy when you heard—"

"When I heard what? That a private investigator had been sneaking around my life—sneaking around *in* my life?" If he'd been controlling his anger at all up to this point, he was through. Compressed with rage, Max's lips thinned to bare his teeth. His chest rose and fell visibly with each heavy breath. "When did you decide to masquerade as a nanny?" He stepped around the table, moving until he was right in front of her. "When did you decide to involve *my children?* Did Loretta give you a bonus for discovering extra heirs?" Standing so close, she could see the loathing in his eyes. D.J. unavoidably flinched when Max grabbed her shoulders. "The pay on this job must be outstanding," he said with silky, menacing smoothness. "Or are you usually willing to sell your body for a song?"

D.J. gasped. Shock supplanted anger for a moment until her natural defenses took over. She raised a hand, aiming it at his shoulder. He was faster and grabbed her wrist before she connected.

"I don't think so," he growled. "I've taken enough hits from you for one lifetime."

He was holding her wrist too painfully, but that was nothing compared to the knife he'd just plunged in her chest. This was the man she had trusted, however fleetingly, with her body and her soul.

"I don't 'sell my body,'" she said, fury making her voice raspy. "To you or anyone else. What happened between us, happened because—"

He arched a brow when she halted. "Don't stop now. I'm all ears."

His sarcasm was a hard-to-breach barrier…hard, but not impossible. And yet D.J. found she couldn't speak. The words froze in her throat. The real barrier, she discovered, was not the one facing her but the one inside. The one piece of information that might…just might…convince him to view things from her perspective was the one thing she couldn't utter.

They stared at each other, adversaries now, with Max holding her wrist and D.J. breathing heavily and painfully from a chest that was too restricted to allow free movement.

Taken individually or together, the facts looked awful. But then, facts without truth seldom told the whole story.

As a child, losing the only people she had known as family had felt like being annihilated. The first time she'd lost her foster parents, she'd been too young to articulate her feelings, but the terror had been real. She hadn't known how she would live…*if* she would live. *Foster* was only a word to a child. Parents were parents and when they rejected you, your soul was adrift with nothing and no one to hang on to. Either you perished from the pain or you built a shell that was strong enough not to crack when rejection happened again…and again…and again.

D.J. had built her shell. Like a pearl surrounds a grain of sand, she'd protected her heart. Bill and Eileen had gotten through…and then Max and his kids. And for him, finally, she'd been willing to face the feelings and the fear that came with loving.

But that was before. Before his anger and resentment had become palpable. To say *I love you* now would be like handing him her heart on a silver platter—with a carving knife.

She tried to fight the resistance, but while she hesitated, Max's lips twisted into what amounted to a smirk. "That's fine, Daisy June—or whatever your name is. The reasons for having sex don't matter. The outcome does." He let go of her wrist. "Every decision I made since you walked into the restaurant has been a nail in my coffin. I played my part to a T, didn't I? Loretta has the ammunition she needs to make me look like an irresponsible jackass."

Self-disgust rose from him like smoke from a fire. "Time to rewrite the script." He reached for the wad of bills he'd thrown on the table. "How much will it take to make you disappear? I'm not just talking about today. I want you gone for good. You don't contact Loretta or allow yourself to be contacted by her again for any reason. You make yourself unavailable for a subpoena. Name your price. I'll pay it in cash."

Emotions assaulted D.J. one after the other, like a volley of tennis balls she wanted to dodge. "Max, you can't be serious. This isn't the way to handle—"

With one step, he was in her face, snarling, "Do not tell me how

I should handle this situation. You helped create it. All I care about now is getting me and my kids out of it." He fanned out ten one-hundred-dollar bills. "I'm not kidding myself that a thousand will be enough for you, so let's call this an appetizer. I'll have access to more this evening. Give me a dollar amount," he demanded again. "What will it take to make Daisy Holden nothing more than a mistake from my past?"

In the end it wasn't so hard to get rid of Daisy, Max reflected, standing on his porch, staring moodily at the darkening sky, a Seagram's on-the-rocks in his hand.

The kids were still at Cleo's, thank God, so he hadn't had to explain Daisy's absence. Yet. She'd left without a fuss.

The fact that she had said nothing—just walked stiffly to the bedroom to collect her things—jerked his string more than if she'd been brazen or apologetic or flip. Her subdued dignity had left him feeling almost churlish.

Furious that *he* felt guilty, he'd been afraid to stay in the house, so he'd gotten back in his car and returned to work, but, of course, he hadn't been able to concentrate on anything but Daisy and her betrayal. She hadn't touched a dime of the money he'd thrown down, irritating him more than if she'd demanded continued payment in large bills for the next twenty years. If she refused his money, then she still intended to work for Loretta and would no doubt testify for his grandmother if the custody case went to court.

Finishing the bourbon, he slammed the glass on the wooden porch rail. How could he have been such an ass? How could he have been duped so completely? After waiting twenty-eight years for the kind of love his parents had shared, the kind of love you fought to keep no matter the cost, he'd fallen for a total fraud.

And he'd put his family, the most important thing in the world to him, in jeopardy.

Suddenly he hoped Terry couldn't see the mess he'd made of things. He'd always thought she was the one who'd made poor choices regarding love. But at least she'd gotten four great kids out of her misbegotten relationships.

An owl hooted from a cedar tree, reminding Max that night was fast descending and that it was time to go get the kids.

Tonight he would tuck them into bed by himself for the first time in weeks, but he would wait until morning to explain that Daisy was gone for good. If Loretta did take him to court, if he did lose custody, he only hoped to God the kids would never have to know that Daisy had been the tool Loretta used to destroy their family.

D.J. lay curled on the worn cushion of her living room futon and stared morosely out her second-story window. Morning sun glistened on the rooftops and trees, adding highlights to the myriad shades of green, gold and brown on her otherwise pedestrian block. It was going to be another beautiful day.

Portland weather sucked. You couldn't count on it. D.J. wanted rain. She wanted gray, low-hanging skies. Dampness and drizzle. A storm sent by ticked-off gods. She wanted the kind of weather that made a person fear she might drown if she dared to look up, not a day out of Mr. Rogers' Neighborhood.

Sighing, she tried to summon the energy to shift. Her right hip had gone numb hours ago, during a 5:00 a.m. infomercial about wrinkle cream. She'd been lying here, looking out her window or at the TV since she'd arrived home yesterday evening. She'd risen only to use the bathroom. And she'd phoned Bill, leaving a message on his machine to say she was home, needed to catch up on sleep and would see him in a couple of days.

Mostly, though, she'd lain awake, wondering how she could have made such a mess of her life. And worrying about how long it was going to take to get back to normal. Because even with hundreds of miles between them, even with the sound of his fury and his rejection ringing in her ears, D.J. still wanted Max with every fiber of her being.

Groaning, she pushed her stiff body to a sitting position, stretched her legs out to loosen her hamstrings, then gave up on comfort and hugged her knees to her chest. The truth was she felt better curled into a ball…closed up…self-protective. She'd feel a whole lot better still, if her mind and emotions went as numb as her hip.

After leaving Max's house, D.J. had felt too raw to see Loretta, but she had phoned from the road and asked the housekeeper to deliver the following message: that as far as D.J. was concerned, her association with Loretta was over; never, not in a million years, would she help the woman steal custody of *Max's* children. She was still shocked that Loretta had thrown such a volatile twist into an already heated situation.

With her point adequately—she hoped—made, D.J. had driven the three hundred miles home.

Foodwise, she hadn't consumed anything more sustaining than nondairy creamer since she'd left southern Oregon. Her stomach was now howling in protest. She doubted that another hit of heavily milk-and-sugared caffeine would fill the bill. Coaxing herself to get off her duff and head to the neighborhood grocery for food, D.J. was waylaid by a knock on her door.

She stood with effort, feeling a couple of decades older than her twenty-six years as she hobbled to the door on stiff legs. The man on the other side of her threshold didn't bother to hide his surprise when he saw her.

"I thought you said you were going to spend a day resting up," Bill Thompson said by way of greeting. "You look about as fresh as a ten spot in a teenager's pocket."

D.J. pictured a sweaty, crumpled ten-dollar bill and winced. She ran a hand through her tangled hair and tried to smile. "You look way better than that," she told him, happy to mean it.

Obviously, Bill's last vacation had done him good. He looked as if he'd gained a few pounds, and the sparkle missing since Eileen's passing had reentered in his eyes. Eyes that rapidly assessed his former foster daughter before he held up a white bakery bag and slipped past her into the apartment.

"I brought cinnamon Danish from Francie's," he said, knowing the sweet, cream-cheese-filled pastry was her favorite breakfast food. "If the mountain won't come to Muhammad," he said, winking. "Do you have coffee?"

"Um, no. I haven't gone shopping yet."

"S'all right. I brought orange juice, too." Setting the bag on the coffee table, Bill opened it, and the aroma of still-warm Danish filled the small living room. Bill plopped himself on the futon and picked up a Danish. "So, fill me in on this job you've been working."

D.J. grimaced. When she hadn't been obsessing about Max and the children during the past thirty-six hours, she'd been wondering how to tell Bill about the job she had bungled so badly. As the owner of Thompson Investigations, he certainly had a right to know that she had not only jeopardized their reputation but also failed to earn the money to cover overdue rent on their office. She hadn't picked up the money Loretta owed her and didn't intend to.

Closing her eyes briefly, D.J. took a breath and decided it would be best to get the whole sorry mess off her chest in one blunt swoop. She turned toward the man who once had assured her, "There's no punishment worse than a guilty conscience."

"I screwed up, Bill," she said without preamble. "I screwed up really, really badly."

Picking up the pastry he'd set on the table and hadn't touched while D.J. spilled her whole sorry tale, Bill began to eat again when she finished speaking.

Wiping her nose and eyes on a napkin, D.J. waited for her foster father to lecture her on ethics or business sense…or something. For the longest time, though, all Bill did was eat. Finally, as he stuck a straw into his bottle of orange juice, D.J. broke the silence. She couldn't stand her own tension anymore. "Say something!"

Bill smiled. "You did good." He put the straw in his mouth and sucked up at least half the small bottle of juice.

D.J. gaped. "Bill," she said, too upset now to worry about offending him. "Do you understand what I'm telling you? I've put our reputation at risk. If I testify in court for Loretta, Max could say I…had a relationship with him to get information. If I don't testify—and I can't because there is no way Max should lose those children—then Loretta can use what she knows to rip us to shreds. Either way, we're toast. And—"

D.J. looked at her knees, utterly miserable about what she had to say next. "I can't take Loretta's money, not now, knowing that her agenda is to sue for custody. It would just make me sick."

Bill nodded approvingly. "That's decent of you. Makes sense to me."

That was not the right response. Panic should have lit Bill's eyes at the news. "Bill, giving the fee back—it puts us in a really precarious position. We'll have brought in no money for weeks."

"We'll get by."

"No we won't!" Nerves tight as drum skins, D.J. decided the time for pussyfooting around their problems had come to an end. She looked him in the eye. "I know about the rent, Bill. Why didn't you tell me the books were so bad? I could have gotten a second job, helped bail us out—"

"There's nothing wrong with our books. We got plenty to fall back on."

Frustrated, D.J. jumped to her feet. "For God's sake, don't try to protect me. I spoke to Charlie Hensel. He says you haven't paid the rent since March. We're five months in arrears."

"Aw, Charlie Hensel can kiss my—" Bill stopped himself, but he looked angry enough to spit bullets. He reached up to pat D.J.'s hand. "Listen, baby, I told Charlie I wouldn't pay a dime more on our lease until he repainted the exterior of the building—the right way. Cheap old codger hasn't stripped a coat of paint off that building in forty years. He'd be a slumlord if his tenants let him get away with it. We have this same fight over one thing or another every couple of years. He'll come around."

Shocked, D.J. asked, "You haven't paid the rent *deliberately?*" She put her hands over her face and shook her head. "I don't understand. Why didn't you tell me what was going on?"

Bill shrugged. "I've always handled Charlie my own way. I didn't think he'd drag you into it." A scowl soured Bill's expression, but his features shifted quickly from grim to mischievous. "Hey, old Charlie must be more frustrated than usual if he went crying to you. Good. I can wait him out. I always do."

"What about the utilities, then?" D.J. still wasn't sure what to believe. "We're a month behind on them."

This time, Bill looked embarrassed. "Yeah, that was my fault. Eileen used to take care of that, you know, same time she took care of the household expenses. I've been kinda inconsistent, but I'll work out some sort of system. All it takes is a routine."

D.J. felt dizzy. She closed her eyes for a moment. The fact was she might never have taken an out-of-town job to begin with had she not been so concerned about the agency. "So, we're okay?" she asked. "Financially, I mean?"

"I've been in business a long time, Daisy girl. Hell, I've been alive a long time. Learned all I need to know about rainy days because I got caught in them once or twice. Business could go flat for a year, and we'd be okay. I've got a nice retirement put aside, too. Eileen saw to that. So…" Bill picked up a napkin, wiped his mouth and hands and stood. "I suppose all that's left is to decide what you want to do about Max."

The by-now-familiar frustration filled D.J. This morning was destined to leave her with a headache. "What can I do about him? If Loretta's lawyer tries to subpoena me, I'll say I have no intention of helping her make Max look like an unfit guardian. I'll say I don't think Loretta should get custody. That's bound to make them back off."

"Not necessarily. Lawyers can word their questions to ferret the answers that'll help their clients. Seems to me you left Mr. Lotorto in a heap of trouble."

Physical pain knifed through D.J.'s chest. Before she could respond, Bill added, "You said he's a good man."

"He is. But what can I do, Bill? I know I made a horrible mistake—"

"What mistake?"

D.J. blinked, bemused. "What mistake? I got involved with a subject."

Bill snorted. "You did not get involved with a subject. The woman I hired—the one I raised—wouldn't do that. I'd say you got involved with a man, and that's going to take a lot more work than fixing a botched job. First thing you have to do is decide whether you love him."

D.J. lost her breath as surely as if someone had reached in her chest and squeezed her lungs.

"Hear me out a minute," Bill continued, striking while D.J. was still speechless. "I've watched you grow up—not from the beginning, but close enough—and I figure I've had a hand in helping you along. That ought to entitle me to a little dad speech every now and again."

Bill paused then to allow D.J. time to stop him if she really, really wanted to. Wrapping her arms around her middle, she nodded, inviting him to continue.

Bill stood across from her, his posture relaxed, his voice soothing. "I loved Eileen from the moment I set eyes on her, and I never stopped. Don't imagine I ever will. We had a good life together. When you came into our lives, good turned to great."

D.J., whose eyes had started to tear up the moment Bill talked about Eileen, gave a watery laugh. "You've got to be kidding. I was such a little pisser when I moved in with you."

Bill laughed. "You were a corker, I'll give you that. Wouldn't have missed a day of it, though. We celebrated a lot of happy Mother's Days after you came to live with us." The corners of his mouth lifted at the memory. "The only regret I have is that I was never able to give Eileen what she wanted most."

D.J. tilted her head in question.

Running a hand over the head of hair he kept neatly combed, Bill looked out the living room window and sighed. "For years I debated telling you this. Seems foolish now that Eileen is gone. But maybe not. I hope not," he murmured almost to himself, then fixed his gaze on D.J. " Every year I used to ask Eileen what she wanted for a gift. Every year it was the same thing." He smiled gently, but the expression behind his eyes was intense. "Eileen wanted to hear you call her Mother."

"Mother? But I…I—" A lump the size of a cannon ball filled D.J.'s throat. Until this moment she hadn't thought about what she called Eileen…or Bill. "It never occurred to me to—" Abruptly she stopped.

It *had* occurred to D.J. to call Eileen Mom and Bill Dad. Of course it had. But that was so long ago….

Nearly a year after she had come to live with them, Bill and Eileen had thrown her a surprise birthday party. They'd invited the whole neighborhood, closed off the street, set up a barbecue on the front lawn, hired a disc jockey and told him to play music a teenage girl would like. They'd even danced together to a Gloria Estefan song.

There'd been a big banner across the front of the house that read, HAPPY THIRTEENTH BIRTHDAY, DAISY JUNE. WE LOVE YOU.

We love you. In twelve-inch-high block letters God and the whole neighborhood could see. That was probably the only time in her life D.J. had liked seeing her full name. And that evening, as Eileen and Bill had wished her good-night, she had wanted so badly to call them Mom and Dad she'd actually felt the words knock against the back of her lips.

D.J. sank to the couch before her trembling legs gave out on her. She put her elbows on her knees and pressed the heels of her palms into her eyes. "I was afraid," she moaned. "I was afraid that if I said the words…" She shook her head, unable to finish. Even now the fear coiled inside her, a big ugly snake that choked the good feelings.

Bill was beside her in an instant. He put a hand on her back and rubbed. "You were afraid maybe it would still end?" He spoke for her, naming her worst fear. "I know, Daisy girl, I know. Eileen and I, we tried to tell you we'd never leave, tried to show you. But there are some fears no one can settle for you. You've gotta feel them and know they won't kill you before you can put them to rest." He squeezed her arm.

"We knew you loved us, even understood, I think, why you always seemed to hold a part of yourself back. You were so hell-bent on showing the world you didn't need anyone. We wanted to adopt you, you know. Officially. But your birth mother never signed the relinquishment papers, and we got some bad advice from the social worker. She thought we were too old. And…well, we should have fought to make you our daughter legally. If you'd have wanted us to."

D.J. wondered how many breaks a heart could take in a two-day period before it just cracked open altogether. "I'd have wanted you to," she said, not caring that her voice gurgled with tears. "I definitely would have wanted you to."

Reaching for Bill, she laid her cheek on his shoulder and hugged. He smelled like spearmint gum and cinnamon Danish and the Downy fabric softener Eileen had taught them to use on their clothes.

D.J.'s smile trembled through the tears that rolled silently down her cheeks as she thought of her foster mother. Eileen had loved quietly and steadily. Just like Bill. In that moment of holding and being held by the only father who really counted in her life, D.J. realized she'd never doubted the Thompsons' love, not really, but rather her own ability to be loved.

"I wish I'd called Eileen Mother," she whispered. Pulling back enough to look Bill in the eye, even though hers now swam with tears, D.J. said, "I know who my real mother and father are. With or without a piece of paper that says so."

Bill nodded and swallowed hard. "Seems like there were a lot of mistakes made all the way around. Things that weren't said and should have been. Speaking for myself, I'm ready to make new mistakes, not the same ones over and over.

"Why did you leave Gold Hill?" he asked, urging the truth with his gentle eyes, with the acceptance she saw there.

Like a geyser the words began to bubble up from her gut, until the need to let them spew forth overcame the urge to bottle them inside. "I love Max."

There. She'd said it out loud for the first time. Cymbals didn't crash. Lightning did not cleave her in two; she was still whole, a little more whole, perhaps, than she'd been a few seconds ago.

"It's true," she insisted, more for her own benefit than her father's. "I wasn't looking for a man. I've never seen myself as the family type. But with Max…I just…I don't know." She hugged her clasped hands to her chest, feeling too cold and absurdly hot at the same time. "How *I* feel doesn't matter, though, not anymore. I lied to him. Every second I was there without telling him who I was I lied to him. And I gave Loretta information that could cost Max everything he cares about. He hates me now, Bill. I know. I could see it in his eyes. And I couldn't stand it, so I left."

"A man can be angry without hating. Besides, you left without telling him the whole story. And you left him with a heap of trouble on his plate and no solutions."

Almost desperately, she looked at Bill for answers. "I know I should have told him how I feel. I *know* it. But he's not going to care what I feel while his life is still messed up because of me. What solutions can I offer him? I've racked my brain and all I can come up with is that I should stay away. Isn't that the best thing I can do for the custody case?"

Bill shook his head. "Her lawyer can compel you to testify. They can label you a hostile witness, but if you're called to give a deposition or to go to court, there's no good way out of it."

"And if I don't talk, they can make mincemeat of our reputation." D.J. could see local press having a field day with the story of the female P.I. who went "under the covers" as a nanny. Loretta would probably be happy to give her lawyer that information if D.J. refused to play ball. She cringed and once more covered her face. "God, Bill, I'm so, so sorry. There's no way to fix this. I blew it. And now one way or another, someone's going to pay."

"Not 'someone,'" Bill responded, his voice thoughtful. "You."

D.J. looked up. Bill nodded at her. "I think there's a way to get us all out of this mess, Daisy June. But only you can do it."

Chapter Eighteen

After debating the merits of calling first, D.J. decided she needed the element of surprise when she saw Max again, if only to make sure he didn't refuse to see her.

When she approached the door to Nonna's Cucina four days after she'd left Gold Hill, she was relieved to note that the sign announcing the date of the grand opening was still in place. He was proceeding as usual. D.J.'s heart knocked against her breastbone as she opened the door, gripping in her other hand a shopping bag filled with gifts that Bill…her *dad*…had helped her pick out for the kids. A little bribery never hurt; she had no idea what Max had told them about her abrupt departure and no idea how they'd felt about it, but when she put herself in their places, she knew she'd be mad at her for leaving without even a "Goodbye, I think you're swell."

Inside the door D.J. slid her sunglasses to the top of her head and looked around, realizing when her chest began to hurt that she was holding her breath. Two workmen were repairing a booth in the back of the restaurant. Someone, presumably a new waitress, was seated at a table, filling individual salt and pepper shakers from industrial-size containers of the same. She looked up when D.J. walked in.

"Hi, we're not open yet—" she began, but D.J. cut her off.

"No, I know. I'm looking for Max…Mr. Lotorto…"

Mr. Lotorto stepped into the restaurant at that moment, deep in conversation with his bartender from next door. An entryway festooned with a surprisingly attractive garland of elephant garlic bulbs joined the restaurant and tavern.

Max looked at D.J. immediately, as if he sensed her there, though his eyes showed clear surprise—and no small degree of displeasure.

"We're closed."

Oh, boy. D.J.'s fingers tightened around the handle of the shopping bag. Her free hand curled protectively, like a pill bug. It would have been unseemly to roll the rest of her body into a protective ball, so she stood as straight as she could. Bill had always told her, *Daisy girl, any time you have to face the music, do it as if you were marching in a band.*

"Hello, Max," she said as calmly as she could. Being vulnerable in front of Max was one thing; copping to her feelings in front of an audience was quite another. "I need to speak with you."

"A request I'll have to decline."

"Which is why I didn't ask." D.J. had played enough penny-ante poker to be able to bluff when she had to. Standing before Max and two of his staff in a royal-purple spaghetti-strap sundress that fell to just below her knees, she knew she appeared more bold than repentant. That was fine. She'd already apologized, and though she would do so again, she wanted Max's first impression today to be of a woman who knew what she was doing and was not easily daunted. "Let's use your office," she told him.

The bartender was visibly intrigued, and the new waitress was rabidly curious. Max, on the other hand, exhibited only a sardonic humor. With no word for the woman who had driven three hundred miles to see him, he handed his bartender some papers, gave him a brief instruction then turned and headed to the swinging door, which led to the kitchen and office. He walked quickly. D.J followed behind, toting her shopping bag and almost sorry she'd worn heels.

Once they were in his small office, the door closed behind them, even the wry smile Max sported slipped from his face. He leaned against a desk covered with invoices, crossed his arms and cocked a brow. "Looking for a job again? We're all through hiring."

A smile shivered at the corners of D.J.'s mouth. "No, not looking for a job…exactly. How are you, Max? How are the kids?"

Lowering his head, he shook it slowly. "Boy, you are some piece of work." When his eyes lifted to hers again, they were hot with anger, cold with rejection. "You and I have said all we need to say. And I'm busy here, so—"

"I know. I figured with the opening you'd be swamped. Where are the kids?"

"None of your damned business." The small room could barely contain the energy now oozing from him. "What do you want?"

D.J. felt her pulse flutter at her throat. "I want to explain…*how* things happened. I want to tell you why—"

"Not interested."

Remembering her father's advice about always distinguishing between the truth and the facts, D.J. appealed. "There are things you need to hear, things I need to say. Right now all you know is the situation."

"Which is more than enough. Look, I don't know what your motive is for being here." He leaned forward marginally, a distinct menace in his voice. "My guess is that you've figured out I can make mincemeat of your reputation if you go to court for Loretta." He nodded. "And I will. Live with it, baby. You've had four days to think about what you want to say. I won't believe a word of it."

"And you've had four days to turn into a thick-skulled—" *Shmuck* was what she wanted to say, but controlled herself in time. Max's resistance and her own tension were decimating her well-thought-out speech. "I came back here because I know I put you in an awful position." She pushed ahead before he could stop her. "And I could never live with myself if anything bad happened to you or the kids. I didn't know Loretta was going to sue for custody. And I'll never help her get it. I'm here because I want to help *you* keep custody. I want to make sure that you and the kids are safe. And that your business is safe, too."

Now that she was on a roll—and Max hadn't bodily removed

her yet—D.J. set the shopping bag of gifts on the floor. "I know how much the legal fees can be if she takes you to court. I want to help. I know you've still got to maintain your business and child care, that all of that is going to be really important to the social worker and judge."

D.J. was speaking so rapidly now, trying to get it all out, that she felt a little breathless and had to pause. Concerned that Max might take the opportunity to invite her to leave again, she was relieved when he said, "Go on."

She nodded. "Opening a new business and securing day care are expensive. I imagine that's one of the main cards Loretta will play—that she has the funds to provide for the kids without putting herself in financial jeopardy. Just like she has the funds to hire lawyers and drag you through court." D.J. paused, knowing this was where her nerves would really kick in. "Of course, there may be a way for you to win without going to court."

Max's arms were still crossed, his face an impossible-to-read mask, but instead of kicking her out again, he said, albeit in a clipped tone, "I'm all ears."

Okay, D.J. thought. *Okay. Remember you are trying to help.* Bill was right: she was about to offer Max the best option, perhaps the only option he had to stop Loretta in her tracks.

Feigning confidence she hadn't quite internalized, she stated, "Wives can't be made to testify against their husbands. And a two-parent family has got to carry more weight than a great-grand-mother with a houseful of servants."

Max's eyes narrowed as he tried to glean some personal value from D.J.'s proclamation. When understanding dawned, he looked about as pleased as if she'd suggested rat poison to cure the hiccups. "Do they have therapists where you're from?"

"Obviously it's not what you had in mind, but if you'll hear me out—"

His brows rose. "When it would be so much more gratifying to *kick* you out? Naw." He reached over to the door, grabbed the knob, twisted.

"Your morals may be called into question because you and I... had sex."

"And I suppose Loretta knows about *that?*"

"No. Not exactly. But I think she suspects." D.J. rushed on. "Since that situation is partly my fault—"

Max laughed harshly.

"Partly," she repeated. "And since I feel responsible even though I had no idea Loretta was going to sue you for custody, I want to make this right."

"And you honest-to-God believe that marriage to a woman who's been playing me from the first moment I met her is going to take all my cares away?" Another bark of laughter held equal parts derision and humor. "Like I said, Daisy, get therapy." He opened the door. "And get out. I've got work to do. While this is entertaining, to say the least, it's also wasting my time and starting to piss me off. Go tell Loretta, I don't feel like playing today."

"I'm not working for Loretta now!" D.J. insisted, digging in her heels when Max took her arm and tried to cart her out. "Don't manhandle me. I know how to fight back." She yanked her arm free, whirling to face him one last time before he really did manage to jettison her from his office. "My relationship with Loretta is finished," she reiterated. "Believe me, my reputation is at stake, too."

Max's head reared back, exposing a strong neck that, inappropriately under the circumstances, reminded D.J. of the kisses she had placed on it the last time they'd made love. His next words dragged her back to the present.

"Ahh, now we're getting somewhere. You think marriage might cover *your* tracks. Trading sex for information does tend to tarnish one's professional integrity." With a retaliatory glare, he added, "Find another chump. I'd rather go to court on my word alone than be legally tied to a woman who wouldn't know the truth if it spit in her face."

D.J. withstood, as best she could, the jolt of pain and anger his words evoked. "You've got to be the most stubborn—" She halted her new attack abruptly, before it got a proper launch, as she once more recalled Bill's lessons about distinguishing the facts of a case from the truth.

"All right, I'll leave," she said, walking toward Max, but stopping short of the door. Raising her chin, she decided to enlighten him whether he liked it or not. "You know all the facts, Max, and they don't look good. But you don't know the truth yet. The truth is I took this job because I needed the money and because it seemed like I was doing a good thing—uniting a family. Keeping families together is important to me…more than I realized. Loretta's a wealthy woman, and she genuinely wanted to see you again. I still believe that," she insisted when he looked as if he was about to say something sarcastic. "She's lonely, and she's scared, which is a dangerous combination when you top it off with pride. Trust me."

She shrugged. "At first I thought the job would be pretty simple, but it got complicated when I realized how you felt about Loretta. And then—" She forced herself to speak despite the stony expression Max maintained. "I started falling in love with you. And with the children. And I got scared. I have a problem with rejection where family is concerned, if you want the *whole* truth. And I think I've developed an antacid addiction since I met you." She looked away a moment, plowing fingers through her hair and feeling old after four nights of next-to-no sleep. "I'm not offering to marry you to save my reputation. I messed up—I'll take my lumps. I'm offering because it would kill me to see you and the kids split up. A two-parent family will have a better shot at gaining full custody than a man alone. Also, it will be a lot harder for Loretta to use 'loose morals' as an argument if you and I are together legally. You can say you planned to marry me all along. I don't think we'd have to be together all the time, or for very long. Only until a judge grants you custody and you get child care in place so that everything is running smoothly."

She'd come to the end of her pitch. Out of breath and increasingly exhausted from the stress of the past days, D.J. figured she'd said it all. She definitely got the feeling Max would try hard to think of an alternative that did not involve marriage to her. His face had remained a mask throughout her monologue.

Beginning to feel depressed, D.J. wanted to get back to her motel room, go for a run, cry. She was getting really good at crying lately. Judging by his expression, she hadn't accomplished anything good here today.

Dropping the name of her motel in Medford, she told Max

she'd be staying overnight, asked him to give the kids the gifts she brought if he thought it was appropriate and said goodbye. Then she turned to walk through the kitchen and restaurant, heartbreakingly aware that he shut the door behind her. As far as she could tell, she had just driven six hundred miles back to Gold Hill only to piss Maxwell off some more.

Daisy had finally lapsed into a restless sleep around 2:00 a.m. She'd opted for an early dinner at a Dairy Queen and a *Lara Croft, Tomb Raider* video she had rented from the tiny video library at the motel's front desk. Halfway through the movie, she'd raided the motel's vending machine out of sheer boredom and so she would have something other than Max to obsess about. Peanut M&M's had proven no match against thoughts, however, so at 11:00 p.m. she'd put herself through a series of calisthenics that would have shamed army troops into picking up their pace.

Her junk-food-fed, exercised, showered body had been sleeping approximately four hours when the first knock on her door jolted her awake.

Only the faintest lavender glow peeked from behind the closed curtains; a lone bird warmed up for its morning serenade.

The knock sounded again, this time followed by a lighter but rapid-fire assault on the panel. D.J. stared groggily at the digital clock: 6:05 a.m. *Oh, good God.* She'd asked for a wake-up call at eight. *Eight.* And weren't wake-up calls usually accomplished over the phone?

Pushing the covers back, she slid her legs out of bed. After last night's impromptu thigh-butt-and-abs routine, she could barely stand, much less drag her sorry self to the door. *Should have done more chocolate and fewer squats.*

"Hey! Neighbors, I've got neighbors," she grumbled as the next spate of door knocking began. The folks in the next room had arrived home late after an almost four-hour *Hamlet* at the Oregon Shakespeare Festival; she doubted they would appreciate the barely dawn reveille.

Blearily, D.J. flipped the security bolt but left the chain in place. Even before she opened the door, she heard the whispers. Giggly whispers. Changing her mind, she removed the chain and opened the door. Three juvenile alarm clocks looked up at her.

"Surprise!" Sean and James chorused as soon as they saw her. Anabel stood behind shushing them and holding out a single rose whose stem was encased in a wet paper towel and tin foil.

"Good morning." Anabel looked at D.J. "This is for you," she said shyly.

Her hair was plaited neatly into two braids, and her eyes were big behind her glasses. D.J. was caught off guard, but not so much that she didn't notice the tentative smile Anabel sent her over the tops of the twins' heads.

As D.J. accepted the rose, she couldn't help but search the area directly behind the children. "This is a great surprise," she said, and it was. "Um, where's Livie?"

"She left her magic princess wand in the car," James said while Sean rolled his eyes to indicate his opinion of girls and their princess wands. "We're here to kidnap you."

D.J. laughed. "I beg your pardon?"

"Yeah!" Sean stepped in front of his brother to announce, "We're kidnapping you to breakfast, and you have to go just like you are."

"Hey, I could hear you all the way at the car. What did I say about raised voices?" Max rounded the corner with Liv in his arms. Dressed in her impossibly pink fairy princess costume, she carried a wand with an explosion of multicolored foil streamers on one end. When she saw D.J., her face lit with joy.

"My wand worked! My wand worked! I told you she'd come back if I waved my wand!"

"Shhh. Not so loud, fairy princess," Max cautioned again. "Most of your subjects are still sleeping." He looked at D.J.

Freshly showered, Max's hair was still damp and his face newly shaved. He wore jeans and a light sweater that showed off the full breadth of his shoulders. His gaze, so hostile yesterday, seemed devoid of enmity today, though wariness remained. At the moment the wariness was softened by a hint of apology.

"We should have called from the front desk."

D.J., feeling a little shy in her boxer-style pajama bottoms and a tank top that read Not As Soft As I Look, shrugged.

"We woke you up," Max said.

The relief D.J. felt at seeing them all here, outside her door, compensated for the missed sleep. His comment, though, vaguely amused her. "It's six-thirty. Did you think there was a chance you might *not* wake me up?"

Slowly Max shook his head. "I suppose I wanted the element of surprise," he admitted, reminding her of how she'd felt yesterday. "And the kids were anxious to see you."

She looked at their smiling faces, then arched a brow. "To kidnap me?"

"For breakfast!" Sean agreed. "It was Anabel's idea. Last year a girl in her school got 'kidnapped' and had to eat at Elmer's in a dumb nightgown."

"That's a scary fate," D.J. murmured. Even after only four days, she wanted to soak in the sight of the children's faces. Seeing Max there, however, tended to command attention. "And you? Are you here to kidnap me, too?" she asked, striving to keep her voice relatively even as her heart beat a tattoo of hope against her ribs.

"Somebody's got to drive," Max said. Before she could respond or ask another question, he put a hand on Anabel's shoulder. "Why don't you take Livie and the boys to the motel lobby? They have free juice and doughnuts in the morning. Tell the lady at the front desk you're my kids." The twins cheered—before Max shushed them again—and ran off.

"But we're going to breakfast," the ever-practical Anabel argued, lagging behind. "Doughnuts will ruin our appetites."

Max lowered Liv to her feet, turning the littler girl over to her sister. "I want to talk to Daisy for a few minutes. Do me a favor and stall the boys for a while. Pretend you can't decide which doughnut you want."

"I already can't decide!" Liv crowed, thinking about the treats already. Then, with no warning, she threw her arms around D.J.'s knees, hugging her tightly.

As D.J. reached down to return the squeeze, Anabel walked in close to Max and cautioned in a worried tone, "The last time you talked to her, she left."

Max crouched to look Anabel in the eye. "Give me another crack at it, okay? I've been practicing."

Blatantly dubious, Anabel nonetheless carted Liv after the boys.

Which left D.J. standing in her skivvies, alone with Max in a motel doorway.

"May I come in?" he asked.

She stepped aside, closing the door as he passed her.

The soberly decorated motel room, modest in size when she'd first moved in, seemed to shrink to claustrophobic proportions with Maxwell's presence. D.J. hovered near the door, curling her bare toes into the rug as she wondered what he had come here to tell her. The presence of the children made her hope for a truce, at least. When she considered that he might actually take her up on her offer of marriage, her pulse throbbed so persistently she felt dizzy.

"I've never been proposed to before," Max said for an opener, which didn't help D.J.'s heart one bit. "You caught me off guard."

"I suppose." Not a brilliant response, particularly as she had to clear her throat a couple of times before she was able to issue it.

"I thought about what you said—and the way you said it—after you left. I decided my response was rude. And…premature."

It was impossible to read Max's expression. He spoke in a low tone, his words slow and deliberate, like a very calm lawyer.

"I realized that your intention is to help. I appreciate that, Daisy." Walking to the small table and armchair across the room, he sat then nodded toward the bed, which offered the only other seating. "Why don't you relax? You look tense."

He had D.J. on pins and needles and she figured he knew it. Though the morning was sultry, she decided she didn't want to be the only one of them barelegged, not to mention braless, so she walked to her suitcase to drag out a pair of light sweats, which she put on right over the boxers. Then she tossed a thin, hooded jacket over her tank top and ran the zipper all the way to her neck. Crossing to the bed, she perched on its edge.

Max regarded her attire with a skeptical eye but didn't comment. "The owners of this motel, Janis and Frank Whalley, are neighbors of mine on Sardine Creek. They'll stuff the kids full of doughnuts before they send them back to the room. We may be here awhile. Do you mind?"

"No. No, I don't mind."

"Good," Max said, still in an annoyingly neutral tone. "I've thought about your suggestion, the…what would you call it? Marriage of convenience?"

Feeling her chest constrict, a feeling she was beginning to suspect might be chronic around Max, D.J. loosened the neckline of her jacket and cleared her throat. "Um…yes. I suppose that's what you'd call it."

"That's a big sacrifice on your part, agreeing to a marriage with all the baggage—relocation, instant family—and none of the perks."

None of the perks? Had they even discussed perks yet? "Well… I want to make amends."

"Marriage is a pretty drastic form of amends. What about your career? You work in Portland, right?"

"Yes. But I work for my foster father." Because that didn't sound right, not anymore, D.J. corrected, "I work for my dad."

Briefly she told him that Bill owned the P.I. firm and that she had mistakenly thought the business was going under. She tried to convey to Max how important it had been to her to find a way to help her father, and that the fee Loretta was willing to pay had seemed like a godsend. Then she attempted, in a stumbling, somewhat stilted explanation to relay what she had discovered: that saving Bill's business had been a misguided attempt to prove she loved him…that Bill had shown her no "proof" of love was necessary; the words alone, uttered sincerely, more than sufficed.

"My dad had no idea what I was doing here," she concluded, wanting Max to think well of Bill even if they never met.

He listened to her whole tale this time without interrupting. Other than a lowered brow when she mentioned that she'd taken Loretta's job to help Bill, Max showed no reaction except to comment, "Your father sounds like a wise man."

"He is. It was his suggestion that marriage would make it a lot harder for Loretta to win a custody case, and that she might drop it altogether."

"So marriage was your father's idea?"

"Yes." Something about the way his eyes narrowed made her add hastily, "I agree with him, of course. Our getting married is the only thing I can think of to make everything up to you. Of course, I never intended for Loretta to know that you and I…that we…"

"Had sex."

"Yes."

"Twice."

"Yes. Naturally, I don't usually…I mean I've *never*…on a job…"

"How did Loretta find out, by the way?"

"She thought I was being evasive, so she hired a second P.I. I don't know if he spied on the house or if Loretta just took a lucky guess."

Slowly, thoughtfully, Max nodded. Still successfully hiding his thoughts, he rose from the chair. "Loretta may be able to make a case for her ability to provide for the children, but I love them, I helped Terry raise them, and they belong with me."

He took a few steps and then turned. "I appreciate your desire to help, Daisy. But I've never thought of marriage as a neighborly gesture. I don't intend to let fear dictate when or how I get married."

In other words, a marriage of convenience would not be added to his day planner.

The news should have come as a welcome relief. Who wanted to upset her whole life, her career, her emotional balance as a favor, for crying out loud? Not D.J. She'd never put marriage high on her to-do list, in any case.

So she nodded in response to Max's declaration. Her chest felt full and her mind, fuzzy. In a moment she realized that more tears were on their way, dammit all.

D.J. stood, determined that if she was going to cry, she would damned well do it in private. "Thank you, Max…for…well, for coming over here to accept my apology. I'm going to be heading back to Portland in a little while, so I guess I should say goodbye now."

"Before the kids come back?"

"Oh. No. Of course, I'll say goodbye properly this time. I just mean…" She glanced at the door. "The kids will be back soon, I'm sure."

Max made no move. In fact, he appeared to relax. "You know," he said, "last night I was thinking about one of the things you said the day you came back. The comment you made about falling in love."

D.J. shook her head to indicate she didn't want to talk about it. Max chose to interpret the gesture as *I don't remember.* "Let me see if I can remember your exact words." His gaze drifted, in the manner of someone reminiscing. "'I was falling in love with you.' That's what you said. You said the reason you'd made love with me was that you were falling in love."

D.J. stood ramrod stiff, wondering where he was going with this and whether her racing heart could take it.

"Verb tense is a funny thing," Max continued as if the intricacies of grammar were uppermost in his mind. "Completely changes the way you hear something, the way you interpret it. Let me give you an example. Suppose I said to you, 'Daisy, I *was* falling in love with you.' To me that implies an emotion that's passed. It's over. On the other hand, the statement 'Daisy, I'm *falling* in love with you' suggests feelings occurring in the present." He held up a finger, a man with an important point. "Even better—'Daisy, I'm *in* love with you.'" For several beats all D.J. heard was the breath she tried to calm. Then Max said soberly, "That's a strong statement."

He stood. Slowly he approached until they were standing face-to-face. "Daisy, I'm in love with you," he repeated, his voice husky, rich. "*In* love, a process that has already begun but is nowhere near over. Never will be."

Max reached for D.J.'s arms, which she'd folded tightly across her stomach. He worked them loose until he held both her hands in his. "I love Daisy June Holden. Now I want to get to know D.J. If she thinks she can fall in love with me and four kids."

The tears D.J. had hoped to forestall until Max left her room began streaming now, though for a very different reason. "Not 'can fall,'" she said, in response to what she knew was a question. "D.J. already fell…" Sniffling, she wrinkled her nose. "Has fallen? I have fallen… I am falling… Oh, whatever!" Pulling her hands from his, she flung her arms around his neck, pressing her body against his. She was right where she wanted to be.

With no thought for the heart she had always been too scared to break, she admitted, "I love you, Max. I love your kids. Obviously, I won't be able to help them with their grammar, but I love them." She leaned back just enough to look at the man who had wrapped his arms around her tightly the instant she'd come into his.

"I'm so sorry for the way we met," she told him. "Sorry that I didn't tell you who I was as soon as I realized how wonderful you are. Sorry I entered your home on false pretenses to begin with." Remorse came through loud and clear in D.J.'s voice; she actually blushed. "Going undercover is just an all-around mistake for me. From now on I'll stick to missing persons."

Max had heard enough. He ended the apology with a long, thorough kiss.

Feeling drugged by the end of it, D.J. stood in his arms a moment, regaining her bearings. She still wanted to make amends for the subterfuge and decided that she could repay him best by being honest. "I think we should reconsider the marriage of convenience option," she told him quite seriously.

The suggestion brought an immediate frown to Max's face. "Nothing doing—"

"Hear me out." Mustering her courage, D.J. opened her heart with no guarantees that it wouldn't get stomped. "I won't risk losing you or the kids—the morals issue has me worried." She placed a finger on his lips, shushing him until she could finish. "The thing is, I've never said 'I love you' to anyone before. And, well…" Her voice dropped to a whisper even though they were the only two people in the room. "I'd like to say it to you while we're making love. And I'd like to do it soon."

Desire flared in Max's eyes…and throughout his body. "Now that you mention it, we should set a good example for the kids."

D.J. nodded. "We got carried away before."

Turning her hand palm up, he placed a kiss in the middle, then reached up to cup her face in his hands. "The kids would probably enjoy going to a wedding."

D.J. slipped her fingers through Max's hair to cradle the back of his head. "Yeah. Kids love that stuff."

When they kissed, bells went off in D.J.'s head and fireworks sparkled behind her closed eyes. For the time in her memory, she pictured herself in what was unmistakably a wedding gown.

By the time the kiss ended, she'd seen the flowers, the food, the music and the guest list. She was breathless.

"Max?" she asked as he lifted his head, "I think Loretta will come around when she sees that you don't want to shut her out completely."

He frowned. "Do you really want to talk about her? Now?"

"She brought us together."

He swore. "You're not going to tell me we have to invite her to the wedding?"

D.J. decided to wait a bit before telling him that her vision clearly showed Loretta in the front row at the ceremony. Instead she said, "I think, deep down, she mostly wants a family. And she's not sure how to get it. I think she's running scared."

Max's response was a bit impolite, but D.J. didn't chastise him. Instead she reminded him, "Everyone needs family, Max. Only, some of us are so frightened of being rejected, we can't admit it. I'm not saying I'm right about Loretta, just that it's a possibility."

"Maybe." He looked troubled. "I don't want you to be frightened anymore."

A machine-gun peppering of knocks rattled the door. The kids were back.

Max looked frustrated, but D.J. smiled. "I'd be an idiot not to be a little frightened," she said. "I want to be part of your family more than anything. I want it forever. I love you all so much, it *is* scary."

Max gave her one more hard, deep kiss before he stepped back. "The kids are going to knock that door in if we don't answer it." He held out his hand. "Most things are less frightening if you do them together. Let's go tell our kids we're willing to bet on forever."

Content with the odds that they might actually make this work, D.J. put her hand in Max's. They'd touched as lovers and as strangers. Now they could add "friends" to the dimensions of their relationship.

Hand in hand they walked to the door, opening it to four grinning kids who were balancing orange plastic trays piled with doughnuts, juice and lidded cups of hot cocoa. James grinned hugely. "That lady in the lobby said we should bring stuff back to the room."

"That's because Sean stuck his finger in three of the doughnuts to see if they had cream." Anabel shook her head.

The adults stepped back to let the children in with their booty. Together, amidst chatter that began immediately, they set the little table with breakfast.

D.J. caught Max's eye over the tops of the kids' heads and felt something deep inside her stir and then settle.

Peace. With no guarantees about what would happen tomorrow and no way to erase the past, D.J. knew a peace that had eluded her until now.

Strangers…lovers…friends. She and Max had covered a lot of territory so far.

Now they were about to traverse the most wonderful territory of all.

Family.

* * * * *